Kaleidoscope

by

Alan Woodruff

authorHOUSE

1663 LIBERTY DRIVE, SUITE 200
BLOOMINGTON, INDIANA 47403
(800) 839-8640
www.authorhouse.com

© 2005 Alan Woodruff
All Rights Reserved.

No part of this book may be reproduced, stored in a retrieval system, or transmitted by any means without the written permission of the author.

First published by AuthorHouse 04/08/05

ISBN: 1-4184-0896-4 (e)
ISBN: 1-4184-0897-2 (sc)

Printed in the United States of America
Bloomington, Indiana

This book is printed on acid-free paper.

DEDICATION

To Sandy and Lanna, patrons of the arts,
for their friendship and support.

AUTHOR'S NOTE AND ACKNOWLEDGMENTS

The fictional stories we tell and the characters who live them, whether the product of research or our imaginations, are all colored by our experiences and the people we know. Although portions of this story have similarities with the real life experiences of the author and his clients, not all of whom have lived their lives entirely within the bounds of the law, the events and characters portrayed in this novel are entirely fictional. Anyone who thinks he or she is characterized in this story is mistaken, guilty of wishful thinking, or simply a captive of their own overactive imagination.

For possibly obvious reasons, some of those who have contributed ideas to this novel would prefer not to be named in these acknowledgments and I respect their wishes. Nonetheless, special acknowledgments are owed to: my friends and law school classmates, Arthur Lester, Donald Bell and Pan Arthur; my friends Michael Ward, Nancy McCluskey and Joel "Smith" Bromberg, longtime editor of my legal reference books and other legal publications, who have been kind enough to read various drafts of this story and share their suggestions, stories and experiences. Finally, I owe a special thanks to Abe Gausted, my writing coach, and Michael Garrett, my editor, without whose tireless criticism of drafts this book would not be what it is.

Kaleidoscope

1.

Martin Bower, CEO of Coastal Regional Hospital, stood by the picture window of his fifth floor office. For twenty minutes, he had remained on the same spot, trying to interpret the events of the last three hours.

The five o'clock call announcing a special meeting of the board wasn't unusual. The merger talks were moving ahead swiftly, and board decisions were required with increasing frequency. What now concerned him was the vote, taken at the beginning of the meeting, to convene in an executive session—from which he was excluded.

In the courtyard below his window, the first signs of spring could be seen in the new grass. In another week, the orange and grapefruit trees would be in bloom. Friends and families visited with patients on the lawn, and candy stripers attended a few patients in wheelchairs. On any other night, he would have smiled at the scene. Tonight, he hardly noticed.

When he was hired, fifteen years ago, the hospital wasn't anything but a dream. Fifteen years of long days and longer nights—weekends and holidays. It cost him two marriages and a heart attack, but the state-of-the-art facility he had built was the pride of the community. Now everything was all slipping away.

The hospital was in financial trouble. His aggressive expansion plans were straining its resources. Reductions in government reimbursements and insurance payments were squeezing revenues. Board members who had rubber-stamped his plans when the cash was coming in torrents were now running for cover—and pointing fingers at everyone but themselves. The merger seemed to be the only way out.

Bower turned from the window, crossed the room and retrieved a pack of cigarettes from his deck. His hand shook as he held the match to the cigarette and inhaled. He took one drag before cramming the remainder of the cigarette into the ashtray. He crumpled the half-empty pack and hurled it into the brass trashcan beside his desk.

The events of the past weeks had taken their toll. The committee responsible for renegotiating his employment contract—and the multimillion-dollar severance package he would receive if the merger went through—had canceled several meetings without explanation. The hospital's lawyers had also, for no apparent reason, renewed objections to terms previously agreed to. They said it was just business, but he knew something personal was involved.

His ruminations were interrupted by a knock on the door. 'We're ready to start,' the board chairman announced. His voice was cool and distant; not the voice of someone Bower had worked with for fifteen years and considered to be a friend.

Bower trailed the chairman down the hallway. Outside the boardroom, two guards were waiting. Bower didn't recognize either of them, but that wasn't unusual. He knew everyone on the medical staff—doctors, nurses, technicians, but others were responsible for the rest of the hospital operations.

The guards followed Bower and the chairman into the room and closed the door.

Kaleidoscope

None of the usual smiles and friendly comments greeted him as he took his customary seat at the end of the conference table. Instead, the heads of all of the board members were bent over; intensely examining what appeared to be a one-page meeting agenda. Even Kathryn Ward, his personal secretary, who was also secretary to the board, refused to look at him.

'Let's make this quick.' the chairman said. Without looking at Bower, he began reading from the paper in front of him. 'The executive committee has proposed that, as a result of the discovery of serious irregularities in the hospital's financial records, the services of Martin Bower as chief executive officer be terminated immediately.'

It took a moment for Bower to register what the chairman had said. *Fire*d**.** He could feel his heart pounding, and fought to control his breathing. His hands clinched the armrests of his chair. He was only vaguely aware that the chairman was still talking.

'The committee further recommends that state and federal authorities be asked to investigate the theft of approximately three million dollars from the hospital.'

Bower couldn't believe what he was hearing, and was no longer listening when the chairman said, 'All those in favor, signify by saying 'aye.''

Eleven solemn 'ayes'. Through the tangle of thoughts that filled his mind, Bower was only faintly aware of one 'nay'. He looked across the table at the grim face of Dr. John Wiley. Wiley shook his head. His look said more than words. *There wasn't anything I could do*.

Bower's eyes circled the table, hunting for . . . something. Whatever it was, he didn't find it in the looks of the board members who, buoyed by the power of their collective action, were focused on him.

Why hadn't he seen it coming? The signs were there, if only he had paid attention.

He knew they expected him to say something. He *wanted* to say something. Within him, words stirred and sentences formed, but none were worthy of voice. There wasn't any point. No words could change what had happened. It was over, and he knew it.

'The guards will escort you out of the building.'

As he headed for the door, Bower saw Joe Morgan, in-house counsel, and Randall Harrington, outside counsel, sitting together in the corner. Morgan was studying the floor, avoiding eye contact. Harrington started directly at Bower—an imperious smile on his face.

Bower couldn't avoid thinking, is that what Judas looked like?

Kaleidoscope

2.

Forty miles off the Florida Keys, the *Not Guilty*, Lucius White's sixty-five-foot motor yacht, rocked quietly at anchor over the Cay Sal Banks. The light of the full moon, reflecting off the ever-changing surface of the sea, danced in ghostly patterns on the ceiling of the cabin. A cool sea breeze, the remnants of an unseasonable cold front, floated through the portholes of the master stateroom. The air was clean and pure with only the lingering aroma of passion—and sex.

At 0030 hours, the tranquil night was interrupted by the shrill chirping of the marine telephone. White dismissed the noise as part of a dream, rolled over and ignored it. The woman beside him nestled closer and moaned softly.

The insistent ringing wouldn't stop.

Finally, he surrendered and groped for the receiver. 'This better be damn important,' White muttered into the mouthpiece, still half asleep.

'This is Marty.'

White was immediately alert. 'What happened?'

'I was *fired*.'

'Damn.' White muttered. 'Start from the beginning. What happened?'

'It was a set-up. The bastards had security waiting to throw me out the door.'

White searched his memory for clues that would explain the hospital's unexpected action. 'When?'

'Early this evening. They called a special meeting of the board and, just like that, they canned me.'

'Did they give a reason?'

'Hell, yes. They claimed I embezzled millions of dollars.'

White sat up and, ignoring the sense of foretelling that enveloped him, asked, 'What's *that* all about?'

'I don't have a clue.'

As he listened, White fumbled for the clock. 'It's 12:30. Where are you?'

'I've been driving around,' Bower said slowly, fatigue and the strain of the night's events beginning to take their toll. 'I don't know how to tell Karen.'

'Why didn't you call me sooner?'

'I'm sorry, I . . .'

'It's okay, Marty.' White knew what Bower was thinking. After twenty years as a defense lawyer, he knew the feelings that overwhelmed clients facing criminal charges for the first time. Bower was angry and confused. That was to be expected. By morning, he would be overwhelmed by different feelings. Bewilderment. Fear of the unknown. The helplessness of knowing that his fate now rested in the hands of someone else.

'I guess . . . I just couldn't believe it. I've been . . . I don't know.'

Nothing White might say would make any difference. He could console Bower in the morning. 'Go home.' White said. 'Meet me in my office at ten o'clock.'

* * * * *

White pressed the button on the intercom to the captain's private cabin.

Kaleidoscope

'Yes, sir,' the captain mumbled, barely coherent.

'Set a course for Marathon,' White said. 'And have the plane waiting when we get there.'

Minutes later, the twin ten-cylinder, turbo-charged diesels that could power the *Not Guilty* to over thirty knots rumbled to life. White heard the clank of the chains as the windlasses raised the two Danforth anchors and felt the boat shutter as it plowed forward, turned slowly to starboard and accelerated. As it headed north, the *Not Guilty* ran parallel to the line of deep swells, rolling from side to side as alternating crests and troughs passed beneath the hull.

The throaty pulsing of the muffled exhaust echoed through the stateroom. On any other night, it would be a lullaby. But not tonight. Any hope of sleep was in the category of wishful thinking.

'What was the call about?' the woman beside him murmured as she snuggled against him and laid her head on his bare chest.

'The shit just hit the fan at the hospital.'

Leslie Halloran rolled to her side and propped herself on her elbow, allowing the sheet to fall from her shoulder revealing her nakedness. 'What happened?'

'They fired Marty. I'm meeting him in the morning.'

No further explanation was necessary. Leslie knew that Martin Bower was one of White's oldest and closest friends. She also knew White had no choice; he had to be there for his friend. But she also knew that Martin Bower's future wasn't the only thing at stake.

The week away with Leslie was intended as a time for introspection—a time to think about the future. His future; their future.

In the beginning, White represented only defendants he believed were being wrongly charged by overzealous prosecutors. Few of his clients could afford his services, but that wasn't important. He wasn't doing it for the money. He was doing it because he hated the power of the government.

He was doing it to expose the corrupt misuse of power by prosecutors. He was doing it for his father.

Now he represented only those defendants who could afford his minimum fee of $50,000 for a criminal defense. He was no longer fighting for the people he had become a lawyer to defend. He was no longer protecting the system he loved. He was merely using it. What started as a motivation had become an obsession. He hated what he had become.

Leslie snuggled against White, listening to his breathing.

Minutes later, White began to relax.

Leslie turned her face to him and smiled. 'Is there anything I can do?'

'No,' White responded, his voice soft and distant. 'The rest will have to wait.' He drew her against him, feeling her warm nakedness.

'Are you sure you're up to it?'

'I don't have a choice.'

* * * * *

Joe Morgan, the hospital's in-house counsel, and Randall Harrington, a partner in Johnson, Kutter & Stump, the hospital's outside counsel and chief architect of Bower's termination, toasted each other with twelve-year-old single malt scotch.

Harrington sat erect in one of the two wicker plantation chairs on the balcony of Morgan's beachfront condominium. His custom-made alligator shoes rested on the white wrought iron table. His monogrammed silk shirt, still crisp and wrinkle-free after his twenty-hour day, was open at the neck.

'It was like leading lambs to the slaughter,' Harrington said as he puffed on his Arturo Fuente Diamond Crown cigar.

'But who were the lambs, Bower or the board?' Morgan asked, his voice subdued and troubled.

'Both.' Harrington smiled. 'Bower didn't have a clue what was coming, and the board went where we wanted them to go.'

Morgan paced the balcony, occasionally leaning against the railing and staring into the dark night. He shared Harrington's satisfaction with the results of their attack on Martin Bower, but the decision to make their move had been forced on him by circumstances. 'I'm still sorry we had to screw Marty like that.'

'It couldn't be helped. The board was getting too curious.'

'I still think we acted too soon.'

'We didn't have a choice,' Harrington responded in a measured tone bordering on arrogance. 'The merger talks were getting too serious, and the feds were taking too long getting an indictment. We had to slow things down—and divert the board's attention.'

'There were other things we could have done.'

'We've been all through this. Bower wouldn't give in. He deserves whatever happens to him. Let the great Lucius White get him out of this one.'

Morgan looked at Harrington. He knew Harrington hated White; hated White's success; hated the fact that White would not give in to the demands made on behalf of the hospital. They both knew White would represent Bower in whatever came next. But for Harrington, Bower was now just a pawn in the game. 'What do we do if the U. S. Attorney wants to see the original records?'

'She won't. All she wants is a conviction. As long as we give her what she needs, she won't ask questions. Bower will get convicted; the deal will go through and we collect a million dollar fee.'

That's easy for you to say, Morgan thought. *You still don't know everything. You don't know what's at stake.*

That much was true. Harrington didn't know that the thefts were only part of the story. The sale would go through only if the rest of the plan—the part Harrington didn't know about—worked as Morgan had promised. But Harrington would do anything to ensure Bower's conviction. If he knew the whole plan, he would use it against Bower.

Bower didn't know the whole story—but he knew enough to ruin everything. Morgan had to keep anyone from discovering the real plan. Two of the others were already dead. Morgan had no desire to join them.

3.

The offices of Lucius A. White & Associates, attorneys and counselors at law, were located in a converted warehouse on the edge of the Caloosahatchee River, four blocks from downtown Fort Myers. The warehouse had been built around the turn of the century to store goods shipped by boat into the small community on the site of what had once been a frontier fort. Until early in the twentieth century, Fort Myers remained isolated from the main populations of Florida—by the Everglades to the east and Charlotte Harbor and the Peace River to the north—and the waterfront was an active part of the town.

In the 1920's, the railroad arrived, and ship-borne trade began a precipitous decline. Over the next sixty years, the waterfront warehouses slowly succumbed to the ravages of time, neglect and decay. By early in the 1980's, only the warehouse that now housed the offices of Lucius J. White & Associates remained. It had become the property of the city—seized for unpaid property taxes. The city had no interest in, or use for, the dilapidated warehouse and was more than happy to sell it to White.

The warehouse had been gutted and turned into two floors of offices and the apartment that occupied the entire third floor. All that remained of the original warehouse were the brick walls and the giant wooden beams that supported the original floors and ceiling. The few original floorboards that could be salvaged were used on the floor of the main reception area. The remainder of the building had been painstakingly restored using the same tools and construction methods used to build the original. No detail was overlooked. A blacksmith's furnace had been built on the site to make nails as they had been made in Florida's early frontier days. Floor planks had been cut on an original steam-powered saw White acquired for his project and later donated to the city historical museum.

The first floor of the warehouse was occupied by his firm's main reception area, the file storage room, the main conference room and offices for White's associates. The offices of Lucius White and Harry Harris, White's partner, were located on the mezzanine.

A wide balcony extended from the mezzanine around the two-story atrium over clerical areas of the first floor contained the firm's law library. Most legal research is now done on computers, but White had a special fondness for his library. He loved the rows of law books, the mahogany tables with their Tiffany-shaded brass table lamps. The library was White's link to times past, when the practice of law was still a noble profession.

* * * * *

White arrived at his office shortly before ten o'clock. Grace Matthews, his longtime office assistant looked up quietly. She knew the circumstances of the early return from his much needed vacation, and, after fifteen years together, she knew when to leave him alone with his thoughts. She handed him a note announcing the hospital's televised news conference scheduled for ten o'clock. 'Mr. Brower is waiting in your office.'

White glanced at the note before dropping it in the trash and accepting the cup of coffee that Matthews offered. No matter when he arrived in the office, Matthews had a fresh cup of coffee waiting. How she did it—how she knew when he would appear—was a mystery. Perhaps it was a special kind of telepathy that had grown out of their years together. Or maybe it was true, as Grace claimed, that it was part of the *ju ju* she brought with her from her native Jamaica.

Martin Bower was slumped against the arm at one end of the leather sofa, facing the entertainment center—a custom-built piece made of weathered wood recovered from the wreck of a late-nineteenth century sailing ship. A cup of coffee, ignored and growing cold, sat on the end table.

Bower's eyes were bloodshot and framed by dark circles. He was unshaven, and what little hair remained around the sides of Bower's balding head was barely combed and seemed even grayer than when White had last seen him only a week before. His normally ruddy complexion was pale and waxen. Even as he sat, his six-foot frame looked shriveled.

Bower stood as White walked into the room. White greeted him with a supportive hug. 'How are you holding up?'

'Relative to what?' Bower said. His voice was strained, as if the act of forming a complete thought required great effort.

'Right,' White responded, acknowledging that his question was superfluous and its answer self-evident. 'How's Karen taking things?'

'As well as can be expected, I suppose.' Bower returned to his place on the sofa and hung his head. 'We were up most of the night. We spent a lot of time telling each other it was going to be okay and everything would work out.'

White sat on the arm of the sofa next to Bower.

Harry Harris rolled into the room and parked his wheelchair beside the sofa just as the newscast began.

The chairman of the hospital board walked directly to the podium in the hospital's auditorium. He looked straight ahead, and without any preliminary greetings or introductory remarks, began reading from his prepared text.

> *'Last night the board of trustees of Coastal Regional Hospital voted to terminate the employment of Martin Bower, president and chief executive officer.*
>
> *'This action was taken after a six month investigation by the board and its independent legal counsel uncovered widespread irregularities in the hospital financial records.*
>
> *'It is possible that further action, including legal action and criminal charges, may be forthcoming.*
>
> *'Joseph Morgan, the hospital's in-house counsel, will assume the duties of chief executive officer.'*

When he completed his statement, the chairman left the podium, ignoring the shouted questions of the assembled media.

Throughout the announcement, White watched Bower's eyes as he stared, unmoving, at the television screen. The chairman's words didn't appear to have any meaning. Bower seemed to be trying to decide whether to believe what he was hearing.

As seconds passed, Bower's face grew flush. His jaw tightened and twitched until he suddenly exploded, 'Bullshit.' He slammed his arm and clinched fist against the back of the sofa. The suddenness, and violence, of his action took even White by surprise.

'Those fucking bastards.' Bower erupted from his seat and stomped angrily around the room. Finally, he stopped beside the window. For a minute, he stood still, clinching and unclenching his fist as he stared silently at the empty river and sky. Finally, he turned and crossed the room. 'They can't say that stuff about me, can they?' he asked no one in particular as he sank back onto the sofa.

White waited. He knew the signs. Bower needed time to collect his thoughts before he could focus on anything White might say.

'I'm really beginning to hate those guys.'

'Save it, Marty. Hate is a wasted emotion. Most of the people you hate don't know it, and those who know don't care.'

As he spoke, White stood and, rather than use the television remote control, walked across the room and pressed the power button turning off the television. Like many trial lawyers, he thought best on his feet. From the corner by the television, he slowly paced the length of his office organizing his thoughts. As he reached the corner of the office, he stretched his arms over his head, arched his back and yawned.

For a full minute he stood at the far end of the room, his arms folded as he stared at the floor. Finally, he began nodding. Imperceptibly at first. Then in more pronounced movements, as if concluding a conversation with himself, before returning to the sofa where he stopped, looking down at Bower.

At five-foot-ten and one-hundred-seventy pounds, White wasn't a physically imposing figure. Nor would he be described as handsome. His face was creased and weathered with angular features. His nose, broken in a childhood accident and reset by his father, was uncentered beneath his dark eyes. His brown hair, now flecked with strands of gray, was worn long, and frequently unkempt, in a rugged western way reminiscent of his formative years in Ketchum, Idaho.

But he had a presence, a don't-tread-on-me look, and a voice, deep and resonant, that commanded attention, even when he whispered.

'Let's start from the beginning,' White said.

Bower hung his head, marshaling his thoughts. 'I just don't know what happened.'

'Neither do I. But some faction of the board isn't happy with your refusal to give in to their demands. You wouldn't give up what you'd been promised. This is your punishment.'

'You can't let them get away with this.' Bower's voice trembled as he spoke. 'I wasn't prepared for this. I don't have any savings. We could lose the house. What am I going to tell Karen?'

It wasn't a pretty sight. Watching a client fall apart was never easy—especially when it was a friend. White and Harris found something on the floor that demanded their full attention. Finally, Bower looked at White. 'You said they can't withhold my severance benefits.'

'That's what the law says. What they think they can get away with is something else. The hospital's attorneys haven't shown much respect for the law so far, and I don't expect them to change.'

'Do you think they fired me to keep my severance benefits?' Bower asked.

'That's probably not the main reason. Just an extra benefit.'

'Then why?'

'The oldest reasons in the world,' White said. 'If you were set up, it was so someone could gain money or power—or both—by getting rid of you.'

Bower shook his head. This wasn't really happening to him. 'But . . . who?' Even asking the question seemed to be a strain.

White frowned. 'That's what we need to find out. The chairman said the investigation has been going on for six months. That means someone has been planning this for a while. If we can figure out who gains from getting rid of you, and what they gain, we should be able to determine the real reason you were fired.'

Kaleidoscope

Bower nodded. 'So what do we do now?'

'You have three choices.' White said, his tone calm and reassuring. 'First, you can crawl in a hole and go away.'

As he spoke, he studied Bower's eyes for any response.

Bower shook his head slowly. Maybe in frustration. Maybe in disbelief. Maybe rejecting the first option. White couldn't tell which.

'Second, you can sit back and wait. After everyone has had time to calm down, we can approach the board about some kind of settlement.' Again, White paused, waiting for a reaction.

Bower responded with a vague look of uncertainty.

'Or you can go on the attack.'

Slowly, Bower raised his head, as if being pulled out of a trance, and looked at White.

'I'm sure the hospital would prefer you take the first choice—and the board's attorneys are arrogant enough to think they can run you off. If you go that way, you lose your benefits. But, if you back off, the hospital might not pursue criminal charges.'

White paused, waiting.

No response.

'The second choice is probably not realistic,' White continued. 'The vote to terminate you was almost unanimous, so I don't see much hope for a compromise. They probably expect you to do something, but don't expect you to take any action right away. They're playing this as a public relations issue. We need to make the community see the board members as the bad guys.'

'What do you have in mind?' Harris said, speaking for the first time.

'I suggest we file suit immediately. They won't be expecting it so soon, and we'll have the tactical advantage. If this is going to blow up, we need to know what's going on.'

Bower continued to look at White with uncomprehending eyes.

White sat on the arm of the sofa beside Bower and began to explain. 'If we're only fighting a criminal issue, we're limited in what we can discover. We can't force witnesses to talk to us. But if we start a *civil* case, we can get information the hospital can withhold if we are just preparing a defense to a criminal action.'

Harris nodded his agreement.

'What do you think, Marty?' White asked

'What am I supposed to say?'

'It's your ass that's on the line. I thought you might like to have a say in how we're going to save it.'

Bower shifted uneasily in his seat before responding, 'Whatever you think is right.'

'Good,' White said firmly as he walked to the conference table and retrieved a yellow legal pad. 'For the time being, this is a civil case. If the hospital *does* file a criminal complaint, we'll have to shift gears. But for now, Harry will be managing the investigation.'

Bower nodded.

'Let's take a break. Then we can get started.'

White was standing beside Grace Matthews's desk when Bower returned from the men's room and signaled him to a corner of the reception area.

'Ah . . . Lucius . . .' Bower muttered uneasily. 'I know Harry is your partner . . .'

'I know what you're thinking, Marty,' White said. 'You're concerned about being represented by an attorney in a wheelchair.'

Bower looked at the floor.

'Let me tell you something about Harry,' White continued before Bower could say anything. 'There was a time when Harry was probably the best trial lawyer in the circuit. About five years ago, a drunken teenage driver broadsided his car. His wife and daughter were killed instantly, and he was left a paraplegic. The losses hit Harry hard. He got addicted to pain killers, antidepressants and booze. I finally got him into rehab, and eventually brought him in as my partner.

'He tried to resume his trial practice, but his stock in trade was pure theater—gestures, postures, dramatic movements around the well of the court room . . . .' White's eyes gleamed with recaptured memories. 'He was Hamlet with a briefcase. But he couldn't do it any more.'

Bower interrupted. 'So why—'

White ignored him and continued. 'I don't go into a courtroom in a major case without Harry. I'm the quarterback, but he's the sideline coach. Harry Harris is the most extraordinary legal tactician I've ever known. He never forgets a fact, and he's an expert at managing the mountains of documents produced in any investigation.'

'I'm sorry. I shouldn't have . . .'

'No,' White said. 'You shouldn't have.'

Bower didn't need to know the rest. He didn't need to know about the demons, or how much White depended on Harris when his obsession overwhelmed him.

4.

White and Bower returned to their places on the sofa in White's office.

Harris maneuvered his wheelchair to a position in front of Bower and began. 'All right, Marty. Let's start at the beginning. What's all this about financial irregularities?'

Bower shook his head. 'I don't know. I really don't know.'

'There has to be *something*.' White said. 'Why would anyone be looking into the accounting system *now*?'

Bower studied the floor before looking at Harris. 'I don't know if it means anything, but . . .' Bower began, before pausing and taking a deep breath. 'Six months ago our chief financial officer told me that some expenses in the executive operation account—things like travel and entertainment, community relations—were out of line, and had been for several years.'

Harris interrupted. 'If they've been out of line for several years, why weren't they brought to anyone's attention earlier?'

'I don't really know,' Bower muttered, seemingly embarrassed by his own ignorance. 'We were never particularly concerned with the details of individual sub-accounts.'

'What about the accounts themselves? Is there anything special about the accounts where the irregularities were showing up?'

'Like what?'

'Well, you mentioned the executive operation account, the travel and entertainment account and the community relations account. What do they have in common?'

Bower shook his head. 'I don't know. What are you getting at?'

'They all sound like accounts that would be under your control.'

'Not really. They were used by all of the executive officers.'

'But you were responsible for managing the executive budget, weren't you?'

'I . . . suppose.'

'Marty,' White interrupted. 'How did the accounting discrepancies come to anyone's attention?'

Bower paused, brushing his hair back before responding. 'When we started talking about a merger with a national hospital chain, Joe Morgan thought we needed an audit, just to be sure our books were in order.'

'And this audit was proposed by *Morgan*?'

'Yeah,' Bower muttered. 'But I think the idea came from the lawyers Joe brought in to do some other work.'

'Why did anyone think there was a need for an audit?' Harris asked.

Bower leaned forward, his elbows on his knees and his head bowed. When he finally spoke, his voice was soft and distant, like thoughts that had somehow escaped. 'The board was starting to split into two factions. One faction wanted to stay independent. They wanted to hang on the golden goose that was providing them with status and a lot of benefits. The other faction knew we had to do something. They wanted to merge with a bigger organization.'

'That's interesting,' Harris said. 'But it doesn't explain the need for an audit.'

Bower shrugged. 'I guess it was because of the accounting discrepancies I asked Joe Morgan to look into.'

'So you asked *Morgan* to look into the discrepancies.'

Bower nodded slowly

'Why *Morgan*?'

'Joe brought in this outside firm, Johnson, Kutter & Stump. They had a whole department that specialized in health care law. When Joe suggested the audit, it seemed like a reasonable idea.'

'But a minute ago you said *you* asked *Morgan* to look into it.'

'I guess. I mean, I mentioned it to Joe, and he suggested we use the outside specialists.'

'So the audit was originally *Morgan's* idea?'

'Yeah, I guess so,' Bower said. His tone was uncertain; as if he wasn't sure he understood the question. 'Is that important?'

'It's too early to know what's important,' Harris said. 'Go on.'

'There isn't anything more,' Bower muttered, still looking at the floor. 'The next thing I know, I'm out on my ass and the hospital is claiming I stole millions of dollars.'

Harris looked at White with arched eyebrows and a shrug. *He's all over the place.*

'He's tired,' White mouthed.

Harris shook his head and returned his attention to Bower. 'Marty, let's go back to the accounts for a minute.'

Bower nodded.

'When the chief financial officer brought the discrepancies to your attention, how far out of budget did he say the accounts were?'

'Not that much. Maybe a hundred thousand dollars.'

Kaleidoscope

'But the hospital claims you embezzled *millions* of dollars.'

'Maybe they found something else they're trying to blame me for.'

'Millions of dollars isn't just 'something',' Harris said flatly.

Bower pressed the heels of his palms into his eyes. 'I don't know what it could be. I never heard anything from Joe after I asked him to look into the accounting problem.'

'Maybe I can fill in some blanks,' White said. 'Six months ago the hospital started negotiating with Marty about revising his employment contract. He has a five-year contract and will be entitled to payment for whatever remains of the contract term if he is terminated. The board wanted to reduce it to two years and eliminate the million-dollar lump sum severance provision. This was about the time the hospital started serious merger talks.

'Two months ago, the hospital advised Marty to retain independent counsel. That's when he first came to us. I met a couple of times with some of the board members and the hospital's attorneys. At first, we seemed to be making progress. Then, everything suddenly changed. At the time, I only thought they were being unreasonable in their demands.'

'And now you think they were delaying?' Harris said.

'That's what it looks like.'

'But why did they want to get rid of Marty? And why did they decide to do it *now*?'

'Both good questions. I'm open to suggestions.'

For half a minute, no one spoke. Finally, White turned to Bower. 'Something must have been happening in the last few months. *Something* made it necessary for the hospital to get rid of you. *Think*, Marty. What could it have been?'

'Damn it. I *have* thought about it,' Bower said, his face flushed and tense. 'It's all I've thought about since last night. I *don't know*.'

'Take it easy, Marty,' White said, placing a hand on Bower's shoulder. 'Remember, we're on your side.'

Bower shook his head. 'I'm sorry. It's just that . . .'

'We know how you feel, but let's stick with the facts.'

'Could it have been a simple power play?' Harris said.

'Like what?' Bower asked, his attention still not entirely focused on Harris.

'Well,' Harris said, 'Joe Morgan *was* named the chief executive officer after you were fired. Maybe he just saw a chance to help himself by getting rid of you.'

'It's a possibility, but I don't think that's all there is to it,' White said. 'I'm convinced Marty's termination had something to do with the merger.'

'But what?'

'Marty,' White said, 'has *anything* out of the ordinary, other than the merger talks, happened in the past few months?'

Bower thought for a moment before responding. 'There is one thing.' He hesitated, seeming to search for relevant facts in a chaos of thought—the nugget of beef in a bowl of soup-kitchen stew. 'About six months ago, the hospital by-laws were changed to give me an automatic tie-breaking vote on the board. Since there were an even number of board members, and I was a voting member under the provisions of the old by-laws, I basically had two votes if the board was tied.'

'But that would give you *more* power in the case of a tie vote,' Harris said. 'Why would giving you *more* power just six months ago explain your termination?'

'It *wouldn't*,' White said. 'They didn't give the power to *Marty*; they gave the power to the *chief executive officer—whoever that* is.

'Think about this,' White said, as he rose and walked to the window. 'At the time the by-laws were changed, the merger talks were just beginning, and the board was split. Marty was on the side favoring a merger. It you take those facts alone, it looks like the change in the by-laws worked to the advantage of those board members who favored the merger.'

Harris nodded. 'But what if replacing Marty with someone who opposed the merger was the plan from the beginning?'

'Exactly.'

'Jesus Christ.' Bower slammed his fist on the coffee table. 'Those bastards have been planning this all along?'

'Hold on, Marty. We don't know anything right now. We're just listing possibilities.'

'Son of a *bitch*.'

White and Harris waited for Bower to regain his self-control. Finally, White asked, 'Was Morgan for or against the merger?'

Bower closed his eyes, straining to recall seemingly irrelevant events from six months before. 'I think he knew some kind of change was inevitable, but he wasn't in favor of the merger we were considering.'

'And now he has the controlling swing vote.' Harris said. 'That sounds like a good reason to get rid of you.'

'*No*.' Bower said. 'You can't think *Joe* got me fired. We've been friends since college.'

'It sounds like he had motive,' Harris said.

'You don't understand,' Bower said. 'You're assuming Joe would have replaced me. He wouldn't have been the board's choice to replace me when the by-laws were changed.'

'Maybe not then. But he *was* named the chief executive officer after you were fired.'

White stopped taking notes and began tapping the end of his pen on his yellow legal pad. 'Morgan isn't the issue,' he said. 'The problem isn't who replaced you, Marty. What we need to know is *why* you were fired *now*. What was the status of the merger when you were fired?'

'We were getting close to a vote. We might have already voted if things hadn't gotten bogged down with the audit.'

'That's another thing that puts Morgan in the middle of things,' Harris said. 'He's the one who was investigating the accounting problem, so he's the one who would have the ammunition to justify your termination. The question is, what did he find?'

'I don't have any idea. He never told me anything.'

For the remainder of the morning White, Harris and Bower reviewed the facts needed to prepare a civil complaint. By noon, Bower's concentration was waning, overtaken by his anxiety and lack of sleep.

'Marty, go home and get some sleep,' White said. 'And for God's sake, shave. You look like crap.'

* * * * *

Harris looked up from his notes of the morning meeting and summarized the facts to be included in their suit for wrongful termination. 'We still have to decide who to name as defendants. We need to name the hospital and the board members, but Marty doesn't want to sue Dr. Wiley. Wiley is an old friend, and he was the only one who voted against Marty's termination.'

White leaned back, considering Harris's suggestion. 'Wiley's a member of the board. He may be an indispensable party.'

'What do we have to lose by leaving him out? We can add him later if we have to.'

White selected a cheroot from the humidor on the corner of his desk. He no longer smoked in the office, or his apartment—an accommodation for Leslie, but still found comfort in the feel of the butt in the corner of his mouth. 'Okay,' he finally agreed. 'Wiley's out.'

Harris made a note on his pad and looked at White. 'Anything else?'

'Yeah,' White said as he continued to study his own notes.
Harris waited.

'I didn't want to get into this when Marty was here, but there's a bad-boy clause in Marty's employment contract. If Marty is terminated for committing a felony, he doesn't get *any* of his severance or retirement benefits.'

'So *that's* why they accused him of embezzlement.'

'Probably. But that's not all there is to it. The way the agreement is written, he only loses his benefits if he is *convicted* of a felony.'

'So the hospital has an interest in seeing to it that Marty is actually *convicted*.'

'And a motive for manipulating the facts.'

5.

After watching the early news with Harry Harris, White climbed the stairs from his office to his apartment. Sherlock, White's caramel mixed-breed retriever, was waiting at the head of the stairs. Her tail pounded against the open door like someone knocking. She could easily have come down the stairs to greet White, but she never did.

Sherlock was an only dog, and she seemed to like it that way. She had birds to bark at and squirrels to chase when she was in the mood. And she had White and Leslie well trained.

White retrieved a handful of treats from the kitchen cabinet and held them, one by one, in front of Sherlock's nose. With each offering, Sherlock sat motionless, staring cross-eyed at the treat and drooling on the floor until White said 'Okay.' Each treat vanished in a single gulp, and Sherlock sat patiently waiting for more.

'That's all there are,' White said when the last treat disappeared.

Sherlock didn't believe him.

'Honest. That's all there are,' White repeated.

Sherlock wasn't convinced.

'Have it your way.'

Dogs and women. They both think they can get what they want with a little guilt. Unfortunately, they're both right.

White poured himself a Diet Pepsi, squeezed two slices of lime into his drink and walked out onto the wooden deck. Sherlock followed his master onto the deck where White sank into one of the lounge chairs, propped his cowboy boots on the railing and lit his cigar.

The setting sun hung on the western horizon, painting the undersides of the low clouds in shades of salmon, peach and sulphur.

Sherlock laid her head on White's leg, waiting to be scratched. White obliged.

'So what do you think, girl?'

Sherlock looked up with sad brown eyes.

'Is this what we're supposed to be doing?'

Sherlock pawed at his hand.

'Do you really think so?'

Sherlock licked his hand before lying down and stretching out on the deck.

'Let's hope you're right.'

The *Not Guilty* was moored at the end of the wharf in front of the warehouse

Restoring the old wharf was the most difficult part of the warehouse conversion. White wanted to preserve the historic integrity of the property by using timbers like those used for the original wharf. The Corps of Engineers, whose approval was required because the river was part of the federally maintained inter-coastal waterway, insisted on a concrete pier. White took the Corps to court, where he prevailed on the argument that the Historic Structures Preservation Act prevailed over regulatory requirements. His victory was so satisfying that he had the court's opinion framed and hung on the wall in his study.

White had suggested that Leslie spend a few extra days on the boat, but he hadn't expected her to stay away. She loved going cruising, but only when White was with her. Now he was curious where Leslie was, White returned to the apartment and walked to his study. As he expected, he found a note taped to the back of his leather chair. He unfolded the note, written on Leslie's personal stationery—she wasn't anything if not socially correct—and read her perfect script.

> *What's a girl to do? I screw your brains out and still you leave me to my own devices. You owe me, Big Boy. You better have a make-up dinner plan. I'm shopping for something special. We'll decide who it's special for when I get home.*

Sounds fair. When Leslie bought something special, it was usually something they could both enjoy, whether batteries were or were not included.

White and Leslie knew every restaurant within fifty miles, and they were constantly on the lookout for something new. A special meal didn't mean anything fancy. When they went out for dinner, it was most likely in search of an exotic barbeque. Wild pig at a fish camp thirty miles deep in the Everglades was White's personal favorite.

When they wanted fine dining, there wasn't a restaurant in southwest Florida that could match what they prepared in White's gourmet kitchen. White was the cook. Leslie's main contribution to meal preparation was selecting the wine—for herself, White didn't drink—and slipping snacks to Sherlock.

Early in their relationship, Leslie had confessed to being 'domestically impaired.' She justified her lack of skills in the kitchen with the simple observation that "I have talents appropriate to many rooms. The kitchen just isn't one of them.' White conceded both points.

White returned to the apartment. Sherlock followed him past the picture windows and French doors opening onto the wooden deck to the intimate sitting area in front of a large

Kaleidoscope

stone fireplace. The fireplace wasn't part of the original warehouse, but it was a necessity for a boy from Idaho. The fourteen foot high brick walls were covered with an eclectic mixture of Native American carvings, Ansel Adams photographs, modern art—all originals selected by Leslie— and a few stuffed animal heads.

White dropped into one of the barrel chairs in the grouping in front of the fireplace. Without thinking, he found himself studying the grotesquely contorted bronze sculpture in the corner of the room. *Life.* That's what the artist called it. *Maybe so,* White thought.

Soon he was asleep.

White was awakened by the sound of the elevator. *Time to see what kind of surprise I'm in for.*

The elevator stopped before reaching his apartment. *That's odd. Maybe she's checking to see if I'm still in the office.*

A minute later, the elevator resumed its trip.

Leslie stepped into the apartment and posed for White. Her long legs, honed by a childhood of country club tennis, were slightly apart. Her hands were on her hips and her head tilted back, accentuating her long neck.

She was five-feet-six-inches and one-hundred-twenty pounds of Irish femininity. Red hair that cascaded recklessly in soft curls over her shoulders and half way down her back. Emerald eyes, large and captivating. She was sexy in a way that men dream about and women envy.

'I bought some new boots.'

'So I noticed.' It was hard not to notice her new boots. She was wearing nothing else.

'Is that all you can say?'

'How about 'ride 'em, cowboy'?'

'That's more like it. Would that be before or after dinner?'

'Do I have to choose? Why not both?'

Leslie laughed. 'Been on the range for a while have you, cowboy?'

'It's been a long day.'

'You can tell me about it later,' Leslie said as she came to White and kissed him softly before heading for the bedroom, exaggerating the sway of her hips as she moved. 'You owe me big,' Leslie said as she sat on the bed and drew her thin panties up her shapely legs. As usual, she didn't wear a bra. 'How do you plan to make up for ditching me on the boat?'

'How about a monster truck rally?'

'In your dreams, stud.'

'Okay. How about dinner? Anywhere you'd like?'

'Let's make it Anthony's on the waterfront in Boston. I'm in the mood for Maine lobster.'

'I was thinking of something a little closer to home.'

'Then you pick.'

'Well, it's road kill night at the Lazy Gator.'

Leslie grimaced. 'It's *always* road kill night at the Lazy Gator.'

'Yeah. Fine country eatin',' White said, grinning. 'You can always get the four basic food groups—dead animal, grease, green weeds and alcohol.'

Leslie wrinkled her nose as if she had just inhaled some noxious fumes. 'You know, you don't exactly fit in among the rednecks.'

'Not a problem,' White responded. 'It's not that different from Idaho. All I have to do to fit in is wear a John Deere cap, scratch my ass, call all animals 'critters' and drive me a big honkin' pickup truck.'

Leslie shook her head and rolled her eyes.

'Besides, it's also a good place to catch up on gossip.'

'And here I thought you wanted to go to the Gator because you loved me.'

'That, too,' White said as he sat on the edge of the bed.

'So tell me about the thing with Marty,' Leslie said as she sat at her dressing table and began brushing her hair.

'There isn't much to tell—yet,' White said. 'He was fired and the hospital has threatened criminal prosecution.'

'Do you know why he was fired?'

'Not the real reason.'

'Do you know what kind of crime he's supposed to have committed?'

'Only what they claim.'

'Do you know who's behind it?'

'Haven't a clue.'

'Do you know what you're going to do about it?'

'We have some ideas.'

'That's a relief,' Leslie said. 'For a while there I thought you didn't have everything under control.'

White laid back on the bed and folded an arm over his eyes as Leslie continued stroking her hair. 'You don't have to take the case,' she said softly.

For a moment, White said nothing.

'Lucius?'

'He's a friend.'

'Maybe that's why you shouldn't represent him. Are you sure you want to know if he's guilty?'

White lapsed into a thoughtful silence.

Leslie stopped brushing her hair and looked at White in the mirror. 'It isn't about him.'

White knew what she meant. Thoughts of his father had been their constant companion during the week away. He was only sixteen when they came to arrest his father, a survivalist and outspoken opponent of everything governmental. Four cars full of government agents, guns drawn, storming the house and dragging his father away. Two years later, his father was dead—stabbed in the back in the prison yard by a drug dealer. There was no investigation of substance, and the drug dealer was released less that six months later, almost two years before he was first eligible for parole. White knew it was more than a coincidence. He knew, as an article of faith, with the same certainty a devout Christian believes in the Holy

Trinity, that the government was responsible for his father's death.

'Maybe not,' White said. 'We'll see.'

Leslie turned from the dressing table, folded her hands in her lap—and waited.

'This is Marty. The other thing will have to wait.'

'This isn't what you decided on the boat.'

White sighed. 'I know.'

'It has to start sometime.'

'It will have to wait.'

'Are you sure?'

'I'm not sure of anything. I just know I have to represent Marty.'

* * * * *

The Lazy Gator, referred to locally as 'Billy's' after Billy Reynolds, the cook, was, it was universally agreed, the most unusual eating place in five counties. And it was by far the least accessible. If you didn't already know where the Lazy Gator was, you would be lucky to find it. Typical directions would be, 'Go east on highway 17 about five and a half miles until you come to a gravel road on the left just past an isolated stand of pine trees. Take the gravel road until it forks. Take the left fork until you come to a big boulder on the right. About a hundred yards further, take the dirt road on the left and stay on it until you come to a big shack and you're there.' Along with the directions would be the admonition. 'Don't try the road unless you have a high clearance vehicle—and four wheel drive if the weather is bad.'

They were met at the door of the Lazy Gator by Ruth Huckins. She was a local girl with a Daisy Mae image, complete with ragged cutoff jeans turned into short-shorts that barely covered her ass, and a loose blouse with the top three buttons opened. Her breasts were tantalizingly concealed by her cascading blonde hair.

Ruth greeted White and Leslie like the old friends they were. 'To what do we owe the pleasure?'

'Lucius owed me a special night out,' Leslie said. 'He's making up for deserting me in Marathon this morning.'

'And he brought you *here*?' Ruth responded. 'Girl, you have some training to do,' she added in a stage whisper to Leslie.

'Give me credit,' Leslie said. 'I have him up to Cro-Magnon Man. When we met, he was a Neanderthal.'

Ruth laughed and led them to their usual booth.

'What's good tonight?' Leslie asked.

Ruth gave her a 'you-have-to-be-kidding' look.

The menu at Billy's was as unorthodox as the rest of the establishment—there wasn't one, not even as a listing on a blackboard. For starch, you had a choice of 'spuds' or 'noodles'—never referred to as pasta—prepared subject to Billy's whims and discretion. Your vegetable was either 'greens'— which might be spinach greens, collard greens or dandelion greens—or beans cooked with a slab of fatback. The closest you could come to an order of your choice was the entrée: 'meat,' 'fish' or 'bird.' Having specified your category of choice, you got whatever Billy had available—cooked however Billy chose to cook it. The sole exception to these choices was Billy's Seminole Special—gator pounded until it was tender, sautéed and served covered with a chutney of plums and peaches, making the colors of the Florida State University Seminoles. Billy loved the Seminoles.

Billy's entrees were local game, birds and fish, not all of which were necessarily in season. In response to charges of ignoring hunting and fishing laws, Billy claimed he was serving road kill, and was actually doing the state a favor by cleaning up its highways. How this explained the inclusion of out-of-season fish on Billy's menu was never clear. But it didn't matter. Everyone who was anyone in local government was a 'member' of Billy's fish camp, and had probably bagged some game or fish out of season in their time

Leslie ordered bird, greens and noodles. White ordered meat, greens and spuds. White also ordered his customary Diet Pepsi with lime. Leslie ordered a beer. It wasn't necessary to specify the brand because Billy carried only one brand at a time. It varied depending on the price he could get from his distributor.

'Where is everyone?' Leslie asked when Ruth had taken their orders and was about to leave. The only other people in the room were three men at the bar playing liars' poker, swilling beer and swapping stories, in the tradition of fisherman everywhere, about the big one that got away. 'It's Thursday. You're usually packed on Thursday.'

Ruth shook her head. 'It's been this way for a couple of months'

'Billy?' Leslie asked.

'Yeah. It's gotten really bad.'

'I'm so sorry,' Leslie said, taking Ruth's hand in her own.

'Sometimes these people make me so mad. They've known Billy for years, and now this.' Tears began to well-up in Ruth's eyes. 'I'm sorry, I can't talk about it,' Ruth muttered as she hurried away toward the kitchen.

Leslie started to say something when her hand shot to her mouth and she gasped. 'Oh, my God.'

'How are my favorite shyster and social do-gooder?' Billy Reynolds greeted them hoarsely as he shuffled across the room to their booth.

'Billy.' Leslie said, forcing herself to sound happy as he leaned over to kiss her on the cheek. So much had changed since she last saw him less than a month ago. The pale scarecrow beside their table was so unlike the Billy she knew. She wanted to cry. Instead, she gave him a warm hug. "How are you?'

'Hanging in there,' Billy said weakly. He made no secret of his condition. In the culture of the country, where everyone knew everyone else's business, it would have been useless to try. There was a time when Billy would have treated AIDS victims as the leper his former friends now treated him. But Billy had come to terms with his condition. White could see the sadness in her face as Leslie considered how much Billy had deteriorated.

Her melancholy returned after Billy headed for the kitchen with the promise of a special surprise. 'He doesn't have much time left,' Leslie murmured softly. White reached across the table and held her hands. He had comforted her through such moments before, and would surely do so again.

The painful times went with her job Leslie was an AIDS activist, an attorney who now worked with support groups and clinics throughout the country, suing states and the federal government for the funds so often promised during election campaigns but which rarely materialized. Billy volunteered in the counseling programs offered by the clinics where Leslie worked. It was there they had met and become friends.

'I talked with Sharon Martin this afternoon,' Leslie resumed after Ruth served their meals.

'Sharon Martin?'

'She's executive director of the network of clinics I work with. You met her at the clinic open house.'

White nodded.

'Something's going on in Sarasota.' There was a new strain in her voice. Not like when she spoke about Billy, but just as personal. 'According to Sharon, the usual source of the newest drugs has dried up. There's been a rash of thefts from the clinics.'

'What's the connection between the thefts and the shortage of new drugs?' White asked. 'The clinics don't have the really new stuff, do they?'

'Sometimes they do,' Leslie said. 'The *really* new stuff is limited, but we get enough to treat a few patients. There's always been a black market for the latest AIDS drugs, especially among the wealthy. The rich are willing to pay top dollar for the new drugs, and the anonymity that goes with being treated by their own doctors.'

'How does that have anything to do with the thefts?'

'I don't know, but I need to go up there and look into it.'

White was beginning to understand Leslie's concern. 'Are you sure that's a good idea?'

'What?' Leslie said sharply. 'Going up to the clinic?'

'You know what I mean,' White responded. They had suffered through this conversation before. He dealt with criminals every day, but he didn't like it when Leslie was required to deal with anything involving criminals.

'Yes. I know *exactly* what you mean.'

Help.

'Sometime you can be . . .' She caught herself before saying something she would be sorry for.

'Billy's dying,' she began again. Her voice turned hard and harsh. 'He's dying because he couldn't get into the trials for the newest drugs. Now, even the basic drugs we have at the clinics are disappearing. If I don't do something, more people are going to end up like Billy. Is *that* what you want?'

'That . . .' He thought better of what he was about to say and, instead, concluded, 'isn't the point.'

'I *know* what the point is.'

'I . . .' The only place for the conversation to go was down. White looked at his plate, toying at the greens with his fork. 'I want to watch the news tonight. Maybe it will have something we don't know.'

Leslie studied him for a moment before relaxing. 'You need to work on your segues,' she said, now smiling, 'But since we've changed the subject, I wasn't aware the media worked for you.'

'Every little bit helps. All we know so far is that someone is trying to ram a giant stick up Marty's ass.'

'*God*, you can be crass,' Leslie said, shaking her head and giving him a look of mock indignation. 'May I remind you that I am a lady of good breeding, and I *do* have my standards.'

'What can I do to make it up to you?'

'You could take me to bed.'

White smiled. 'Is sex your answer for everything?'

'Everyone needs a hobby. And I haven't heard you complain.'

'I can do that. I was just thinking about grabbing your ass and whispering 'How about it'?'

'I've heard more romantic approaches, but that might work.'

6.

'Good evening, ladies and gentlemen. This is Action News. I'm Lynn Thomas with today's lead story.

'The Coastal Regional Hospital today announced the firing of Martin Bower, president and chief executive officer. A hospital spokesman stated that the terminations were made following discoveries of financial irregularities. Action news has learned that the financial irregularities were discovered when a routine audit uncovered what one hospital board member described as a pattern of misappropriation by Mr. Bower going back five years. According to the hospital spokesman, criminal charges are possible.

'In other news . . . '

'Good newscast, people,' news director James Murphy announced as the news anchors tried to look busy while the closing credits rolled.

Kaleidoscope

Murphy waited at the side of the set. As the on-air talent began to leave, he wiggled a finger toward Thomas.

'What is it, Jim? I'm a little busy right now.'

'The hospital story.'

She smiled. 'It looks like it's going to be an important story.'

'That's what I wanted to talk to you about.'

Thomas waited.

'I got a call from the station's lawyer.'

'He didn't waste any time.'

'He's worried.'

'The lawyers are always worried.'

'Maybe. But he thinks the story is going to turn into something big. He wants to be sure we know exactly what we're talking about . . . and don't say anything that may come back to haunt us. We need to coordinate our information and handling of these stories, and make sure that anything even marginally questionable is run past legal first.'

Thomas shook her head.

'None of us like it,' Murphy consoled her. 'But that's the way it has to be.'

'That's ridiculous. We can't hold off on a story until the lawyers review it.'

Murphy shrugged. 'I've delivered the message.' He began to leave but stopped, turned back to Thomas, and smiled. 'Of course, what you do about it's up to you.'

7.

As was their custom, White and Harris met at the end of the following day to review the status of pending cases. Harris, who supervised the files handled by White's associates, did most of the talking. White made a few notes, but generally just listened.

Harris could read White's moods almost as well as Leslie could. Whatever White was thinking, it wasn't about their daily briefing. 'So I told the associates they could all have a month off, with pay,' Harris said.

'Whatever you think best.'

'And we're going to paint the offices black.'

'Yeah. Okay.'

'*Lucius*. You haven't heard a word I said.'

'Huh?' White said, looking at Harris. 'I guess I let my mind wander.'

'No shit.'

White leaned back in his chair and brushed his hair back with both hands. 'Marty called a little while ago.'

Harris closed the file he was holding and laid it on the conference table. 'I assumed as much.'

'He's been getting a lot of harassing phone calls. Some of them threatening.'

'We should have anticipated that. Tell him to get an unlisted number.'

'That's what I suggested.'

'What else?'

'He's not holding up very well.'

'That's to be expected,' Harris said.

'I suggested he see a psychiatrist.'

'But that's not all you have on your mind.'

White looked at Harris expectantly.

'You think Marty's being framed.'

'It's a possibility.'

For several minutes, neither of them spoke. White sat motionless at the end of the table—his eyes open, but closed.

'Lucius. This isn't about your father.'

White looked up. 'That's exactly what Leslie said.'

'Leslie's a smart lady—and she's right.'

White nodded. 'But it's about everyone like him—everyone who is the victim of others who hold more power. That's why we do this.'

'We do it because someone has to. It's not personal.'

'Isn't it?'

Harris shrugged. 'Leslie's concerned about you.'

White tensed. 'What are you doing talking to Leslie about it?'

'Like I said, she's concerned.'

'I can't talk to her about the case.'

'She knows that. But it's not just about Marty's case.'

'Then, God damn it, let's stick to Marty's case.'

Harris said nothing.

'I'm sorry. It's . . .'

They were interrupted by Grace Matthews' soft knock on White's door. 'If there isn't anything else, I'll be leaving now.' Matthews rarely left the office before White, and seemed embarrassed when she did.

'That's fine, Grace. Have a nice weekend.'
'The news is about to start.'
'Thanks for the reminder.'

> *'In further developments in the Coastal Regional Hospital scandal, Action News has learned that the hospital has filed a criminal complaint with the State's Attorney charging Martin Bower, the fired chief executive officer, with embezzling more than three million dollars over a period of five years. Action news has also learned that the financial crisis at the hospital may require massive layoffs. A hospital spokesman said that the possible layoffs were the result of mismanagement by Martin Bower.'*

'It looks like the board is going to try the case in the press,' White grumbled, taking another long drink of Diet Pepsi.

'Then maybe we should do some of the same.'

'Tell me you have a plan to make those guys squirm.'

'Okay. How's this?' Harris said. 'Today is Friday. The story of the day is the criminal complaint filed by the hospital. Nobody pays attention to the news over the weekend, so the hospital's action is going to be the only story people talk about until Monday.'

White nodded.

'This is going to be the lead story again on the late news,' Harris said. 'We need to get our story in front of the jury pool. Maybe we can even turn up the heat on the board and let them be the ones sweating out the weekend.'

'Got a plan?'

'Let's get with the reporter now.'

White walked across the room to the mini-refrigerator and retrieved another can of Diet Pepsi while he mulled the idea over. 'And you think we can do this in time for the late news?'

'If you were Thomas, wouldn't you do anything to get an exclusive?'

White nodded thoughtfully, a smile forming on his lips. 'What do we have to lose? Call her.'

8.

Lucius White escorted Lynn Thomas into the living room of his apartment and introduced her to Harris and Bower. In spite of her experience as a print and television journalist, Thomas was unprepared for this meeting.

She had no illusions about the reason for the invitation. She knew she was going to be the subject of manipulation. The purists in her profession might profess the neutrality of the press, but everyone in the room knew the importance of public opinion. That was the only reason she was there.

After five minutes of the obligatory chitchat, Thomas couldn't contain herself any longer. 'Gentlemen,' she said abruptly. She was already the informal center of attention, so nothing more was needed to call the inevitable next stage of this gathering to order. 'I enjoy sharing a good scotch with good company as much as anybody, but I can't help noticing the only topic we have in common hasn't been mentioned. Let's put our cards on the table. You want some good press, and you think I can give it to you.'

Her statement was greeted by a poignant silence. It wasn't the reaction she expected from her take-charge gambit, and

Kaleidoscope

she was perturbed by the lack of response. Surely an acknowledgement. At least a denial. Something.

White was the first to speak. 'You misunderstand. We do not intend to sway your opinion. In fact, this is the only time you will hear from any of us until this case goes to trial.'

Thomas' expression said this wasn't what she expected to hear.

'Your observation,' White said, 'is correct. We would like good publicity. However, this case will be tried in the courtroom, not in the press.' White now spoke in a detached manner, more like a lecture than the not-so-subtle attempt to increase her curiosity that it was. 'We all know the hospital has undertaken an aggressive campaign to manipulate the press—and public opinion. We don't condone such conduct. Although I don't know you personally, I've been assured of your competence . . . and your ability to independently unearth the truth.'

'Then why am I here?' she asked, the question sounding more like a plea than she intended.

White smiled. 'Why, to share some of my excellent scotch and meet the public enemy,'

'And to get an *exclusive*,' Harris added.

The magic word had Thomas' attention.

'At four-thirty this afternoon,' Harris began, as if reading a press release, "Martin Bower filed suit against the Coastal Regional Hospital.' As he spoke, he handed Thomas a copy of the complaint that had been filed only hours earlier. "Mr. Bower charges Coastal Regional Hospital with wrongful termination and violating federal law by improperly depriving him of severance benefits owed to him. The value of the benefits Mr. Bower claims exceeds two million dollars.

'Furthermore,' Harris continued, 'Mr. Bower denies any wrongdoing as alleged in the criminal complaint filed by the hospital.'

The only thing White and Harris knew about the criminal action was what Thomas had reported on the early news, but that wasn't important. Bower was going to deny whatever the hospital alleged.

'Finally, you may inform your viewers that Mr. Bower believes the charges against him have been fabricated by certain members of the board, who, for their own purposes, oppose the merger of the hospital with an as yet undisclosed entity. Such a merger, and you may quote me, would deprive them of the substantial financial benefits they enjoy as members of the board.'

White and Harris had not decided on a defense strategy, or even a theory for the defense. They didn't even know what they were going to be defending against. The only thing they knew was that pointing fingers at the board would be involved. They also knew that, because discussions of the possible merger of the hospital had been a closely guarded secret, disclosure of these negotiations would be an embarrassment to the board and would focus the public's immediate attention on the hospital rather than on Bower.

Thomas' expression showed her surprise at the news of Bower's lawsuit. But the suit was now a matter of public record and was available to every other newsperson in town. The possible merger of the hospital was another matter.

'What about the merger? Who is it with? What does it mean for the hospital?' Thomas threw out questions as fast as she could think of them.

'That's all we can tell you for now,' White said. 'As I said before, we're not here to control the news. That's up to you. You're going to have to do your own digging.'

'Will you at least answer questions about what I come up with on my own?'

'We'll consider that when the time comes,' White said. 'And now, although I am sure we all enjoy your company, I believe that you may have a newscast to prepare for.'

* * * * *

Kaleidoscope

The story was the new lead for the late news.

> '*Martin Bower, fired yesterday as the President and chief executive officer of Coastal Regional Hospital, struck back today by filing suit against the hospital and its Board of Trustees, claiming that he had been improperly terminated and deprived of more than two million dollars in severance benefits owed to him. In an exclusive interview, Bower said that his termination had nothing to do with the administration of the hospital or the alleged embezzlement of hospital funds, an allegation Mr. Bower strongly denies. Mr. Bower contends that his termination was brought about as a result of a division on the Board relating to previously undisclosed discussions of a merger.*
>
> '*Sources familiar with mergers in the health care industry suggest that such a merger would, if it occurred, lead to massive layoffs. Members of the board contacted by Action News refused to comment on the merger talks or any plans to lay off hospital employees.*'

White pressed the mute button on the remote control. 'The lady has been busy.'

'The board members are going to be taking a lot of antacid this weekend,' Harris said.

'And their lawyers will be plotting a response,' White muttered. 'We need to find out what they're going to do next.'

9.

According to his birth certificate, his name was Jim Bob McGee, but no one ever called him that. Jim Bob earned the name he claimed as his given name in the maternity ward at Baptist Regional Medical Center in the panhandle of northwest Florida. The explanation came from his father, who had been known to drink on occasion and lack a clear recollection of all facts. As the story went, on the occasion of his birth, his mother, in an unkindly reference to the circumstances of the moment, announced, in a voice that could be heard by all of Santa Rosa County, 'My God, I'm giving birth to a horse.' And that was that. Henceforth, Jim Bob McGee was known to one and all as Horse.

It was a name that fit. Horse McGee started life big and kept on growing. By the time he was seventeen, Horse McGee was six-feet-three-inches tall and two-hundred-forty pounds of farm-raised muscle. According to his teachers, he had the academic interest of his namesake. His only reason for going to school at all was football.

As fortune would have it, Florida's flagship university had flexible admission standards for a linebacker who needed help completing the admission form, but could bench-press any fullback, and run down any tailback, in their conference. Horse fit right in. Class attendance wasn't required as long as he made a lot of tackles, and Horse was good at holding up his end of this arrangement.

Earning a spot as a starting outside linebacker as a freshman is rare enough in major college football. Horse did more than just start. Five games into the season he was already the talk of college football, and the next game was on national television against archrival Tennessee.

On the third defensive play of the game, Horse was in pursuit of the Tennessee tail back when his legs were taken out from behind. The penalty flag, which was in the air before Horse hit the ground, was little consolation for the cracking sound Horse heard as he rolled under the weight of Tennessee's All-American offensive guard. Horse knew that his season, and maybe his career, was over. This wasn't the way he had planned for it to end.

Broken leg and all, Horse staggered to his feet, grabbed the offender's facemask, tore his helmet from his head and, with all the considerable strength he could muster, put a large fist directly into the offender's nose.

Eighty-six thousand fans cheered as Horse took a bow and collapsed to the field. The majority of those who witnessed the event were thrilled. Unfortunately, the minority included his own head coach and the president of the university. Horse's college football days were over.

Without football, Horse had no reason to stay in school, so he joined the Army.

In spite of his marginal academic record, the Army discovered that Horse had a special aptitude and trained as a computer programmer. Horse found his niche, and a reason to learn. He also discovered the joys of hacking. It wasn't a skill the Army encouraged, but one for which it had a use. Horse was assigned to the National Security Agency, and was soon an expert at breaking into the secret records of his country's friends and foes alike.

By the time his second enlistment was over, Horse had endured enough. He left the Army and joined the F.B.I., where he applied his skills to the investigation of the financial transactions of members of the underworld. It was there that Jim Bob "Horse' McGee came to the attention of Lucius White.

White was defending a major money-laundering case. Much of the government's case was based on Horse's investigation of the money trail White's client had left while moving his profits into legitimate businesses. When the case against his client was dismissed on a legal technicality, White offered Horse the opportunity to apply his skills in support of the work of defense attorneys. Horse accepted, and moved into White's recently renovated warehouse to establish his own computer security and investigation firm.

* * * * *

It was just after noon when Horse McGee walked across the outdoor deck of the T&A bar on Fort Myers Beach.

On any weekend afternoon or evening, the deck of the T&A was filled with suntanned bodies. Now, however, it was virtually empty. Horse McGee found a seat at a table on the far corner of the deck, under the shade of the Tiki hut away from the main bar. A few gulls hopped from the railing to the various wooden tables and benches searching out scraps. Someone at the bar threw a french fry onto the middle of the deck, and a dozen birds descended on it in a flurry of thrashing wings and screeches. Horse watched as the victorious gull sprang into the air, the french fry in his beak, and headed out across the sand with the remainder of the flock in hot pursuit.

As he waited, Horse reviewed his conversation with Morgan. Horse had asked for a meeting away from the hospital, but Joe Morgan was eager to oblige. In fact, it was Morgan who suggested the T&A. He made a note to ask

Morgan about his choice of meeting places, but he was more concerned with what he had told Morgan.

For Horse to accomplish his objective, Morgan had to think that he was part of the team investigating Martin Bower. But impersonating a law enforcement agent was a crime. All Horse had said on the telephone was he needed to fill in some gaps. *Yes*, he thought, *that was true enough.* He never said that he was with any particular agency. So far, he hadn't crossed the line, although the line wasn't far away. It wasn't that an occasional venture over the line was foreign to Horse. But Morgan was a lawyer, the enemy's lawyer, and extra caution was required.

Horse didn't have long to wait. Five minutes later, Joe Morgan's heaving bulk appeared by the bar. A brief, but apparently friendly, exchange between Morgan and the bartender told Horse that Morgan was probably a regular patron of the T&A.

Morgan's pause at the bar gave Horse an opportunity to size him up. With the exception of an apparent aversion to exercise, Morgan was the image of success in his tailored suit, silk shirt and polished shoes made out of the skin of some deceased reptile. He wore a gold Rolex watch, and the diamond in his pinky ring could have been mistaken for an ice cube.

Horse stood and raised his arm. Morgan nodded, finished his brief conversation with the bartender and lumbered toward Horse. As Morgan approached his table, Horse stood and extended his hand. 'I'm Paul Smith,' Horse said, using the name he had given Morgan during the call to arrange the meeting.

'My pleasure,' said Morgan. 'I hope I can be helpful.'

The greeting caught Horse by surprise. Every comment tells a story, and Horse knew no one was ever in a hurry to become involved in a criminal investigation. Even victims, the people who have the most at stake, have reservations about talking with the police and are rarely completely forthcoming.

Morgan had no such hesitancy. He acted as if he were looking for an opportunity to tell what he knew.

'Thanks for meeting me here,' Morgan said. 'Our outside counsel thought it would be a good idea if we didn't meet in town. Besides,' he said with a man-of-the-world smile, 'I'm a tit man, and the viewing here is always worth the drive.'

A woman in a thong bikini brought them drinks. Beer for Morgan and an iced tea for Horse. He would have preferred a beer, but it would have been out of character for 'Paul Smith.'

'It's not a bad place for an ass man either,' Morgan said, grinning has he studied the departing waitress.

For ten minutes, Horse and Morgan engaged in the ritual of introduction, getting to know each other in anticipation of an extended working relationship. Finally, Horse asked, 'Why was your outside counsel concerned about our meeting?'

'Oh, he wasn't concerned. In fact, he wanted me to meet with you,' Morgan said. 'He just didn't want to make our cooperation too obvious.'

'Uh huh.'

'I assume you saw the news on Friday.' Morgan said, more a statement than a question.

'Hard to miss it,' Horse said. 'Doesn't look like they're going to take it lying down.'

'We expected the lawsuit,' Morgan said, confirming the assumption White had made about the hospital's strategy. 'It doesn't have any effect on what you're going to be doing, does it?'

'Don't know why it should. Doesn't change your cooperation with us, does it?' Horse asked, testing the extent of any agreement between the hospital and the authorities.

'No. The board wants to make sure you get Bower. We'll do anything we can do to help.'

'Suppose you fill me in.'

'The hospital already gave the U. S. Attorney all the information we have. I don't know what else I can tell you.'

Kaleidoscope

Damn. Horse had no idea what the hospital had already disclosed, and anything he might say could tip Morgan off.

'Suppose you tell me about Martin Bower.' Horse had no interest in learning more about Bower. He wanted to know about Morgan's role in Martin Bower's termination, but direct questions would be too obvious. What Morgan chose to talk about, and what he chose to withhold, would tell Horse a lot about Morgan and where he stood.

For thirty minutes, Morgan talked about his history with Bower: how they met as college roommates; how they stayed in touch over the years and how Bower hired him as in-house counsel at the hospital when Morgan decided to leave private practice. But whenever Horse asked a direct question about the hospital, Morgan responded with a confused look.

Horse made one more try. 'One thing I didn't see in any of the reports. There's no indication of how you uncovered Bower's actions in the first place.'

'We got the documents from the banker—the one who set up the account the money was transferred to.'

'But how did you discover the account?'

Something floating in Morgan's drink required his undivided attention. 'I . . . don't remember.' Morgan took another swallow of his drink. 'Someone in the accounting department must have found it.'

Horse knew Morgan was lying. 'Who in the accounting department discovered the account?'

Morgan scanned the deck, looking for a distraction, before responding. 'I'm not sure.'

'What about the banker who gave you the documents. Who was he?'

'It was a while ago,' Morgan responded evasively, returning to an examination of his drink.

What are you hiding? Horse chose not to press the issue and moved on to more general questions. After half an hour, Horse ended the interview with an agreement to meet again when 'Paul Smith' needed more specific information.

* * * * *

As Joe Morgan pulled out of the parking lot of the T&A and turned north on San Carlos Boulevard, he pressed the speed-dial on his car phone. In less than five seconds he was connected to Randall Harrington and summarizing his meeting with Paul Smith.

'Did he tell you anything about their investigation?'

'I couldn't get anything out of him.'

'I'm not surprised,' Harrington said. 'Communications with the F.B.I. are always one way. They listen to what you say, but they don't tell you what they know.'

'Maybe. But I think this guy was a rookie. He must have some cop skills, but he seemed a little lost in the investigation.'

'Maybe we can use that to our advantage. If he's a rookie, he doesn't want to screw up on his first major case. He may be interested in any extra information we can feed him— and not quite jaded enough to question what we give him.'

Kaleidoscope

10.

Lou Hamilton was tall, thin and drawn with deep-set dark eyes, a narrow nose and a look that made you think his parents were closely related. He was originally from Maine and, even after twenty years in Florida, he retained the distinctive accent peculiar to the region—the languid 'down east' drawl found nowhere else.

Hamilton's look and voice had served him well as an investigator. He was so unlike the public's image of a policemen that witnesses were lulled into a false sense of security. His easy manner made him one of the best investigators in the State's Attorney's office, until a drug dealer's bullet left his right arm partially paralyzed and qualified him for disability retirement. His injured arm didn't prevent him from doing his job, but it was a good excuse for getting out of a position with which he had become increasingly disillusioned.

Hamilton lived alone at the end of a gravel road on the outskirts of St. James City, a small, misnamed enclave on the south end of Pine Island, ten miles down the river from Fort Myers. His small house sat on the edge of Pine Island Sound. The left side and rear of his property were bordered by thick stands of red mangroves, federally protected trees that were the nursery to the many species of fish that spawned in the warm, shallow waters of the Sound. To the right of the property was the narrow channel leading from the Sound to the small marina and restaurant that were the center of what little social life existed in St. James City. Hamilton's battered bass boat rocked gently on the light swells as they rolled into the canal from the Sound.

'Good to see you, Lou,' White said when Hamilton answered the door. 'It's been a long time.'

'Too long.' As usual, Lou held a cigarette in the nicotine-stained fingers of his left hand. White couldn't remember ever having seen Hamilton when he didn't have a lit cigarette. Why Hamilton, a four-pack-a-day smoker for more than thirty years, had not long since succumbed to lung cancer was a mystery that would never be explained. 'Since you turned into a big-shot lawyer, you've forgotten your old friends.'

'It hasn't been that long.'

'Now you're being defensive. It's a sure sign you're feeling guilty.'

'Don't you ever stop being an investigator?'

'If I did, you wouldn't be here.'

'Touché.'

'And now you're up to your ass in alligators,' Hamilton said as he led White through the kitchen and out to the screened porch at the rear of his house. The screen was superfluous. Lizards and flies passed freely through large tears in the screen and helped themselves to the remnants of pizza, at least a week old, sitting in the box on the rusting remains of a patio table.

White eased into one of the wrought iron chairs and accepted the Diet Pepsi Hamilton pulled from the cooler beside the table. 'You don't forget a thing, do you?'

Hamilton shrugged. 'I hear you represent the hospital guy.'

White wasn't surprised that Hamilton knew that he represented Martin Bower. Local law enforcement agencies had more leaks than a pack of dogs with bad kidneys, and Hamilton knew where every dog lifted its leg.

'Looks that way. I'm just not sure what he's going to be charged with.'

'How you going to find out?'

'The usual. Ask a lot of questions; listen to a lot of answers; turn over a lot of rocks. Something will pop out. Maybe even a defense.'

'And you think I might know something?'

'The last I heard, you knew everything worth knowing around here. A butterfly can't fart without you knowing about it.'

'I hear things,' Hamilton admitted.

'What do you hear about my case?'

'It looks like an open-and-shut case for embezzlement.'

'Based on what?'

'Your client is either a brilliant crook or the stupidest administrator in history.'

'I'll take stupid. That's not criminal. What do you have?'

'A couple days ago I had lunch with Bob Wells. He's an investigator in the State's Attorney's office.'

'I know him. Dull and plodding, but generally quite thorough.'

'That's him. I don't think he's had a creative thought in the last twenty years. But when it comes to digging out facts, he's their best.'

'What kind of information has he dug up?'

'The way I hear it, $50,000 a month was stolen from the hospital and deposited in a corporate account set up by your client. The interesting thing is that the corporation that's supposed to have opened the account doesn't exist in Florida.'

'Maybe an out-of-state corporation?'

'Could be, but the feeling seems to be that there never was a corporation.'

'So? Where is the money now?'

'Nobody knows. When the funds were transferred into the account, they were immediately wired out to some other bank.'

'What bank?'

'Wells didn't know yet, but he thinks it's probably offshore.'

'Does he know where?'

'No. They don't have the resources to trace international transfers. When they need that kind of thing done, they go to the feds.'

'It's probably the Caymans or Panama. They've got the strongest bank secrecy laws.'

Hamilton grinned. 'And they say you're just another pretty face.'

'It could also be the Bahamas or Belize,' White suggested.

'Not likely. They have the laws on the books, but anyone with a few bucks can get all the information they want.'

White studied the table and nodded. 'Anything else?'

'Just that when Wells started nosing around, the bank admitted they didn't have any documentation for the account.'

'What do you mean by *no documentation*?'

'Nothing signed by Bower. No account cards or signature authorization cards. Nothing.'

'And the bank didn't realize that until the hospital asked for it.'

'That's what Bob said.'

'How did they know it was Bower's account?'

'Oh, his *name* was on the account.' Hamilton said. 'There just wasn't anything with his signature.'

'When did all this come out?'

'Apparently it was discovered a couple of months ago.'

White hid his surprise, a skill mastered after years in the courtroom where the first rule was to never show surprise. 'If the hospital had the information months ago, why did it wait so long before acting on it?'

Hamilton shrugged, his hands extended, palms up.

'And how did the State's Attorney get this information so fast?'

'I'd like to say you underestimate the skills of local law enforcement, but they can't take all the credit. The fact is, the hospital gave the State's Attorney all the documents. Apparently they were enough to make an open-and-shut case.'

'Then why hasn't Marty been charged with anything?'

'My guess . . . The State's Attorney is waiting for the federal Grand Jury to come out with an indictment. Then he is going to cede jurisdiction to the feds.'

White couldn't completely avoid reacting. It was so slight it wouldn't have been noticed by most people, but Hamilton had read faces for a living. Hamilton roared with laughter. 'You didn't know about the Grand Jury, did you?' Hamilton stammered between laughs.

White did his best to cover his surprise with a neutral look.

Hamilton continued to laugh. 'Counselor, if that's your best poker face, I have a regular Friday night game you'd be welcome to attend. Just bring a lot of money.'

White shrugged.

'If you didn't know about the Grand Jury, you'll *really* be happy with this. The Grand Jury is being run by the Ice Princess.'

'*Elizabeth Powell.*'

'None other.'

White shook his head and wrinkled his nose. 'That's just great.'

'Yeah. It's about like putting a pedophile in charge of the day care center.'

'What have you heard?'

'She's out for blood, if that's what you mean.'

'And?'

'She's ambitious, and this is a high-profile case.'

'I haven't had any dealings with her, but I've heard rumors. I hear she isn't big on following the rules.'

'Only if you consider fabricating evidence and threatening witnesses to be not following the rules,' Hamilton said.

White gave him a puzzled look.

'Lucius, things have changed since I started working as an investigator. Used to be the authorities really wanted to find the truth. There was something noble about being part of the justice system. Now it's all politics. Getting a conviction is all that counts. These new prosecutors will stop at nothing. That's one of the reasons I took my pension when I did.'

'I've wondered about that.'

'It's one thing to dig through trash—and I mean that both figuratively and literally. It's another thing to break the law while you're doing it. We may have gone a little overboard on occasion, but we knew what we were trying to do. We played by the rules, but the courts kept changing the rules. Maybe we weren't always as current as we should have been, but at least we tried.

'This new breed of prosecutors, all they want are convictions. They start out with what they have to prove, and they only want to know about evidence that proves it. In the old days, back before prosecutors had to turn everything over to the defendant's attorney, the prosecutors wanted to know everything. Now they're afraid they might discover something that will help the defendant. They just close their eyes and don't even try to get all the facts.'

White nodded absently, his thoughts suddenly on his father's trial. White wasn't permitted to attend the trial, but everyone in the community knew about the fabricated testimony by paid informants and others who made deals to avoid prosecution.

Hamilton shook his head before returning to their conversation. 'Do you remember the first time you cross-examined me?'

White suppressed a smile. He remembered.

'You were still a rookie lawyer back then. I figured you didn't know shit.' Hamilton grinned. 'I was ready to jerk you around and make you dance.'

'I thought so.'

'You cut me to ribbons.'

'I felt bad about that, Lou.'

Hamilton laughed. 'No, you didn't'

White laughed with him. 'You're right, I didn't.'

'You earned your spurs, Lucius. The cops respect you. They may not like what you do, but they respect you. Especially the old guys who know you're just doing your job.'

'Sometimes I wonder about that.'

'About what? Whether you're doing your job?'

'Whether any of us are doing our jobs.'

'I know the feeling . . . ,' Hamilton said, searching his pockets for a fresh pack of cigarettes. 'But enough of this sentimental crap. What else can I do for you?'

'Are there any interesting skeletons in the Ice Princess's closet?'

'I'll ask around. Are you looking for anything in particular?'

'I don't have any idea.'

'What's in it for me?'

'The joy of knowing justice is being done.'

'Since when is a criminal trial about justice?'

'There's a first time for everything,' White said.

Hamilton shrugged. 'I might be able to come up with something. Are we looking for facts or dirt?' Finding facts was something Hamilton could do as a matter of course. When he was looking for dirt, he was a pig on a truffle hunt.

'Just let me know what you come up with.'

When he next spoke, all signs of humor had left Hamilton's face. 'Lucius, watch your back with this one. The Ice Princess she likes nothing better than carving up defense attorneys and hanging their johnsons in her trophy case.'

'Nice imagery. I'll be sure to wear a cup.'

11.

One of the advantages of being a bank's largest individual customer is that the bank manager always has time to talk with you. It didn't hurt that Lucius White had also helped the bank manager's son avoid having a criminal record by getting him into a diversion program after he was arrested for possession of marijuana.

'Good morning, Mr. White. Can I get you some coffee?' the receptionist offered with a smile as soon as White stepped off the elevator.

At the mention of White's name Connie Baker, the Regional Manager of Gulf Coast Bank, looked up and signaled that she would be with him as soon as she could get off the phone.

'No thanks. But a Diet Pepsi would be nice.'

'I believe Ms. Baker keeps some Pepsi just for you,' the woman said with just the right amount of emphasis to assure White that he was a valued customer.

The receptionist placed the drink on a coaster beside White just as Connie Baker emerged from her office. She was five-foot-five-inches tall. She wore a tailored suit that gave her a professional look. Her dark brown hair was cut short. Her clear complexion, bright brown eyes and warm smile made her look younger than her forty years.

'Lucius. How are you?' Baker asked warmly. They had known each other for years.

'Couldn't be better, unless you could advance me a couple million interest free.'

'Not likely.' Baker laughed. 'John and I missed you at the club pig roast,' she added as she led White to the sofa in her office.

'We intended to be there,' White responded easily. 'but Leslie and I needed to get away for a while.'

'Oh?'

'Nothing special. I've just been feeling a little burned out lately. We were on the boat when the shit hit the fan.'

'How's Marty holding up?'

'About like you'd expect.'

'I feel sorry for Karen and the kids.'

'It's hard for everyone,' White agreed.

'I just can't believe it.'

'Can't believe what?'

'You know . . . what they're saying about Marty.'

White nodded noncommittally and took a sip of his soda.

'You don't think he did it . . . do you?'

White made a dismissive move, somewhere between a nod and a shrug. 'I'm his lawyer. It doesn't matter what I think.'

'But you're also his friend.'

'You're his friend, too,' White said, evading the question. 'What do you think?'

'No way.' Baker said. 'Not the Marty Bower I know.'

'Money does strange things to people.'

'I suppose. But I can't believe Marty would do anything like that.'

'Marty was a big spender.'

'What are you suggesting.'

'Nothing. Just making an observation.'

'You can't be serious,' Baker said as the implication of White's statement became clear.

'Defending a friend isn't easy. Part of me doesn't want to know anything that points to his guilt, but I can't defend him if I don't know everything.'

'Marty isn't the type.'

'Maybe I can get you on the jury.'

'Lucius,' Baker said, no longer smiling. 'I'll be happy if you can just keep me off the witness stand.'

'Is there a problem?'

Baker's look turned serious as she continued. 'I think I know why you're here. So before you ask, I have to remind you that I can't tell you anything about the Bower accounts.'

'But you talked to the F.B.I.'

'They're the F.B.I. Besides, they had a subpoena—not that they needed it.'

'What do you mean, *not that they needed it*?'

'They already had everything,' Baker said, making no effort to conceal her awareness that the information was important.

'And?' White prodded.

'Lucius, I can't . . .'

'It was worth a try,' White said. "How about this? I'll tell you what I know, and you can go into a laughing fit when I say something that isn't accurate.' White didn't know anything about the transactions Bower had been accused of masterminding. All he had to go on was what Lou Hamilton told him and some assumptions based on past cases involving money laundering.

'No guarantees. But it might be interesting to hear your theories.' Her expression was more serious than her words.

'My guess is that none of your records have been signed by Marty.'

Baker said nothing, but there was a slight curl at the corners of her mouth.

Kaleidoscope

'I'm also guessing that no deposits were ever made in the account except wire transfers.'

Baker's smile became more pronounced.

'... and that there was only one transfer into, and one transfer out of, the account per month'

Baker nodded.

'... and the transfers into and out of the account were virtually simultaneous.'

Baker smiled and shook her head in mock disbelief. 'How did you figure all that out?'

White shrugged. 'I confess. I already knew about the deposits and transfers. I was just guessing about the process. But automatic wire transfers was the only logical explanation.'

Baker laughed. 'Is there anything else you want to tell me while you're showing off?'

'Not unless there's something else I should know . . . without you telling me.'

'If I could, I would. But you know how it is.'

'Yeah, I know.'

'As it is, the legal department is all over this. It's only a matter of time before the bank examiners land on us. You can be sure a bank manager will soon be looking for a job.'

'Jesus. I'm sorry. I should have realized this would be a major bomb. I'm sorry I asked you anything.'

'Don't worry about *me*. If you want to show sympathy, save it for the poor slob at the Sarasota office where the account was opened.'

'*Sarasota?*'

'I *thought* you might find that interesting,' Baker said. 'I *can* tell you that the F.B.I. made the same assumption you did. They assumed that the account had been opened *here* because the hospital accounts are *here*—and we had all the records on the Bower account. I didn't tell them any different. The bank wants to stay as far away from this as it can, and we're not volunteering anything.'

'You said the F.B.I. didn't need its subpoena because it already had the bank records when they came to see you.'

'That's right.'

'Did anyone at the bank give the documents to the F.B.I.?'

'No.'

'How can you be sure?'

'We wouldn't have released any records without a subpoena, and I would have known about it.'

'But they got the records from someone.'

'Not legitimately.'

That much was obvious. It was equally apparent that Connie Baker didn't know how the F.B.I. had obtained the account documents, and didn't want to talk about the matter.

White changed the topic. 'So why does someone from here open an account at a bank in Sarasota?'

'No one did. At the time, the Sarasota bank was the Peoples Bank of Sarasota. The account was opened there. We acquired Peoples Bank three years ago. The person who opened the account, Brian Lester, was transferred down here. He brought the account records with him.'

'Why would the hospital open an account at a bank in Sarasota?'

'Good question.' Baker said. 'I wish I had an answer. The F.B.I. seems to think the account was opened *here*, without any documents being signed, as an accommodation to the hospital.'

'Why would a bank in Sarasota open an account, without any documents being signed, as an accommodation to the hospital?'

'I doubt if they would,' Baker said. 'But that's not the point. The F.B.I. didn't know about the Sarasota bank. They assumed that *we* opened the account.'

'Would *you* have opened an account without documentation?'

'Not under normal circumstances. But, if Marty needed an account opened for some sort of emergency transfer, and said he would be over in an hour to sign the papers, I'd probably accommodate him. Whoever opened that account had to be *very* important to the officer who opened it.'

'Brian Lester would know.'

'Presumably. But he's no longer with the Bank.'

'Where is he now?'

'He retired about two years ago and left town.' Baker said, bowing her head as she considered what else to say.

'And . . .?'

'I was a little curious about his retirement at the time. He was still a young man. Mid-forties or so. Our retirement plan isn't that good.'

'Maybe he had another source of money.'

Baker looked up.

'Did he have another source of money?'

'What do you have in mind?'

'Nothing. Just thinking to myself. But it looks like Mr. Lester is the key. Do you have an address for him?'

'It won't help. He's dead.'

12.

August days in southwest Florida are hot and humid, even in the early evening. The daily summer rains had come on schedule late in the afternoon, adding to the humidity.

White and Horse jogged slowly along the waterfront past Centennial Park, the warm-down after their regular evening run. It was an unstated rule that during their run they were not lawyer and investigator, just two competitive runners with a common background—on the gridiron and in the military—each trying to force the other to his physical limits. The final quarter-mile sprint from the new Edison Bridge to the statues of the Three Friends—Thomas Edison, Henry Ford and Harvey Firestone, Fort Myers' most famous seasonal residents—was serious business.

Sherlock was waiting by the gate in the fence surrounding White's warehouse. The fence had been made necessary by the event that earned Sherlock his nickname, "The Idiot Dog.'

Shortly after being rescued from the city pound, Sherlock discovered pelicans. True to her instincts, Sherlock took it upon herself to keep the area free of intrusive birds. In his first effort to protect his new homestead, he raced down the wharf, yapping at the birds at the top of his puppy lungs. The birds took flight—soaring low over the river. Sherlock followed.

Kaleidoscope

With legs flailing, and what had to be a look of extreme bewilderment, she charged off the end of the wharf and into space and landed ten feet out in the river.

The fence along the seawall was installed the following day.

As they collapsed in the patio chairs beside the seawall, Horse started to tell White about his meeting with Joe Morgan. 'Something just wasn't right,' Horse said. 'Morgan was eager to talk about Bower, but nothing else.'

'What's so surprising about that? We assumed the hospital was cooperating with the authorities.'

'It's not that. He didn't deny that they were working together. But the hospital's outside counsel seems to be running the show. Morgan said that the outside counsel suggested we meet where we wouldn't be seen together. That struck me as a minor detail for the outside-counsel to be concerned with.'

White nodded and rubbed his chin.

'And another thing,' Horse continued. 'Morgan kept saying he was sorry he was hurting Marty. He went out of his way to say he was only doing what he had to do for the hospital.'

'Do you believe him?'

'I don't know. If he believes what he's saying, but he isn't letting it get in his way.'

'What do you think? Is he feeling guilty about something?'

'You'd have to get a shrink to answer that one,' Horse said. 'But, yeah. It was something like that.'

White leaned forward, elbows on his knees, hands clasped in front of him and head bowed in thought.

'And there was something else.' White looked up as Horse spoke. 'I think Morgan was trying to point me in the direction of something else—but without really saying anything. I think he knows something else, but he wants the feds to discover it on their own.'

'Like some other documents . . . or hospital operation?'

'That's the funny thing. Whatever it is, I don't think it's *directly* connected to the hospital. It might even be outside the investigation.'

'Anything specific to go on?'

'Not really. But he kept talking about Marty's SCUBA diving.'

'Why was that strange?'

'Well, here's a guy who was Marty's college roommate. They've known each other for thirty years. He has to know that Marty is a golf addict. But the only thing he wanted to talk about was Marty's SCUBA diving trips. It was like he didn't know anything about Marty except that he liked to SCUBA dive in Belize and Grand Cayman.'

'Interesting.' White said. 'A drug transit country—with no criminal extradition treaty, and a tax haven—with strict banking security laws. How often did he say Marty went diving?'

'Couple times a year. And he made a point of saying Marty went diving with someone named Jim Worthington.'

'Is that someone from the hospital?'

'I don't think so. I figured we could ask Marty, so I didn't push it.'

'Why would Morgan want us to know about Worthington?'

'I don't know, but I don't see why Marty's diving could be important. That leaves *where he dived* and *who he dived with*. Like you said, Belize and Grand Cayman make interesting connections.'

'Any ideas?'

Horse shrugged. 'Morgan didn't say anything specific, but he definitely wanted to put Worthington on our radar screen. It was like he was trying to create a diversion.'

'That's not consistent,' White said. 'If they're trying to help nail Bower, why would they want to create a diversion?'

'Maybe *diversion* isn't the right word.' Horse stood and walked to the fence. 'Let's assume that Marty is being framed by the board. Morgan knows it, but he wants to save Bower. He can't come right out and tell everything he knows because he would be betraying his employer.'

'So he does the next best thing,' White said, picking up Horse's thought. 'He points the authorities in the direction of someone else.'

'It's a possibility.'

'Or, maybe he's just creating a false lead to keep the investigation from going in some other direction.'

'Maybe there's something else the hospital wants to hide?'

'It could just be something else *Morgan* wants to hide.'

'What could Morgan want to hide from the hospital?'

'It was just a thought,' White said. 'Anything else?'

'Maybe. Morgan went out of his way to say he was available anytime. He even volunteered his personal cell phone number. He wrote it on the matchbook I gave you back at the office.'

'The matchbook from the Turtle Reef Hotel on Grand Cayman?'

'Yeah.'

'Did Morgan say if he had ever been to the Caymans?'

'When I commented on the matchbook, he said he had been to Grand Cayman with his wife about a year ago. And there's one other thing,' Horse said, turning to White. 'When he was talking about being available to help, Morgan made a specific reference to past cooperation. It sounded like the cooperation with the feds didn't start with Marty's firing.'

White nodded.

'You look like you already knew that.'

'I suspected it. Lou Hamilton mentioned a federal Grand Jury.' White paused before continuing. 'I'd like to know what the Grand Jury is up to. According to Connie Baker, the F.B.I. came to her with a subpoena for records, but they didn't need to copy anything. They already had all the documents.'

'So they must have gotten them from Morgan.'

'But how would he have gotten them?'

'Morgan said he got them from the banker who set up the account,' Horse said. 'He told me he gave them to the government.'

'Are you sure that's what he said?'

'Yeah. Why?'

'Connie said the banker who opened the account left the bank two years ago. She also said the records had never been released. Morgan must have gotten them unofficially.'

'That fits,' Horse agreed. 'The whole subject seemed touchy—like something Morgan hadn't been asked about by the authorities and didn't want to discuss.'

'Maybe he knew he had violated some banking laws and just didn't want to get into it?'

'Maybe,' Horse said. 'But I think there's more to it than that. I think he had something to hide.'

Horse waited while White mulled over some thought. 'According to Connie Baker, the account officer was a guy named Brian Lester. He left the bank a couple of year ago . . . but he may be dead now.'

'You want me to look into him?'

White shook his head. 'Later. It's a loose end, but not a high priority. I need to know everything about the transfers of funds.'

'Anything else you need while I'm nosing around in their system?' Horse asked. It would never occurr to him that he might not be able to break into the computer system.

'Not for now. Just find out how the money was transferred.'

Kaleidoscope

13.

Lucius White's War Room was a windowless conference between White's and Harris's offices. In the middle of the room was an oak conference table surrounded by eight chairs. At one end of the room was a white marker board. The side walls of the room were covered with corkboard. Early in every case, seemingly random facts were recorded on white cards and posted on the corkboards walls. As patterns later emerged, facts were transferred to colored cards, each color representing facts that related to different events.

The corkboard walls were still empty when Lucius White, Harry Harris, Martin Bower and Horse McGee gathered for their first meeting since the announcement of Bower's termination.

White stood and walked slowly to the end of the room, organizing his thoughts. 'Let's start with what we know.' White held up a hand, all fingers extended, and beginning to list what they had discovered. 'First, we know Marty is going to be accused of using the hospital's computer to make transfers from the hospital account to a bank account supposedly opened by him.'

Bower nodded. Harris jotted notes on a yellow pad. Horse began filling out white 3x5 cards.

'Second,' White continued to fold down fingers as he spoke, 'we know there is no *direct* evidence that Marty actually opened the account.'

More attentive nods.

'Third, we know the hospital knew about the money transfers for more than a month before Marty was fired.

'Fourth, we know the hospital was already working with the U.S. Attorney when Marty was finally fired.

'And fifth, I think we can assume Marty's firing had something to do with the hospital's merger plans.'

White bowed his head and continued to pace. 'What we don't know is how these facts are connected.' His voice was soft and pensive, as if he was thinking out loud. When he reached the end of the room, he stopped and turned to the others. 'There seem to be two alternatives. One is that the people who wanted Marty fired just stumbled onto the thefts, and are using the discovery as justification for the firing.' White paused, seeming to consider the logic of the first alternative before continuing. 'The other possibility is that whoever orchestrated Marty's termination is also behind the thefts and is trying to frame Marty.'

'What makes you think the same people are behind both matters?' Harris asked.

'Right now it's just a hunch. But someone at the hospital obtained copies of bank records without going through official channels.'

'Maybe,' Harris said. 'Maybe they didn't do anything to get the bank records. Whoever opened the account would have those records. Maybe they already had them.'

'Then all we have to do is find out who opened the account,' Bower said hopefully.

'It isn't that easy,' Horse said. 'The documents the hospital turned over to the State's Attorney show that the account was a business corporate account opened in the name of . . . I have it here somewhere . . . Walco, Inc.'

''Let me guess,' Harris said. 'Walco used a post office box as its mailing address. There is no such corporation, and post office records don't get us anywhere.'

Horse smiled. 'Right. But you don't get any points for that one. It was too easy.'

Bower looked from Horse to Harris and back at Horse.

'So where does that leave us?' Harris asked.

'I don't know, but there have been some other developments. While Andy was meeting with Lou Hamilton and Connie Baker, I met with Joe Morgan. He didn't give me anything that Andy didn't get from Hamilton, but he said something about Marty making SCUBA diving trips to Grand Cayman and Belize. He seemed to want the feds to look for something in Grand Cayman or Belize, or something connected to a guy named Jim Worthington who went diving with Marty.'

Bower suddenly stiffened and looked at Horse.

'What is it, Marty?' White asked.

'It's . . . ah . . . nothing.' Bower said. 'You just caught me off-guard. Jim is an old friend. We've known each other since we served together in Vietnam. And, yes, we go diving together . . . just about every year.'

'How would Morgan know about Worthington? And why would the hospital want the authorities to look at him?'

Bower hesitated, studying the grain of the table before responding. 'Like I said, I've known Jim for a long time. A couple of years ago he had a cocaine problem and I helped him out.'

'But how does Morgan know about Worthington's past?'

'Jim got arrested on drug charges about five years ago. He needed money, and he came to me for help. I arranged for him to do some consulting work for the hospital—to help with expenses—and I got Joe Morgan to represent him.'

'Why Morgan?'

'Joe was still in private practice at the time, but he was already doing some work for the hospital . . . and some of the board members. In fact, he was representing Nat Sommers' kid about the same time he was representing Jim. But I don't know what that could have to do with me now.'

'It's probably nothing.' White said. 'I didn't mean to upset you.'

'I'm not upset,' Bower said, his words contradicted by his tone and look. 'It's just that Jim has had some tough times. I can't imagine why his name even came up.'

'It probably doesn't have anything to do with Mr. Worthington,' White said. 'They were probably just using your diving to make a connection to the Cayman Islands.'

'But why would *that* be important?'

'I think we're coming to that,' White said, turning to Horse.

'After you talked to Lou Hamilton and Connie Baker, we knew the money was being transferred from the hospital to an account in a Sarasota bank. The records the hospital turned over to the State's Attorney show transfers of $50,000 a month.'

'How were the transfers being made?' Harris asked.

'Actually, it was pretty simple.' Horse said. 'Every month, the hospital's computer sent the bank's computer a message telling it to transfer money to the Walco account in the Sarasota bank. But that's not the most interesting thing. As soon as the money arrived in Sarasota, it was wire-transferred to another bank. The bank records we got from the State's Attorney show wiring instructions for transfers from the Walco account to a bank in the Cayman Islands.'

As he spoke, Horse stood and walked to the marker board where he wrote:

> 1. Wire transfers from hospital account to account in Peoples Bank. [$50,000 per month]

Kaleidoscope

2. Simultaneous wire transfers from Peoples Bank to a bank in the Cayman Islands.

'That reminds me, Marty,' White interrupted. 'Have you ever done any business with the Peoples Bank of Sarasota?'

'Never even heard of it,' Bower said. 'Why?'

'That's the bank where the money was originally sent. Peoples Bank was later acquired by the Gulf Coast Bank,' White said. '*That's* why everyone thought the transfers were made between two accounts in the same bank.'

'Is that important?'

'Right now it's just a fact, Marty. It's too early to know what's important.' White waited until he was sure Bower was focused, then nodded to Horse to continue.

'At that point I came to a dead end, so I went back to the beginning to find out how the transfers started. I went into the hospital's computer system, and found the subroutine that made the wire transfers. The interesting thing is that the same program made random adjustments to various executive operating accounts.'

As he spoke, Horse wrote:

1. Money transfers reduce hospital cash account.
2. Corresponding amounts allocated to executive accounts as expenses.

'And that produced the accounting discrepancies Marty mentioned?' White said.

'That's what it looks like.'

White leaned back in his chair and sighed. 'Okay. At least we know how the plan worked. Now we have to—'

'Not so fast, Lucius,' Horse said.

White looked up. 'There's more.'

'A *lot* more.'

White rubbed his temples. 'I'm not going to like this, am I?'

'Probably not.'

White ran his fingers through his hair. 'Okay. Let's have it.'

'The program I'm talking about did one other thing,' Horse said as he wrote:

1. Drug inventory account *reduced* by $50,000.
2. Accounts receivable *increased* by $50,000 as payments due for drugs sold.

'The way I figure it, *this* part of the program was supposed to make it look like the hospital had sold drugs and was awaiting payment.'

White looked at Bower. 'Who would the hospital be selling drugs to?'

'Maybe one of the out-patient clinics.'

'Were drugs actually being sold to subsidiaries?'

Bower shrugged and made a helpless gesture with his hands. 'I don't know.'

'Horse?'

'I don't think so,' Horse said. 'But the hospital was *receiving* money that it recorded as payment for drugs.'

White, Harris and Bower all looked at Horse with blank expressions.

Horse concentrated, trying to find words to simplify what he knew was a complex transaction. 'I knew the computer was recording artificial drug sales, and increasing the accounts receivable to account for the sales. If that had been going on for five years, without any payments being received, the accounts receivable for the drug sales would have been huge. *Someone* would have noticed the increases. I figured something was being done to keep that from happening.

Kaleidoscope

'When I dug a little further I found that the hospital was *receiving* monthly wire transfers of $50,000 from a New York bank. *These* transfers were being recorded as payment for the drugs that were *supposed* to have been sold to one of the hospital's subsidiaries.' As he spoke, he continued to write on the marker board.

1. $50,000 recorded as receipt from New York bank.
2. Accounts receivable *reduced* increased by $50,000 to reflect payment for supposed drug sales.

'Wait a minute,' Harris said. 'Are you telling us the hospital was receiving payments for drugs it never actually sold?'

Horse grinned. 'That's right.'

'What the hell . . .' Harris said, shaking his head. 'Why is some New York bank making payments for drugs that were never sold in the first place?'

'It isn't.' Horse paused, giving the others time to absorb his statement before continuing. 'The money coming in from the New York bank is the *same* money that was initially transferred to the account at Peoples Bank—and from there to the bank in the Caymans.'

'*Jesus.*' White said. 'Let me see if I understand this.' He approached the marker board and began adding the new facts to Horse's list.

1. Wire transfers from hospital account to account in Peoples Bank. [$50,000 per month]
2. Simultaneous wire transfers from Peoples Bank to a bank in the Cayman Islands.

3. *From the Caymans, the money it goes to a bank in New York.*
4. *From the New York bank, the money comes back to the hospital.*

'Is that right?'

Horse nodded.

'So no *money* is actually being stolen. It just leaves the hospital, circles through other banks, and comes back to the hospital.'

'Right.'

'And the real scheme was to steal *drugs*.'

'That's what it looks like.'

'But what was the point of cycling the money?' Harris asked.

White stepped away from the marker board and sat on the edge of the conference table, studying the list of transactions. 'My guess,' he said, slowly, 'is that the money cycle was set up as a diversion. In fact . . . it's pretty clever.'

'Clever? How?'

'First of all, the theft of drugs alone wouldn't have any obvious suspects. By building a system that started out with the transfer of money to a bank account with Marty's name on it, the scheme created a trail to an obvious suspect—Marty.

'Plus, the only thing that would appear to be leaving the hospital was money. If there was ever an audit, there wouldn't be any reason to investigate the drug accounts because the sales and receipts all balanced out.'

'But even if that's true,' Harris said, 'it doesn't explain why the hospital has only accused Marty of taking money. Why wasn't the rest of the scheme disclosed?'

White thumbed the edge of his legal pad as he considered the question. 'I can think of a couple of reasons. The obvious reason is that they don't know everything. The audit of the accounting discrepancies gave them what they needed to get rid of Marty—and they had no reason to look for anything else.'

'Or,' Harris interrupted and completed White's thought, 'they already knew what else was going on and didn't want it disclosed.'

'As far as Marty goes, I think Lucius is right,' Horse said. 'But if we're going to figure out who's behind the scheme, there are some other things we need to consider.

'Two years ago, the wiring instructions for transferring funds from the Sarasota bank to the Caymans were changed. Now the money is being sent to a *different* account in the Cayman bank—not the same account that received the funds, and sent them to the New York bank. After the change was made, no more money went into the *old* account at the Cayman bank, so there wasn't anything to be transferred to New York—and routed back to the hospital.'

White approached the marker board and corrected the summary of money transfers.

1. Wire transfers from hospital account to account in Peoples Bank. [$50,000 per month]
2. Simultaneous wire transfers from Peoples Bank to a bank in the Cayman Islands.
3. ~~From the Caymans, the money it goes to a bank in New York.~~
4. ~~From the New York bank, the money comes back to the hospital.~~

'So, for two years,' he said in a soft voice, almost as if he were talking to himself, 'money has been getting sent to a new account in the Cayman Islands and it's just sitting there?'

'Unless someone has moved it,' Horse said.

'Amazing.' Harris muttered.

'How do we know this happened two years ago?' White asked. He had a feeling the timing meant something, but he didn't know what.

'There weren't that many transfers into and out of the Sarasota account. Just one in and one out each month. I did a trace on the outbound transfers and recorded the date of each. The destination bank account code changed two years ago.'

'But the money was still leaving the hospital until it discovered the program and fired Marty. Is that right?'

'That's what it looks like.'

'Which means that $1,200,000—$50,000 a month for twenty-four months—left the hospital but never returned.'

'Yes.'

'What about the drugs? Have they stopped leaving the hospital?'

'I don't know for sure,' Horse said. 'I looks like the transfers stopped about six months before Marty was fired.'

'Now we're getting somewhere,' White said. 'Now we know what was happening and when the deal stopped.'

'But do we know when it started, Horse?' Harris asked.

'The coding in the original program gives us some idea of when the scheme started,' Horse said. 'The software has a system for recording the date of program changes. The date of the last recorded change in the money transfer subroutine is five years ago.'

'But do we know this scheme started five years ago?' White asked as he stood, walked to the marker board at the far end of the room and picked up a colored marker which he twirled idly as he paced.

'Not exactly. The master program only records the date of the most recent version of the subroutine. All we know is the last change to the program was made five years ago. There may have been an even earlier version we don't know about.'

Harris began tapping his index finger softly on the arm of his wheelchair. 'Maybe we do know that the scheme started five years ago.' He paused before continuing. 'The hospital claims Marty stole three million dollars. We know the program transferred $50,000 a month.' Nods. 'That's $600,000 a year, and three million over five years. But the statute of limitations for grand theft is *seven* years. If the thefts had been going on for more than five years, the hospital would have claimed a greater loss.'

'You're probably right,' White agreed as he stood and walked to the mini-refrigerator where he recovered a Diet Pepsi. He opened the can and sipped slowly as he paced the length of the conference room.

'So? Where does this leave us?' Horse asked.

'I don't know. But I don't think we have a paddle,' White said absently. 'We seem to know what happened, and we can assume that whoever is behind the transfers is also responsible for getting Marty fired. But we're no closer to knowing who they are—or why they needed to get rid of Marty.'

For several minutes, they all studied the marker board. Finally, Bower broke the silence. 'Can't we just go to the other banks and find out who opened the accounts?'

'It's not that simple,' White said. 'We already know the Sarasota bank records won't get us anywhere, and the Cayman Island banking secrecy laws will prevent us from getting much information on *that* account.'

'What about the New York account?'

'We *could* subpoena the information from the New York bank. But the bank would have to tell the account holder about the subpoena. Once the bank did that, the bad guys would know what we had discovered. We may have to do that later, but, for now, I don't want to let anyone else know what we've discovered. Besides, what we really need to know is who programmed the hospital computers.'

'Maybe . . .' Harris interrupted. 'Maybe it would be worth chasing down the other side of the trail—the drugs. Do we know what drugs were disappearing?'

'No. All I could find was the number of the drug accounts. It's here somewhere,' Horse mumbled as he shuffled through his papers. 'Here it is. XA999-01.'

White turned to Bower. 'Does the number mean anything to you ?'

'It's an account for experimental drugs.'

White sat up, instinctively aware that they had stumbled onto something significant. ''What are those accounts for?''

'The hospital is involved in a number of clinical drug testing programs. We do them under contract to the Food and Drug Administration in connection with the medical school at the University of Miami. Because those drugs aren't part of the hospital's regular treatment programs, they're inventoried in separate accounts. The 999 designates an experimental drug account, and the 01 designates the year it was established.'

'What does the XA mean?' White asked, fearing the answer.

'AIDS drugs,' Bower said.

White tensed. 'Oh, shit.'

* * * * *

After Bower left the meeting, White continued his discussion with Harris and Horse. 'It looks like we have at least two separate problems to solve.'

Harris stopped shuffling his papers and looked at White. 'Two?'

'Yeah. First, we have the money transfers Marty has been charged with.'

Harris nodded. 'Okay.'

'Then we have the real theft, the drug transfers that no one else seems to know about yet.'

'No one except whoever is behind them,' Harris corrected.

'Right.'

Kaleidoscope

'But those aren't our only problems,' Harris said. 'We still don't know why Marty was fired. If he's being set up, he's being set up for a reason. There isn't anything connecting the drug thefts and Marty's firing?''

'You don't think they're connected?'

'No. I agree they're connected. But it's still possible Marty is behind the thefts. Maybe the discovery of the thefts just gave the Board a convenient reason for firing him— something they wanted to do anyway.'

'You're not convinced Marty is being framed?'

Harris drummed his fingers on the arm of his wheelchair. 'I'm a little concerned about Marty's reaction this morning.'

'You noticed.'

'Yes. He didn't register any surprise when Horse mentioned the computer program stuff—or the bank accounts.'

'What are you thinking?'

'Maybe he already knew.'

'You don't know the half of it,' Horse said.

White rubbed his eyes. 'Why do I have the feeling you aren't about to give me some good news?'

'I don't know what kind of news it is,' Horse said, slipping onto the sofa. 'Maybe nothing. But I did a work-up on Brian Lester, the banker who supposedly set up the Walco account.'

'I'm not going to like this, am I?'

Horse shrugged. 'Connie Baker was right; he died about six months ago. They found his body sitting in his car at a shopping center in Sarasota. Officially, he died of an overdose of pain killer. Nothing about his death seemed significant until Marty just told us about the drug account.'

'The experimental AIDS drugs.'

'Right. According to the detective I talked to, Lester was being treated for AIDS.'

White released a soft whistle.

'But, according to the doctor who was treating him, Lester was never given a prescription for any kind of painkiller.'

'If he was a drug user, he could have gotten painkillers anywhere in the street.'

'That's the logical assumption, and that's what the detective figured—at first.'

'At first?'

'According to the autopsy report, Lester showed no signs of long-term drug abuse.'

'That might explain the overdose,' White said. 'Without much experience, he could have just taken too much.'

'Maybe. But the detective didn't think so. Lester's body was found in a parking lot. But the amount of drugs in his system was too much for him to have driven to the lot after taking the pills. According to the medical examiner, Lester would have been unconscious within minutes of taking the pills.'

'Maybe he connected with someone at the parking lot and took the pills there.'

'Anything's possible. But the detective said it was an upscale suburban parking lot. No history as a place where drugs were traded. The detective is convinced Lester was murdered.'

14.

Lucius White was in the bedroom, packing for his trip to the Cayman Islands, when the elevator door opened and Leslie called, 'Are you decent?'

'Unfortunately, yes,' White answered. 'I'm in the bedroom.'

'Sounds promising so far,' Leslie said as she entered the room and kissed him.

'If you have anything lewd and adventurous in mind, you better be quick,' White said. 'I'm expecting my girlfriend any minute.'

Leslie threw a pillow at him as she dropped onto the bed. 'Planning on sneaking out on me in the middle of the night?'

'It's only noon.'

'Then we have time for some make-up sex before you leave.'

'What do we have to make up for?'

'We'll think of something,' Leslie said, before turning serious and asking, 'Where are you going?'

'I have to run down to the Caymans to check out some things in Marty Bower's case.'

'You'll never make it if you run. There's water in the way. Why don't you take the plane?'

'Very funny.' White picked up the pillow and threw it back at Leslie.

'I try to hold up my end.'

'So we're back to the sex again?'

Leslie smiled. 'You are a dirty old man. Fortunately,' she said as walked across the room, unbuttoning her blouse as she went, 'I like dirty old men.'

White snapped his overnight bag closed and walked into the living room, followed by Leslie and Sherlock. He opened a can of Diet Pepsi for himself, poured a glass of wine for Leslie, and dropped onto the middle of the sofa in front of the fireplace. Leslie curled her legs under her as she sat leaning against the arm of the sofa. Sherlock crawled up on the leather chair opposite them, circled three times and settled in with her head on the arm, watching intently.

'There is something you might be able to help me with,' White said. 'When we were having dinner at Billy's, you mentioned something about thefts of AIDS drugs.'

Leslie sipped her wine and cocked her head to the side.

'The hospital is involved in the trials of some new AIDS drugs.'

'I know. It's a study being conducted in connection with the medical school at the University of Miami.'

'There may be some connection between the money Marty is supposed to have taken and the disappearance of experimental drugs.'

Leslie sat up attentively. 'You don't think Marty is involved in drugs, do you?'

'Not a chance. At least, I don't think so. But the drug transfers stopped about the time you noticed an increase in drug thefts from the clinics.'

'That *does* seem strange.'

White stood and began circling the room. 'If I could get my hands on experimental AIDS drugs, what would I do with them?'

'For one thing you could retire very quickly. The new drugs are worth a fortune on the black market.'

'How so?'

'Well, first of all, they're very expensive. Treatment with the main HIV suppressants costs more than six thousand dollars a year. And that's the cost of the drugs alone. On the black market, the new, exotic drugs go for upwards of twenty thousand a year. The experimental drugs aren't even available through clinics. They're only available to people in the clinical trials. People who have money—and are HIV positive—will pay virtually anything for the new stuff.'

White took another sip of his soda. 'I thought AIDS drugs could only be dispensed through programs.'

'Sometimes yes, sometimes no.'

'Which brings me back to my first question. If I can get my hands on these drugs, who do I sell them to?'

'You would probably sell them to an unethical doctor who specializes in diseases of the rich.'

'And if that supply were to suddenly dry up?'

'There would be an increased demand for drugs from any other source,' Leslie completed White's thought. 'Maybe involving thefts from legitimate treatment programs.' Her eyes brightened at the possibility of solving the problem at the clinics. 'I could ask around . . . find out if any doctors have been treating special clients.'

'No. You better not,' White said, closer to a command than a suggestion. 'But maybe you can give Horse somewhere to start. I don't want you getting involved in anything more than that.'

'Are we going to go through this again?' Leslie snapped.

'Leslie,' White began, his tone unintentionally condescending. 'This isn't something you should be involved in. If we're right, there could be some really bad people involved.'

'And, as usual,' Leslie said harshly, 'you don't think I'm capable of dealing with it because I'm a girl.'

'It isn't that. It's . . .'

'Yes, it is. That's *exactly* what it is. But people with AIDS are victims, not dangerous criminals.'

'Damn it. This isn't about AIDS victims. We're talking about the people who deal in black market drugs. You said it yourself. There's big money involved. We don't know how big this is, but when there's a lot of money at stake, bad people tend to get very upset at the people who investigate their business.'

As it usually did when they discussed her participation in criminal cases, the conversation was going badly, and heading for worse.

'And what makes you think I'm not just as capable of taking care of myself as Horse?'

White was tempted to point out the obvious. Horse was a lot bigger than Leslie and could be just as bad as the bad guys, if necessary. But the discussion was past the point where a logical argument had any relevance.

'Why can't you think of me as just like you, only prettier and smarter?'

'Your sex isn't the point.'

'The hell it isn't. Let's just drop this before we get into another fight—with no chance for any make up sex. Leslie stood and headed for the bedroom.

'Leslie . . .' White called after her.

'I know. I'll talk to Horse this afternoon,' Leslie said curtly as she slammed the bedroom door.

Sherlock looked at White forlornly, as if asking, *what have you done now?*

Kaleidoscope

15.

It was late afternoon when White's Lear 45 started its final approach into Roberts International Airport northeast of Georgetown on Grand Cayman Island. The flight took almost twice as long as a direct commercial flight, but what fun was it to own a private jet if you didn't use it? Besides, White couldn't order a commercial pilot to take a long slow circle around Grand Cayman while he savored the beauty of the shallow turquoise and teal reef extending a quarter mile from the shore before plunging a thousand feet into the black depths.

Ten minutes after touching down, White embraced Sir Hugh Greenfield, former High Solicitor of the Cayman Islands, the equivalent of the U. S. Attorney General, and now one of its most respected solicitors.

'My good friend. How have you been?' Sir Hugh grinned, ignoring the British custom of quiet reserve.

'Sad to think how long it's been. With any luck we can make up for lost time.'

'I've made arrangements for you to stay at the Turtle Reef Hotel. That's where I'm staying while the house is being remodeled.'

'I'm not familiar with it.'

'It's the island's newest hotel. It just opened two weeks ago and already its bar has become the major gathering place for those in search of interesting activities.'

* * * * *

Two hours after his plane touched down, White had checked into the Turtle Reef Hotel and rejoined Sir Hugh at the outdoor bar. White's attention was on a statuesque woman whose more than ample breasts and firm ass were barely concealed by a bathing suit for which she could have been arrested at most public beaches in the United States.

'The natives are attractive,' Sir Hugh said.

'Absolutely.' White agreed. 'It's not how I remember things being in the old empire.'

Sir Hugh chuckled. 'Scandalous isn't it. The Ladies Tea Society is having fits.'

The waitress, herself very pleasant on the eyes, brought them iced tea. As she walked away, there was a little something extra in the way she moved her hips.

'I think she likes you,' Sir Hugh said.

'She has good taste.'

'Still having problems with your confidence, I see.'

White ignored Sir Hugh and changed the subject to the purpose of his visit. 'Were you able to get any information on the banking transactions I told you about?'

'Only a little. As you know, our banking laws are very strict. The Caymans' treaty with the United States allows disclosure of information to your federal authorities in certain criminal and tax matters. Unfortunately, there are no provisions for information to be released to individuals such as yourself, even in the same matters in which information can be released to your government.'

White was familiar with these provisions of Cayman law, but listened patiently as his friend continued. 'As a practical

Kaleidoscope

matter, the rules only apply to *Cayman* banks. Many of the banks doing business here are branches of foreign banks. Information relating to their clients can be obtained from the parent bank, if it is located in another country where the courts can order disclosure of information. When a depositor wants the full protection of the Cayman banking laws, he must deal with a bank that is chartered here and has no branch offices in countries where less strict laws apply. There are only a few such banks. From the wire transfer instructions you sent, I've been able to determine that the funds you seek were transferred to one of these banks.'

'But they won't tell me anything,' White guessed, resigning himself to the inevitable.

'Not directly, I'm afraid.'

'So I'm left with a dead end.'

'Perhaps so; perhaps not.' Sir Hugh said. 'I've arranged for you to meet with an officer of the bank to which the funds were transferred. He won't disclose any information about the account you are tracking, but he may provide you with other useful information.' As he spoke, Sir. Hugh looked toward the door, lifted his hand and raised his index finger. 'In fact, here he is now.'

The banker was tall and gaunt with a narrow face and a thin gray mustache. In spite of the heat, he wore a dark gray suit and vest, complete with pocket watch and chain. No one was likely to mistake him for anything but an English banker.

Sir Hugh introduced White to Nigel Carrington. They chatted briefly about White's flight and the state of island tourism. Finally, Sir Hugh turned the conversation to the reason for White's trip.

'Nigel, I've explained our banking laws, and told Mr. White there is little you can disclose about your customers.'

'Quite right.' Carrington said, without embellishment.

'Mr. Carrington,' White took over, 'I'm involved in a criminal case in which several million dollars have been routed through a series of banks by wire transfers. One of those banks was yours.'

White paused and waited for a response.

Carrington nodded but said nothing.

White realized he would have to disclose more than he had intended. 'We already know that the funds came into your bank.'

Carrington tapped his fingertips lightly on the table. 'Would these transfers, by and chance, be drug related?'

'We don't think so.'

Carrington relaxed, and White continued. 'It's possible the funds were later transferred from your bank to another bank, probably with an automatic wire transfer.'

'Are you saying that no one in the bank would have been involved?' Carrington asked, his expression suggesting that he was concerned about a problem of his own.

'We don't know. Is it possible for such transfers to have been made automatically—without anyone in the bank being involved?'

Carrington considered the question before answering. 'We can accommodate certain of our customers in that way.'

'So a customer could simply request that any funds received in his account be transferred to another bank?'

'Certain customers. Yes. That is correct.'

'Would he have to make this request separately for each transfer?'

'Not necessarily,' Carrington said. 'However, you should know that our bank doesn't engage in such transfers to countries known to be active in the drug trades.'

White removed a photograph, taken at a hospital Christmas party, from his coat pocket. He laid it on the table in front of Carrington and pointed to Martin Bower. 'Do you recognize this man?'

Carrington took the photograph and examined it carefully.

'No. I don't,' Carrington said, still looking intently at the photograph. 'But I *do* recognize this *other* man.' Carrington was pointing at the face of Joseph Morgan, Esq.

* * * * *

When White returned to his apartment the following evening, Leslie was curled up in the corner of the sofa clutching a cushion. A glass of white wine sat untouched on the coffee table. Her eyes were red and puffy, and she didn't look up when he entered.

White sat on the sofa beside her, and waited.

'They took Billy Reynolds to the hospital this afternoon.' Her voice was so soft it was hard to tell whether she was talking to White or to herself.

White accepted the news without response. He had long ago acknowledged the inevitable. He knew and liked Billy, but not in the same way Leslie did.

'He isn't going to make it,' she said. 'It isn't fair.'

'No, it isn't.'

'He couldn't get the drugs he needed,' she said. 'When he was diagnosed, his condition was too advanced for the standard drugs to do him any good.'

White knew there was more.

'The hospital was testing some new drugs that might have helped him. We tried to get him into the program.'

'I didn't know that.'

Leslie retreated to her thoughts as White waited.

'They wouldn't let him into the clinical trials.'

'Why not? Why wouldn't they let him in the trials?'

'Dr. Sommers—he's the medical director for the program—said they just didn't have enough drugs to go around.'

It took a moment for the implications of Leslie's statement to register with White. 'Wouldn't the program have to account for all of the drugs it uses?'

Leslie straightened and turned to face White. 'Of course.'

'How would they do that if the drugs weren't all being used to treat patients in the clinical trials?'

Leslie shrugged. 'I don't know. They have to keep records of all the patients—and all the drugs they're given.'

'So how would they account for drugs that weren't being given to patients in the trials?'

Leslie thought for a moment before responding. 'I suppose they could make up phony patient records. But that would make the clinical trial data useless. Is that what they were doing?'

'It's a possibility,' White said, as he began to explain what they knew about the money transfers and the missing AIDS drugs.

'So they didn't have enough drugs to let Billy into the program because they were stealing the drugs.'

'That's what it's beginning to look like.'

'Those bastards.' Leslie said softly. White held her trembling body. 'Those fucking, thieving bastards.'

16.

White heard voices in his office as he entered the mezzanine. One voice he recognized as that of Martin Bower. The other voice wasn't familiar.

Grace Matthews glared up at White. 'You have visitors,' she grumbled sternly. 'They don't have an appointment.' At times like this, White wasn't sure who really ran the office, but it didn't matter. For Leslie and Grace, the same rule applied: apologize quickly and hope you find out what you did wrong later.

'I'm sorry, Grace. I wasn't expecting anyone.'

Matthews responded with her customary 'hrumph' and the matter was settled.

'I don't think Grace likes me.' Bower said as White crossed the room and took his hand.

'She can be a bit over-protective,' White said. 'She had a bad marriage to an abusive husband. It left her pretty bitter about men in general. It takes her a while to warm up to some people.'

'How long does it take?'

White chuckled. 'About ten years.'

White extended his hand to the man standing beside Bower. 'I'm Lucius White.'

'Jim Worthington.' the man said, taking White's hand. Somewhere in the back of White's mind, a filing cabinet opened and he reviewed what he knew about Worthington. It wasn't much. Just enough for White to know something important was happening. 'I've heard a lot about you,' Worthington added with a smile.

'Don't believe everything you hear.'

'Don't worry, it's all—'

'Lucius,' Bower interrupted nervously. 'I think Jim needs your help. His house was broken into.'

White looked from Bower to Worthington, then back at Bower. 'And you think it may have something to do with your case?'

'I don't . . . I mean, I don't think anything,' Bower said. 'It's just that . . . You asked me about Jim a while ago. You told me it didn't mean anything when Joe Morgan mentioned my SCUBA trips with Jim. But when Jim told me his house had been broken into, it seemed like more than a coincidence, so I came straight to you.'

White also saw the break-in as more than a coincidence, but there was no reason to worry Bower. 'You did the right thing bringing Jim here, but it's probably nothing to be concerned about.'

White thought for a moment, then addressed Bower. 'Marty, I think I better talk with Jim alone. If he does need a lawyer, your presence would breach the attorney-client privilege.'

'But I'm a client, too—and this may have to do with me.'

Why does every client think they know what the law means?

'Marty, the attorney-client privilege only covers communication between an attorney and his client when no one else is present. If you're present when I talk to Jim, our conversation wouldn't be privileged, and I could be forced to testify about our conversation.'

'Okay, okay,' Bower said with resignation.

'And while we're on the subject, nothing you tell each other is privileged. From now on, don't talk about either the break-in or your case between yourselves.'

* * * * *

As Bower left the room, White closed the door and directed Worthington to a seat on the sofa. 'All right, Jim. What happened?'

'Saturday afternoon, while I was out fishing, someone broke into my house. They went through the papers in my study and tried to access my computer. Then they planted a vial of rock cocaine in the tank of the toilet in my guest bathroom.'

White's calm appearance hid his mounting suspicion. It wasn't just the facts. It was Worthington. He had been the victim of a crime, but he remained in total control. He was able to give a concise, emotionless summary of events that would have left most people agitated and disorganized.

White took a legal pad from the stack on the end table and removed a pen from his pocket. 'Start from the beginning. How do you know someone broke in?'

'I have a motion activated video surveillance system. When I came back from fishing, the indicator light was flashing. Everything is on videotape.'

Jesus Christ. I thought I had heard it all. White tapped his pen on the pad, putting his thoughts in order, before continuing. 'Did the police respond to the alarm?'

'There isn't any alarm. That's not the purpose of the system. I don't have anything of value in the house. The security system was installed by the Department of Justice. They're not interested in who tries to steal from me. They just want to know who may try to find me.'

'Wait a minute.' White interrupted. Now it made sense. 'You're in the Witness Protection Program?'

Worthington looked as if he suddenly realized he had revealed something he had not intended to disclose. Without speaking, he stood and walked slowly to the picture window overlooking the river. 'Marty trusts you,' he said cautiously, still looking at the river. 'That's good enough for me. The fact is, I don't exist.'

White sat quietly, straining to show no response to Worthington's unusual revelation.

'Five years ago,' Worthington continued, 'I cooperated with the F.B.I. in an investigation of drug trafficking in Philadelphia. My reward was the Witness Protection Program.'

White made a few notes on his legal pad before looking up. 'Maybe you better start from the beginning.'

'I worked for a computer specialist for a defense contractor . . . and I was a cocaine addict. If my addiction had become known, I would have lost my job—and my career. I was blackmailed into helping drug dealers avoid wiretaps . . . and transfer money out of the country. When I was caught, I exchanged what I knew about the dealers for immunity and witness protection.' Worthington returned to the sofa and sat opposite White. 'When the feds arrested the dealers, I committed 'suicide' by driving my car into a bridge abutment. A little plastic surgery and here I am.'

It took White a moment to absorb this information. He had a dozen questions about Worthington's past, but this wasn't the time to ask them. Instead, he asked, 'How did you and Marty get together?'

'We served together in 'Nam, and we've been friends ever since. When I got my balls in a wringer in Philadelphia, Marty got Joe Morgan to represent me. Marty also loaned me the money to pay my legal bills. Afterwards, he used his contacts to get me into a rehab program. When that was all

Kaleidoscope

over, I needed to get lost for good. Southwest Florida was as good a place as any.'

White rocked in his chair, leaning back and staring at the ceiling while letting Worthington's revelations sink in. 'So now your house has been broken into, and Marty thinks there's a connection to his case.'

'I don't know if there's a connection, but I agree with Marty. The timing is suspect.'

'Do you think you may still be a mob target?'

Worthington made no effort to correct White's assumption that Worthington's prior activities involved organized crime. 'Maybe.'

'Did the intruder find anything in your files?'

'There's nothing anyone would care about. I don't have anything in the house that would reveal my past.'

'Maybe that's not what they were after.'

'Whatever he was after, he didn't seem to find. He didn't show any interest in the papers on my desk. But he did seem irritated when he couldn't access my computer. He cou;dn't have known much about computers. Any teenage hacker could get past my access code.'

'With your knowledge of computers, couldn't you—'

'I could have made it impenetrable. But I'm still subject to the scrutiny of the Department of Justice. They have a right to look in on me, and my computer, any time. If they found too many security measures, they'd have questions.'

White nodded before changing the subject. 'What about the cocaine?'

'A watertight vial in the tank of the john. Maybe one or two grams.'

'Who would want you set up?'

'Maybe my former employers.'

White nodded. That was the obvious conclusion. Maybe too obvious. But drug dealers got rid of their problems. Setting Worthington up for a drug bust would be too subtle.

'What did you do with the cocaine?'

'When I discovered it, I called my case contact at the Department of Justice. He's just as concerned as I am. He's almost certain it wasn't my former employer, but he *was* concerned about leaks in the system. His first inclination was to call in the local authorities. When I told him what was going on with Marty, he decided that any contact by his office would risk exposing me.'

'That's a reasonable conclusion,' White said. 'What did you do with the cocaine?'

'I fished it out of the tank with a pair of kitchen tongs. Then I put it in a plastic bag and sent it to my case contact. He's going to see if there are any fingerprints on the vial, or if he can trace the cocaine. Then I got some rock candy. I put it in a similar vial and replaced it in the tank.'

White couldn't suppress a chuckle. If Worthington's house was ever searched, all anyone would find was candy.

'It's obvious someone is setting you up,' White said. 'It isn't like I want you to get arrested, but it could be a blessing in disguise.'

'Like hell . . . How could getting arrested be a blessing?' Like most victims of the criminal justice system, he saw no benefit to a repetition of the experience.

'If you *are* arrested, we may find a trail back to whoever is trying to set you up. I'd bet my last dollar there's a connection to Marty.'

'I'd like to help Marty if I can,' Worthington said, still agitated. 'But I'd prefer to help in some other way. Besides, what makes you so sure there's a connection to Marty?'

'A couple of grams of cocaine aren't enough to get you serious time. But it's enough to put pressure on you to cut a deal in exchange for anything you know. If someone wanted to make serious trouble for you, they would have planted a lot more.' As he spoke, White made a note on his legal pad. 'Did your videotape record everything the intruders did in your house?'

Kaleidoscope

'No. The system turns on whenever anyone comes into a room and runs for about thirty seconds. The Department of Justice was only concerned with *who* might be there. They knew there wasn't anything in the house that would reveal my old identity, so they had no reason to care what any intruder did while he was inside.'

* * * * *

After Bower and Worthington left his office, White walked into Harris's office and told him about the meeting with Worthington. 'There's something fishy about this,' White said when he completed the story.

'What's that?'

'I don't know. We already knew the hospital wanted the authorities to look into a connection between Marty, Jim Worthington and the Cayman Islands. Now we know Worthington's history includes money transfers. Making a connection between Marty and Worthington would reinforce the argument that Marty is behind the disappearance of the money.'

'But why is someone trying to set Worthington up with a drug connection?'

'Maybe to divert attention from the AIDS drug thefts.'

Harris shook his head. 'That doesn't make any sense. As far as we know, the government doesn't even know about the missing AIDS drugs. Why would anyone at the hospital want to raise a new issue?'

'Like you said, to divert attention from the AIDS drug thefts.'

'But how would a connection to Worthington help?'

'It creates an independent motive for the theft of the money. It could also be made to appear that Marty was stealing the money to finance drug deals with Worthington. That would make the feds spin their wheels looking for a nonexistent drug network.'

'Or maybe your first hunch is right. Maybe someone just wants leverage over Worthington to make him flip on Marty.'

White shook his head. 'Maybe. But that assumes Worthington knows anything. If Worthington isn't involved in anything with Marty, he wouldn't have any information to trade.'

'Maybe there's another reason for pointing the feds to a connection between Marty and Worthington.' Harris paused, looking at his notes before continuing. 'When Morgan first pointed Horse to a connection between Marty and Worthington, he thought he was talking to someone from the F.B.I. Right?'

'Yeah. So what?'

'If the hospital only wanted to create a connection between Marty and the Caymans, they only had to tell the feds about Marty's SCUBA diving trips. But they didn't just do that. Morgan made a point of saying Marty went diving *with Worthington*. I think the drugs were planted to create a reason for the feds to investigate Worthington.'

'So someone at the hospital has another reason for pointing a finger at Worthington.'

'I'm beginning to think so. And it must have something to do with Joe Morgan. He's the only person, other than Marty, who knows about Worthington's cocaine past.'

Kaleidoscope

17.

The call White had been expecting came shortly after ten o'clock on a Wednesday morning. He was leaning against the brass railing of the office mezzanine, discussing the weekend football games with one of the lawyers who leased offices on the first floor, when Grace Matthews signaled that he was wanted on the telephone.

'Do you want to take it here?' she asked. She had a sour look, as if she had just bitten into an unripe crabapple. White knew it was probably not good news.

'I'll take it in my office.' White ended his conversation, went into his office, and picked up the telephone.

Without preamble, Assistant U. S. Attorney Elizabeth Powell announced, 'The Grand Jury indictment has been released. Are you prepared to surrender your client?'

Such a call was normally a courtesy—an accommodation to the attorneys who wanted to save their clients the embarrassment of police cars showing up in the client's driveway and taking him into custody in front of his friends and neighbors. Powell's call was no such courtesy.

'What happens now?' Bower asked, his subdued voice reflecting his obvious concerns, when White called to tell him the news.

'I told the prosecutor you would surrender yourself at two o'clock. I'll be by to pick you up about one-thirty.'

'Then what?' Bower asked hesitantly. White recognized Bower's tone—the fear that came with knowing that this could be his last day of freedom.

'I'm sure the prosecutor has alerted the media. They'll be waiting in front of the courthouse. The U. S. Marshal is going to let me bring you to the side door used by the judges and the court staff. The lot is secured to keep the public out, so we'll be able to avoid the press..'

'Are they going to let me out on bail?'

'I don't know. Probably. The Magistrate agreed to an immediate bail hearing. The charges are serious, but not the kind that makes you a danger to anyone. Your roots are all in the community, and you aren't an obvious flight risk. But just to show your good faith, you should bring your passport and pilots license. You'll have to surrender them in any event, and it may help if we show up ready to comply with any conditions the judge may want to impose.'

Bower was waiting on the deck surrounding his waterfront home when White pulled into the driveway. His wife stood solemnly beside him, holding back her tears. Bower kissed his wife and walked toward White, fighting the urge to turn and wave . . . or something. It would only lead to more tears.

Bower climbed into the seat beside White without speaking, and gave no reaction when White asked, 'Did you remember to bring your toothbrush?'

They spoke only fleetingly on the ride to the courthouse. There wasn't anything to say, and Bower's thoughts were elsewhere.

White knew what he was thinking. What would his wife do? What would happen to the twins, now only two-years-old?

Kaleidoscope

They were not thoughts he could dwell on at home where he had to be strong and confident for Karen's sake. Now he had to deal with reality. White understood his thoughts and left him alone.

As White predicted, there was a crowd in front of the courthouse. Every local news outlet was present. At least a dozen reporters milled around, talking among themselves, each trying to discover what the other knew without revealing any of their own information. Two television camera crews were busy setting up their equipment.

Sorry to disappoint you, but we won't be in front of your cameras today, White thought, pleased at his decision to use Horse's green Ford Explorer rather than his own, better known, truck.

Ed Bailey, a U. S. Marshal White had known for many years, was waiting at the side of the courthouse. Bailey led them through the door and into a corridor almost forty feet long with no doors or windows on either side. The walls were a sterile institutional white. At the opposite end of the corridor was a featureless steel door. All that was missing was a sign saying *Abandon hope all ye who enter here.*

Bower turned to White with a look of helplessness—a look White had seen before and understood all too well.

'I have to leave you here,' White said, giving Bower a pat on the shoulder. 'They'll be taking your fingerprints and photograph and filling out the paperwork. When they're finished here, Ed will bring you to the courtroom for your arraignment.

'Meanwhile, don't talk to anyone,' White reminded Bower. 'They may have to put you in a holding cell temporarily.' White paused and looked at Bailey. The Marshall shrugged his ignorance of what might happen.

'If they do, keep your distance from anyone else. Don't say anything except hello and good-bye. Am I clear?'

'Yes,' Bower said, his mind still elsewhere.

Bower's arraignment and bail hearing were, much to White's surprise, uneventful. White expected the Assistant U. S. Attorney to oppose any bail. To White's surprise, she suggested a reasonable bail, and White immediately agreed.

Martin Bower, now officially a participant in the federal criminal justice system, was released in less than two hours.

* * * * *

White and Bower sat opposite one another at a small table on an area of the sidewalk a Chinese restaurant had taken over as its own. The restaurant was new and had received some favorable reviews, but restaurants in the entertainment district of old downtown Fort Myers had a short life. Six months ago, this location was occupied by a pasta bar. It served good food, but was too trendy and upscale for a location where survival depended on a lunch menu that was fast, cheap and simple. Before that, a salad bar restaurant had come and gone in less than a month. No one mourned its passing, just as, apparently, no one had noticed its arrival.

Pedestrian traffic was light. A homeless man, all of his worldly possessions stuffed into a rusty shopping cart, stopped at the corner, looking hopefully at White and Bower. White removed a ten-dollar bill from his pocket and held it out to the man. The old man shuffled nervously forward and reached out slowly. White pressed the bill into his grimy hand, giving the man a smile he hoped would not be interpreted as condescending. The man nodded a cautious thanks, but said nothing as he took the bill and stumbled away.

The waiter delivered their orders and disappeared.

White took a bite of Kung Po chicken and chewed thoughtfully before speaking. 'Marty, we need to know what's going on inside the hospital.'

'Like what?' Bower asked, having no idea what White was interested in.

Kaleidoscope

'The hospital produced a lot of documents in response to our discovery requests in your civil suit. We've been going over them for the last week, and we've reached a dead end. We have some interesting material, but it has been liberally redacted. They've blacked out almost everything that doesn't obviously relate to the civil suit.'

Bower's look said he didn't understand what White was saying.

'They didn't blacken everything out, just certain sections. There was enough left to indicate the subject of the blacked-out material. Some of it looks like it relates to the hospital's cooperation with the government.'

'What documents are you talking about?'

'The most important ones are the minutes of the board meetings.'

Bower thought for a minute before responding. 'My old secretary prepares the minutes. She's at all the meetings and takes the minutes. Then she sends drafts to the board before each meeting. After the drafts are reviewed by the board, she makes any necessary corrections and prepares the final minutes for the record book.'

'Can we get copies of the draft minutes from her?'

'Not a chance. I called her a couple of weeks ago, just to let her know I'm holding up. She was scared . . . afraid to talk to me.'

'What about the copies circulated to the board?'

'Some of the board members might have kept their drafts.'

'Except that we can't talk to them.' White thought aloud, frustration filling his voice.

'Why not?'

'An attorney can't have any direct contact with anyone who is already represented by another attorney,' White said. 'All the board members are defendants in your civil case, so we can't contact them.'

'That doesn't stop *me* from calling them, does it?' Bower asked, then added, 'Not that they would be interested in helping me.'

'No. The rules say we cannot do indirectly what we cannot do directly.'

'But doesn't that only apply to the people we sued?' Bower asked.

'Yes. Why?'

'We didn't sue John Wiley, did we?'

Thank you, Harry. White smiled as he remembered that Harris convinced him not to include Wiley as a defendant. 'No, we didn't. Do you think he'll help you?'

'I can ask.'

As they stood to leave the restaurant Marty opened his fortune cookie and read: *You will be befriended by a tall dark stranger.*

'Let's hope his name isn't Big Bubba.'

'Your confidence in my future is very reassuring,' Bower said, without humor.

* * * * *

White and Leslie lay in bed, on top of the covers, waiting for the evening news to begin. It was unseasonably cool, even for late September. A once in a century cold front had moved out of Canada, sprinkling an early snow on New England and the upper Atlantic states and dropping temperatures to near freezing as far south as western North Carolina and northern Georgia. In Fort Myers, the early evening temperature was already in the mid-sixties, and a low in the fifties was forecast.

After twenty years in Fort Myers, White considered himself a Floridian. He had sand in his shoes, as the local saying went, but he still missed the crisp cold nights in Idaho. A fifty-degree evening in Fort Myers wasn't the same, but it would have to do. With the windows open, the cool night air blowing through the bedroom was a pleasant reminder of another place and time.

Leslie didn't share White's preference for the cold. She wore a long flannel nightgown, with nothing underneath, the way White liked it, and snuggled against him, wrapping herself around him as best she could.

White turned up the sound on the television:

> *'Good evening, ladies and gentlemen. This is Action News. I'm Lynn Thomas. In today's lead story, a federal grand jury handed down an indictment today against former Coastal Regional Hospital president and chief executive officer Martin Bower. The indictment alleges that Bower embezzled more than three million dollars by causing hospital funds to be transferred to the bank account of a corporation purportedly controlled by Mr. Bower*
>
> *'Mr. Bower voluntarily surrendered himself to federal authorities this afternoon and was arraigned before Magistrate Judge Gregory Simonton, who released Mr. Bower on a $100,000 bond.*
>
> *'Mr. Bower's lawyer, Lucius White, said he was confident Mr. Bower would be cleared of all charges. Mr. White contends that the charges against Mr. Bower were fabricated by the hospital board to justify Bower's termination and avoid paying Bower in excess of two million dollars in severance benefits.*
>
> *'The Assistant U. S. Attorney has refused to comment on the indictment except to say that additional charges may be filed.*
>
> *'In other news . . .'*

'What kind of additional charges is she talking about?' Leslie murmured sleepily.

'I was just asking myself the same question. I think it's time to pay a visit to the prosecutor.'

Kaleidoscope

18.

The new federal courthouse was an attempt to blend the classic dignity of the traditional columned courthouse with modern lines and glass walls. It was generally agreed that the effort failed. The only redeeming feature of the courthouse was that it sat far back from the street—two giant old live oaks and their colony of Spanish moss. Live oaks were not common in this part of Florida, and the magnificent trees, estimated to be well over a hundred years old, gave at least some dignity to the structure.

Eight sets of double glass doors faced the promenade, but only one set was ever unlocked. There was probably some explanation for this, but White had never been sufficiently curious to investigate.

Inside the main entrance was an atrium foyer, two stories high, a hundred feet long and seventy feet wide. It had a dark grey marble floor and was divided in the middle by a mahogany counter. Anyone having business with the various federal agencies located in the building had to pass through a metal detector and be scanned by security cameras before proceeding to the bank of elevators at the opposite end of the foyer. There were always three marshals behind the counter. A major waste of manpower—there were never any women security officers present—White had thought on more than one occasion. But this was, after all, a government building, and someone needed to keep the unemployment figures in check.

Entering the lobby, White couldn't avoid remembering what Lou Hamilton said about changes in the justice system. Twenty years ago, the intricate security measures would have been unheard of—and unnecessary. Now a federal building was a fortress with guards, security cameras and metal detectors at every entrance and throughout the building. White often wondered who, or what, was responsible for this change. Had the criminal element of society become so brazen on its own, or had the justice system become so unbalanced and unfair that it brought out the worst in all elements of society?

White entered a waiting elevator and pressed the button for the second floor where the offices of the clerk of the court were located. He didn't have any business in the clerk's office, but there was occasionally some useful information in the posted announcements and copies of the latest judicial actions.

In the old courthouse, which had been abandoned two years earlier, the clerks worked behind an open counter. In the new building, the clerks were protected from the public by a barrier wall of supposedly bulletproof glass. The glass shield was broken by a series of holes, six-inches in diameter, allowing those on the opposite sides of the glass to communicate. Did someone think a homicidal maniac bent on shooting up the clerk's office wouldn't notice the holes through which he could shoot?

Only one other person was in the clerk's waiting area when White entered. Charles Halperin, one of the federal public defenders, was idly examining the previous day's opinions and announcements. White had, on several occasions, taken special court appointments under the Criminal Justice Act to represent defendants on behalf of the public defenders office. It was something that happened when the public defenders were overloaded or had a conflict of interest and couldn't represent multiple defendants charged with a single crime. In the course of those cases, he and Halperin had become friends.

'Hello, Lucius. What brings you to these hallowed halls?'

'I have a meeting with the Ice Princess. I just thought I'd check up on the files before I went upstairs.'

'That's right. You represent Marty Bower, don't you?'

'Looks that way.'

'Stop by after your meeting and we'll grab some lunch. I may have something for you.'

* * * * *

As White waited in the seventh floor reception area of the United States Attorney, he reviewed what he knew about Powell. Thirty-five years old. Graduated from Vassar but rejected by the top law schools she applied to. Finished in the middle of her class at Stetson Law School. Landed a job with the office of the U. S. Attorney—with a lot of help from family and influential friends. Married into a family of old money and power, with enough of each that she could afford to say 'screw you' to those she didn't like. For the first seven years of her less than illustrious career she prosecuted small time dealers who could rarely afford the services of top defense attorneys. According to the rumors, she had lobbied hard, and called in more than a few family favors, to be assigned to Bower's case.

Lawyers who opposed her regularly described her as cold and unemotional—qualities that earned her the nickname 'Ice Princess.' It didn't make any difference. White wasn't there to make friends. He needed to know how Powell acted, and reacted—what buttons he could push to keep her off balance; what would be most likely to distract her.

White had been waiting for twenty minutes, just long enough for Powell to let him know who was in charge, when the buzzer sounded behind the thick glass partition. The security door in the corner of the reception room opened and the receptionist signaled White to follow her. She was a young woman of Hispanic heritage—attractive and with a pleasant smile.

The receptionist led him down the long hall, past the library and conference room and knocked on the open door to Powell's office.

As he entered, White examined Powell's office. There were no diplomas on the wall and no personal pictures or mementoes on the desk. It was as if she was a visitor, using whatever empty office was handy; a transient who didn't really belong here and would soon be moving on.

Elizabeth Powell—she had long since abandoned the *Beth* nickname she had grown up with and insisted on being called Elizabeth—had shoulder length auburn hair, a decent face and figure and dark eyes. White might even have considered her attractive, but she had cultivated a stony look that conveyed a clear message: *Don't even think about it.* She wore a tailored dark blue suit and silk blouse that spoke for themselves: *If you have to ask you can't afford me.* Her only jewelry was her diamond-studded gold Rolex watch.

Powell stood and reached across the desk. 'Mr. White. Nice to see you.' Her tone said something else; *Why the hell are you here?*

She didn't offer refreshments.

So much for professional pleasantry.

Powell directed White to one of the straight-backed chairs opposite her desk rather than to one of the easy chairs in the sitting area of her large office. White recognized the power positioning—she with the large and impressive desk, he with nothing but an uncomfortable chair.

Kaleidoscope

White sat on the edge of the chair, leaned back, stretched his legs in front of himself and clasped his hands behind his head. 'I'm impressed. You run an efficient Grand Jury.'

Powell studied White, as if searching for some hidden meaning behind his statement.

'No sense wasting the taxpayer's money,' she said finally smugly.

'Less than a month since Marty was fired. That must be some kind of record.' White knew the Grand Jury had been in session for more than two months before Bower was fired, but he wanted to see how much she would admit.

'It's a simple case,' Powell said without emotion, leaning back in her chair as if to emphasize her total lack of concern about any problems in her case. 'The money went into an account controlled by your client. The chief financial officer discovered the problems in the hospital's accounting reports. He told your client that the irregularities had been discovered. Your client told his old friend Joe Morgan to hide the problems and not disclose them to the board. End of story.'

Everything he saw said Powell was trying to present herself as cold and emotionless. But her eyes said something else as they searched White's face for some sign of concern.

It was a wasted effort. White had been playing poker, and reading juries, for too long to let his expression reveal anything. 'Very circumstantial case, don't you think?'

His response wasn't what Powell expected. She leaned forward, resting her hands lightly on her desk in an effort to show a calmness she obviously didn't feel. 'It's enough,' she said without conviction as she picked up her pen and began tapping it softly on the corner of her deck pad. 'Juries have been known to convict on less.'

White chuckled.

'Is something funny?' she asked, harshly. 'This isn't a game.'

'Of course it is. I'm trying to find out what you know, and you're trying to do the same.'

'I don't really care what you know.' Her words were contradicted by the tightening grip of her fingers around the pen in her hand. 'What I know is enough to convict your client for grand theft and Medicare fraud.'

No mention of drugs. White couldn't be sure if it was an oversight, or something she was holding back. There wasn't anything about the drug thefts in the indictment, but it could still be amended to add new charges.

White smiled. 'You make it sound serious.'

Powell stared at White while she struggled to regain her lost composure. 'Face it, counselor,' she said with renewed calm. 'Your client is a thief.'

'I keep forgetting that.'

Powell said nothing as she continued to examine White. She wasn't accustomed to being taken so lightly. 'I've heard about you, Mr. White. You play it close to the edge. Rumor has it the whiz kids you have working for you don't have a full comprehension of rules of discovery . . . and bend a few laws getting their evidence.'

White couldn't avoid the thought of black pots and kettles.

White knew she was posturing, trying to intimidate him. She wasn't very good at it.

'Rumors, you say?' White asked as he removed a piece of imaginary lint from his shoulder. 'They wouldn't happen to come from prosecutors who lost their cases would they?'

Powell scowled.

'Anyway,' White said, 'if prosecutors liked me, I'd worry that I wasn't doing my job.'

Powell's look hardened. 'Are you always such a smart-ass?'

'It works for me. The hours are good, and there's no heavy lifting.'

Powell looked like she wanted to say something, but couldn't find the words—or the courage.

'By the way, where's the money?' White asked, abruptly changing the subject.

Powell stared at White, as if the question had never occurred to her. After a moment's hesitation, she said, 'It doesn't matter. Bower took it. That's all I need to prove. What he did with the money isn't an element of the crime.'

'Maybe not. But the jury might want some proof that it actually got into his hands.'

'The jury won't care.'

'Juries have a way of deciding for themselves what they care about.' White spoke in a solicitous, mocking tone he usually reserved for witnesses he knew were lying. With any luck, she would become angry and let something slip.

'Are you always so generous with unsolicited advice?'

'Just trying to be helpful. . . . But you haven't answered my question. Where's the money?'

White watched, and waited. Powell's delay was itself an admission that she hadn't thought the issue was important, but might be reconsidering.

The silence continued. It was an old game. The first one to speak loses.

'Maybe he hid it until the statute of limitations ran out,' Powell said with none of the conviction she had when presenting her initial summary of the case.

White showed the suggestion of a smile. 'Has it occurred to you that my client might be the victim of a frame-up?'

'That's not my problem; and it's not my concern.'

'You aren't concerned that he may not be guilty?'

'It's your job to prove he's not guilty.'

'What happened to innocent until proven guilty?'

Powell ignored White's attempt to provoke her. 'My job is to get convictions,' she said, as if it were a simple statement of her job description. 'If the jury convicts him, he's guilty.'

'It that all that counts?'

'You don't seem to understand something, Mr. White. The wheel has turned. The public is sick and tired of slick defense attorneys getting scum off on technicalities and blinding juries with phony theories and misdirection just to create reasonable doubt. I get convictions because that's what the public wants, and I do what I have to do to get them.'

And you don't leave much doubt about where you stand. 'How about we talk deal?' Now that White had learned what he needed to know, he wanted to distract her before she realized the focus of his inquiry. The best way to do that was to change the subject. It was a tactic he often used in court to divert the jury's attention from evidence damaging to his client.

'Sure, we can work something out. Come see me the first Thursday after hell freezes over.'

'That soon?' White smiled pleasantly, ignoring her sarcasm and caustic tone.

'If I have my way, your client will get a sentence so long his parole officer hasn't even been born yet.'

'Ah. So we have an offer. How about a counter-offer? Three years suspended and community service.'

Powell looked at White as if she were uncertain what she had heard. 'Were you born an idiot, or is that a quality you developed later in life?'

'They teach it at defense attorney school.' White chuckled, thinking that Powell now had the bewildered look—a cliché to the urban born but intimately familiar to those with country roots—of a deer caught in the headlights of his pick-up truck. 'I'll even throw in a lottery ticket.'

'With an offer like that I could have you arrested for attempting to bribe a federal official.'

'I didn't know you lacked a sense of humor.'

'Mr. White,' Powell said coldly, 'there's nothing humorous about this. That was federal money your client stole. That's Medicare fraud. You may not know it, but the Attorney General has placed a high priority on Medicaid crime. Medicare and Medicaid crime costs the government more than a billion dollars a year.

'The Attorney General intends to stop it by prosecuting violators to the full extent of the law. The attorneys who win these cases have high visibility.'

Powell caught herself before proceeding, but it was too late. Her statement, and the tone with which it was made, told White everything he needed to know.

19.

Lucius White and Charles Halperin were seated at Pancho's, a popular Mexican restaurant a few blocks from the courthouse. It was still early for the lunch crowd. They were the only ones in the restaurant, so they could speak freely.

'I was surprised when I saw you were representing the hospital guy,' Halperin said.

'Oh.'

'I heard you were getting out of the game. Retiring.'

'Where did you hear that?'

Halperin shrugged. 'It's a small community.'

'Ain't that the truth.'

'So it isn't true?'

White shrugged. 'I don't know. It isn't like it used to be.'

'I hear you.'

'I'm tired of the win at-all-costs mentality,' White said, as if he hadn't heard Halperin. 'It isn't why I got into the game in the first place.'

'No doubt about it. Things have changed. You can't even trust the government any more.'

White looked at Halperin, wondering how much he knew about White's history, and what drove him, before changing the subject. 'So what sort of interesting gossip do you have for me?'

'Nothing specific. Just some rumors and goings on,' Halperin said.

Halperin was a career federal public defender. For him, it was the ideal position. His job was to represent clients who were unable to afford a private attorney but had, as the United States Supreme Court had determined in *Giddeon v. Wainwright*, a Constitutional right to counsel at taxpayer expense. Most of his clients were guilty and had little hope of avoiding conviction no matter what Halperin did.

Although the federal public defender and the Assistant U. S. Attorneys were officially on opposite sides of their cases, they received their pay from the same place. The relationship between pubic defenders and the government prosecutors differed from the relationship that existed between those agencies and private criminal defense attorneys. Federal public defenders worked in the same building as the U. S. Attorney, shared the same elevator on a daily basis, and often socialized over lunch or drinks where they discussed their cases and shared gossip and rumors. Charles Halperin was to the federal courthouse what Lou Hamilton was to the local law enforcement community—the ultimate source of reliable inside information and gossip. When Halperin offered information, it was good to pay attention.

'I'm listening.'

'Rumor has it that our esteemed congressman is particularly interested in this case.'

'Richard Marks? Why would he even *know* about the case?'

'Normally, he probably wouldn't. But someone might want him to know about *this* case.'

White returned his burrito to his plate and leaned forard

'He's the number two man on the House Judiciary Committee, and chairman of the subcommittee that considers federal judicial appointments.'

'And the favor of our congressman would be important to an Assistant U. S. Attorney who has aspirations for an appointment to the federal bench.'

'I do believe it would be,' Halperin said, a knowing smile forming on his lips.

'That explains why he *knows* about the case But why would the congressman have any particular *interest* in it?'

Halperin swallowed a bite of taco salad and continued. 'The congressman was on the original hospital board. Some of the current board members were major backers of the congressman.'

'I didn't know that; but it's certainly interesting,' White said. 'Do you think the board is using the Congressman to make sure the case gets the attention the board wants?'

'I don't know, but I wouldn't doubt it. After all, the hospital is the biggest private employer in his district. That's a lot of voting constituents . . . and a lot of people who wouldn't be disappointed if Bower was to be convicted.'

'You're right about that. The board is doing everything it can to point the finger at Bower. But they've conveniently forgotten they were active participants in all the decisions that put the hospital into a financial crisis.'

'No doubt about it. They're running for cover.'

'What other interesting tidbits do you have?' White asked.

'Well, judging from the comings and goings of the hospital attorneys, you'd think the hospital has an office in the U. S. Attorney's office.'

'Who's coming and going?'

'That weasel in-house counsel and their outside counsel meet with the Ice Princess at least once a week.' Halperin paused to pick a seed from between his teeth. 'They're constantly bringing boxes of documents.'

'Maybe they're just responding to subpoenas.'

'Yeah. And I'm rich and handsome,' Halperin said. 'I've overheard them talking. They're definitely working together.'

'I'm not surprised. Do you have any idea where the investigation is going?'

'Not really,' Halperin said. 'Usually I can get something on pending investigations from the F.B.I., but they don't seem to be in the loop.'

'That's curious.'

'Very,' Halperin agreed. 'But the hospital is giving the Ice Princess everything she needs. She doesn't think she needs much investigating by the F.B.I.'

White considered Halperin's statement while he chewed on his burrito. 'Anything else?' he asked between bites.

'Nothing you wouldn't expect. Embezzlement, fraud, tax evasion.'

White was suddenly more interested. 'Tax evasion?'

'You seem surprised.'

'It wasn't in the indictment—and the Ice Princess didn't mention it.'

'You didn't expect her to show you her whole hand.'

'I guess not,' White acknowledged. 'Is that all you've heard?'

'That's it. Is there something Powell hasn't come up with?'

'Who knows?' White said evasively. 'When's the last time a client told you everything?'

* * * * *

Harry Harris was waiting by the staff entrance when White pulled his truck into the vacant parking spot beside the door. There was no hierarchy to parking. It was always first-come-first-served. Nonetheless, the parking spot beside the door was always left open when White wasn't in the building. He was sensitive to the possibility that his staff had unofficially acknowledged that this was a reserved parking spot. When he mentioned it, Harris had disabused him of his concern.

'Lucius,' Harris had said. 'That parking spot is directly below the roof extension where the birds perch. The car parked below them catches all the bird shit. Everyone but you is too smart to park there.'

White still knew that *his* spot was left empty out of deference, but, whenever he felt an entitlement, as the owner of the firm, he remembered Harris's story.

'How did your meeting with the Ice Princess go?' Harris asked as White stepped out of the truck and retrieved his briefcase and jacket from the passenger seat.

'Very pleasant,' White said, 'if you're the sort of person who enjoys having a viper in your shorts.'

Harris chuckled. 'That good?'

'We may have underestimated the Ice Princess,' White said. 'Before our meeting, I only knew she is humorless, heartless, sneaky, amoral and vindictive.'

'And . . .'

'Now I know those are her good qualities.'

* * * * *

White reached for a government telephone directory on the shelf over his desk, thumbed through several pages and placed a phone call. A recorded message guided him through the wonders of voice mail.

'Judiciary Committee,' a live operator finally said.

'Jack Lancaster, please,' White said.

White was put on hold where he listened to financial reports.

Before the telephone was answered, Harris reappeared at White's door. White wiggled a finger, signaling Harris into his office, and quietly mouthed *Jack Lancaster*. White pressed a button on his telephone, switching the phone to speaker-phone just as Lancaster answered.

'Lancaster,' a voice announced.

'Would this happen to be the Jack Lancaster who couldn't pass a course in basic evidence with two lawyers at his side?' White asked.

'No.' Lancaster said, instantly recognizing White's distinctive voice from their days together at the University of Virginia Law School. 'This would be the Jack Lancaster who is actually doing something for the good of the country instead of putting low-life criminals back on the street.'

'God. If I'd known what you were going to do with your law degree, I would never have nursed you through law school,' White said.

'And if I'd known you were going to become an eminent criminal lawyer, I would never have nursed you through your weekly hangovers,' Lancaster responded in kind.

'You must be thinking of someone else,' White countered. 'I'm strictly a Pepsi man.'

'Since when?'

'Since I started going to Alcoholics Anonymous—and since I started worrying about the fate of the nation being determined by someone whose only claim to notoriety is hanging between his legs.'

'Screw you.' Lancaster said, still laughing. 'And now, having duly insulted the only person in your law school class who will still admit to knowing you, I suppose you're going to ask me a favor.'

'As a matter of fact, I am interested in a little information.'

'Imagine my surprise. What do you need?'

'I hear Congressman Marks has an interest in a case down here.'

'That case wouldn't happen to involve a certain hospital executive, would it?'

'That would be the one.'

'Don't tell me. You represent the defendant.'

'Okay. I won't tell you . . . '

Lancaster hesitated. 'Lucius, you know I can't tell you about the Congressman's dealings.'

'But?' White prodded.

'I can tell you this, and only this,' Lancaster continued, ignoring White's attempt to persuade him to disclose something helpful. 'The Congressman has been getting a lot of pressure from somewhere.'

'Where's the pressure coming from?'

'I don't know . . . and I couldn't tell you if I did know.'

'What's the Congressman doing about this pressure?'

'Sorry, Lucius, no can say. But I *can* tell you this isn't just political.'

'Are you telling me the Congressman has something personal at stake?'

'I can't confirm or deny your suggestion.'

Is Jack trying to tell me something? White knew he had touched on something sensitive. 'I suppose it would be too much to ask for a heads-up if anything particularly significant comes up.'

'You suppose right. As far as I'm concerned, we didn't even have this conversation.' Lancaster was suddenly in a hurry to return to the pressing business of governing the masses.

'What conversation?'

'Right.' Lancaster said as he hung up.

* * * * *

Grace Matthews had left for the day, and White was alone at his desk when Harry Harris rolled into his office.

'Do we need to talk?' Harris said.

White laid his pen on the desk, leaned back and ran his fingers through his hair. 'I don't know,' he said in a voice that sounded both thoughtful and sad.

Harris waited.

'When did we stop being able to play by the rules?'

'This isn't about your father.'

'So you keep reminding me.'

'Because you need an occasional reminder.'

'This isn't at all the same.'

'Isn't it? A prosecutor who wants a conviction, and doesn't care how she gets it. What's so different?'

'I . . .'

'Or are you afraid Marty may have done it?'

White bolted to his feet. '*Damn it*, Harry . . .'

'I know. He's your friend . . . and you don't want to think about his guilt.'

'That's not relevant. Most of our clients are guilty.'

'But they aren't personal friends.'

'It doesn't matter.'

'Of *course* it matters. You loved your father, but you couldn't do anything to save him. Now you have a personal stake in the case.'

'What's your *point*? If you have something to say, spit it out.'

'I was just wondering if you came back too soon.'

'It's not like I had a choice. I don't think the hospital was concerned about my mental health when they decided to fire Marty. What was I supposed to do—ask them to put off firing Marty until I had my head screwed on straight?'

Harris waited, without saying anything.

White returned to his desk and dropped into the chair. 'I'm sorry, Harry. I know you're concerned, and I appreciate it.

Harris nodded and smiled. 'A little anger never hurts. It keeps the blood flowing.'

'Yeah . . . thanks.'

'But, Lucius . . . we don't have much to go on. Marty's not looking good. This isn't the time for you to be distracted.'

20.

White accepted his morning coffee from Grace Matthews, walked into his office and was reviewing his messages when his intercom sounded.

'What is it, Harry?'

'Can you come into my office? I have something interesting.'

Harris's office was furnished with a custom-designed desk, computer stand and conference table, all built to accommodate his wheelchair and allow him to work and move about without obstruction. Even his files had motor-driven drawers that tilted when fully extended so Harris could examine document files without having to lean, bend or twist.

When White entered Harris' office, Harris was seated at the side of the conference table covered with documents. 'The hospital attorneys must be having a good laugh,' Harris said as White took a seat by the table. 'The judge told them to give us everything, and they did. They sent twenty boxes of documents, including lunch menus and announcements of meetings of the hospital candy stripers.'

'What did you expect?' White said. 'It's an old trick. Hide the trees in the forest.'

Kaleidoscope

'Yeah. But they've included shrubs, bushes and a few dead stumps.'

White laughed. 'I have faith in you, Harry. What do you have?'

'I've organized the documents according to categories: like board minutes, internal memos and e-mails. Then I went through each category of document and used different color Post-It notes to indicate different categories of information.' As he spoke, Harris handed White a list of information categories and their corresponding color code.

'What have you come up with?'

'It's a little too early to say. I'm still getting a handle on what we have. But I've found some materials that could be important to Marty's criminal case.' Harris placed a file folder, approximately one inch thick, in front of White. 'These are copies of all the documents that contain any direct reference to Bower's conduct, his firing and the bank accounts.'

White began paging through the documents. Harris rolled his wheelchair to the head of the table where he sat waiting to offer an explanation or comment on the documents if White had any questions.

When White completed his examination of the documents, he swiveled to face Harris. 'Okay. What do you think we have?'

'There are three things that seem to be significant,' Harris began. 'First, look at these e-mails.' Harris thumbed through the file and removed copies of three e-mails which he put in front of White. 'All of these e-mails refer to a merger partner for the hospital. But the e-mails *seem* to be referring to a merger with someone other than Hospitals of America—the corporation Marty told us the hospital was considering merging with. I think the hospital's counsel is trying to orchestrate a merger with someone the outside attorneys also represent.'

White rubbed his chin as he considered the possibility. 'And you think there's a connection between this and the fact that Bower was pushing for a merger with Hospitals of America?'

'It would explain why they wanted Marty out of the way,' Harris said. 'It would also explain why the outside attorneys want to keep the focus on Bower, and away from anything going on inside the hospital.'

'It's a possibility,' White agreed. 'What else do you have?'

'The next thing I noticed was . . . These documents . . .' Harris said, pulling another set of documents from the file, 'all have the same blemish on the copy.' Harris pointed to the areas of interest on the copies in front of White.

'It's most likely a mark on the glass of the copier, or a blemish on the copier drum,' White said, with little interest.

'You're probably right. But it may help us figure out who made the copies in the first place.'

'What makes you think that's important?'

'These documents all contain the *same* blemish, but they were copied on at least two *different* machines. *This* set of documents,' Harris said, indicating one pile of papers, 'were produced by the hospital. They were sent directly *from the hospital*. But these other documents,' Harris continued, indicating another pile of papers, 'were produced by the outside attorneys. They came directly *from the lawyers*.'

'So these marks were on the *original* documents from which these copies were made.'

'They must have been. But there's more,' Harris said. 'The documents we received from the hospital were made *at the hospital* after I reviewed their files. I selected documents we wanted copied and they copied them. The other documents—the ones we got from the lawyers—were provided in response to our request for production. Whatever we received from the lawyers should have been the same things we received from the hospital.'

'But they weren't?' White guessed.

'Right. The lawyers sent us several documents that weren't in the hospital files when we inspected them. That means some documents were removed from the hospital file after copies were made by the attorneys.'

White returned to his examination of the documents. 'That would explain why the attorneys had copies of documents that weren't in the hospital's files when you looked at them. But it isn't the only explanation. It's also possible that some of the documents provided by the attorneys—the ones that *weren't* also provided by the hospital—were *never* in the hospital files. My guess is that they were fabricated for Marty's civil case.'

'Or his criminal case,' White suggested.

'Maybe,' Harris agreed. 'Either way, we have to explain the common marks on the copies that came from two different sources.'

'Very interesting. . . . You said you had three things to show me.'

'Yes. Each of the documents with this odd mark passed through the same person's hands at one time or another. It either originated with him, or it was sent to the attorneys by him.'

'Who's that?'

'Joe Morgan. The hospital's in-house counsel.'

21.

Harry Harris was one of the few people who could make Grace Matthews laugh. He was treating Matthews and Horse to more of his stories about growing up in western North Carolina when White and Bower joined them in the War Room.

'You don't really believe all those stories Harry tells, do you?' White asked no one in particular.

Harris drew back in mock indignation. 'I'll have you know that every word is true.'

'Harry,' White said, winking at Matthews. 'The fact that you grew up in North Carolina's quaint little foothills doesn't make you a mountain man.'

'Ah. Grizzly Adams speaks,' Harris snorted, crossing his hands in front of himself as if warding off danger.

Good-natured arguments between Harris and White about the relative merits of growing up in their respective mountain homes were common. Although raised two thousand miles apart, they had so many common experiences that they could have been brothers. Under other circumstances, they might have shared stories, each one better than the last, for hours. But this wasn't the time.

Kaleidoscope

One corkboard wall of the War Room was covered with white 3x5 cards containing summaries of information that seemed important but didn't yet connect to the significant players or events. A second corkboard wall was covered with colored 3x5 cards grouped in categories relating to individuals and/or events.

Each new discovery seemed to lead to more questions. New questions were being raised faster than old questions were being answered. Bower was growing increasingly impatient. After three months, they were no closer to a solution than on the day the criminal charges were been filed.

'Something isn't right about Joe Morgan,' Horse began. 'It's nothing specific, but Morgan has an odd pattern. A couple of nights a week, he stops at the same bar for a drink. He has one drink—scotch. The he goes next door to one of those copying places that has computers. He spends from half an hour to an hour on the computer. According to one of the clerks, he spends his time searching a singles matchmaker site and sending and receiving e-mail messages.

'I wanted to take a look at his messages, so I gave the clerk twenty bucks to look over his shoulder and get his account password. Then I was able to partially trace some of Morgan's contacts. Morgan was equally interested in ads from *women seeking men* and ads from *men seeking men*.'

'So Morgan goes both ways. So what?'

Bower shook his head. 'I've known Joe Morgan since he was a virgin. He's strictly a tits and ass man. I don't think there's any chance he's bisexual.'

'That isn't really the point,' Horse interrupted. 'What's interesting is that all the messages he sends, *and* all the messages he receives, go to and come from the same electronic address.'

'And?' White asked, knowing Horse had something special in mind.

'You didn't hear the magic word—*all*. He's responding to ads placed by women seeking men, and he's receiving mail from men seeking men. But the messages all go to, and come from, the same internet location.'

White thought for a minute before responding. 'It's a blind communication system.'

'That's what I think,' Horse said. 'If anyone is caught in the act, it looks like an innocent search for some action, when it's really a system of hidden communication between specific people.

'When I dug a little further, I discovered that all of his outgoing messages go to a woman named Erica Matheson, and all of his incoming messages come from a man named Parker Boles. I'm sure they aren't real names, but I think this confirms your conclusion that this is a system for blind communications.'

Martin Bower asked the question that was on everyone's mind. "Why did they have to use such a complicated system? Why couldn't they just talk on the phone?'

'Phones can be tapped,' Horse said. 'And phone records can be obtained by the police. Even if they made their calls from pay phones, there would be a record that might give the police a lead. Internet communications, especially when they originate from computers that are available to the public at copy centers, are almost untraceable, unless you're lucky enough to know where to look and are able to intercept a call when the users are on-line.

'I'm trying to find out who is actually on the other end of these messages by tracing the routing on the few documents we've gotten. I haven't had any luck so far. It's possible the messages are erased after they've been retrieved.'

'Can't we read them before they're retrieved?' Harris asked.

'Probably not. When a message is retrieved, the computer doesn't know the difference between retrieval by me and a retrieval by the intended reader. If I tap into the mailboxes, the messages will be erased after I read them. There won't be anything there when the intended recipient goes to retrieve his, or her, mail. If that happens, they may know something is wrong.'

'Can't you replace the message by sending it yourself?' Harris suggested.

'Yes, but then the routing information will be different.'

Harris looked confused.

'Most people don't read the routing information on their e-mail, but these people aren't just anyone,' Horse said. 'They know what they're doing, and they're very careful. They may check the routing. We'd be running a risk of getting caught if we tried to intercept and replace the messages.'

'Couldn't you use Morgan's code and the same computer he uses?'

'Maybe, but I've been following him for a couple of weeks. He always uses the computer at precisely the same time of day. The time may be important, and we can't duplicate the time.'

White stood and began pacing the length of the room. He stopped in front of the wall containing the 3X5 cards and stared at them for several minutes while the others waited. 'Do we know this is even connected to the hospital or Marty's case?'

'I can't be sure,' Horse said. "But I think so.' He picked up another file and opened it. 'The board minutes Harry subpoenaed in the civil case show the dates the board talked about the merger. We only have a few of these references, so I can't be sure there is a pattern. But it looks like Morgan's use of the copy center computer occurs right before and right after these meetings.'

'Meaning that he may be getting instructions regarding the meetings, and reporting on what happened,' White mused out loud.

'But why is Morgan doing all this from a copy center?' Harris said. 'He must have a personal computer at home.'

'He probably doesn't want to make his wife suspicious,' White said. 'Even if it had nothing to do with any personal desires, he wouldn't want his wife knowing he was communicating with women on the internet.'

'That's one possibility,' Harris agreed. 'But I think there's more to it.'

'Let's hold off on that for now,' White said. 'Knowing *why* he's using an outside computer probably isn't important. Not yet. What we need to know is *who* he's talking to.'

'I'll see what else I can come up with,' Horse said.

White nodded. 'In the meantime, what have you come up with in the background of the board members?'

'Not much,' Horse said. 'One doctor on the board, Dr. Sommers, had a bankruptcy just before the money-moving scheme started. He also lost a big medical malpractice case and was investigated by the State Department of Professional Regulation. He almost lost his license. He isn't highly regarded in the medical community and doesn't get many referrals. His medical practice has dropped off quite a bit, but he's living like he is still making a lot of money.'

White looked toward Bower.

'I knew about the bankruptcy and the malpractice suit,' Bower said. 'The hospital was also a defendant in the suit, but we settled for the limits of our liability policy. Summer was naked—he didn't have malpractice coverage—so the judgment really hurt him.'

'Is there anything else we should know about Dr. Sommers?' Harris asked.

'Not that I know of. He's been on the board since the hospital was started. Some people wanted to kick him off the board after the malpractice matter because he had previously said he had insurance—it's required for a doctor to have hospital privileges. His hospital privileges were revoked, but he had too many friends for us to remove him from the board.'

'What about his medical practice?' Harris pressed.

Kaleidoscope

'Without hospital privileges, he's limited to treating patients in his office. I don't know much about his practice.'

'Where did he stand on the matter of the hospital merger?'

'He was against that, too,' Bower said. 'Do you think it means something?'

'Maybe,' White said. 'Right now it's just something to keep in mind.'

'Anything else?' White asked the group generally.

'Just one thing,' Horse added. 'I checked out Jim Worthington.'

Bower's head snapped up. 'Why are you checking on Jim?'

'I told him to,' White said. 'If there is any connection between the break-in and your case, we need to know what it may be.'

Bower started to say something but changed his mind.

White waited. When Bower said nothing, he turned to Horse.

'Everything Jim told you checked out. Up until five years ago, *James Worthington* didn't exist. His driver's license, voter registration card and social security number were all issued when he went into the Witness Protection Program.'

'Isn't that a little obvious?'

'Probably, but it's not unusual. Worthington is a small fish by Witness Protection Program standards. If he had been a major player, like a capo in a major crime family, or a deep cover informant, the feds would have created a complete cover history. Worthington wasn't that important.'

'Anything else?'

'Nothing special,' Horse said. 'Worthington lives on the edge of Charlotte Harbor in Bokeelia, on the opposite end of Pine Island from St. James City. The house and his lifestyle are nondescript and ordinary by Bokeelia standards. That's what I would expect from someone who doesn't want to draw any special attention to himself.'

'But?' White prodded, reading Horse's look and knowing there was more.

'He has a boat that doesn't fit the pattern: a forty-one foot thunder boat. It has about every piece of electronics known to the boating public. It's rigged like a serious fishing boat, but it's designed, and runs, like a drug interdiction boat. All the marinas, and most of the serious local boaters, know the boat and who owns it. That's not consistent with someone who wants to go unnoticed.'

'I agree,' White said. 'See what else you can find out.'

Grace Matthews handed Harris a telephone message slip when he rolled out of White's office. Harry looked briefly at the message, swiveled his chair and rolled back to White's door. 'They're going to run another story on the hospital on the evening news. Lynn Thomas wants to know if we have any comment. Do you want to call her?'

'You call her. I think she's sweet on you.'

Harris gave White a one-finger salute and rolled away toward his own office.

* * * * *

'I'm in the kitchen,' White called when he heard the elevator door open. The sounds of a John Coltrane recording mingled with the sound of White's chopping knife striking the rock maple of the cutting board built into the breakfast bar separating the kitchen from the living room. On the island stove behind him, thick slices of portabella mushrooms were sautéing in garlic butter, filling the room with the aroma of an Italian kitchen.

'Ah. Onions,' Leslie murmured.

'If you knew as much about food as you know about sex, you'd know these are shallots, not onions,' White chastised playfully. 'Onions go on hamburgers, or on bagels with cream cheese, lox and capers. They do *not* go on my famous braised chicken.'

Leslie took a seat on one of the stools in front of the breakfast bar.

Sherlock, as she always did when meals were in the making, settled into her regular post at the end of the breakfast bar—a spot from which he could watch both White and Leslie. Snacks could come from anywhere. It paid to be prepared.

White retrieved a bottle of Pinot Chardonnay from the refrigerator, removed the cork and poured Leslie a glass.

'Nice,' she said after taking a sip.

'I wouldn't know.' White's thoughts were revealed in his longing tone. *Five years, seven months. Two-thousand-thirty-three days. And now back to two meetings a week.*

'I'm sorry,' Leslie said, holding her glass in front of her. 'Would you rather I didn't ?'

White cast a last covetous glance at the wine. 'No. I have to deal with it.'

Leslie took another sip of wine while White busied himself in the kitchen. Finally she spoke. 'Lucius,' she began tentatively. 'Have you noticed anything out of the ordinary around the building?'

White stopped chopping shallots and looked at Leslie. 'Like what?'

'I don't know. It's just sort of . . . a feeling.'

White laid the knife on the cutting board and leaned against the breakfast bar. 'What kind of feeling?'

'I . . . I can't explain it. It's like I'm being . . . watched . . . or followed.'

'What makes you think so?'

'For the last couple of days, I've seen the same blue car parked up the block when I leave in the morning.' Her expression was thoughtful, as if she was trying to visualize the car in her mind. 'I didn't think anything about it until . . .' she hesitated, controlling her sense of fear. 'Lucius, I think I saw the same car outside the clinic in Sarasota.'

'It was probably just a car that looked the same,' White said in a tone meant to be comforting but which didn't conceal his concern. He considered pointing out that this was why he didn't want her involved in criminal cases, but he knew an *I told you so* would only make matters worse. Besides, that wasn't the most important thing on his mind. He didn't believe in coincidences. If Leslie was being followed, it meant only one thing. Someone was interested in the investigation of the missing AIDS drugs. The question was, which investigation were people interested in: the drugs being stolen from the clinics, or the drugs being stolen from the hospital? *Or were the same people interested in both?*

22.

White and Harris watched the evening news in White's office.

> '*Good evening, ladies and gentlemen. This is Action News at six. I'm Lynn Thomas.*
> '*Coastal Regional Hospital today announced the layoff of over two-hundred and fifty employees, approximately one-fifth of its total workforce. The press release issued by the hospital said the layoffs were made as a cost-saving measure required by the hospital's deteriorating financial condition.*
> '*A spokesman for the hospital, speaking on condition of anonymity, said the layoffs were required when the merger talks first reported by Action News following the termination of Martin Bower, the hospital's former chief executive office, were suddenly broken off by the still undisclosed merger*

> *partner. According to the anonymous source, Bower's revelation of the previously secret merger talks made it impossible to conclude the merger. According to our source, and I quote, 'Anyone who is upset by the hospital's action should remember that Martin Bower is the person responsible for this action."*

'Jesus.' White said. 'It looks like Joe Morgan and Randall Harrington have been busy little boys.'

> *'Responding to the accusations that Mr. Bower was responsible for the layoffs, Mr. Bower's attorney, Lucius White, revealed documents, obtained from the hospital in Mr. Bower's civil suit, showing that, in a straw vote taken less than two weeks ago, seven of the twelve members of the hospital board opposed the merger. According to Mr. White, the hospital's claim that the termination of merger talks was caused by Mr. Bower's revelations is nothing more than, and I quote, 'A cheap ploy to poison the community against Mr. Bower.' The documents released to Action News by Mr. White show that the merger was opposed by board members: Joe Morgan, acting chief executive officer and ex-officio member of the board, Kevin Beck, Dudley Marshall, Harris Mathers, Scott Baker, Stephen Boyd and James Williams.*
>
> *'It sounds like there is some difference of opinion about what is going on at the hospital,'* ' Lynn Thomas's co-anchor Peter Willis said with feigned innocence.

> *'I think you could say that.'* Lynn Thomas agreed.

Kaleidoscope

'In other news...'

'Looks like their little ploy may have backfired,' White said.

'Someone should alert the emergency room,' Harris added happily. 'There are going to be some cardiac cases arriving soon.'

'At the very least,' White added, 'there are going to be some board members with a hard-on for Morgan and Harrington.'

'Are you sure they're the ones behind this?'

'Who else?' White said. 'From what I hear, most of the board members want the whole Bower matter to go away unnoticed. There are too many potentially embarrassing things that could come out.'

'At least it looks like whatever plan Morgan and Harrington had to control the hospital merger is moot,' Harris said.

'I wouldn't be so sure,' White said. 'The faction of the board that didn't want the original merger may have prevailed for the time being, but I don't think we've heard the end of the merger plans. Besides, this doesn't eliminate Marty's problems. This merger may be over, but we still have to find out why it was necessary to get rid of Marty.'

23.

Early mornings alone were Lucius White's special, private time. The river, flat and glassy, was a natural tranquilizer. Only the occasional cry of a seagull that had ventured too far upriver from the Gulf of Mexico broke the silence.

White was sitting in the green leather recliner in the corner of his study watching the surface fog drift into the unseasonably cool morning air. Sherlock lay protectively at White's feet, listening for the sound of food.

White's thoughts were interrupted by the sound of Sherlock's tail thumping happily against the floor. When he looked up, he saw Leslie standing in the doorway. She was wearing a light, lime colored negligee and, as White could see from the silhouette revealed by the morning light coming through the picture window behind her, nothing else.

'Could I interest you in a little something to start your day?'

'What did you have in mind?' White said, giving her a roguish grin.

'Something to eat.' Leslie clarified emphatically, in a tone meant to deflect White's leering suggestion.

White continued to grin. 'You'll need to narrow it down a little more than that.'

'I will not dignify that with a response,' Leslie scolded, laughingly, 'because my mother always taught me to be kind to the ill-bred. What I had in mind, you dirty old man, is ham and eggs.'

'With a side of Leslie?' White suggested.

'Not in this lifetime, you uncouth SOB.'

'I don't recall you objecting last night—or earlier this morning.'

'I was obviously suffering a temporary lapse in good judgment. And the fact that I was horny as a reindeer might have had something to do with it.'

'So that's all I'm good for, trimming your horns?'

'Do you have a problem with that? You should always go with your strong suit,' Leslie said as she turned and headed for the kitchen, with a pronounced shake of her rear for good measure.

'On that note, I think I'll take a cold shower while you wrestle up some grub.' White squeezed her ass as he passed.

* * * * *

The telephone was ringing when White came out of the shower.

'Hello.'

'Lucius, I've been arrested.' Jim Worthington announced, without preliminaries, but far more calmly than White would have expected.

The arrest itself wasn't a surprise. The drugs planted at Worthington's house had obviously been intended to set him up. If there was any surprise, it was how long it had taken the authorities to arrest Worthington.

'I'm at the county jail. Do you know where that is?'

What kind of a question was that? White certainly knew where the county jail was. What surprised him was that

Worthington was being held at the county jail. Bower's case was federal, and White assumed that any set-up involving Worthington would be connected to the charges against Bower. If his assumption was correct, Worthington should have been picked up by the F.B.I. But federal prisoners were held in the city jail, not the county jail.

'Who arrested you?'

'Two sheriff's deputies came to the house about two hours ago.'

Sheriff's deputies? That confirmed that Worthington had been arrested under a State warrant.

'Stay put, and don't say anything to anyone. I'll be there as soon as I can.'

White returned the phone to the cradle and said, 'That was Jim Worthington. I have to meet him at the jail.'

'But it's Sunday,' Leslie protested.

'What do you want me to tell him? Should I have said I can't bail you out today because it's Sunday and I'm about to get laid?'

'Tell him my PMS has kicked in,' Leslie suggested, ' and I'm being a bitch about you leaving me alone. And if that doesn't work, tell him you're about to get laid.'

White was still puzzling over this latest development when he called the court duty officer and was informed that the on-call judge was Judge Stanley Mitchell. At least that was good news. The sheriff had probably chosen to arrest Worthington on Sunday morning expecting him to have to spend at least one night in jail, just to soften him up before he could be brought before a judge for a bail hearing. Fortunately, Judge Mitchell was a friend of White's, and he had little tolerance for such obvious tactics. The judge agreed to a bail hearing at one o'clock, just as soon as he could get to the courthouse from church. *At least I can ruin the State's Attorney's Sunday too.* White thought as he placed the next call advising the State's Attorney of the one o'clock hearing.

Kaleidoscope

* * * * *

The State was represented by Assistant State Attorney Robert J. Klein, Esq. He was one of the younger attorneys in the office of the State's Attorney, but by no means the lowest man in the office hierarchy. White wondered whether Klein's presence was a measure of the importance the State's Attorney attached to this case, or merely the fact that a more senior States Attorney, who might later have responsibility for the case, didn't want to ruin his Sunday afternoon with a simple arraignment appearance.

White knew Klein only vaguely, but it never hurt to treat opposing counsel as an old friend. White greeted Klein warmly before asking, 'What's your position on bail, Bob?'

'You know our position on drug cases, counselor.' Klein replied. His expression, and the use of the term *counselor*, suggested that he couldn't remember White's name.

Good. Keep him off balance. 'What kind of weight is my client supposed to have had?' White asked.

'I'm not exactly sure. He was only arrested this morning and the final report hasn't been typed. I believe he was in possession of a couple of rocks of crack.'

'So we're looking at misdemeanor possession at best.'

'Hey. This is crack we're talking about.'

'Allegedly crack,' White said, emphatically.

Klein smiled and rolled his eyes. Word games and subtle distinctions were the defense attorney's stock in trade, and Klein seemed to be amused that White was playing the game. In this conversation, such distinctions were irrelevant, and Klein took the comment, as White had intended, as collegial posturing.

'Okay, Bob, let's get serious. It's minor weight. You don't even *know* it's crack, and it's a first offense. I'm thinking release on his own recognizance.'

'Lucius,' Klein said, having finally placed the face and remembering White's name, "normally you might be right, but I have my marching orders.'

So someone higher up the pecking order is calling the shots.

The door to the judge's chambers opened and the bailiff sprang to his feet intoning the time-honored call to order: 'All rise. The Court for the Twentieth Circuit of the State of Florida is now in session. The Honorable Stanley Mitchell presiding.'

'Be seated,' the Judge said, waving everyone to their seats.

The judge held his index finger up to the court reporter, indicating that he wasn't ready to go 'on the record.'

'Mr. White,' the judge said, sliding his glasses down until they perched on the end of his nose. 'Do you have the donuts?'

Judge Mitchell was known for his of sense of humor, a characteristic generally appreciated by the lawyers who appeared in front of him. When in his judicial mode, Judge Mitchell didn't tolerate any nonsense in his courtroom. But he went out of his way to discourage overzealous adversary tactics and remind lawyers that they were just doing a job, not going to war. Beginning proceedings in a casual, *we're all in this together*, manner was one of his better known quirks.

'That was this morning, Your Honor,' White responded in kind. 'I'm afraid we're all out.'

'Bailiff,' the judge called to the courtroom bailiff. Even on Sunday, when the courthouse was otherwise locked and there was little risk of violence, the rules required a bailiff be present whenever court was in session. 'Don't we have some procedures for disciplining attorneys who call me in on Sunday and don't bring donuts?'

'Yes, Your Honor,' the bailiff said, sounding serious but smiling as he spoke. He was well acquainted with Judge Mitchell's style and fully vested in the spirit of the proceedings. 'We have a little room in the basement where we run an education program for such attorneys. But I don't think the Court wants to know how we administer our training.'

Worthington watched the exchange in bewilderment.

The judge nodded to the court reporter, indicating that he was ready to go 'on the record.'

'Let's make this quick, gentlemen. Appearances, please?'

White and Klein rose and stated their names, and the names of the party they represented, for the court reporter.

'Okay. This is the arraignment of James R. Worthington, arrested this day on the charges of possession of a controlled substance, to wit, crack cocaine; possession with intent to distribute a controlled substance, to wit, crack cocaine, and money laundering. How does the defendant plead?'

'Not guilty, Your Honor,' Worthington said flatly.

'So entered. What about bail, Mr. Klein?'

'Your Honor, this is a serious crime. Drugs are pervading every segment of our society and—'

'Cut the crap, Mr. Klein.' Judge Mitchell was a good-old-boy whose occasional lapse into the language of the fish camps was generally overlooked. He had been on the bench for so long that hardly anyone even noticed. 'I've already heard my sermon for the morning, and there's no one here for you to impress with the righteous indignation speech. *Now*, what's your position on bail?'

'Your Honor, the State requests bail of one hundred thousand dollars.'

White was immediately on his feet. 'Your Honor. The State's bail request is totally unjustifiable. My client has no criminal record. In fact he doesn't have so much as a traffic ticket. He has resided in the community for more than five years and isn't going anywhere. Even if he was in possession of crack, which we dispute, the amount was extremely small. A street punk would get low bail on these facts. In this case, I request that my client be released on his own recognizance.'

'Your Honor,' Klein jumped in. 'Considering that one hundred thousand dollars was found in Mr. Worthington's home . . .'

Only his experience in controlling his response to surprises kept White from grabbing his client and demanding an explanation.

'. . . He can certainly afford bail in that amount. Besides, what Mr. White says is true, and that is just the problem.'

Klein's curious, rehearsed phrasing had the judge's attention. Klein waited a moment to allow his statement to sink in before continuing.

'Mr. Worthington has no record,' Klein paused for effect, '*at all*. He has no criminal record and no traffic tickets . . . *anywhere*. Until five years ago, he had no voter registration and no driver's license—*anywhere*. We don't even *know* he is who he says he is. He also has no known source of income. The State believes Mr. Worthington is a significant flight risk.'

This summary had the judge's attention. He looked to White, expecting a rebuttal argument.

Klein's statement caught White off-guard. White never doubted the Assistant U. S. Attorney would discover Worthington's past, but he was surprised that the information had been shared with the State's Attorney.

The look on Judge Mitchell's face told White the judge had serious reservations about releasing Worthington without bail. 'Mr. White?'

'The defendant has faith in the Court's discretion.'

The judge smiled. 'Nicely put. Bail is set at twenty thousand dollars, cash or bond. Anything else?'

'Yes, Your Honor,' White said. 'My client requests an immediate probable cause hearing.'

The judge consulted his calendar. 'Probable cause hearing is set for Friday—two o'clock. Anything else?'

'Yes, Your Honor,' White said. 'Given the short time before the probable cause hearing, there may be some problem in locating the necessary witnesses, particularly the police officers who obtained the search warrant and the officers who searched Mr. Worthington's home and made the arrest. We ask that the State's Attorney be required to produce all of these officers at the hearing.'

'Any problem with that, Mr. Klein?' Judge Mitchell said in a voice that made it clear he wasn't asking a question.

'No problem, Your Honor.'

'So ordered. Anything else?'

'No, Your Honor,' White and Klein said in unison.

'Then we are adjourned.'

* * * * *

By the time they left the courthouse, the temperature had dropped and a light drizzle had begun to fall. It was one of those rare rains that fell from high clouds unaccompanied by any wind. The waters of the river were smooth and flat. The rain fell in fine but distinct drops, each of which left small splashes giving the river's surface a look of coarse, dark sandpaper.

The mood in the War Room reflected the weather, gray and dreary.

'You sure know how to louse up a Sunday afternoon, don't you?' Harris said, sarcastically, trying to lighten the moment.

'It wasn't my idea,' Worthington said

White was about to brief Harris on the events of the day when Worthington asked, 'How did they know about my history?'

White made a mental note of the fact that Worthington was more concerned about the disclosure of his past than the charges against him.

'Let's worry about that later,' White said. 'For now, I want to know everything that happened.'

It took a minute for Worthington to gather his thoughts. 'About six-thirty this morning,' he began, still trying to focus, "two cops were banging on my door. I opened it and they said they had a search warrant.'

White, who had already examined the search warrant, handed a copy of the warrant to Harris.

'Were there only two cops?' White asked.

'Uh, yes,' Worthington said, then corrected himself. 'No. There were two at the front door, but there were two cop cars. I guess the others were somewhere else.'

'Probably at the back of the house, making sure you didn't slip out,' Harris suggested.

White nodded and signaled Worthington to continue.

'One of them told me to stay where I was, and the other one went into the house. He came back a minute later with the stuff from the toilet.'

'How long was he gone?'

'Not long. Maybe half a minute.'

'Did you watch him when he went into the house?'

'Yes.'

'Did he go directly to the bathroom?'

'Yes.' Worthington was beginning to understand. 'They knew *exactly* where to look, didn't they?'

'Apparently,' White said. 'What happened next?'

'They told me I was under arrest and put handcuffs on me.'

'Did they read you your *Miranda* rights?'

'No . . . Yes . . . Maybe. I don't remember. I wasn't thinking.'

'That's okay,' White assured him. 'Then what?'

'They took me into the study and told me to sit down,' Worthington said, closing his eyes and trying to visualize the scene. 'One of the cops stayed with me . . . in front of me . . . while the other rummaged through my desk.'

'Did they find anything that seemed to interest them?'

Kaleidoscope

Worthington closed his eyes, trying to focus. 'No. The cop seemed to be looking for something he couldn't find. It was like . . .' Worthington paused. 'You know how you move stuff around when you're looking for something specific and aren't interested in the stuff you're moving?'

White and Harris nodded.

'It was like that. He wasn't even looking at the stuff he was moving.'

'What could he have been looking for?'

'I can't think of anything.'

White and Harris waited, looking at Worthington but saying nothing.

'Nothing. I swear.'

White and Harris remained silent, thinking. Finally, White spoke. 'How did they find the money?'

'Wait a minute.' Harris interrupted. 'What money?'

'Sorry. I didn't have time to catch you up on that,' White said. 'They also grabbed a hundred thousand in cash.'

'*Jesus Christ.*' Harris said.

Harris's outburst stunned Worthington.

'While we're on the subject,' White said, 'do you want to tell me where the money in your safe came from?'

'Not particularly.'

'Humor me—or would you prefer to get a new lawyer?'

'Sorry,' Worthington said. 'It's just that I didn't exactly tell the authorities about all my money when I cut the deal to testify in Philadelphia. I was supposed to forfeit everything I had. Some of the money didn't happen to get included.'

'So you really had money when you went to Marty for help?'

'Yeah,' Worthington said, his attention now focused on the floor. 'I guess I knew I was using Marty, but I had to convince the feds that I didn't have any other money of my own.'

White looked at Harris. He wasn't buying the story either.

'Go on, Jim.'

'When the cop finished with my desk, he started looking all over the room. Finally, he found my safe and told me to open it.'

'And you opened it?'

'Yes.'

'Did you object before you opened the safe?'

'No,' Worthington said softly. 'Hell, I was about to take a dump in my pants. I knew what was in the safe.'

'Okay. Then what happened?'

'I opened the safe.'

'Then what did the cops do?'

'God. You'd think it was Christmas morning. They were grinning like the proverbial cheshire cat.'

'Did they say anything?'

'Yeah, something. I don't remember what.'

'*Think*. Did they give *any* indication they expected to find the money?'

'I don't think so. It seemed like it was a big surprise.'

'What happened then?'

'They put me in the squad car and took me to the jail.'

'Did they say anything to you on the way to jail? Ask you any questions? Anything?'

'Not that I recall.' Worthington paused again, trying to think. 'They did call in on the radio, I think. I remember them saying something about finding the mother lode.'

'What happened when they got to the jail?'

'They booked me. You know, fingerprints, picture, all that stuff.'

'Did they give you your *Miranda* rights after they had you in jail?'

'I think so. Yes, I'm pretty sure they did.'

'Too bad,' Harris said.

'Yeah,' White agreed before returning his attention to Worthington. 'Did anyone say *anything* to you once you were at the jail?'

'No. In fact . . .' He paused, apparently trying to coax his memory. 'It was almost like they didn't care about me.'

'It sounds like they already knew everything they needed,' Harris said 'Maybe they didn't want to risk revealing anything by asking questions that might alert us.'

'When is the last time you ever heard of a cop not asking any questions?'

Harris nodded. 'Never happens.'

'Ten bucks says they were told not to ask anything. Someone didn't want to risk a *Miranda* violation'

'You're probably right. But *who* told them not to ask anything?'

24.

Lucius White and Jim Worthington finished the sandwiches Grace had ordered so they could eat while they prepared for the probable cause hearing. White gathered the wrappers, crushed them into a ball and threw it into the wastepaper basket in the corner.

'It sounds like we're going to be trying my case now,' Worthington said.

'To some extent, we are,' White said. 'We're going to try to make the State show that they have sufficient evidence to justify your arrest. We don't have to argue any of our defenses, but *they* have to convince the judge they have enough evidence against you to justify a trial.'

'So what are we trying to get out of this?'

White stopped stuffing files into his briefcase and sat on the edge of the conference table. 'First of all, I want to know how this all came about. Somebody set you up. I want to know who, and I want to know why. I also want to know whether this is something that's targeted on you alone, or something that has a connection to Marty. By making them disclose the basis for their warrant we can find out where this action came from.'

Kaleidoscope

'And you think you can find this out at today's hearing?'

'I hope so. You see, in a trial we'll be focusing on evidence and legal issues regarding the admissibility of evidence. In a probable cause hearing, there's more opportunity to make the prosecutor disclose his theory of the case. The prosecutor isn't likely to have prepared for the probable cause hearing as carefully as he'll prepare for a trial. He may let something slip.'

* * * * *

As White and Worthington entered the courtroom, White spotted Paul Parker, the State's Attorney for the Twentieth Circuit. *Interesting. The State's Attorney himself is handling this case. Not one of his minions. Someone is seriously interested in this case.*

The bailiff called the court to order and judge Stanley Mitchell took his place behind the bench, waving the parties to their seats as he took his own.

'All right. What do we have here?' the judge asked impatiently.

White was immediately on his feet. 'Your Honor. As you may recall from Sunday's hearing,' White began to refresh the judge's memory and build the foundation for his argument.

'I may be old, counselor, but I'm not completely absent-minded,' Judge Mitchell said. 'I was there? Now, what's your position?'

'Your Honor. The defendant contends that his arrest was improper because it was made incidental to an unlawful search.'

'How so?' Judge Mitchell inquired in a tone suggesting that. in his twenty years on the bench, he had heard it all and nothing surprised him.

'My client was arrested when the police discovered what they *thought* to be cocaine in his home. However, the only basis on which they were in his home was that the Court had issued a warrant to search for cocaine.'

'Did I authorize the search warrant?'

'No, Your Honor. The warrant was signed by Judge Carlin.'

The judge wrinkled his nose and shook his head. 'Go on.'

'It's the defendant's position that the search warrant was improperly issued because it wasn't based on sufficient evidence.'

'What evidence was offered in support of the warrant application?'

'The warrant was issued solely on the basis of an affidavit of Officer David Grey.'

When the judge didn't ask anything else, White continued with his analysis of controlling law.

'If an affidavit offered in support of a request for a search warrant contains intentional false statements or statements made with reckless disregard for the truth, the trial court must excise the false material and consider whether the affidavit's remaining content is sufficient to establish probable cause. If the false statement is necessary to establish probable cause, the search warrant must be voided and the evidence seized as a result of the search excluded.' White delivered his argument with precision and authority, and it had the judge's attention.

Parker knew he needed to divert the judge from the search warrant.

'Your Honor, the question regarding the warrant is moot,' Parker said, as if the law was so clear that no argument was necessary. 'The police officers found something exactly where the informant said they would find it. That alone is sufficient to establish the informant's credibility.'

Judge Mitchell glared at the State's Attorney. 'You'll have your turn.'

'But while we're at it . . .' The judge paused, considering whether to change the direction of the hearing at this point.

Kaleidoscope

'You say you found *something*,' Judge Mitchell said, confirming his reputation as a judge who was alert to every nuance. 'Just what kind of *something* did you find?'

White could barely suppress a smile. *Thank you, judge.*

Parker busied himself looking at the papers in front of him. White knew what he was thinking. He was wishing that he was anywhere but in this courtroom at this time.

'A sealed vial in the tank of the toilet in the guest bathroom.' Parker finally said, hoping his response would satisfy the judge.

The gods were not with him.

'And what was in the vial, Counselor?' Judge Mitchell pressed on.

'Uh,' Parker mumbled. 'Candy, Your Honor.'

'What was that?' Judge Mitchell asked. He had obviously heard the answer and felt some need to make an unambiguous record of the answer.

'Candy.' Parker repeated more loudly.

White knew that his point had been scored for him and chose to save the State's Attorney further embarrassment by quickly moving on to the next point.

'Your Honor, Judge Carlin authorized a search for evidence of cocaine based on Officer Grey's affidavit. In that affidavit, Officer Grey stated that an informant had disclosed that there was cocaine in my client's home. Obviously the informant's information wasn't accurate, because the only thing the authorities was found was candy.

'Moreover,' White continued before the judge could interrupt, 'my client was arrested because the police thought they had discovered cocaine. As the State's Attorney has now admitted, my client wasn't in possession of anything more than candy. Therefore, there was no justification for his arrest.

'Furthermore . . .' White had the judge's attention and wasn't about to give up center stage. 'The controlling issue is not what was found, but what was known at the time the warrant was obtained. Subsequent events, and information subsequently discovered, do not validate an otherwise invalid search warrant. If the warrant wasn't valid when it is signed, nothing else matters.'

'He's right, Mr. Parker,' Judge Mitchell said. 'What do you have to say to that?'

Parker knew he had lost this argument, but made a final attempt to salvage his position. 'That's not the issue, Your Honor. The police were acting in good faith on the basis of information they believed to be accurate.'

'Which brings us back to the original issue, doesn't it?' Judge Mitchell said. 'Just what was the source of the information on which your affidavit was based?'

Parker wasn't happy with the inference that the affidavit was his own, but this wasn't the time to argue the point.

'The information was provided on a confidential basis, Your Honor. As the Court is well aware, the police cannot function if the identity of their informants is made public, particularly when it is put in the record of a judicial proceeding. Public policy requires the police to be able to protect the identity of their informants.'

Parker wanted to continue this argument, but the judge was growing impatient.

'Thank you for the civics lesson, Counselor, but in my courtroom you answer my questions.'

'Your Honor . . .' Parker protested, until the judge cut him short.

'*The name*, Counselor.' Judge Mitchell demanded.

'There is a question of federal law here, Your Honor. The information was provided by the Assistant U. S. Attorney.'

White was immediately on his feet, ready to argue the credibility of second-hand information, but the judge waved him off.

'Not exactly a confidential informant, Counselor,' Judge Mitchell said with a hint of sarcasm. More words were not necessary. Judge Mitchell wasn't pleased with Parker's attempt to mislead him.

'Well, the information was provided on a confidential basis,' Parker argued lamely. 'In fact, the information was originally provided to the F.B.I. by a confidential informant.

'As the Court is aware, when an individual in not under arrest, the F.B.I. has the authority, under federal law, to grant immunity to undercover informants without the consent, or even the knowledge, of the U. S. Attorney. After a suspect has been arrested, the U. S. Attorney's agreement is required to give a suspect immunity, but that is not the case here.'

Judge Mitchell interrupted Parker and began to summarize. 'So you are saying that the F.B.I. obtained information from a confidential informant, whose identity they didn't even disclose to the Assistant U. S. Attorney. Then *she* passed this information to the local police. Then the police obtained a search warrant based on information supposedly provided by a reliable informant, even though they had no idea where the information actually originated.'

'It isn't like you make it sound, Your Honor. The police had every reason to believe that information provided by the U. S. Attorney was accurate. In fact—'

'Save it, Counselor.' Judge Mitchell said.

'Well, that doesn't change the facts. The police had a good faith basis for the facts stated in the affidavit. If anything, the fact that the information came from the Assistant U. S. Attorney makes it more credible than any information they might have obtained from a street informant.'

It was a reasonable argument, and it seemed to calm the judge.

'And since the police *had* a good faith basis for their initial search,' Parker said,' the cash they discovered in the course of their search was properly discovered incidental to a valid search for drugs.

'The warrant authorizes a search for evidence of possession of cocaine or trafficking in cocaine. The courts have specifically held that, and I quote, *A description is sufficiently particular when it enables the searcher to reasonably ascertain and identify the things authorized to be seized.'* Parker handed a copy of his case authority to the judge and, with some smugness, dropped a copy of his case on the table in front of White.

'Mr. White?' Judge Mitchell said, indicating that he was ready to hear White's argument.

'Your Honor.' White started as he slowly stood. 'The prosecutor makes a great argument, and his authorities are directly on point.' Parker relaxed, a hint of a smile beginning to form until White continued. 'Unfortunately, he is in the wrong court.'

Parker spun to face White.

The judge leaned forward.

'The prosecutor has correctly stated the law as it applies in *federal* court.' White said, now knowing that the U. S. Attorney had prepared Parker's argument based on federal law, without considering the possibility that a different standard applied in state court.

'Under *state* law, the standard is whether the warrant is so specific that any document, found and examined by an officer, can be readily recognizable as being, or not being, a document described in the warrant, and nothing should be left to the discretion of the officers executing the warrant as to what should be seized and taken. If the original source of information on which the search warrant affidavit relies cannot describe existing objects or things other than in terms of generic reference such as *papers* or *documents*, the information is too vague and indefinite upon which to authorize a search.'

White walked confidently to the bench and handed the judge copies of his case authorities.

Judge Mitchell slid his reading glasses down his nose as he thumbed through the cases White handed him. Finally the judge looked at Parker. 'These cases seem to be directly on point. Do you have anything to add?'

Parker hung his head. 'No, Your Honor.'

Kaleidoscope

White grabbed his opportunity. 'Your Honor, inasmuch as the warrant doesn't cover the search that uncovered my client's funds, the discovery of the cash is the fruit of the poisonous tree.'

'Right again, counselor.' Judge Mitchell said. 'Make your motion.'

'Because the State has no admissible evidence to support the charges against my client, I move that all charges be dismissed.'

'So ordered.' the judge announced. 'We're adjourned.'

As they left, a heavy set man with the dark complexion, long black hair and black leather jacket sitting in the corner of the last row of in the courtroom gallery folded his newspaper and followed them from the building.

* * * * *

Elizabeth Powell was in her office, reviewing the status of her pending cases with Managing Assistant U. S. Attorney Dwight Madison, when her secretary announced that Paul Parker was on the line.

Powell, anticipating good news that would improve her standing in the office pecking order, switched on the speakerphone . 'Good afternoon, Paul,' she greeted Parker in what passed for her cheeriest voice before Parker had a chance to say anything. 'I trust you have good news.'

'Good news, my ass. What in the hell did you think you were doing to me?'

'*What?*' Powell sputtered. 'What happened?'

'What happened?' Parker shot back. 'What *happened* is that you sent my cops out in a search for sugar candy.'

'*What the* . . ..'

'You heard me, lady. The package in the toilet was sugar candy. The judge damn near laughed in my face when I had to tell him what we found.'

'But that can't be,' Powell stammered.

'It can . . . and it was.'

'But it was good information—and a good warrant.'

'Not according to Judge Mitchell. Where the hell did they teach you to draft search warrants?'

'That was a standard form warrant,' Powell fired back indignantly. 'We've used it a hundred times.'

'Maybe it works in federal court, but it's not enough in this circuit of state court. You sent me in there with federal case authorities and I had my ass handed to me.'

'But you got the seized money in, didn't you?' Powell asked, fearing the worst.

'In your dreams, little girl. Didn't they teach you about the fruit of the poisonous tree in law school?'

'Damn.' Powell muttered to herself, but overheard by everyone.

'You said that right,' Parker said. 'The next time you want to put someone in harm's way you can march your own ass over here.'

'Now, listen here. I don't have to take that kind of crap from you,' Powell nearly screamed.

'Oh, yeah? Just what kind of crap do you have to take?'

Powell had no answer.

'The next time you need a favor, don't call me,' Parker said and hung up.

'I think,' Madison said as Powell slumped back in her chair, 'that both of you need a little work on your people skills. Now, let me see if I have this right.' Madison stood and leaned against the wall. 'You talked the State's Attorney into raiding the home of Martin Bower's friend because you *thought* he might find some drugs. Instead of drugs, the police find candy and $100,000 in cash. But they can't keep the cash, because it was discovered during an illegal search based on *your* improper warrant. So we now know Worthington, who we never really suspected of anything, is probably involved in money laundering or illegal currency transactions. But we can't do any thing about it because we only discovered these facts by virtue of an illegal search. Is that about it?'

'Yes,' Powell said, her voice barely audible.

'Well, your day is certainly ending on a high note, isn't it?' Madison asked rhetorically and he headed for the door.

'Dwight, I . . .' Powell began feebly.

'Save it,' Madison muttered and left the office without turning around.

There was no one left to hear her when she muttered, 'Don't worry. I'll nail that son of a bitch—one way or the other.'

25.

Joe Morgan paced in circles in an empty corner of the hospital parking lot, becoming increasingly agitated as he waited for Randall Harrington to answer his phone. *A half a million dollars a year in billings and he keeps me cooling my heels while he talks to his wife. I deserve better than this.* Morgan's irritation was due more to what Elizabeth Powell had just told him than by Harrington's delay, but he didn't want to admit that to himself. Besides, Harrington was an easier target for his wrath than Powell.

'Joe. Sorry to keep you waiting,' Harrington answered.

Yeah, sure you are. 'We have a problem,' Morgan said without preamble.

'So. If we have a problem, we'll take care of it. That's why you pay us the big bucks,' Harrington said, not willing to be drawn in by Morgan's anxiety. 'What's up?'

'I just got off the phone with Elizabeth Powell. It seems that Lucius White is representing Jim Worthington.'

There was a brief pause before Harrington responded. 'So what?'

'They had a probable cause hearing this morning on Worthington's arrest. The State's Attorney got his ass handed to him by the judge. The State's Attorney read Elizabeth

Powell the riot act, and now she's pissed at us—particularly me.'

'What's she pissed at you for?'

'She blames me for giving her bad information on Worthington.'

'How can she blame you for that? You only suggested that she *look* at Worthington. The F.B.I. dug up the information about his supposed drug dealing. Besides, he was only supposed to be a red herring in the first place.'

'Bullshit. We need her to focus on a connection between Bower and Worthington.'

'Not *we*. *You*,' Harrington said. 'It was *your* idea to point Powell toward Worthington. I told you we should limit things to Bower and let nature take its course.'

Morgan started to respond, but thought better of it. He had his own reasons for wanting to keep the government's attention on Worthington, but it was still too early to disclose them to Harrington. Instead, he said, "Well, you went along with the Worthington plan.'

Harrington changed the subject. 'What happened that got Powell so upset?'

'The judge threw everything out because the search of Worthington's safe wasn't covered by the warrant. That's what Powell is most pissed about. Now she knows Worthington is involved in something, but she's stuck with a poisonous tree problem, and she doesn't have any other grounds for going after him.'

'Dumb ass cops.' Harrington muttered. 'Don't those guys know anything about search and seizure? How are we supposed to be responsible for that?'

At least he's back to '*we*', Morgan thought with some small satisfaction. 'It hardly matters at this point. What matters is that Powell isn't likely to be responsive to anything we give her for a while.'

'So we ignore her and feed the next piece of information to your buddy, what's his name, the rookie at the F.B.I.'

'You mean Paul Smith?'

'Yeah . . . him.'

Morgan kicked a can in the corner of the parking lot and watched it sail into the street before continuing. 'That's our second problem.'

'What do you mean?'

'I mean I tried to call him. There is no such person at the Bureau.'

The consequences of this revelation were immediately apparent, something Morgan recognized in Harrington's silence.

'That's right.' Morgan said smugly. 'The guy I talked to after Marty was fired was someone *posing* as an agent. Nothing I told him ever got to Powell. She only connected Bower and Worthington because Bower posted Worthington's bail. Everything I told the guy posing as Paul Smith went to someone other than the Bureau. It doesn't take much imagination to figure out who that is.'

'Lucius White.'

'Your grasp of the obvious is amazing,' Morgan said. "Now White and Bower are one step ahead of the feds, and our credibility for feeding anything to Powell is bordering on zero.'

Harrington paused before speaking. 'I don't know if the Worthington plan is dead, but it's going to have to be left dormant for a while. In the meantime, we have to focus on Bower.'

'No shit.'

Morgan continued pacing the parking lot, considering how much he should tell Harrington. The people in Philadelphia were not happy. The investigation into the theft of AIDS drugs from the clinics in Sarasota was making them nervous. The clinic thefts didn't have anything to do with them, but it was too close to home. It also wasn't anything White should be interested in, but White's girlfriend was involved—and that

Kaleidoscope

was too close to White. Morgan's instructions were clear, *Make sure that no one connects us to the AIDS drugs.*

Morgan was frightened. He, more than Harrington, knew what their client was capable of doing to avoid discovery. He understood what their client meant when they told him to take care of a problem. If he didn't put a stop to the investigation in Sarasota . . . Morgan didn't want to consider the alternative.

Morgan's thoughts were interrupted by Harrington. 'Joe,' Harrington said, speaking as if he was explaining something basic and obvious to a kindergartner, 'Elizabeth has her blinders on, and we're her only eyes. She'll forget about Worthington soon enough.'

'But what about Bower's lawyers? They don't have blinders on, and they're capable of looking everywhere they damned well please.'

'Then we feed then some leads and let them chase their tails around in blind alleys.'

'Like what? What are you going to do?'

'I'll have Sommers pretend he doesn't like what has been going on and feed Harris a lead or two.'

Morgan abruptly stopped pacing. 'Why Sommers?' *How did you know about Sommers?*

'Didn't Dr. Sommers treat White's partner for a while after his accident?'

Morgan began breathing again. 'Yeah. I think so.'

'I'll call you when I get it worked out,' Harrington said and hung up.

Morgan slammed his cell phone closed and started across the parking lot toward the hospital, still wondering how much Harrington knew.

26.

Kelly's was a cop bar in the finest tradition of cop bars. Owned by Sergeant Michael Kelly, retired, formerly of the Boston Police Department, Kelly's is located on Fort Myers' main north-south artery, approximately equal distance from the courthouse, the central office of the Fort Myers Police Department and the Lee County Sheriff's office. That made it a convenient place for both formal and informal meetings of officers from both jurisdictions.

The distinction between the Irish and all others didn't have the significance in Fort Myers that it had in Boston. In Fort Myers, the only relevant distinction between classes of people was the distinction between native rednecks and every-fucking-body else. Nevertheless, when they were in Kelly's, everyone who wore the uniform was an honorary Irishman.

From the afternoon shift change at four o'clock until early evening, and again late in the evening when the night shift came on, Kelly's was populated mostly by law enforcement officers. It was undoubtedly the safest place in town to go drinking.

When White entered Kelly's, a haze of blue-gray smoke hung over the pool table that sat like green mushroom in the middle of the room. A short man wearing a Police Benevolent Association T-shirt, his belly hanging over his belt and the edge of the table, looked up from his shot and examined White. Like a chain reaction, all conversation ceased as the other patrons stopped talking and directed their attention toward White.

Outsiders were tolerated at Kelly's, but not made especially welcome. Lawyers, at least those recognized as members of the criminal defense bar, were generally unwelcome.

It wasn't that law enforcement officers had any more loathing for lawyers than the general public. It wasn't even that defense lawyers occasionally got criminals off on some technicality. What made defense attorneys particularly loathsome was the defense *de jur*: sloppy police work tainted all evidence, and law enforcement agencies were staffed all by ignorant morons who had never heard of the Constitution.

Lucius White was an exception. On those rare occasions when he tried a case in state court he was at least polite to law enforcement officers. More importantly, when officers found themselves in trouble in their official capacity, White represented them *pro bono*. His fight was with the prosecutors, and an occasional favor for the men in blue was a small price to pay for cooperation from the police when he needed it. Over the years he had represented enough officers to be personally known by many, and his name was known favorably by many more.

White didn't know the person who called his office and suggested this meeting. He didn't even recognize the name, and, because the call had come after the afternoon shift change, he was unable to contact any of his regular sources to check on the caller. He would find out what he needed to know soon enough.

White sat at the end of the bar, drinking his customary Diet Pepsi with two squeezes of lime, and watching faces as people moved through the short vestibule inside the large, solid wood doors. It wasn't as if a few additional seconds of preparation would make any difference, but old habits die hard.

'Are you White?' A deep baritone voice sounded over White's shoulder.

White swiveled his bar stool until he was facing a tall, well-dressed, and physically fit, African-American. White was tempted to ask, *Are you black?* but thought better of it.

'Yes,' White said, extending his hand. 'I'm Lucius White.'

The black man took White's hand in a firm but friendly grip, not a test of strength as some cops did with lawyers.

'Nice to meet you, Mr. White,' the black man said.

'Call me Lucius.'

'All right. Lucius it is,' the black man agreed. 'Call me Tony.'

White wasn't sure if Tony was his real name, but it didn't matter. If it became important, he could check on it later. After all, how many six-foot-four-inch black men with a gold-capped front tooth and scar on his cheek worked in local law enforcement? One thing was certain; he wasn't an undercover officer. He was far too memorable and easily identifiable.

'Let's talk in the corner,' Tony suggested. 'We can have some privacy.'

There was an unwritten rule in Kelly's that the corner furthest from the bar, windowless and dimly lighted, was reserved for private conversations. Even when the bar was packed three deep and every table was filled, the corner would be empty—waiting for those who needed privacy.

'Lou Hamilton says nice things about you,' Tony began. 'He told me about your visit after Bower was fired.'

'Tell Lou I appreciate it. I say nice things about him too.'

'He says you're one of the good guys.'

'I'm never sure what that means, but I'll take it as a compliment.'

'It was meant as one.'

Kaleidoscope

'Then, thank you. I'll do my best not to blush.'

'I couldn't tell back here.'

'No, you couldn't,' White agreed.

Neither man said anything while the waitress brought Tony a longneck beer. When she left, White began. 'If we're going to dance, shouldn't someone put a quarter in the jukebox?'

Tony smiled. 'Lou said you were a smart-ass. I like that.'

'What kind of an ass are you?' White said.

Tony laughed. 'You're okay.'

'I'm glad you're pleased.'

'You were with the Bureau for a while, weren't you?' Tony asked, changing the subject.

'No, but I spent some time with the D.E.A.'

"I was misinformed.'

'Are we going to do Bogart now?' White asked.

Tony smiled again. 'You worked with Sandy Donaldson, didn't you?'

'Are you fishing, or telling me what you know?'

'Sorry. Just asking. In fact, I talked to Sandy this afternoon. He speaks highly of you.'

'He's a good agent. We spent some time together, but that was a long time ago.'

'It must have been. He transferred from D.E.A. to the F.B.I. almost fifteen years ago. He was one of my trainers at Quantico.'

Was that a slip or a test? When Tony called, he gave every indication that he was with local law enforcement, but Quantico was the main F.B.I. training facility at Quantico, Virginia. Did this mean that Tony was F.B.I., or had he merely taken one of the many courses taught by the F.B.I.?

'Give him my regards.'

'I will,' Tony said.

'But you didn't invite me here to bring me up to date on an old acquaintance.'

'No, I didn't,' Tony said. 'Forgive me for trying to get a feel for you.'

'It's an occupational hazard. You can't help it,' White said. 'But while we're on the topic, just what is your occupation?'

'Detective. County Sheriff's office. Presently on special assignment.'

'And I suppose this special assignment has something to do with me.'

'You could say that.'

'And what is this special assignment?'

'You. You're being followed.'

Leslie was right.

'You don't seem surprised.'

White ignored the implied question. 'Who's following me?' he demanded. He wasn't in a mood for playing games. Not where Leslie might be involved.

Tony smiled. 'Me.'

'*You* are following *me*?' White said, far louder than he intended. A few faces at the bar turned in their direction.

Tony merely nodded.

'You're following me, and you asked me here to tell me that you're following me?'

'That's right.' Tony smiled more broadly.

'Well, I'm impressed with your approach. If you're going to tail a guy, it's easier to go drinking with him than sit outside on a rainy night wondering where he's going to go next.'

'My thoughts exactly. If I hadn't told you, you never would have suspected me.'

'You have me there,' White said. 'Any other interesting tidbits you'd like to share? For instance, why are you following me? And why are you telling me that you are following me?'

'As a matter of fact, yes,' Tony said. 'A couple of weeks ago we started following you and Mr. McGee—and Mr. Worthington. I didn't know it at the time, but Paul Parker had been offered a high-profile drug case by the Assistant U. S. Attorney.'

'The Assistant U. S. Attorney doesn't give anything away without getting something in return.'

'We were supposed to let her know if we came up with anything relating to your guy . . . Bower.'

'Let me guess. The soon-to-become high-profile case—the one that was going to put Parker in the public limelight in this election year—was Jim Worthington.'

Tony nodded as he took another swallow of his beer. 'And Parker was less than happy when he was carved up by you and the judge.'

'No hard feelings, I hope.'

'Not against you. In fact, he was impressed. But the same can't be said for his feeling about the Assistant U. S. Attorney.'

'So Parker decided to get even by letting me know he was having us followed.'

'That's about it.'

'But if Worthington was such a prize, why did she give him to Parker?'

'I thought that was a little strange,' Tony said. 'The story she gave the State's Attorney was that her people were all tied up with the investigation of your man.'

'You say that like you don't believe it.'

'I think Attorney Powell has been watching too much television,' Tony said. 'The F.B.I. and local law enforcement may not always cooperate in the big cities, but this is a small town. We don't go out of our way to share information, but we do talk. The way I hear it, the boys from the Bureau don't have much involvement in her investigation of Bower.' Tony took another long drink from his bottle of beer and looked around the bar, nodding to some acquaintances.

'Well, thanks for the head's up,' White said, assuming the conversation was over.

'That's only part of it,' Tony continued, regaining White's attention. 'We follow bad guys for a living, but we don't usually follow attorneys unless there's a good reason. And you being who you are . . .'

'And who am I?'

'A lot of cops know you. A lot of cops like you because you've supported them when they needed it.'

White tried his *aw shucks* look.

Tony ignored him and continued. 'Anyway, it turned out we weren't the only ones watching your people.'

Jesus. 'How do you know?'

'After the fiasco at Worthington's probable cause hearing, Parker ended all cooperation and called off the tail. Lou Hamilton knew what was going on and asked us to keep an eye out for you and your lady friend. Some patrol officers got curious about vehicles parked where they didn't belong.'

White began tapping a finger on the table. 'Who are they?' White asked, his tone far more relaxed than he felt. 'You already said the Bureau didn't seem to be involved.'

'Amateurs. All they needed to make their disguise complete was a neon sign.'

'But who?'

'I don't know. But if I were you, I'd be careful.' Tony suddenly became serious. 'I ran the license plates and found they were driving rental cars. The drivers licenses they gave the car agency are phony.'

'Any ideas?' White asked, controlling his anxiety.

'Good guys don't generally need phony driver's licenses,' Tony said seriously. 'And whoever they are, they haven't found whatever they're looking for.'

'What makes you think so?'

'They're still here,' Tony said, as if that said it all.

'So we could still be in danger.'

'Like I said, I'd be careful.'

'Why are you telling me this?'

'Orders,' Tony said, nonchalantly. 'Parker was pissed at the feds. When the Worthington case blew up in his face, he told me to tell you what was up.'

While White considered this, Tony slid to the edge of the seat in the booth, ready to leave.

'Just one thing,' White said.

Tony paused.

'These other guys playing junior sleuth, are you sure they're tailing *my* people?'

'Do you have something else going on that would make anyone want to tail you?'

White thought for a moment before responding. 'No. Forget I asked,'

Tony stood and extended his hand. 'As much as I enjoy playing mind games about this, I have a lovely lady waiting for me.'

'Yeah,' White said absently. 'Look, I'd like to return the favor and help you out. Is there somewhere I should fax my schedule to make your tail easier? Maybe help you locate me if you lose me?'

'No thanks,' Tony said. 'My men need the practice. But just in case something comes up, here's my card. It has my office number, my cell phone and home phone.'

White looked at the card and then at Tony. 'Am I going to need your numbers?'

'I'd bet on it.'

27.

Congress wasn't in session. The President was on vacation. No wars were being fought. No planes had crashed.

In the absence of any real news, Bower was confronted with a daily dose of speculation by journalists with too much time on their hands. There was inevitably something in the news to ignite Bower, and the strain was showing.

This morning the big story was Worthington's probable cause hearing. The State's Attorney's had admitted that Worthington's arrest was based on information provided by the Assistant U. S. Attorney. With nothing else to report, the media had turned a nothing story into another major issue in the continuing investigation of Martin Bower. The lead story in the morning paper was filled with theories and innuendo. The Assistant U. S. Attorneys refused to comment on the hearing. Although consistent with the government's policy of not commenting on any ongoing investigations, her refusal merely added fuel to the reporter's speculation.

White expected Bower to be out of control over the news story. He wasn't disappointed.

'What's this all about?' he shouted, waving the morning paper.

'Just fine, thanks, and yourself?' White said, ignoring Bower's outburst.

'Jesus, Lucius. What the hell is going on?' Bower asked more reasonably as he began to calm down, his outburst having quenched his need to be angry at someone.

'That's what we're here to figure out,' White said. 'We've had a couple of new developments. I wanted you to listen in, just in case something jogs your memory.'

White turned from Bower to Horse. 'What do you have on Congressman Marks?'

'Not much. He was on the original board of the hospital, but he was only there for a couple of years after Bower was hired. That was almost fifteen years ago.'

'What do we know about his personal life?'

'He was married for a couple of years. Got divorced just before Lucius was hired. It was an amicable divorce. His family has serious money, and his ex-wife was well taken care of.'

'Are there any women in his life?'

'No one that stands out.'

'Any drug connection?'

'According to my sources, the congressman did a little recreational coke at one time. Nothing that suggests a habit—and there's no evidence he's still a user.'

'Is there any possibility that the congressman is gay?'

Horse looked up from his notes. 'Funny you should ask. There were some rumors about that, bad jokes actually, at the time of the divorce. But no one I talked to thought much about it.'

'I remember reading that he takes regular hunting and fishing trips. Is it possible the trips were covers for weekends with a boyfriend?'

'Anything's possible. Why are you so interested?'

'The congressman is taking a special interest in this case. The hospital board may be using him to put pressure on Elizabeth Powell.'

'What kind of pressure?' Bower asked.

'I don't know yet,' White said. 'It could be nothing more than making sure the case doesn't get swept under the rug. The hospital has a lot riding on your conviction.'

'I know they want Marty convicted,' Horse interrupted, 'but what do they gain, other than being able to blame all the hospital's failures on him?'

'They probably hope to get an order of restitution. Then they'll claim they're entitled to keep his severance and pension benefits to satisfy the order.'

Bower stiffened at the suggestion that he might actually have to forfeit his severance benefits.

'Marty,' White said. 'Does anyone on the board have influence with the congressman?'

Bower shook his head. 'Probably not anymore. Most of the board contributed to his early campaigns. Back then, the people on the board were important in community. The town's a lot bigger now, and the board members aren't as important in local politics as they were.'

'So you don't think the Congressman owes any favors the board may be calling in?'

'I doubt it.'

'But that doesn't mean that the attorneys don't have any influence,' Harris said

'I don't think that's where the pressure is coming from. They don't have an office in his district.' White said.

'So where does that leave us?'

'I'm still just thinking,' White said. 'We know pressure is being put on Marks. Pressure serious enough to be worrying him. What if the pressure is closer to extortion than a favor? What if the congressman were gay? If something like that got out, the congressman's career would be over.'

Harris understood where White was going, and continued his analysis. 'If Marks is gay, it wouldn't be too far-fetched to conclude that he is also HIV positive, and would want the latest AIDS drugs from a very confidential source.'

Kaleidoscope

'And the congressman may still have closer contacts to the hospital than we know about. Maybe they're close enough to have him involved in the deal,' White said

'A connection to the congressman would explain why Powell wasn't pursuing the drug aspect of the whole arrangement,' Harris added. 'Keeping that part of the investigation quiet could be beneficial to a prosecutor who had higher aspirations.'

'That would explain a lot of things.' White said. 'It's hard to believe the feds haven't been able to close the circle of the money and the drugs. Hell, we were able to figure it out, and we're not that smart.'

'Speak for yourself.' Harris said.

'What I mean is, we had to break into the computer system and rummage around before we found anything. The system was wide open to the prosecutor. The hospital was giving them anything they wanted.'

'Maybe that's just it,' Harris said. 'The hospital was giving them everything they needed, so they didn't have to look inside the computer for themselves. That's consistent with what we've been hearing. Powell is relying on the hospital for information. She's leaving the F.B.I. out of the investigation.'

White stood and walked to the marker board where he picked up a green marker and began twirling it absently. Finally, he stopped and turned to the others. 'How about this? Suppose you knew about the drug side of the deal, and you wanted to use it for your personal benefit. Would you want the F.B.I. guys nosing around and finding out the same thing, or would you keep them out of it?'

'Probably keep it to myself,' Harris agreed.

White nodded and continued to twirl the green marker.

The others waited silently.

White remained standing by the marker board, nodding as if having a conversation with himself before returning his attention to the others and asked, 'What else do you have, Horse?'

'I have some stuff on the Sarasota connection you had me looking into.'

Harris looked up, startled. 'What Sarasota connection?'

'It's a wild idea I was following up on,' White said. 'Leslie told me there's been a rash of drug thefts from clinics in the Sarasota area. After Marty told us that the drug account involved in the money cycle was for AIDS drugs, I told Horse so see if there's any connection.'

'Leslie's people weren't much help,' Horse continued. 'They gave me the names of some doctors who were sympathetic to AIDS victims. I spoke with all of them, but I didn't get anything. They all claim they send their AIDS patients to the hospital program in Sarasota, if they can pay, or to one of the clinics run by Leslie's friends, if they qualify. I believe them. And none of them knew anyone else who might have a private AIDS treatment practice.'

'So we've drawn a blank?'

'Only on the direct approach. When that approach failed, I started looking for a connection between anyone in the hospital administration and anyone in Sarasota. I cross-referenced databases for medical school graduates, residencies, fellowships, grant applications and professional organizations. Then I eliminated matches based on obvious things—membership in the American Medical Society, the Florida Medical Society and the Association of Hospital Trustees. After eliminating people who had those memberships in common, I had a list of about a hundred doctors.'

'That doesn't narrow things down much.'

'No. But something else does. Brian Lester, the banker who supposedly committed suicide, was being treated for AIDS by a Dr. Thomas Hart, an internist.'

'Let me guess,' White interrupted. 'Thomas Hart is on your other list.'

'Bingo.'

'What's the basis for his match?'

'His match is with Dr. Sommers, Nathan Sommers. At different times, they both had National Institutes of Health fellowships to study contagious diseases, and they both attended several of the same Centers for Disease Control seminars on AIDS.'

White stood and walked to the mini-refrigerator where he retrieved a can of Diet Pepsi. He took a long swallow and began pacing across the front of the room. 'What are the chances that a banker with AIDS just *happened* to go to a doctor with a link to the Coastal Regional Hospital board member who is liaison between the hospital and an AIDS drug research study?'

'Slim and none would be my guess,' Harris said.

'Weren't the wire transfer codes sending the money from the Gulf Coast Bank to the Cayman bank changed about two years ago.'

Horse thumbed through his files, and smiled. 'The change was made six weeks before Brian Lester left the bank.'

'So,' White said, continuing to think out loud. 'Try this on for size. Brian Lester knows he has AIDS. He might even know he doesn't have much time left. So he decides to leave the bank. Dr. Hart arranges for Lester to get treated with the latest experimental AIDS drugs. In exchange for this favor, Lester changes the transfer codes so the money goes to a new Cayman bank account.'

'It's an interesting theory,' Harris agreed. 'What do we know about Dr. Hart?'

'That,' Horse said, a broad smile filling his face, 'is where things get interesting.'

White and Harris leaned forward.

'Dr. Hart was a diabetic. Six months ago, he took an accidental overdose of insulin.'

'Dead?' White asked.

'As dead as you can get.'

White stood and resumed pacing. 'How the hell could a doctor take an overdose of insulin?'

'Maybe the same way a banker with no history of drug abuse, and no obvious access to pain killers, commits *suicide*.'

'With a little help,' White muttered.

'It's a possibility.'

'And when did you say Dr. Hart died?'

'Six months ago.'

'Just about the time the hospital accounting discrepancies were discovered and the drug transfers were stopped.'

'Quite a coincidence,' Horse said.

'What do you think?' Harris asked.

'I think,' White said after a long pause, 'that someone is getting rid of loose ends. The problem is, I don't know if it's anything we can use.'

'What do you mean?'

White paused, gathering his thoughts. 'Our theory is that someone *other* than Marty is the bad guy. But what we know only helps if the disappearance of the AIDS drugs is part of the government's case. So far, it doesn't look like Powell even *knows* about the missing drugs. If *we* raise the drug issue, and she doesn't already know about it, we'll be giving her another charge to bring against Marty—and another theory for her case.'

'How sure are we that she doesn't know about the drugs?' Horse asked.

'All we know is that there's nothing related to the drugs in the indictment.'

'But,' Harris interrupted, 'we've assumed Powell is staying away from the AIDS drug issues to protect Congressman Marks. If she doesn't know about the drugs, our theory about the importance of *his* interest in the case gets shattered.'

'Not entirely,' White said. 'She doesn't have to know about the drugs to want to keep the congressman happy.'

Kaleidoscope

As White thought about this, he saw that Bower was concentrating on something else. 'Do you have something, Marty?'

'Maybe,' Bower said. 'It may not mean anything, but about the time this whole thing started we were making some changes to the computer system. Sommers doesn't know anything about computers, but the board wanted a doctor on the committee to advise on the medical aspects of things.'

'What sorts of *medical* issues were involved in the financial accounting?' Harris asked.

'You have to understand, none of the board members knew anything about running a hospital. They were only on the board because they were part of the community leadership that started the hospital. Someone on the board had just come back from a conference and had the bright idea that we should be able to account for all of our expenses by medical category. Nat Sommers was supposed to advise on the categories of expenses that we needed for patient cost accounting and analysis.'

'Was he sufficiently involved to have the money transfer routine built into the *new* system?' White asked.

'I doubt it. I don't know why he would have been.'

'But he would at least have known about all the accounting categories?'

'Yes. That's what he was on the committee for—to identify the categories we needed to track expenses.'

'This connection to Nat Sommers may be something,' Harris said. 'I received a curious call from Nat yesterday,'

'Why would he be calling you?'

'It's not usual. He treated me after my accident and he's sort of stayed in touch, just to see how I'm doing.'

'Did he have anything interesting to say?' White asked.

'He started out just checking on how I was doing, the sort of questions I might have expected. But then he started asking about the case against Marty. I had the feeling he wanted to tell me something.'

'What?'

'I don't know. As soon as the conversation turned to the hospital, I reminded him that he was a defendant in the civil suit. I told him I couldn't talk to him because he was represented by an attorney. But he wanted to talk to me anyway. Nat claimed his attorney knew about his call and said it was all right.'

'It sounds like they're trying to spread some disinformation.'

'I didn't think so at the time. But, considering what we've just discovered, I think you may be right.' Harris paused before continuing. 'There's something else that's bothering me.'

White put down his pen and leaned back.

'We've been assuming Morgan is at the center of everything. But nothing Horse discovered about the AIDS drug issue has any ties to Morgan. In fact, there's nothing to connect Morgan to *anything* other than the plan to convict Marty.'

'What are you getting at?'

'What if the two conspiracies are totally separate?' Harris suggested. 'What if the original money circle and AIDS theft thing is something only Sommers is involved in, or Sommers and someone we haven't identified yet? What if Morgan is only involved in the frame-up of Marty and the plan to control the hospital?'

'That's what I like about you, Harry,' White said. 'You can always find a way to trash a nice tight theory. Unfortunately, you're also right.'

Horse and Harris chuckled.

'One last thing,' White said, abruptly putting aside the question of Nat Sommers. 'I met with one of the local cops at Kelly's last night. He told me that some of us may be under surveillance.'

'*Who?*' Harris asked.

'I'm not sure.'

'Bower?'

'I don't know.'

'Leslie?' Horse asked.

White clinched his jaw at the suggestion but didn't respond.

'Are you sure this has anything to do with Bower?' Harris asked.

'I'm not sure of anything,' White said. 'It sounded like the interest was in Worthington.'

'Do you think they're following Worthington?'

'That would only make sense if the government knew about the drugs . . . and thought there was a connection between Bower and Worthington,' White argued. 'I can't think of any other reason for their interest in Worthington.'

'But what would make them interested in Worthington in the first place?' Horse asked. 'Only *we* know Morgan was trying to stir up some interest in a connection between Bower and Worthington.'

'I still think it was all a false lead. They needed to keep the investigation away from the computer system.'

'That's not the point,' Horse said. 'We only know about a connection because Morgan fed it to us. But, when he told me about the connection between Bower and Worthington, he thought I was a federal agent.'

'And having already told one F.B.I. agent, there would be no reason to tell another.'

'Right,' Horse agreed. 'If he ran around dropping the same hint to too many people, someone could get suspicious.'

'But if the government didn't learn about Worthington from Morgan, what got them interested in him?'

'Good question.'

'Worthington was just unlucky enough to have the money in his safe discovered during the search of his house,' White mused. 'If the government wasn't seriously interested in him before the break-in, the money got their attention.'

'Great.' Harris said. '*We* know there's no connection, but the government doesn't know that.'

Horse returned to the subject of the surveillance. 'Do you want me to try and set up whoever is following us?'

'What do you have in mind?'

'It's easier to detect a surveillance when the person being followed is on the move.' Horse said. 'I could arrange for us to be followed by one of my people whenever we go out. With a little luck we'll pick up whoever else is out there.'

White thought for a moment before responding. 'Let's try it. Whenever you go out,' White instructed the others, 'let Horse know so he can put one of his people on you.'

'And try not to let them get a picture of you scratching your balls in public,' Harris added.

When the meeting disbanded, White motioned for Horse to remain. White closed his door and spoke in a confidential tome. 'I'm not sure that whoever is following us is interested in either Bower or Worthington,' White said, pacing the room as he spoke. 'Last week, Leslie said she had a feeling she was being followed. She said she saw the same blue car up the street a couple of times, and was sure she saw the same car outside the clinic in Sarasota the last time she was up there.'

'And you think *she's* the one who's *really* being followed?'

'It's a possibility. I didn't want to say anything with Marty here, but the cop I met at Kelly's said these guys were using phony Pennsylvania driver's licenses. Whoever they are, they're not government.'

'Why would anyone be following Leslie?'

'I don't know, and that's what bothers me,' White said. 'She's the one who reported the thefts from the AIDS clinics, and I know she's talked to the police about the investigation. Maybe someone thinks there's a connection between that and our investigation.'

'It may be more than that,' Horse said. 'When I was first nosing around in Sarasota, I didn't find anything connecting our investigation to the thefts from the clinics. Now we know there's a connection between a hospital board member and Dr. Hart in Sarasota. And we know that *someone else* is concerned about the investigation in Sarasota. I can't see a couple of people from Pennsylvania being interested in a few thefts from AIDS clinics. That has to mean there's a connection between Marty's case and something else that's going on in Sarasota.'

'It also means Leslie might be in danger,' White said.

'Can't you tell her what's going on and keep her home for a while?'

'She already knows what's going on. And as for trying to keep her home . . .'

'I get the picture. Do you want me to have someone keep an eye on Leslie?'

'Yes,' White said. 'And, Horse, make it someone good. I don't want the bad guy to pick up on the tail. If Leslie isn't already being followed, I don't want her to spot your guy and have her worst fears confirmed.'

* * * * *

Harry Harris was waiting in White's office when White returned from lunch. He was thumbing through a pad of notes, frowning and shaking his head.

'Something bothering you, Harry?'

'The same thing that should be bothering you.'

'What's that?'

'In spite of everything we've discovered, we still don't have anything to rule Marty out. The only thing we *know* is that there's more to the case than even the government seems to know about. We know other people are involved. We even know who they probably are. But we can't use anything we know because it doesn't clear Marty. What we know only establishes a larger crime, and opens up the possibility of more charges against Marty.'

'We've been through this before. But you're right . . . As far as Marty's concerned, we still don't know any more than we did when this thing started.'

'That's not entirely true,' Harris said. 'We do know a lot of people are trying to point the finger at him.'

'So? How does that help?'

'Try this on for size. Suppose you're involved in a conspiracy *with* Marty. Would you want to bring *part* of it to light—knowing that a thorough investigation could reveal the remainder and involve you?'

'Not likely,' White said as he stood and walked slowly toward the window. 'But what if I had no choice?'

'What do you mean?'

White stopped by the window and turned. 'Suppose you're right. Suppose you're Morgan, and you and Marty are involved in a conspiracy, but no one else knows about it. Suppose, also, that the rest of the board is desperate to get Marty out of the way.'

'Which we know is true,' Harris said.

White nodded before continuing. 'Then, suppose you think you can expose Marty's role while controlling any investigation, or confining it to the parts that point only to Marty.'

'You'd be running a big risk,' Harris concluded after some thought. 'If Morgan *was* involved with Marty in the beginning, but decided to double-cross him, he couldn't be sure Marty wouldn't turn around and double-cross *him*. Marty could cut a plea for his own benefit in exchange for disclosing Morgan's involvement.'

'But what if you could be sure Marty wouldn't turn on you?' White said. 'What if you had some major clout?'

'Such as?'

'Suppose you had a congressman in your pocket, and the congressman could make sure the investigation was limited to Marty?'

'It wouldn't be enough,' Harris said. 'Even if you could limit the investigation, you couldn't keep Marty from going public with his side of the story.'

'Unless you paid Marty off . . . convinced him to take the fall.' White said. 'If you had enough influence to limit the investigation, wouldn't you have enough influence to assure Marty that he would get a light sentence?'

'It's a possibility. But, if that's true, why was Powell so adamant about not considering a plea?'

'That was early in the game. Maybe the clout hadn't been asserted when I first talked to her.'

'But that doesn't explain Marty's own opposition to a plea,' Harris said.

'Maybe he's hoping we can pull a rabbit out of the hat and get him off—knowing that his worst case is a light sentence.'

'That's a lot of *ifs* and *maybes*.'

'I'm afraid there's one more possibility we have to consider.'

'What's that?' Harris asked.

'What if Marty *is* involved, but only as a minor player in someone else's plan.'

'Then I'd say someone has plans for Marty to join Brian Lester and Dr. Hart.'

28.

Grace Matthews was beyond annoyed when she pressed the button on the intercom to White's office. 'Mr. White, there's a man on the phone who won't give his name. He insists it's important that he talk to you.'

'Take a number and tell him I'll call back.'

A moment later, Matthews was back on the intercom.

'Mr. White, he won't leave a number and he won't give his name. I think it's *him*.'

'Thank you.' White smiled. *Him* could only be one person, the only client Matthews truly disapproved of. 'Tell him I'll be right with him.'

White waited twenty seconds before he picked up the phone. 'Hula, amigo.'

'Counselor, so nice to hear your voice,' the caller said. 'But you should not keep old friends waiting.' The caller's voice was all too familiar, a voice White had come to know well during two years of trial preparation and a month of trial. 'Are you still fighting the good fight with the federales?'

'You know I am. Nothing ever changes.'

'I understand you have the day off tomorrow. We should share a tequila.'

'I never have an off day. But we don't have court tomorrow, if that's what you mean. How did you know?'

'I like to be informed of things involving my friends.'

'And your enemies?'

'Even more so,' the caller said. 'The internet is a wonderful thing. Even a child from a poor village in Columbia can look at a court calendar and know what is happening miles away.'

'And why would you be interested in such things?' White asked with increasing curiosity.

'I hear things. I ask questions. Sometimes information comes to my attention. I ask myself if this is something I could share to help an old friend.'

'Very good.' White said cheerily. 'Excellent imitation of Brando doing Don Corleone.'

Unlike the majority of the caller's countrymen who White had occasion to represent, Manuel Rodriguez was highly educated. He had undergraduate and graduate degrees from Georgetown University and spoke English with very little accent. Nonetheless, he delighted in imitations of, alternatively, a mafia don—or what he thought a mafia don would sound like based solely on his viewing of the *Godfather* trilogy—and the headmaster of a British boarding school. It was something of a joke between them and, under most circumstances, was the source of shared laughter. The fact that these were not normal circumstances for White was of little concern to Rodriguez who, White knew, had chosen to remain in character and have some fun at White's expense.

'And helpful information is always appreciated,' White continued, speaking in a way he hoped would fit into the *Godfather* script Rodriquez was following, and would show his understanding that the receipt of helpful information created a debt to be honored.

'And as it happens,' Rodriguez continued, 'I know of an individual who did a favor for the F.B.I. in exchange for, I believe the term is a *quid pro quo*.'

'What might that favor have been?' White asked, much more calmly than he felt, as he rummaged through the clutter on top of his desk for a pen and pad of paper.

'Certain information has come to my attention regarding a break-in at the home of one of your clients.'

My God. Worthington. 'And the source of this information . . . Would he be available to talk with me . . . and testify?'

'He believes it is his civic duty to share his knowledge.'

'Would I prefer not to know how he came to this conclusion?'

'I do not know why you would be interested in such matters.'

'How can I be sure he won't change his mind regarding his civic duty?'

'There are many things to consider when making such decisions. He is a religious man, and he has concluded that his truthfulness will benefit him in the hereafter.'

I really do not want to hear any more of this. Unless Rodriguez had recently been deified, religion was unlikely to have played a part in any decision to testify. The person White needed to speak to probably had good a reason to believe his confrontation with the hereafter was likely to be imminent if he didn't co-operate.

'Perhaps a tequila or two with an old friend would be a good idea.'

* * * * *

The Three Flags Marina was named for the flags flown by sport anglers when they have scored a triple by landing all three of the major billfish: a swordfish, a sailfish and a marlin. It was located on the Manatee River just west of Interstate 75 midway between White's office and his friend's home in Tampa. Mutually inconvenient, as Rodriguez described it.

Kaleidoscope

The sweltering heat of the afternoon was beginning to surrender to a cooling evening breeze. A jazz combo was setting up on a stage on the corner of the lounge.

White was waiting at the bar when Manuel Rodriguez came in, alone, and signaled White to a table by the window overlooking the docks.

'It's been a long time, friend,' Rodriguez began, smiling.

'I'd ask if you've been keeping yourself out of trouble,' White said as they shook hands and took their seats. 'But since I haven't heard from you I must assume you have.'

'Life goes on. Things happen. The kids grow up. Same old, same old.'

The conversation went on for several minutes; two old friends catching up after a long separation. It reminded White that his clients, regardless of what they did, or were accused of doing, were people with friends and families and family problems just like everyone else.

'But enough of this,' Rodriquez said, abruptly changing the subject. 'The person you want to meet is in the car.'

Rodriguez's black Cadillac limousine was parked in the far corner of the parking lot. Rodriguez' driver, who White knew only as Jake, stood by the door. He was squat and ugly, with dark, emotionless eyes under heavy brows. He didn't look the sort to wear a jacket, and White assumed that the large bulge under his arm wasn't a wallet.

White had seen Jake every time he met with Rodriguez, and every day throughout his month long trial, but he couldn't remember ever hearing Jake say a word.

Jake opened the rear door and White slid into the seat opposite a man whose face he had seen a dozen times on the tape of the break-in at Worthington's house. Rodriguez took a seat beside the man and Jake closed the door.

'Tell him,' Rodriguez ordered.

The man hesitated, not knowing what to say and afraid of saying the wrong thing. Finally he spoke. 'What do you want to know?'

'Suppose you start with your name,' White said.

The man looked at Rodriguez. Rodriguez nodded.

'Steve Hogan,' he said, his voice dark and hesitant.

'And were you involved in a break-in at the home of James Worthington?' White asked, sounding very much like he was conducting an examination of a hostile witness.

'I don't know whose house it was, but I did a break-in.' As Hogan spoke, he looked at Rodriguez. White was asking the questions, but he knew who had to be satisfied with the answers.

'Why?'

'Why did I do the break-in?' Hogan asked. He knew his answers had to be right, and he didn't want to answer the wrong question.

'Yes.'

'My lawyer told me to.'

'What lawyer was that?' White probed.

'Mr. Davis. James Davis. He's a lawyer with Johnson, Katter & Stump.'

This was suddenly more interesting than White had anticipated.

'What was Mr. Davis representing you for?' White asked, as if he had all the time in the world and wanted to cover every relevant detail.

'Possession . . . with intent,' Hogan said. 'Crack,' he added quickly, not wanting to risk leaving anything out.

'How long had Mr. Davis represented you?' White asked.

'It was the first time. He's been my attorney for about a month.'

'How did Mr. Davis come to be your lawyer?'

'He volunteered,' Hogan said, uncertain why this was important or where it was going.

'How did he volunteer?'

'He showed up at the jail . . . Said he would be my lawyer. He said someone I knew asked him to represent me.'

'Who was your mutual friend?'

'I didn't ask,' Hogan said. 'If I was supposed to know, someone would tell me.'

'Wasn't that a little unusual?'

Hogan hesitated, looking cautiously at Manuel Rodriguez. 'Sometimes the people I work for take care of these things.'

Rodriguez nodded, confirming Hogan's answer.

'Did you ever find out who asked Mr. Davis to represent you?'

'No.'

'How did you come to break into Jim Worthington's house?'

'What do you mean?'

'Did Mr. Davis tell you to commit the break-in?' White clarified.

'Yeah. He said I was supposed to do something that could be used in a plea bargain.'

'Whose plea bargain?'

'He didn't say. Not then. Turned out it was mine.'

'So the break-in was intended to give you something to use in a plea bargain?'

'That's not exactly what he said, but that's how it turned out.'

'What were you told to do?'

'I thought I was supposed to break-in and steal something. Turned out I was supposed to plant something in the house.'

'What were you supposed to plant?'

'Some rocks of crack . . . in the john. And I was supposed to stick some papers under a drawer. You know, tape them to the bottom of a drawer.'

'And did you?'

'Yeah.'

'What kind of papers where you supposed to plant?'

'I don't know. It was just an envelope. I didn't look at what was in it.'

'Weren't you curious?'

'It's not good to be too curious.'

White nodded. 'Then what happened?'

'Then Davis cut me a deal. I was supposed to tell the feds about my supplier and tell them where they could find the stuff in his house. Then they was supposed to drop the charges against me.'

'Which federal agency was this deal made with?'

'The feds in Tampa,' Hogan said, irritated at what he now considered to be a meaningless question. 'How the hell should I know which ones? The F.B.I., the attorney, the judge for all I know.'

Rodriguez was about to rebuke Hogan when White nodded him off. 'And did you tell the authorities what you had done?'

'Yeah. I told them about the house where I planted the crack. I said I didn't know him good myself, but I'd been to the house with another guy and knew about the stuff.'

'Did they want to know who the other guy was?'

'Yeah. I told them it was a drug guy who'd got whacked . . . so they couldn't check my story.'

'And did they drop the charges against you?'

'Hell, no. They changed the deal. They said they'd only drop the charges if my story checked out, but Davis got them to lower my bail.'

'Who posted your bail?'

'Davis.'

'Then what happened?'

'Nothing. I was going to get as far away from here as I could.'

White nodded. 'But here you are.'

'Yeah, here I am,' Hogan said. 'Before I could get moving, Jake come and got me. Said Sr. Rodriguez wanted to see me 'bout something.'

Kaleidoscope

'Did you know Sr. Rodriguez before that?'

''Course I knew who he was,' Hogan said. He didn't want to offend Manuel Rodriguez by implying there was anyone who didn't know who he was

'What happened then?'

'I tol' Sr. Rodriquez what I jus' tol' you. And, like you say, here I am.'

White asked a few more questions, but didn't learn anything useful. Hogan had never heard of the hospital or Martin Bower.

When White seemed to have concluded his examination, Hogan asked, 'Is that all?' He could care less about White, but he wanted to be certain Manuel Rodriguez was satisfied with his cooperation.

'Do you need Mr. Hogan any more?' Rodriguez asked.

'No. I think we can say Mr. Hogan had done his civic duty.' White didn't know, or want to know, what plans Rodriguez had, but knew he would sleep better if he put in a good word for Mr. Hogan. 'However, I don't think it would be a great idea for you to disappear. You're free on bail, and I don't think the authorities will be concerned with you, even if your information isn't as good as they wanted it to be.'

White knew that, in the aftermath of the sugar candy fiasco, the authorities would not be in a hurry to admit having any connection to Worthington's arrest.

'Besides, if you have any more problems with the authorities, Sr. Rodriguez knows how to reach me.'

Manuel Rodriguez raised an eyebrow and looked toward Steve Hogan out of the corner of his eye. His expression asked, *You would be willing to represent him?*

White nodded openly, not trying to keep his silent communication private. He would prefer that Hogan knew he was being guaranteed representation. It would keep him from running—as if Rodriguez's interest in the matter wasn't enough. But, even more, it would give White access to information relating to everything Davis and the government had done.

'Then I believe the time has come to depart,' Rodriguez said.

At precisely that moment, Jake opened the door. *Has he been listening? Almost certainly not. Did Rodriguez send him some signal? Possible, but how?* White filed the question with the many others that would likely never be answered.

'Stay in touch,' White said as they hugged. "And thanks.'

'Be careful, my friend. These lawyers cannot be trusted. They represent many clients who do not have common interests,' Manuel Rodriguez said, his serious expression saying more than his words.

A warning? What else does he know? White knew better than to ask. If Rodriquez could tell him, he would have.

* * * * *

As he pulled out of the parking lot and turned east on state road 64, heading for Interstate 75, White ordered his voice-activated telephone to call Horse's home phone. The call was answered on the fifth ring by a female voice.

'Hello,' she said lazily.

Doesn't he ever slow down? If he keeps this up, he'll wear himself out before he's forty.

'This is Lucius White. May I speak to Horse?'

'Just a minute. He's in the shower.'

White heard muffled voices. A minute later Horse was on the phone.

'What's up, Lucius?'

'I just had an interesting conversation with the master break-in artist. I'll fill you in on the details later, but there's something you need to do.'

'Shoot.'

'In addition to the drugs left at Worthington's, my new friend left an envelope taped under a drawer of Worthington's desk. Worthington didn't say anything about the police finding it, and it wasn't mentioned at the probable cause hearing. I think our friend forgot to mention it to the police, or they forgot to get it. I want you to go over to Worthington's and see if you can find it.'

'I'll take care of it right away. Should I call Worthington first?'

White thought for a moment before. 'No. Just go over there and get it.'

'Okay. Is that all?'

'Yes. And I'm sorry I interrupted your evening.'

'No problem. I was beginning to wonder how I could avoid having to cook her breakfast.'

Both men chuckled as they hung up.

As White drove south on Interstate 75, a blue Chevrolet Caprice with rental car license plate accelerated past a tractor-trailer and pulled into the line of traffic three cars behind him. The driver removed a cell phone from his pocket and pressed a series of buttons. 'It's me,' he said after the phone was answered with a curt, 'What?' 'He just left a meeting with the Spick and some guy I didn't recognize. I'll e-mail the pictures from the motel.'

29.

On the last Friday of October, Lucius White hosted his annual Tyler Maxwell Day party. It was a celebration of the case that made him a rich man.

Tyler Maxwell was an electrical engineer. He and White had become friends when they served together in the Army, discharging the obligations of the R.O.T.C. scholarships that paid for their college education. While White used his G.I. benefits to go to law school, Maxwell had, for three years after leaving the service, spent his nights and weekends working on new electronic devices in his garage. His efforts led to the invention of a compact version of a device used for storing electronic data. Maxwell had the foresight to obtain a patent on his creation, the forerunner of the hard-drive now found in every personal computer. But he was ahead of his time, and he couldn't interest any established computer manufacturer in his invention.

Less than a year later, a start-up computer company announced the introduction of a revolutionary new desk-top computer based on Maxwell's creation, without the benefit of Maxwell's permission. The lawyers Maxwell first consulted showed little interest in filing suit over the use of an obscure

Kaleidoscope

device whose only application was in a product that didn't yet have an established market. Eventually Tyler Maxwell came to his old friend, Lucius White.

True to the defense lawyer's credo, the attorneys for the company that had stolen Maxwell's invention engaged in a battle of delay, hoping Maxwell and White would tire of the battle and go away, or settle for a nominal sum.

Their time-tested strategy backfired. By the time Maxwell's case came to trial, the desktop personal computer was being hailed as the technological breakthrough of the millennium. The little device for which other lawyers saw no significant value was now critical to an industry worth billions of dollars a year. On the eve of trial, by which time the defense attorneys had consumed as much of their client's money as they could, the case was settled for twenty-one million dollars.

Tyler Maxwell Day was so entrenched in the legal community that it was penciled onto every lawyer's schedule as soon as each new year's calendar arrived, a full ten months before the annual gathering. Over the years, the event had evolved—no one was exactly sure how or when—into a costume affair: Halloween for lawyers. Lawyers came as their favorite advocate. Famous English barristers of centuries past, such as Lord North in his traditional wig, mingled with famous early American lawyers. There were always several Clarence Darrows and identifiable modern icons, such as William Kunsler and F. Lee Bailey, and numerous television lawyers. No one infringed on Harry Harris' exclusive right to be Ironsides, the wheelchair-bound lawyer played by Raymond Burr. Lucius White dressed as Gerry Spence, the famous Wyoming lawyer known for his western attire.

Even judges made a point of attending the annual gathering. Generally, judges lead a lonely existence. Their only peers are the other lawyers from whose ranks they came. But the need to avoid even the appearance of bias often prevented them from socializing with former colleagues who appeared before them in their official capacities. Tyler Maxwell Day was a sort of unofficial holiday from the rules. Like a meeting of some secret fraternal society, everything said within the sacred walls of White's warehouse remained there.

The center of attention was, as usual, Tyler Maxwell himself, who never seemed to tire of regaling envious new lawyers with the story of his own suit. Like stories told by fisherman, the story got better with each passing year. Young lawyers listened with rapture. Older lawyers, who had heard the story many times before, laughed heartily with each year's new embellishment.

Bars were set up in the reception area outside White's office and in his apartment. Tables were laden with food ranging from bar-b-que to Oysters Rockefeller and cracked Dungeness crab. Throughout the office and apartment, lawyers were swapping war stories.

'. . . Honest to God. The judge found her guilty of prostitution and fined her $250, and she asked if she could pay her fine in trade.'

'. . . You have to remember, Judge Gillian was a visiting judge and didn't know Pete. So the judge says, just as stern as he could, 'Why are you wearing dark glasses in my courtroom?' And Pete says, totally straight-faced, 'Because I'm blind.' There just wasn't a hole big enough for the judge to crawl into.'

'. . . So she said, 'I can't answer that 'cause it's hearsay.' And the judge says, 'what do you mean, it's hearsay' and she says, 'cause I hear him say it.''

'. . . The judge was about to sentence my client for DUI and he asked my client if he had anything to say for himself. My guy says 'Your Honor, I had to drive 'cause I was too drunk to walk.''

'. . . She was trying to talk her way out of the speeding ticket, so she looks at the cop and says 'I bet you stopped me to sell me a ticket to the policeman's ball.' And the trooper says, 'Lady, State Policemen don't have balls.''

White and Leslie were mingling with their guests on the deck outside White's apartment when Diane Flynn caught White's eye and nodded toward his study. White excused himself and followed Flynn.

Diane Flynn was also a criminal defense lawyer. Most of her cases were drug related, and she had a reputation as an expert in pharmaceuticals.

When they were alone, Flynn came directly to the point. 'Lucius,' Flynn began. 'I have some information you may be interested in. I've been hearing rumors about some new players in the trade.'

'New players?'

White rarely represented street dealers. For one thing, he abhorred drug trafficking on principle. For another, few street dealers could afford his fees. The closest he came to drug cases was when he represented clients, such as Manuel Rodriguez, who, although their crimes may have been related to the drug trade, were charged with more sophisticated crimes: money laundering, illegal currency transactions and tax evasion. The nature, and limits, of his practice were well known, and he was curious why Flynn thought he would be interested in new players in the street level trade.

'From what I've heard,' Flynn said, 'someone new—someone from out of town—has been asking a lot of questions about the local players. The interesting thing is that he, or they—I don't know if it's the same person—has been asking questions all along the coast from Tampa south.'

'How do you know this?' White asked casually, his interest still being only academic.

'I was at a conference a couple of weeks ago, and some other defense attorneys mentioned that they had heard the same rumors.'

'Does anyone have any idea what it means?'

'I don't really know. But there's something you have to understand about the street. There isn't a lot of crossover between serious druggies—crack heads and heroin junkies—and the people who are into prescription drugs. They're almost separate cultures.'

'And this person you think is moving in. Which side is he on?'

'From what little I know, it seems to be on the side of controlled pharmaceuticals. I think someone has access to controlled drugs, prescription type drugs, and is looking for an outlet—a mass outlet.'

'Moving in on someone else's territory isn't a good idea,' White said. 'People have been known to lose body parts—or simply disappear.'

'True,' Flynn agreed, 'if the new people are viewed as competition.'

There was something tantalizingly suggestive in Flynn's tone.

'Maybe it would be help if I take a step back. When the public thinks about drug crimes, their first thoughts are usually about cocaine, heroin and other drugs targeted in the war against drugs. In fact, prescription drugs, from narcotics to sleeping pills, are far more prevalent in the drug subculture than their more publicized cousins. The thing is, from a legal perspective, we really have two different types of drugs. On one hand, we have controlled substances, drugs that are legal but whose distribution and use are subject to strict controls. Then we have illegal drugs, drugs that cannot be legally prescribed or possessed.

'From the standpoint of dealers, this difference is important because of how they're prosecuted. All drug offenses are subject to prosecution under both state and federal statutes, but federal authorities rarely concern themselves with the street trade in prescription drugs. The only time the U. S. Attorney gets involved in cases of trafficking in prescription drugs is when the government wants

Kaleidoscope

to make an example of a doctor who's prescribing them. The rest of the time, cases of possession and distribution of controlled substances are prosecuted in state court.'

'That's all true, but what makes you think it has anything to do with my client?'

'I'm getting to that,' Flynn said. 'We all know that the Columbians control the highest levels of the cocaine trade, and heroin isn't what it once was—at least not here. Now the big growth industry is the illegal trade of pharmaceuticals. Up north, organized crime is into pharmaceuticals in a big way. The states aren't really equipped to deal with the problem, and the feds are too busy with their war on cocaine to pay much attention.'

White was beginning to understand where Flynn was going. 'So there's less chance of getting caught by state authorities, and state penalties are less when you do get caught.'

Flynn nodded. 'That's one reason why the trade in pharmaceuticals is getting so big. There are rumors that the new players may be someone from up north. It also seems like they have an arrangement with the locals. Probably the Trafficante crime family in Tampa.'

'What makes you think it's the Trafficante's?'

'Nothing specific,' Flynn said. 'It's just that the Trafficantes pretty much control the drug trade on the west coast.'

'You might be right.' White agreed, without mentioning that his own client, Manuel Rodriguez, would be equally interested in anyone dealing in drugs.

'I don't know if it means anything for your case,' Flynn said, 'but you know what the press is saying about Marty Bower. The hospital people stopped talking, and the feds never say anything. The press has to say something to keep its ratings up.'

White nodded, but he was only half listening. AIDS drugs obviously fall into the category of drugs Flynn was talking about. *What if . . .* His attention returned to Flynn.

'Some of our local journalists have vivid imaginations. I haven't heard anything specific yet, but if one of them picks up on any of what I've told you, he's likely to add one and one and get three. He'll think he's discovered a major conspiracy.'

'That would be a good bet,' White agreed. He could do his own arithmetic, and he didn't like how things were adding up

30.

Professor Arthur Lawson, head of the department of criminology at Florida State University, was one of the nation's foremost authorities on document authentication. White easily found Professor Lawson's corner office on the second floor of Hecht House, a plain, two-story red brick building with a white wrought iron balcony on West Call Street, and introduced himself to the secretary. She confirmed his appointment and offered him coffee. White declined the offer and took a seat in one of the comfortable chairs in the waiting area.

Five minutes later, Professor Lawson came out of his office, handed some papers to his secretary and walked across the room.

'Mr. White,' he said, briskly. 'Nice to meet you. Please come into my office.' Professor Lawson had an air of energy and intensity, a Type-A personality who focused on tasks with little time spared for idle chitchat. His manner left no doubt he had already investigated White and found him worthy.

When White and Professor Lawson were seated on the sofa, Professor Lawson came straight to the purpose of the meeting. 'I've examined the documents you sent me, and I think I can answer at least one of your questions about the letter you sent.'

He was referring to the three-page letter White had received in an envelope postmarked in Tampa. There was no return address. The letterhead, salutation and signature were masked, and the origin of the letter itself was a mystery. The substance of the letter was ambiguous. The part that concerned White was the reference to Joe Morgan as chief executive officer. It could have been a letter to the hospital, but it read more like part of a negotiation for a position for Morgan with another organization.

Harris was convinced it was a hoax, a deliberate attempt to mislead them. White conceded the possibility. Whether the letter was real or a hoax, they agreed it had probably come from someone having a connection to the hospital's outside counsel. This hypothesis was supported by Professor Lawson's next observation.

'If you look carefully at this copy of the letter you sent me,' Professor Lawson continued, 'you'll see a faint watermark.' Lawson held the paper up to the light and pointed to what he was referring to. 'This tells us two things.

'First, it is unlikely that a *draft* of the letter would have been made on watermarked paper. What you have is a copy of a final document. Moreover, a watermark wouldn't show up in a copy made on most office copiers, so whoever made this copy has access to some high quality copying equipment.'

'Does the watermark tell us anything?' White asked.

'Probably not. But I've done some research. The paper the original letter was written on is fairly common. It's a top of the line linen paper.'

'The kind of paper that would be used by a major law firm?' White asked.

'Possibly,' Professor Lawson acknowledged. 'But it would also be used by any number of people and organizations who want to convey success and prestige. It isn't unusual enough to limit the source of the letter, but it's unusual enough to be relevant evidence of the source.' Professor Lawson paused momentarily, waiting for White to indicate his understanding, before asking. 'Do you think it came from a law firm?'

'It's a possibility,' White said. In fact, it was more than that. White already knew the hospital didn't use watermarked stationary.

'The reason I ask . . .' Professor Lawson paused, looking down at his desk as if embarrassed to continue. 'It's hard to examine a document without reading it, even when the text isn't important to my analysis.'

'I understand,' White assured him, curious where this was going.

'I'm not a lawyer,' Professor Lawson said, shifting uneasily in his chair. 'But it seems to me the letter is a sensitive legal document. Isn't that sort of thing a privileged communication?'

'Only communication between a client and his attorney is privileged,' White said. He already knew the sensitive nature of the document, and was all but positive it had originated with the hospital's attorneys. He and Harris had spent hours trying to determine who had sent the letter to them. Certainly not the attorneys. And employees of the law firm were equally unlikely—unless they had no choice.

'Is there any way to identify the copier that was used?' White asked.

'Probably not, at least not to the extent the identification would be useful as evidence. This is obviously a copy of a copy. I assume that *this* copy is a duplicate of the document you originally received. Knowing that, I could testify with some certainty that *this* particular copy was made on *your* machine. However, the document you received was, at best, a copy of the original. My guess is that what we have here is a copy of someone's file copy of the original letter. That means the copy you received was at least a second generation copy— a copy of a copy.

'Every time you make a copy, minor details of the original are lost or altered. I wouldn't be able to testify as to the source of the original, even if you could get a sample of the copies made on the machine where the first copy was made.'

'So that's probably a dead end.'

'I'm afraid so. Someone with more sophisticated equipment than I have—the FBI laboratories at Quantico for example—might be able to do better. But I assume you're on the opposite side of this case from the F.B.I.'

'Unfortunately,' White confirmed. 'Could a private laboratory do anything for us?'

'I've already had the document reviewed by the best private labs.'

White had hoped for more, but hadn't been optimistic. 'What about the other documents?' he asked, turning his attention to the records of the bank accounts.

'Ah, now that's another story,' Professor Lawson said. 'I agree with your conclusion that these markings on the corner are significant. It's my opinion that these marks represent a tiny flaw on the printing drum of the copier. Such a flaw is like a fingerprint. It's almost beyond the realm of possibility that two copiers would have this same flaw.'

'Can you rule out a manufacturing defect?'

'Not entirely. But I've examined these documents carefully, and I think they were made on a high-end machine—not the sort of machine that would use cheap drums.'

'Can you identify the machine these copies were made on?'

'If you gave me a sample copy from the machine, I could give you an opinion with a sufficient degree of certainty to be useful.'

'Frankly, Professor, at this point I'm not trying to prove anything about the copies, although that may change. What I need to know is where the documents came from.'

'All I can tell you is this; I believe that this copy came from a high quality desktop printer.'

'What makes you think that?'

'The drum markings,' Professor Lawson said. 'If you look closely, you can see indications of a second and third blemish mark, here and here.' Professor Lawson pointed to barely visible marks on the copies. 'The spacing between these markings indicates that the printer drum was small, probably an inch and a half in diameter. Large printers, the kind you would find in an office, use a much larger printing drum, eight or more inches in diameter. If these copies had been made on an office copier, the blemish marks would be much farther apart. This copy was definitely made on a desktop printer—an old one.'

'How do you know it's an old machine?'

'The newer desktop machines use toner *cartridges*. Drum-based desktops haven't been made for a couple of years.'

'That could be helpful.'

'Don't get too excited. These small machines generally use an assembly that contains both the toner and the printing drum. The flaw we're discussing is only on the drum that was in the machine when these copies were made. As soon as the toner is exhausted, the whole assembly would be replaced.'

'And the new drum wouldn't leave these marks,' White completed the professor's thought.

'Right.'

'So, in order to identify the source of the documents we have to get a sample that was made on the same machine *and* was made around the *same time* the copies had been made.'

'Unless this machine is being used for business purposes, or the owner has a lot of children writing term papers, it's quite possible that the toner and drum assembly would not be replaced more often than once a year.'

So there is a chance we might get lucky. White's concern was evident from his expression.

'There is one other thing that may be useful,' Professor Lawson continued. 'These two documents . . .' Professor Lawson resumed, placing copies of the bank statements filed with the State's Attorney and the bank statements found in Worthington's desk in front of White. 'Notice the alignment of the text on these copies. The original from which these copies were made didn't feed through the copier straight. It was slightly out of alignment. The odds against an original passing through the copier *twice* with precisely the same degree of misalignment are astronomical. These copies were made at the same time.'

White nodded, but said nothing.

'Does that mean something to you?' Lawson said.

'It means I know who made the copies.'

31.

Dr. John Wiley sat opposite Lucius White and Martin Bower in a booth at The Ship restaurant on highway U.S. 41, south of Fort Myers.

Wiley wasn't anything like White pictured him from Bower's brief biography—a West Point graduate with three commendations for bravery in Viet Nam. He was approximately five-foot-ten-inches and slender, about one hundred and fifty pounds. His hair was dark brown, bordering on black, thin on top and severely receding at the temples. He had a dark, almost olive, complexion. He wore dark rimmed classes and he had a scholarly, competent look. But he still had a military bearing that White knew instilled confidence in his patients.

'I know this is difficult for you, Dr. Wiley,' White began. 'If it wasn't important, or if there was any other way, we wouldn't be putting you in this position.'

'Mr. White.' Wiley said. 'Marty has already told me some of what you've learned.' His look said he knew he hadn't been told everything. 'And I'm concerned about what I've heard. If it's true, the truth has to come out, even if it hurts some of my friends. I agreed to discuss your concerns, but I may not answer some of your questions if I feel it would be inappropriate to do so.'

'Fair enough, Doctor,' White said. 'I think we already know the answers to most of my questions. I'd just like you to confirm what we know.'

'If I can,' Wiley agreed.

'All right. First of all, we think Marty's termination was being orchestrated by a faction of the board for quite a while before he was finally fired.'

'That's at least partially correct,' Wiley said. 'Some of the board members began lobbying for Marty's termination a couple of months before he was actually fired.'

'How did the movement to terminate Marty get started?'

'I don't think there was a single event.' Wiley examined his drink for a moment before continuing. 'Mainly, I think, it was Marty's desire to pursue a merger with Hospitals of America. Some of the board members agreed with him, but the more vocal board members opposed the merger.'

'Why?'

'I don't really know, but the members who initially opposed the merger may have been motivated by their own interests.'

'What interests were they trying to protect?'

'I'd prefer not to go into that. I'm sure Marty knows everything I know.'

White nodded. 'But there's something I don't understand. If these board members opposed a merger Marty favored, why did they amend the by-laws to give Marty the swing vote in the event of a tie on the merger vote?'

Wiley pressed his lips together. 'That's an interesting question. Marty asked the same thing, and I've given it some thought. As I recall, the amendment was proposed by some of the people who most opposed Marty's position on the merger.'

'Didn't you think it was odd that they gave Marty *more* power at a time when they opposed his position on the merger?'

Kaleidoscope

'Not really. The two events didn't occur at the same time. The change to the by-laws was made almost a month before we had a serious merger proposal.'

'Then why did the matter of the by-law change even come up?'

'That was something Joe Morgan and our outside counsel suggested. The hospital has a twelve-member board. The attorneys recognized the possibility of an evenly divided board on any number of issues. *They* suggested the change to give the CEO a tie-breaking vote.'

'Was *any* merger under consideration when this change was proposed?'

'Not actually,' Wiley said. 'We . . . by that I mean the board . . . were dealing with problems relating to the hospital's financial condition. The need to consider some sort of merger had been mentioned, but there wasn't anything specific.'

'Who first suggested a merger?'

'As I recall, Joe Morgan and the outside counsel started us thinking about a merger.' Wiley paused, as if hearing his own words had made something else clear. 'As you probably know, the first merger proposal fell through. What you may not know is that the hospital was approached by another potential merger partner. In fact, the new proposal is still under consideration. I probably shouldn't be telling you this, but some of what Marty told me has caused me to have some concerns.'

'Tell me about the new merger partner.'

'Well . . . first of all . . . it's not actually a merger.' Wiley said. 'It's an outright sale . . . to a corporation from Philadelphia. They want to get into health care. They're buying up troubled hospitals and consolidating them into a network'

'This is a strange time to want to be getting into the health care business,' White said. 'A lot of good hospitals are struggling. Why do they want to buy you?'

Wiley shrugged. 'Those are all good questions. But they appear to have a lot of cash and know what they want.'

'Have you met any of the management of this corporation?' White asked, not sure where he was going.

'No. We've been meeting with a man named Harry Levine. He's the attorney representing the buyer.'

Levine? Levine? I know that name. White thought about the name for a moment but couldn't place it and returned to Wiley's original topic. 'You said that what Marty told you made you have some concerns. What kind of concerns?'

'If your theory is right—if Johnson, Kutter and Stump is promoting this sale to another client—I have to wonder whose interests are really being represented. I've also had some concerns over the fact that Joe Morgan will become the chief executive officer of the hospital if the sale goes through.'

'Why is that a concern?' White asked. 'Wasn't he appointed chief executive officer after Marty was fired?'

'He was. But that was a temporary solution to an emergency situation. What concerns me is that Joe wasn't initially in favor of the sale. Then, he switched sides and became an advocate of the sale. I didn't think much about it until Marty mentioned that letter—the one you call the *Tampa letter*. Most of what was in that letter corresponded to what Morgan and Harrington were promoting, and I started thinking about Joe's change in his position. That's when I realized Joe changed his position about the time of that letter . . . after he had reached an agreement to keep him on as the chief executive officer.

'At first, I thought that was just unethical. Then Marty told me what you discovered about the movement of money.'

'But the hospital is blaming Marty for that.'

'I know. But when Marty told me what you found out about the money transfers, I started thinking about the facts that led to Marty's termination. That's when I realized that all the information used to justify Marty's termination came from Joe Morgan and the outside attorneys. In fact, the board never saw anything directly implicating Marty. We only knew what the attorneys told us. When I realized that, I stopped trusting any of the information we were being given.'

'How do you feel about it now?' White asked.

'I think something else is going on—something Joe is trying to hide or cover up. I was never convinced that Marty did anything wrong. I've known him for too long, and I just couldn't believe what Joe and the attorneys were telling us. That's why I voted against his termination.'

Martin Bower silently smiled his thanks.

'Anything else?' White asked.

Wiley leaned forward, looking into White's face. 'The board is scared. Marty has sued them personally for millions of dollars, and they're afraid that they're going to end up looking like ignorant fools. They've ignored Marty's advice for years. Now the hospital is paying for it. They'll do *anything* to keep the public from finding out who's *really* responsible for the hospital's financial condition.

'The attorneys have assured the board they have nothing to worry about, and the board has given the attorneys what amounts to a blank check to protect them. But the board members are still restless.'

'Do you know anything about the fabrication of documents to convict Marty?'

To White's surprise, the question seemed to be expected.

'I would prefer not to comment on that,' Wiley said firmly. 'But I wouldn't bet against it,' he added.

'Why not?'

'I don't trust Joe Morgan or Johnson, Kutter and Stump.'

'Did you know the hospital has been working closely with the Assistant U. S. Attorney in the criminal case against Marty?'

'I wasn't aware of anything along those lines until Marty told me about your suspicions,' Wiley said. 'After Marty filed his suit, the board formed a litigation committee to coordinate things relating to its defense. I didn't think much about it until

Marty called the other day. After we talked, I asked about the committee. That's when I realized that the people who were on the litigation committee were the same ones who had been pushing for Marty's termination. I don't exactly know what they're doing, but it wouldn't surprise me if they're actively participating in the investigation.'

'Do you know anything about contacts with Congressman Marks?'

'Why would he be interested in the case?' Wiley asked, without answering White's question.

'I don't know; it's just a question,' White said. 'Can I assume you don't know anything about any pressure the board may have brought on the congressman?'

'I haven't heard anything about that.'

* * * * *

Horse was waiting by the rear door stairway when White returned to the warehouse. Ever since the discovery that someone might be following them, Horse took extra precautions. Whenever White was out of the building and Leslie was left alone, Horse found some reason to remain at the office until White returned. It wasn't something they had talked about, but White knew what Horse was doing.

Horse's expression left no doubt that there was a problem.

'What happened?' White asked, immediately concerned that something had happened to Leslie.

Horse read his mind. 'Don't worry. Leslie's fine. She's upstairs with Sherlock.'

'Then what's up?'

They walked down the short hallway and through the rear door to Horse's office. 'Someone tried to break into our computer system.'

White stopped and looked at Horse. 'Are you sure?'

Horse gave White what had come to be known as the full-Monty look—both eyebrows raised, eyes rolled upward and a disbelieving shake of his head. White knew he was being awarded two ears and the tail in the category of stupid questions.

'What did they get?'

'Nothing,' Horse assured him. 'Client files are disconnected from the rest of the system after business hours. About 8:15, the main computer detected an attempt to get into our system. I designed the system to make initial access easy. That way, someone would think they had gotten in and would spend some time looking around while my system traces the call.'

'Did you find out who was trying to get in?'

'No. But I *was* able to find out where the call was coming from. Unfortunately, it was from a cloned cell phone.'

'How do you know that?'

'The computer was able to trace the number. It's listed in the National Criminal Information Center data system as a stolen number—a cloned phone.'

'So we can assume it wasn't the government, or the hospital attorneys.'

'That's a good bet.'

'How do we find out who made the call?'

'I don't think we can. But at least we know where it came from. The call came through a cellular network in southeastern Pennsylvania.'

'Philadelphia.'

'Probably. You don't seem surprised.'

'Shocked, maybe. But not surprised.'

'Why?'

'I just came from a meeting with John Wiley, one of the hospital board members,' White said. 'He told us that a corporation in Philadelphia is negotiating to buy the hospital.'

'Why would anyone who's buying the hospital want to break into our computer system?'

'Probably for the same reason that someone with a phony driver's licenses has been following us.'

Alan Woodruff

32.

'Good evening ladies and gentlemen. This is Action News at six. I'm Lynn Thomas.

'In today's breaking story, a committee of bondholders today filed suit against Coastal Regional Hospital and its board of Trustees alleging malfeasance and mismanagement and willful failure to disclose the hospital's rapidly deteriorating financial condition.

'The suit followed the hospital's second failure to make quarterly payments of interest on outstanding bonds.

'Officials for the hospital have refused to comment on the suit or respond to growing concerns about the hospital's financial condition.

'Lynn. Did the hospital have anything to say about Martin Bower's role in the hospital's financial condition?' Peter Willis asked his co-anchor.

'No Peter. The hospital was uncharacteristically silent on that.'
'Interesting.' ' Peter Willis said.
'I agree.' Lynn Thomas said.
'In other news . . .'

33.

Harry Harris and Horse McGee were already at work, sorting and classifying documents and marking exhibits, when White came down the stairs from his apartment, crossed the reception area and entered the War Room. Martin Bower was sitting on the side of the table, looking helpless but available for any menial task that needed to be done. There was an air of intensity in the room; the culmination of months of investigation being brought together as facts were summarized and supporting documents were made ready.

'Ah, I love the smell of testosterone in the morning,' White said.

'Balls to the wall.' Harris said. 'We're on a roll.'

White filled his coffee cup and took his seat at the end of the conference table.

The elevator door opened and Leslie emerged with a large box of fresh donuts.

'Do my eyes and nostrils deceive me?' Harris asked in happy mock surprise. 'Does fair yon maiden, preacher of healthy and virtuous eating, come bearing donuts for these weary working souls?'

'Your gratitude is overwhelming.'

'I didn't know you even knew how to buy donuts.'

'I don't. I stood in line and watched what the other people were doing.'

'Do you need help learning how to eat them?'

'I bought a manual at the donut shop. It doesn't look too hard.'

'Here, let me demonstrate,' Harris said, as he put a jelly-filled donut in his mouth and bit down. Raspberry jelly oozed out the side of the donut and dribbled onto his shirt.

Leslie rolled her eyes at a grinning Harry Harris. 'God really screwed up when he invented the male chromosome.'

Harris smiled. 'Girls are allowed to take smaller bites.'

* * * * *

Donuts and coffee in hand, White, Harris and Horse returned their attention to the corkboard walls now covered with 3x5 cards filled with facts and notes. For the next three hours, they rehashed what they knew, tested new theories and reviewed and amended the questions White would ask the government's witnesses on cross-examination. The 3x5 fact cards were moved around as new relationships were visualized and different connections examined. Occasionally, the attorneys conferred with Martin Bower to clarify a point or test an evolving theory. Otherwise, Bower spent most of the time listening with growing apprehension.

The attorneys were not giving him many reasons for optimism. Phrases like *We're screwed* and *If we get lucky*, uttered quietly by his attorneys at the other end of the room, resonated in his ears. Finally, Bower couldn't control himself.

'What happened to innocent until proven guilty?'

By unspoken agreement, the attorneys and the investigator decided it was time for a break. Harris rolled his wheelchair to the coffee table, and Horse slid into a chair and began reviewing documents from one of the many files scattered in

Kaleidoscope

the conference table. White walked across the War Room and pulled out a chair beside Bower.

'Marty,' White began, searching for the right words. 'Once a trial begins, whether or not you're innocence isn't an issue. The prosecutor wants a conviction, regardless of whether or not you're innocent. It's our job to make sure you don't get convicted, regardless of whether or not you're guilty.'

'But I didn't do it.' Bower argued wanly, still unable to understand or accept the truth of what White was telling him.

'It doesn't matter,' White said, as a father would console his son. '*Innocent* and *not guilty* are two different things. Innocent means you didn't do it. But *innocent* isn't one of the choices on the verdict form. The prosecutor wants to prove you're guilty. The verdict form is only about whether the prosecutor proved her case. We only have to keep the jury from agreeing with her. That's all. A trial isn't about the truth—it's about proof.'

The words came without thought. White had said the same thing to so many clients over the years that they came automatically, like a recording. And as always, White saw his father in his words.

'But I didn't do anything.'

White nodded. More words weren't going to make a difference.

White left his place beside Bower and rejoined Harris and Horse. 'Are we about done here?'

'I think we're as ready as we'll ever be,' Harris said.

Horse nodded without saying anything.

'Any last thoughts on the defense strategy?'

White and Harris had already decided they wouldn't put on a case of its own. It wasn't a difficult decision. Bower himself couldn't take the stand because he knew nothing, or so he continued to maintain, and had nothing to offer in his own defense. Besides, innocent or not, they couldn't risk exposing him to cross-examination by the prosecutor. All they could do was attack the sufficiency of the government's case, and hope they could point to enough holes and inconsistencies to establish reasonable doubt.

'We just have to decide what to do with your ace of trump,' Harry said.

White gave him a raised eyebrow, and what he hoped was an imperceptible shake of his head, but Bower had already picked up on the signal. 'You've got something special, don't you?'

White looked askance at Harris. Harris shrugged. 'We might as well deal with it. It may be our best shot anyway.'

White moved to a chair opposite Bower and sat down. He crossed his arms on the table and leaned forward on his elbows, looking directly into Bower's eyes. 'Marty, how much do you trust Joe Morgan?'

'Joe?' Bower said with a vague look of bewilderment. 'What about Joe? What does he have to do with this?'

'Marty.' White paused as he measured his words. 'This isn't easy. I know Joe is a friend, but we've known all along that the hospital is actively assisting the government . . . and may be fabricating evidence. Joe is the only common link between everything we know.'

Bower shook his head violently and slammed an open palm on the table. 'That can't be. Hell, I'm godfather to his son, and he's godfather to my oldest son. We've been best friends for my whole adult life. Joe may be the hospital's errand boy, but I can't believe he's behind the whole thing.'

'That doesn't change the fact that he keeps popping up,' White said. 'You have to face facts. Joe is the key to our alternative theory of what has happened.'

'I can't believe it.'

'That's probably what Julius Caesar thought,' Harris said. *Et tu, Brute* and all that.'

'Marty,' White said, speaking like a concerned friend. 'We don't want to get caught by any surprises. We have to consider all the alternatives, even the least likely and least pleasant ones.'

It was suddenly as if they were back at the beginning. Bower had the same look he had the day they watched the news conference announcing his termination.

'You're asking me to turn on Joe,' Bower said in a low whisper.

White knew what Bower was thinking—and feeling. He was still unwilling to believe what he was hearing. He couldn't let himself believe it. If he accepted what White was telling him, he couldn't have faith in anything he believed in. It was the same feeling White had struggled with from the beginning of the case. He had to believe Bower was innocent, but he couldn't prove it. And Bower wasn't helping. This wasn't the first time Morgan's involvement in the frame-up had been discussed. Bower had to have known what was coming, but he clung to a hope the attorneys would discover something to clear his friend. Letting go of that hope meant turning on his friend. If he did that, he would be no better than Morgan.

'Let me walk you through this,' White said. 'First, most of the documents we have, as well as most of the significant documents the government is going to be using, passed through Joe's hands at one time or another. In fact, many of them may have originated with Joe.'

White pulled a document from a file and passed it to Bower. 'We've had most of these papers examined by a document authentication expert. He believes that these copies were all produced on the same machine, and that the machine was a desktop printer-copier. That would exclude any of the machines at the hospital. We know that Joe is the common denominator for these documents, and we're reasonably sure they were created, or copied, on Joe's own machine.'

Bower remained silent.

'Joe is also one of the few people who knew about your relationship to Jim Worthington. There is no reason why anyone else at the hospital would know about your friendship with Jim.'

'Why is that relevant?' Bower asked.

The case was beyond the point where Bower could make any meaningful contribution to the development of the defense theory. His value now was as a juror surrogate, a role customarily filled by Leslie. If Bower had questions, the jury would probably have many of the same questions.

'When Jim's house was broken into, something other than drugs were planted,' White said. 'Copies of the bank records were also planted in his desk. The police didn't find the documents when they searched Jim's house, so we were able to recover them. They have the same marks that are on all the documents we think were produced on Joe's printer-copier.'

'I don't believe it,' Bower said. His voice was filled with the disappointment that came with surrender to unpleasant facts.

'There's more,' White said. 'When Horse first met with Morgan, right after the criminal complaint was filed in State Court, Joe seemed particularly interested in pointing us toward the Cayman Islands. It didn't seem important at the time because we didn't know about the Cayman bank accounts. Now we know why he was trying to provide a basis for additional charges of illegal money transfers.

'Joe also lied to us about his own presence in the Cayman Islands. Even if he hadn't told Horse he had been there, his picture was identified by an officer of the bank where the funds were transferred.'

'But you said Joe admitted being to the Cayman Islands.' Bower protested, still trying to defend his friend. 'Now you said he lied about it.'

'Joe said he was in the Caymans about a year before I went there,' White said. 'I doubt if the banker would remember someone who had only been there once, a year earlier, even if there was a good reason for his trip.'

Kaleidoscope

Bower took a deep, thoughtful breath. His eyes were open but his expression said he was looking inward.

'I sort of hate to say this, because it isn't anyone's business, but I guess you should know . . .' Bower paused, trying to decide whether to proceed.

'What is it, Marty? We need to know everything.'

'It probably doesn't mean anything, but the last time I saw Joe he was talking about getting a divorce. Maybe he was just hiding his money in the Caymans.'

'If that's the case, it's something for the government to bring up. Our job isn't to explain his conduct. We only bring it into question.'

This seemed to satisfy Bower, and White continued. 'We're also concerned about Morgan's cooperation with the government. It looks like he went out of his way to avoid leaving a record of his contacts with the prosecutor.'

'How do you know that?' Bower asked.

'These are Morgan's appointment logs,' White said, laying a stack of documents in front of Bower. 'From the appointment logs, we know who he meets.'

'What can they tell you?' Bower interrupted. 'Morgan meets with everyone.'

'Exactly. But, in addition to telling us who he meets with, they tell us who he doesn't want it known that he is meeting. For the first three weeks after you were fired, Joe's logs record regular meetings and conversations with outside counsel, the State's Attorney and the prosecutor. Then, all of a sudden, there are no more log entries involving these people. The office telephone logs show they were still calling Morgan, but he didn't take the calls. There's also no record in his telephone log indicating that he ever called them back, or met with them. But we know from other sources that Morgan met Powell regularly in her office. We have to conclude that the lack of any record of these meetings means that he didn't want us to be able to find out about them.'

'But what about Dr. Sommers . . . and that doctor up in Sarasota? I thought *they* were the ones who got the AIDS drugs.'

'They probably did, and we're not ruling them out as participants in the scheme. It's just that we don't have enough to make *them* logical alternatives to you. Besides, the government hasn't charged you with anything relating to missing drugs. We aren't even sure the government *knows* about the drug aspect of the scheme. The last thing we want to do is open up another avenue for attacking you or, charging you with another crime. Because *we* have to avoid the drug part of the scheme, we're left with Joe Morgan as the only viable alternative that the jury can wrap its hands around.'

Bower shook his head.

White and Harris, seeing that Bower was thinking about something, waited silently.

Finally, Bower spoke. 'It couldn't possibly be Joe.' There was something in the quiet conviction of Bower's voice that told White a major problem was about to be exposed. 'You know that the scheme started about five years ago. Right?'

'Yes,' White agreed, cautiously. He knew something unpleasant was coming.

'Joe *couldn't* be behind it. He didn't work for the hospital when the scheme started. In fact, he didn't have any contact with the hospital until I hired him three years ago.'

White turned slowly, walked to the corner table and poured himself another cup of coffee, buying himself time and hoping Bower wouldn't see the stress in his face. 'That doesn't necessarily change our strategy.' White said, far more calmly than he felt. 'He could have had some other connection you didn't know about.'

'But we don't *know* that,' Bower said.

'We don't have to,' White said. 'We can't prove that Joe was involved when the scheme started. We don't even know how he may have been involved. But we don't have to prove anything. We only have to create reasonable doubt.'

Bower couldn't contain himself. "I thought this was supposed to be a search for justice.'

'That's right,' Harris smiled. 'We want the evidence to be had by *just us*.'

White ignored Harris's attempt at humor and sat on the edge of the table beside Bower, not sure he wanted to know the answer to the question he had to ask.

'Marty,' White asked calmly, not wanting to let on how important his question was. "Where did Morgan work before he came to work for the hospital?'

'He had a private practice in Sarasota.'

34.

White and Harris, now alone in White's office, were trying to salvage their case. Ever since Bower had gone, White had been pacing the War Room like a caged animal.

'That's great. That's just *fucking* great.' White said, slamming his clinched fist into the wall. 'We're two days away from trial, and we still don't know if our client was involved.' Again, he hit the wall. 'We know what really happened, but we can't use anything we know because the government hasn't charged our client with the real crime. We know who was involved in the real crime, but we can't use any of what we know. We know who orchestrated the frame-up, but we can't even prove there was a frame-up. We have the perfect alternative suspect, and our own client shows us why he couldn't have been involved.'

White threw his pen on the desk and watched it bounce and fall to the floor. 'We spend months preparing our case based on an alternative theory. Then, on the eve of trial, we find that our alternate theory is impossible. Hell. I even *knew* Morgan was in private practice five years ago. That's when he represented Jim Worthington.'

'We saw this coming,' Harris said.

'Jesus Christ, Harry. Is that supposed to make me feel better?'

Harris exhaled deeply before responding. 'When Horse first told us about the connection between Sommers and Hart, we tried to find something connecting them with Joe Morgan. We couldn't find anything, and we still haven't found anything connecting Morgan to the AIDS drug part of the scheme. We even talked about the fact that his only involvement might have been in the frame-up by the hospital.'

'Thanks for reminding me,' White muttered. 'That helps a hell of a lot.'

'On the other hand, maybe it wasn't all us,' Harris said.

'What the hell is that supposed to mean?' White demanded, still angry at himself.

'Maybe we have to accept the fact that Marty did it,' Harris said. 'Face it, in spite of all we know we've never been able to rule Marty out. I don't like it any better than you do, but we've considered this before. Nothing Marty said today changes the facts—he may have been involved in this, along with Morgan, from the beginning. He didn't react when we first told him about the system for transferring the money. He wasn't surprised by our discovery of the drug deals. He's made excuses for Morgan at every turn. He even gave Morgan an alternate reason for being in the Caymans.

'He's also had plenty of opportunities to clear Morgan. He could have *told* us about Joe not working for the hospital until three years ago, but he never said anything. We know someone had to open the account at the bank in Sarasota. Now we know Morgan had an office in Sarasota. That makes an arrangement between Marty and Morgan even more likely.'

'I don't know,' White said softly, rubbing his temples in an effort to alleviate the pounding that was beginning in his head.

'Think about it,' Harris continued. 'When the Chief Financial Officer brought the accounting discrepancies to Marty's attention, Marty went to *Morgan* to investigate the problem. Why Morgan? The Chief Financial Officer had responsibility for the accounting system. He would have been the logical person for Marty to have looking into the problem. Why did Marty go to an attorney to investigate the discrepancies if it wasn't to cover them up?'

'God, I hate it when you're right.'

'Besides, if you were going to set up a complicated illegal transaction, who would make a more trusted co-conspirator than a friend you've known for more than thirty years? Especially if the friend was someone you could hire to work for the institution you were stealing from, and protect you from discovery.'

'You build a strong case against our client,' White said. 'Maybe you should be working for the prosecutor.'

'I'm just trying to face facts.'

'But there's still a problem with your analysis,' White said. 'If Marty already knew that the problems in the accounting records were caused by the money transfer program, why would he have wanted them investigated at all?'

'Maybe he really didn't ask Morgan to investigate them. We only have Marty's word for that,' Harris said. 'Powell's theory is that Marty went to Morgan to be sure that the accounting problems were never disclosed to the board. Maybe she's right. If she is, it means that Morgan has double-crossed Marty.'

'How could we have been so stupid?'

'We weren't stupid,' Harris said softly. 'We were just blind.'

'What the hell is *that* supposed to mean?'

'Isn't it obvious? We were so determined to beat the government that we lost track of our responsibility to Marty. We figured out the plan, but the government doesn't even *know* about what was really going on.'

'Or doesn't care.'

'But that's *not* the point.'

'Then what the hell is the point, Harry?'

'You know what the point is. Powell wants a conviction, at any cost. And you want to show the government up.'

'That's what we do.'

'But that's not our job. Our job is getting Marty off. You've been so preoccupied with proving that Powell is part of a frame-up that you've lost sight of our objective.'

White slumped into the chair behind his desk and rubbed his eyes.

It had been coming for months.

The timing couldn't be worse.

Harris waited.

'It's happening again.'

'I know,' Harris responded, in as soothing a tone as he could muster.

'*Damn*,' White said softly. 'So what do we do now?'

'We don't have a choice. We have to go after Morgan.'

'Why? Just because we can . . . We know he couldn't have been involved when everything started. Marty just said so.'

'Not our problem. Morgan represents reasonable doubt.'

'We're not supposed to destroy someone we know isn't involved, just because we can.'

'We're not doing it because we *can*. We're doing it because we *have* to. Our job is to defend Marty. It's what we do. Besides, we know Morgan is involved in something. We just don't know what.'

'But ignoring what we know to be true is *not* what we do. It's what prosecutors do. We're supposed to be better than that. We used to be better than that.'

'You can't change the system, and you know it.'

'*Someone* has to. It has to start somewhere.'

'And where has trying gotten you?'

'Damn it, Harry. There are rules.'

'Tell that to your father.'

White stiffened and glared at Harris.

'I'm sorry. That was out of line. I'm sorry.'

White relaxed. 'I know. And I know you're right.' White closed his eyes and leaned back in his chair. 'I can't do this anymore.'

35.

As Horse expected, he found White and Harris in the War Room. Trial preparation was completed by the middle of the afternoon, and there was no reason for them to still be there, except that it was a tradition, and maybe a little superstition.

White and Harris were munching on sandwiches Leslie had brought them, and chatting idly about the college football standings—anything to take their mind off the case—when Horse came into the room.

'I think I have something you'll want to look at,' Horse announced with an air of excitement.

'Do you have the scores for next Saturday's games?' Harris asked.

'Maybe better than that.'

'Well then, by all means, let's have it.'

'You need to come down to my office.'

'Oh, no. Not that,' Harris said. It was a running joke. Harris was an expert in the law of electronic communications, but he wasn't computer literate. In fact, he was wholly overwhelmed by what Horse was able to do with his mystery boxes, as Harris called them.

'One of these days we're going to have to do something about your computer phobia,' White teased Harris.

'I don't have a phobia about computers,' Harris said, defensively. 'I'm just afraid of them.'

White and Horse laughed as they all headed for the elevator.

'When I came down to my office after our meeting, I had an e-mail message waiting,' Horse began. 'I don't know who it was from, and for now that probably isn't important. We may want to chase the source down later, but I don't think it will lead anywhere. Whoever sent this message is very good and doesn't want to be found.'

'Pretty mysterious, so far,' White said. 'What was the message?'

'The message contained three things,' Horse said. 'An e-mail address, a set of gatekeeper codes and access instructions.'

'Is there something in the air around all this electronic stuff that makes it impossible for you to speak English?' Harris asked.

Horse ignored Harris and continued. 'The electronic address was for a subprogram inside the computer matching service Morgan has been accessing from the copy center.'

Now even Harris was attentive. He had no idea what Horse was talking about, but it seemed to be leading somewhere interesting.

'Was this an address you couldn't find on your own?' White asked.

'I could have found it, all right,' Horse said. 'But, unless I knew what I was looking for, it wouldn't have meant anything. I already spent a lot of time nosing around the matchmaking services' program trying to follow the trail of Morgan's messages, but nothing got me anywhere. I'm talking about the printouts that were included, probably by accident, in some of the discovery documents we got from the hospital.

They gave us the basic message routing information, but access to the routing center was controlled by user inputs.'

'You're speaking in tongues again,' Harris said.

'Okay. Let's try this again,' Horse said. 'You've seen the routing information that appears on the bottom of e-mail messages?'

'Yes.'

'Well, that information describes the route the e-mail took from the sender to the receiver.'

'Okay,' Harris said understanding, but not fully comprehending what Horse was saying.

'Now,' Horse continued, 'think of the e-mail routing instructions as driving instructions with one turn, either the first or the last, missing. The information we already had didn't have the last instruction on the trail back to the point of origin. In terms of travel instructions, we could trace the route back to the state, city and street of origin, but we didn't have the street number.'

Understanding nods.

'That's one of the things that was in the e-mail. Now we know where the messages originated. They came from a program that could only be accessed by going through the matchmaker service program.'

'How does that help us find out who was sending the messages?' White asked.

'I'm coming to that,' Horse said. 'But before we deal with that you need to understand how someone gets access to the program we just discovered.' Horse was showing off, and White and Harris knew it, but tolerating Horse's occasional displays was a small price to pay.

'When we decided that this was a blind communication system, I assumed it would be protected by some serious encryption technology.'

'Which it wasn't,' Harris guessed.

'Right,' Horse said. 'Access to the system was by password. But it was controlled by a complicated password access system.'

'What's the difference?' White asked.

'The difference is in what you get to see and how you get to see it,' Horse said. 'Encryption technology is intended to keep someone from reading your data by storing the data in coded form. Even if someone can get to the data itself, they can't read it without the encryption code.

'Access technology is a different thing. It protects data, and whole computer systems, by keeping intruders out and preventing them from getting to your data in the first place.'

Now it was Harris's turn to show he wasn't entirely computer illiterate. 'I thought new encryption coding was virtually unbreakable.'

'Only in theory,' Horse said. 'Besides, encryption security has one fatal weakness. If all your information is stored in one coding format, anyone who discovers the code has immediate access to *all* your data. And there isn't anything you can do to stop them.'

White and Harris continued to listen attentively.

'Access coding is different, because you can change the access codes any time you want and still protect everything. If you think someone has broken your code, you simply change the access code without having to recode all your data. The people we're dealing with have a sophisticated access coding system that can be changed in a matter of seconds.'

'All right,' White said. 'You have my attention. Now, how does this system work?'

'Think about a door that is controlled by a keypad entry code. If you know the code, you can open the door. Even if you don't know the code, you can still open the door by trial and error, by trying every possible combination of codes until you hit the right one.'

Harris rolled his eyes.

Kaleidoscope

'It turns out that the access code is a sixteen-digit number.'

'Jesus Christ,' Harris muttered. 'I can't remember my social security number. How is anyone going to remember a sixteen-digit number?'

'That's an obvious problem,' Horse said. 'If it was a number that couldn't be easily remembered, the users would have to write it down somewhere.'

'Which means that it could be discovered,' White said.

'Right. But these guys thought about that, and came up with a clever solution. Take a look.' As he spoke, Horse wrote a number on a sheet of paper and placed it in front of White and Harris.

$$1012149207041776$$

White studied the number for a moment before saying, 'I give up.'

Horse smiled. 'Would the number be any easier to remember if I wrote it as 10/12/1492 and 07/04/1776?'

'I'll be damned. Columbus and the Declaration of Independence.'

'Right. Now, instead of having to remember a sixteen digit sequence, a user only has to remember two dates. But if you don't know the number, even if you had a computer that could test a billion combinations a second it would take almost six months to test all the possible combinations.'

Harris tapped his fingers impatiently on the edge of the table. 'Let's cut to the good part. Can we now trace the internet correspondence Morgan was involved in?'

'Better than that,' Horse said, no longer able to control his excitement. 'We have the damn whole plan to take over the hospital.'

It took several moments for the initial shock of Horse's announcement to wear off. White and Harris alternated between staring, with disbelief, at each other and at Horse.

'We have everything in these printouts.' Horse grinned as he slid the papers toward White and Harris.

Like starving dogs going after a steak, White and Harris grabbed for the pile of papers Horse handed them. For half an hour, they pored over the documents, uttering statements of amazement with each turn of the pages, and stopping occasionally to assure each other that this wasn't a dream and the documents really did say what they appeared to say.

'I see it, but I'm not sure I believe it,' Harris finally said.

'I'm having a hard time believing it myself.' White agreed. 'But there it is.'

White fell silent as he continued to stare at the printouts.

'You have that look, Lucius,' Harris said.

'Yes,' White said, nodding. 'A big piece just fell into place.'

'Don't keep me guessing.'

'When I met with John Wiley, he told me that the people discussing the purchase of the hospital were represented by a Philadelphia attorney named Harry Levine. I knew the name rang a bell, but I couldn't place it. Now I can. Harry Levine is reputed to be the main lawyer for a Philadelphia crime syndicate.' White sat quietly, staring at the papers spread over the table in front of him, and thinking.

'It all fits,' White continued. 'We're being followed by people from Philadelphia. Someone from Philadelphia tried to break into our computers. This is the real thing.' His voice was tense. 'Morgan was selling the hospital to the mob.'

'My, God. It's amazing.' Harris said. 'What a plan.'

'I don't get it,' Horse interrupted.

'The mob was going to buy the perfect front,' White said, thinking aloud as he spoke. 'Owning a hospital would let them launder money and have legitimate access to controlled drugs.'

'I still don't get it'

'Think about it.' White said. 'Hospital bills can be big. A twenty-thousand dollar hospital bill would be nothing unusual.

Kaleidoscope

All they would have to do was create an electronic patient—someone who existed only in the computer—and a set of patient records. Give the patient an expensive operation and you have justification for large payments. And what better way to get drugs? You want morphine; the electronic patient was given morphine. You get your drugs to sell on the street, and the records all balance. If the D.E.A. audits your drug records, everything balances out and no one is any the wiser.'

'Could they really pull it off?'

'I think they've already been doing it,' White said. 'In the clinical trials of the experimental AIDS drugs, they had to keep records on all their patients to account for the drugs they used. We know drugs were being diverted from the program. The only way to account for the missing drugs would have been to create phony patients and say the drugs had been given to them.'

'And you think the AIDS drug thing was just a test of a system for stealing other drugs,' Horse said.

'I didn't think so—not at first,' White said. 'The AIDS drug thefts have been going on for a long time; too long for them to have been just testing a system. But this answers a question that's been bothering me. I haven't been able to figure out why only AIDS drugs were disappearing. Now I think I understand. Dr. Sommers was the medical director for the clinical trials, so he was in a position to control the creation of phony patient records to account for the missing drugs. But he could only control the records for the experimental AIDS drugs. They couldn't expand the program to other drugs because there was too much risk of discovery. But if they controlled the whole hospital, they could do whatever they wanted.' As he spoke, White stood and began pacing. 'This also explains what Diane Flynn told me about new players asking about street sales of controlled pharmaceuticals,' White continued. 'Someone was doing a damned marketing study.'

'I hate to rain on anyone's parade,' Harris said. 'But this only tells us why it was necessary to get rid of Marty and control the merger. We have a trial starting in two days, and we still don't have anything that clears Marty of the original embezzlement—or tells us who was behind the original scheme. We may be great detectives, but so far we've solved the wrong crime.'

'But we have enough evidence to muddy the water,' Horse said.

'That's not the problem I'm concerned about right now,' White said. 'The people who've been watching us are still out there somewhere. Whoever they are, we have to assume they represent the mob. It's fairly obvious they murdered Brian Lester and Dr. Hart to make sure they didn't talk.'

'They won't be very happy if they think we've figured out their plan,' Harris added. 'These aren't people who take disappointment lightly. They can't risk letting us put any of this into evidence.'

'Horse . . .' White started to say.

'I'm ahead of you, Lucius. I'll get some people to look out for all of us until the trial is over.'

'Who …' White started to ask who Horse would use, but thought better of it. Some things he didn't want to know. The lifestyle of the people Horse used as watch dogs was more likely to qualify them as White's clients than as his employees. In fact, some of them had once been clients of the firm, and owed favors that Horse called in when it was necessary. They weren't likely to be invited to dinner, but, if anyone posed a danger to Leslie, he was happy to have one of Horse's larger friends looking out for her.

'Just be sure they're careful'

36.

The chambers of Judge Horace Greene, United States District Judge, were as grandiose as the rest of the new federal courthouse. His office was paneled in rich golden oak and had a plush deep blue carpet. It was furnished with a large mahogany desk with matching credenza and conference table extending from the front of the desk. At the end of the room, by the picture window overlooking the river and the city marina, there were two sofas, a coffee table and two end tables on which stood modern polished brass lamps.

Judge Greene was tall and thin. His hair was white, not gray or silver, and worn cropped close to his head, like the marine recruit he had once been. He sat ramrod straight, another remnant of his years in the Corps. In his nearly thirty years on the bench he had acquired a regal authority that left no doubt that he was confident in his status and would not tolerate any nonsense in the legal proceedings brought before him.

Lucius White and Elizabeth Powell sat silently on opposite sides of the conference table. A court reporter sat at the end of the table, ready to record the proceedings.

It was understood that the judge and his law clerk, who sat behind and to the right of the judge, had reviewed the pending motions and researched the case law cited in the pre-trial briefs submitted by the attorneys. Nonetheless, the judge once again scanned the pleadings to be discussed.

'All, right,' the judge began abruptly. 'Let's begin with the evidentiary matters. Am I correct in my understanding that the parties have exchanged document and exhibit lists and have agreed to the admissibility of those document and exhibits?'

'Your Honor,' White said. 'We have agreed to the authenticity of the documents. But we reserve the right to dispute the admissibility of certain documents on the grounds that they have no relevance or that their prejudicial effect outweighs their probative value.'

'Is that correct, Ms. Powell?' the judge asked.

'The government believes that all of its documents are relevant and admissible,' Powell said.

'I'm sure you do,' the judge said, mild irritation in his voice. 'But my question was whether you agree with Mr. White's statement regarding the documents and exhibits that have been exchanged.'

'Yes.'

'Fine. Now,' the judge said, looking at White. 'I believe you have a motion regarding mandatory *Brady* disclosures. According to your brief, you believe that the government has failed to disclose all exculpatory evidence. What do you have to support this claim?'

'As the Court may be aware, my client has a pending civil suit against Coastal Regional Hospital. In that case, the hospital has asserted several counterclaims against my client based on the same alleged conduct that is the subject of these criminal proceedings. In the course of discovery in the civil case, we have obtained numerous documents that we believe are exculpatory but which have not been provided by the prosecutor.'

'If you've already discovered the documents, why is it necessary for the prosecutor to disclose them?' the judge asked.

'There are two issues, Your Honor. First, the fact that we have independently discovered the material doesn't relieve the prosecutor of her duty of disclosure. She has no way of knowing what we have, or haven't, discovered on our own, so her failure to turn over exculpatory evidence is not excused by our independent discovery of it.

'Second, we have no way of knowing how much material may have been withheld. The fact that we have discovered *some* relevant material that wasn't turned over to us is an indication that the prosecutor has knowingly violated the strictures of *Brady*.'

Under other circumstances, White would have made a more lengthy argument, identifying and discussing relevant case law and arguing the issues of public policy on which the Brady decision was based. Judge Greene was acknowledged as a legal scholar, and was known to appreciate a good policy argument, but his lack of tolerance for unnecessary argument was equally well known. White opted for a short presentation of his position.

'Ms. Powell,' the judge said, signaling that he was ready to hear Powell's rebuttal.

'Your Honor, the government is only required to turn over material it recognizes as exculpatory. It is not required to turn over every piece of evidence it has before the trial begins.

'I,' Powell continued, reverting to the personal pronoun rather than refer to the prosecution as the government, 'can assure the Court that I do not have any undisclosed material that appears to be exculpatory.'

'So, we have a conundrum,' the judge summarized. 'The defense says you have material, but can't prove it because it doesn't know what you do and do not have. The government says it doesn't have anything it should have turned over, but its position is based on its own determination as to what information in its possession may be exculpatory. Is that about right?'

White and Powell nodded.

'Well, I can't order the prosecution to turn over what it doesn't have,' the judge said. 'However,' he said as he turned to face Powell, 'I can, and I will, enter a trial order of dismissal of all charges if it becomes evident that the government has withheld exculpatory evidence. Ms. Powell, you are now on notice that I will not tolerate any games in my court. If you have anything that is even remotely exculpatory, you had better disclose it to the defense by close of business today. Do I make myself clear?'

Properly advised and chastised, Powell acknowledged her understanding.

'Now let's talk about the defense's motion to enter documentary evidence by stipulation.' The judge picked up another file and turned to White. 'As I understand your motion, Mr. White, you're willing to stipulate to the authenticity and relevance of documents relating to certain bank accounts and transfers into and out of those accounts. It that correct?'

'Yes, Your Honor.'

If the documents could be admitted by stipulation, it would be unnecessary for the prosecutor to call witnesses to authenticate them. Jurors tend to overlook, or at least give less weight to, documents that have not been discussed by witnesses. If he could get the government's documents admitted by stipulation alone, he would have an edge. He didn't really expect Powell to agree to his proposal, but that wasn't his objective. The real purpose of his motion was to make Powell explain why it was necessary to have the documents authenticated by witnesses. Maybe she would slip and say something that would help in his cross-examination of her witnesses.

Kaleidoscope

'And you want those documents admitted without the testimony of records custodians to authenticate the documents. Do I understand your position?'

'Yes, Your Honor.'

'And the prosecution objects to this; is that correct, Ms. Powell?'

'Yes, Your Honor. It is the government's position . . .' Powell began to argue, reverting to references to the prosecution as *the government* in an effort to make her argument appear to be the position of a neutral party having no bias.

Judge Greene interrupted. 'If the documents can be admitted on stipulation, why should I waste the time of the court and the jury with unnecessary witness testimony?'

'Your Honor. The government believes the witnesses have more to offer than merely authenticating documents. It's the government's belief that the circumstances surrounding the creation of these documents has significance independent of the documents themselves.'

'Your Honor,' White interjected. 'I believe that an offer of proof is in order. Unless the prosecutor can show that the witnesses have something extra to offer, allowing her to call witnesses to authenticate every document would impute excessive significance to the documents.'

'If that happens,' Powell said, addressing Judge Greene while glaring at White, 'the court can always give a jury instruction regarding the witness.'

'Your Honor,' White said dragging the words out with exaggerated calmness. 'We all know that once the jury has heard something the court cannot wipe it from their mind with a jury instruction. The bell just can't be unrung.'

'This is just a cheap trick to make the government disclose portions of its case,' Powell objected, louder than she should and directing her statement to White.

'Ms. Powell, I remind you to address your comments to me.'

'Of course, Your Honor.'

The judge continued looking at Powell, assuring himself that his message had been understood before continuing. 'As tempting as your suggestion is, Mr. White, I'm going to deny your motion. The prosecution may call witnesses to authenticate the documents. But you,' he addressed himself to Powell, 'are going to be on a short leash in this matter. Understood?'

'Yes, Your Honor.'

'Any other evidentiary issues?' the judge asked.

'Yes, Your Honor,' White said. 'We have a motion to exclude the testimony of Joseph Morgan, the hospital's in-house counsel.'

'I've read your motion,' the judge said. 'Let's take it up next.'

'Your Honor,' White began. 'Mr. Morgan was the defendant's college roommate. They have been friends for more than thirty years. The defendant is godfather to Mr. Morgan's oldest son. The defendant hired Mr. Morgan to work for the hospital based on their long personal relationship. When the defendant disclosed facts to Mr. Morgan, he believed he was speaking with his own attorney. Therefore, everything he discussed with Mr. Morgan is subject to attorney-client privilege, and anything that may have been discovered as a result of disclosures made to Mr. Morgan by my client is the fruit of privileged communication and is also inadmissible.'

'Your Honor.' Powell was flushed, barely able to control herself. 'This is nothing more than an end run around my case. Mr. White knows that Mr. Morgan was the hospital's attorney when the defendant spoke with him. He also knows that, as the hospital's attorney, Mr. Morgan had a duty to tell the hospital board anything he learned about the defendant's misconduct.'

'That's *enough*, Ms. Powell,' the judge said, cutting the prosecutor short.

Returning his attention to White, the judge asked, 'Has Mr. Morgan ever been hired by the defendant to act as his attorney in any matters prior to Mr. Morgan being hired by the hospital?'

'That may be a question of degrees,' White said.' 'I don't know if there was ever any formal engagement, but Mr. Bower did regularly consult with Mr. Morgan regarding personal matters, and Mr. Bower regarded Mr. Morgan as his legal advisor. As the Court knows, the test of whether or not an attorney-client relationship exists is based on the subjective understanding of the party. The defendant *believed* Mr. Morgan was his personal attorney, and that's all that matters.'

'That is *not* all that matters.' Powell sputtered.

'I've warned you, Ms. Powell,' the judge said sternly. 'I'm not going to warn you again. Another outburst and I cite you for contempt.'

'But, Your Honor. . . .' Powell sputtered.

'*Enough*, Ms. Powell.'

Powell's face took on the color of boiled ham, but she didn't dare argue.

The judge rolled his chair to the side and spoke quietly with his law clerk who made some notes on his legal pad.

'I'm going to reserve ruling on this motion until I've done some additional research. If either of you has any additional case authorities to bring to my attention, you may do so no later than five o'clock this afternoon.

'When do you expect to call Mr. Morgan?' the judge asked Powell.

'He's third on our witness list, Your Honor. Depending on how long Mr. White drags out his cross-examinations, I expect to call him on the second day of the trial.'

'Fine. I'll have a ruling before you call Mr. Morgan. Anything else?' the judge asked.

'No, Your Honor,' White and Powell said in unison.

'Then we are through here,' the judge said, dismissing White and Powell and wiggling a finger at his clerk, summoning him to the side of his desk.

* * * * *

White was on the telephone when Harris rolled into his office and took up a position in front of White's desk.

'So how did the pre-trial conference go?' Harris asked when White put down the telephone.

'Fair,' White shrugged. 'Maybe better than expected.'

'How so?'

'We didn't get anywhere with the *Brady* argument,' White said.

'We didn't expect to,' Harris said.

'No. But we got what we wanted out of it. The judge is aware of our position. He also let Powell know, in no uncertain terms, that she was on a short leash. He told her that he'd dismiss the case if we can show any significant *Brady* violations.'

'Can we?'

'That remains to be seen. She has to have *some Brady* material. Every good prosecutor does. I'm just going to have to get one of her witnesses to say something helpful to us, and then admit that it had been disclosed to the government.'

'Do you think the judge will actually give us a directed dismissal?'

'It will have to be a serious *Brady* violation, but he's a stickler for compliance with the rules.'

'Did you get Powell stirred up?'

'I was my usual brilliant self,' White said. 'She came close to exploding a couple of times, and the judge read her his version of the riot act. He even threatened her with a contempt citation. If she errs, I think it will be on the side of caution.'

37.

Lucius White sat alone at his desk, preparing his opening statement to the jury, when his private telephone rang. The caller identification showed the call was from Horse's cell phone.

'What's up, Horse?'

'Are you ready to meet the guy who's been following Leslie?'

White sat up abruptly. 'Where is he?'

'He followed me when I went to Sarasota to check on a few things this afternoon,' Horse said, never content to give a simple answer when he had an opportunity to explain how he had accomplished his mission. 'I lost him on the way back by making a quick lane change and getting off the interstate. Then I jumped back onto the highway behind him. Either he didn't expect me to do a reverse on him, or he didn't care where I went when I got back to town, because he went straight to a motel off Exit 24. I waited for a while, and when he came out, I followed him to Crazy Alan's. It's a sleazy bar on Fowler Street.'

'I know where it is. Is that where you are now?'

'I'm parked just down the street in front of the convenience store just north of Winkler Avenue. What do you want me to do?'

'Wait for me. I'll be there in ten minutes.'

Eight minutes later, White pulled to the curb behind Horse's Ford Explorer. Horse came out of the shadows of the parking lot beside the convenience store and climbed into the passenger seat of White's truck.

'What do you have in mind now?'

'Tell me about our friend.'

'Medium height, about five-nine, heavy set, maybe two-hundred-ten pounds, dark complexion, long black hair slicked back. No facial hair, but he looks like he hasn't shaved for a day or two. No glasses. No visible facial scars, but I wasn't close enough to be sure. He's wearing jeans, a blue shirt and black leather jacket. He wears his watch on his right wrist so I assume he's left-handed. He looked like he could have been on the cover of *Hoods Quarter*ly.'

'Is he armed?'

'I couldn't tell, but it's too warm for a leather jacket . . . especially if he's from Pennsylvania like your cop friend thinks. Northerners who come down here think it's warm even when we think it's cold.'

'So you think he's armed?'

'Probably.'

White sat looking at the door to the bar, considering what he should do. 'Where did he park?'

'In the lot.' Horse indicated the small lot on the side of the bar facing them. 'The blue Chevy Caprice near the back of the bar. It's a rental,' Horse added. 'You can tell by the license plate numbers.'

'There are only four cars in the lot,' White said. 'Have you seen much street traffic?'

'No. A couple of people have left since he got here, but no one has gone in.'

Kaleidoscope

'So there isn't likely to be a crowd in the parking lot when he comes out,' White thought out loud. 'Park your car on the other side of the bar and slip around to the back, beside where his car is parked. I'll wait here.'

They didn't have long to wait. Fifteen minutes later the man came out of the bar, lit a cigarette and walked toward his car. White left the shadows where he had been waiting by the side of the convenience store and crossed the parking lot.

'Hey, mister. I wonder if you could help me?' White asked—just another lost tourist asking for directions. Nothing to alarm the man as White approached.

'Can't help you,' he said, glancing only casually at White as he continued toward his car.

White was ten feet away when he asked, 'Can you tell me which way Cleveland Avenue is?'

The man turned from the half-opened door and spat, 'I told you I can't help, asshole.'

So much for polite discussion.

White stepped to the rear bumper of the Chevy, boxing the man between his own car, the car next to his and the wall of the bar and cutting off his escape. 'Then maybe you can tell me about your day in Sarasota.'

Slowly, White's statement registered with the man. 'What the fuck? Who the fuck are you?'

With his attention focused entirely on White, at the rear of the Chevrolet, he didn't see Horse slip around the corner of the bar and through the space between the wall and the front of his car.

'Just someone looking for some information.'

'Well, I'll fucking information you . . .' the man said as his left hand quickly moved under his coat and around his back.

Horse's right fist connected with the man's kidney at the same time his left hand grabbed the man's wrist, twisted it against his back and slammed the man against the car. As he pinned the man against the car, Horse reached under his jacket and removed a Glock 9-millimeter automatic pistol from under the belt at the small of the man's back.

'Nice toy,' Horse said as he spun the man around. 'Now answer the man's question.'

It took a moment for the man to recognize Horse. 'You! What the fuck do you want?' he demanded.

'Playing tough guy isn't going to get you anywhere,' Horse advised as he sent the man to his knees with another blow to his solar plexus.

Horse raised the man roughly by his collar and again slammed him against the car.

The man spat at Horse. Horse brought his head back and snapped it forward, his forehead connecting with the bridge of the man's nose. A stream of blood began flowing down the man's face.

'You ain't gettin' nothin' from me,' the man hissed.

'That isn't your wisest course of action,' White said, calmly injecting himself into the confrontation.

'Who the fuck are you?' he demanded, glaring at White.

White stepped in front of the man with no more urgency than he might stop to check his tie in a mirror. 'My name is Lucius White,' he said softly. 'I am an attorney, and right now I can be either your best friend or your worst enemy. Your choice.'

At the mention of White's name, the man stiffened and his face took on a look of confusion and concern. White recognized the change in the man's expression.

'You know who I am?' White said. It was both a statement and a question.

The man stared at White defiantly before answering. 'Yeah. I know who you are.'

'Now we're getting somewhere. Why are you following me?'

'I don't gotta tell you nothin'. Besides, I wasn't followin' *you*.'

'Okay. Then why were you following my very large friend with the bad temper?' White said, nodding toward Horse.

Horse twisted the hand holding the man's collar. The collar bit into his throat cutting off his breath. The man gagged and tried to speak, but he was unable to form words. Horse loosened his grip and the man coughed as his airway cleared.

'What do you care? I wasn't going to hurt anyone.'

'Then what were you doing?'

'I was jus' supposed to find out who you was talking to in Sarasota.'

'Who wanted to know who we were talking to?'

The man glared at White, then at Horse, but said nothing as he considered what to do.

Horse tightened his grip on the man's collar.

'Aw right.' the man gasped.

'That's better,' White said calmly. 'Now, who are you working for?'

'I don' know.'

Horse tightened his grip.

'Honest. I don't know. A guy called me and told me to get down here and find out who you're talking to and what you know about stolen drugs.'

'*A guy* called you,'' White said. 'That's *it*?'

'That's the way it works. Honest. I get an order, and I do what they tell me.'

'You said you were supposed to *come down here*. Where did you come down here from?'

The man stared at White for a moment, thinking, before responding. 'Philadelphia.'

White considered this information while he stood staring at the man and letting him worry about what was coming next. In the dark, neither Horse nor the stranger could see the muscles of White's jaw twitch at the mention of Philadelphia.

Seconds became minutes as the man grew more nervous. When the tension became too great he blurted, 'And I was supposed to leave you and your lady friend alone.'

White relaxed while he considered this revelation. The man saw White's reaction and, knowing he was moving onto safer ground, said. 'You got a godfather somewhere down here. You're off-limits.'

White nodded to Horse who relaxed his grip on the man's collar.

'Who's my godfather?'

'I don' know. I just know you got a big one. My orders was real clear. If you got so much as a paper cut while I was tailin' you, I was responsible.'

White considered this for an additional minute before opening his cell phone and dialing a number.

'Tony? It's Lucius White.'

'Lucius,' Tony said pleasantly. 'I didn't expect to be hearing from you so soon.'

'I have a present for you.'

The stranger seemed to suddenly realized his troubles were not over and struggled to get away. Horse held him tightly, threw him into the car and forced his hands through the steering wheel where he handcuffed them around the steering column.

'One of our friends with the rental car wants to have a chat with you.'

'Not voluntarily, I assume.'

'No. He took some persuading.'

'Where are you?'

'He'll be in a blue Chevy Caprice in the parking lot of Crazy Alan's bar.'

'I'll send a car right away.'

'The keys to the handcuff will be in the back seat, along with a Glock semi-automatic.'

'Shit,' Tony muttered. 'It sounds like you're playing with a rough crowd.'

Kaleidoscope

'Not by choice,' White said as he considered Tony's comment. 'I need a favor.'

'If I can.'

'You said you thought there were two guys down here from Pennsylvania.'

'Yeah.'

'The other one's still out there somewhere. Can you get a car over to Martin Bower's place and keep an eye on things until I make other arrangements?'

'Do you think he's a target?'

'I don't know. Maybe I'm just being paranoid.'

'A little extra caution never hurts. I'll take care of it.' Tony said. 'What about you and your people? Do you need coverage?'

'Thanks for the offer, but Horse has already taken care of that.'

'I assume you don't want the records to connect you to your new-found friend.'

'I'd rather not. Why?'

'Unless you press charges, we won't be able to hold him for long.'

'What about the gun? Won't that be enough?'

'We'll confiscate it. But without your testimony, he'll just claim someone attacked him and planted the gun. I can hold him for a day or so while we try to find out who he is, and I'll make it clear that we're looking out for you. That's about all we can do.'

* * * * *

The shower was running when White returned to his apartment. He was tense, angry and concerned and needed a long shower to relax and recover. He stripped out of his clothes as he walked across the bedroom and stepped into the shower with Leslie. She was facing the wall, her head under the shower rinsing her hair, as White ran his hands over her shoulders. She turned and fell into his arms, burying her face in his shoulder and making an odd sound, not a sob or a sigh but something in between.

'Andy,' she whispered. 'I'm scared. I know I'm being followed.'

'You don't have to worry about it anymore,' White said calmly. 'Horse found the guy, and we had a little chat with him. The police have him now. There won't be any more surveillance.'

'Oh, God!' she sobbed. 'So it wasn't just my imagination. I've never been followed before. I didn't know what to do.'

'I know,' White said softly.

A moment later, Leslie stepped away and looked at him. 'You aren't telling me everything.'

White turned away, reaching for the soap.

'Lucius! What aren't you telling me?'

'What makes you think there's anything more?'

'After five years together don't you think I can tell when something's bothering you?'

White forced a smile. 'You always have.'

'Then talk to me, damn it.'

White sighed and hung his head.

'It's what we talked about on the boat, isn't it?'

'Maybe . . . Yes . . . I don't know.'

'Is it the trial?'

White shook his head; his faced contorted in angst and indecision. 'I don't know if I'm ready.'

Leslie wrapped her arms around him and whispered, 'You are.'

38.

Neither Lucius White nor the Elizabeth Powell was completely satisfied with the jury. Both identified jurors they were sure would favor their side, and other jurors who would present problems. White used all of his peremptory challenges—challenges that permit either side to excuse potential jurors without giving a reason—to eliminate several retired engineers from the jury. Analytical people, like engineers and scientists, are every defense attorney's nightmare. They're trained to solve problems, and they tended to fill in gaps based on logic and experience rather than see gaps in the evidence as the source of reasonable doubt. He still had concerns with some of the jurors, but it was time to put them behind him.

Opening statements were scheduled to begin at one o'clock. First by the prosecutor, then by White.

White arrived at the courtroom at twelve-thirty. As usual, the room was empty when he arrived. He sat alone at the defense table, allowing himself, in a zen-like way, to become one with the room. Whatever the judge might think about his own place in the order of things, the room belonged to White.

Alan Woodruff

At ten minutes before one, the gallery was still only half full. There were a few courthouse employees killing time during their lunch hour, but most of the spectators were reporters. The real media people—the camera crews and the on-camera reporters who introduced and summarized stories against the visual backdrop of the attorneys and the defendant entering and leaving the courthouse—were outside the courthouse.

Leslie and Harry entered the courtroom and took their designated places: she in the back of the gallery, he at the defense table. Everyone had their assignments. White would monitor the jury. Their responses to questions and answers would dictate much of his trial strategy. Harris would monitor the witnesses for indications of nervousness, excessive coaching by the prosecutor and anything else that might be a sign of weakness to be attacked on cross-examination. Leslie would monitor the judge. Judges are not supposed to give any indication of their feelings in the presence of the jury, but they're human. Their responses generally go unnoticed because everyone's attention is focused on the witness. But subtle indications of their feelings can be invaluable in the preparation of proposed jury instructions at the end of the trial. White had won more than one case based on Leslie's reading of the judge.

Elizabeth Powell marched through the double doors at the rear of the courtroom, down the center aisle, past the ten rows of benches that comprised the gallery, and through the wooden gate that separated the spectators from the *real* courtroom. She wore a vivid garnet suit accented with a gold scarf. Her suit would have made her stand out in any crowd, and that was exactly the point. For her opening statement, she wanted all eyes focused on her. During the presentation of her case, when she wanted the jury to focus on witnesses and exhibits, she would wear more subdued attire. It was also significant that, as she had learned from the juror questionnaires, four of the

Kaleidoscope

jurors had attended, or had children who attended, Florida State University, whose school colors were garnet and gold. School loyalties run deep in the South, and every edge counted. None of the jurors had connections to the University of Florida, so her choice of color schemes was unlikely to offend anyone.

Lucius White walked to the side of Powell's table, leaned over and said, 'Could I have a moment?'

'Don't mess with me, Mr. White. I have an opening statement to deliver in less than ten minutes and I don't intend to be distracted by your last-minute games.'

'Sorry,' White said with a false attempt to show remorse. 'I just thought I should give you my amended witness list as soon as possible.' White slid a paper across the table. 'We'll be calling Michael Metz. You know him, don't you?' White asked, trying to conceal his feeling of triumph. 'He's the F.B.I. agent who told you about the drugs that were planted at Jim Worthington's house.

'We'll also be calling Kevin Wilson.'

'Who the . . .'

You don't know him yet. He's a former associate with Johnson, Kutter & Stump. He now works for a friend of mine, and he'll testify about all the dealings between the hospital's attorneys and your office. I just thought you'd want to know.'

White didn't mention Jim Davis, the Johnson, Kutter and Stump attorney who had represented Steve Hogan and arranged for him to plant the drugs.

'Oh, and we'll also be calling Congressman Marks,' White added, as if it was an afterthought. 'I'm sure he'll remember you fondly when you try for a seat on the federal bench.'

White turned his back to Powell and walked to the defense table, wishing he could see the look on Powell's face when it dawned on her that White knew everything—and her career as a federal prosecutor could be measured in the time this trial would last.

One of Powell's assistants signaled for the courtroom deputy, who had been watching the scene from her position by the door to the judge's chambers. The deputy hurried across the room to the prosecutor's table. She spoke briefly with Powell, then stepped to White and tapped him on the shoulder.

'The prosecutor would like a fifteen-minute delay,' the deputy said without explanation. 'Do you have any objection?'

'Not at all,' White said before the deputy trotted across the courtroom and into the judge's chambers.

When Powell approached the podium to make her opening statement, her face was still ashen. Her concentration had been shattered by White's ploy, and her delivery was half-hearted and flat. The only thing that saved her was that it was the first day of the trial. Everything was new and the jury was still alert, no matter how boring the presentation. Otherwise, the jury would have been asleep midway through Powell's opening.

Throughout Powell's opening statement, White, Bower and Harris sat quietly at the defense table, showing little interest in the prosecutor's story. It is a cardinal rule of defendant preparation: no matter what the other side says, never show emotions. Never show surprise; never show anger; never show concern, frustration or doubt.

White began his opening statement while seated at the defense table. It seemed, he had always believed, a little more casual, and it relaxed the jury. There is an old adage: juries vote for the side whose attorney they like the best. The adage probably has little validity, but anything that made the jury more comfortable with him was a help.

'Good afternoon, ladies and gentlemen. My name is Lucius White, and I am counsel for the defendant, Martin Bower.' White's words were strong and clear, the epitome of confidence.

Kaleidoscope

'The government has told you,' White said, as he slowly stood and walked to the podium, 'what it *thinks* it is going to prove. The government has described to you the evidence it is going to present. The government has told you what its witnesses are going to be telling you. In short, the government has told you how it is going to occupy the next two to three weeks of your lives.

'The government is going to tell you a very interesting story. It's a real life mystery, and you are going to be captivated by it. But there is one thing missing from the government's story. The government is missing any provable connection between Mr. Bower and the scheme the prosecutor has described to you.

'Mr. Bower doesn't contest most of the facts the government is going to present.' White said, reverting to a casual, folksy tone intended to convey the message that he and, by extension, Martin Bower, were just ordinary folks. 'In fact, when documents are offered by the government, we will stipulate to their authenticity because we have no desire to keep anything from you.

'The government will *reject* those stipulations,' White said, pausing to let the jurors consider his statement. 'The government wants you to sit through endless testimony about how it obtained its evidence and how it preserved its evidence and how it analyzed its evidence.' As White knew they would, at least half of the jurors looked at Powell, their eyes asking, *Are you really going to waste my time with this*? It never hurt to start off with the jury questioning the prosecutor.

White's tactic wasn't unknown to Powell, or even unique to White, but it kept the prosecutor off-balance throughout the trial. If White stipulated to all facts that a witness was likely to offer, the prosecutor would be seen as wasting the jury's time. However, never knowing what testimony or evidence White might object to, the prosecutor had to prepare every witness for a vigorous cross-examination. That took time away from the preparation of other witnesses whose testimony White may be more intent on attacking. It was all part of trial strategy. Keeping the other side, and its witnesses, off-balance was as much a part of the trial as the evidence itself.

'But do not be misled by this government tactic,' White said, emphatically. 'The weight of the evidence is not measured by how long the prosecutor takes to present its case, or the number of dull and boring witnesses the prosecutor presents.

'You heard the prosecutor refer to my client as *the defendant*. It's a nice, anonymous term to remind you he is accused of being a bad person. But Mr. Bower is a person, just like you.' White stepped back from the podium and turned to look at Martin Bower. With an exaggerated sweeping of his arm, he dragged the juror's eyes to his client.

During the course of the trial, the jury might occasionally look at Bower to gauge his response to particular testimony. Otherwise, he would be largely ignored. It is a quirk of the jury system, easily explained but not really understood, that the person having the most at stake, the defendant, was the least important participant in the trial. Unless he chose to testify, no one would pay much attention to him.

White used the most of this opportunity to make the jury like his client. Bower was dressed in a conservative brown suit, white shirt and simple print tie. His attire was carefully chosen to contrast with the dark power suits worn by the attorneys, and to emphasize that he wasn't a member of the privileged elite as Powell attempted to portray him.

'As you will learn in this trial, Mr. Bower is a good person. You will learn a great deal about Mr. Bower and his leadership in building an institution the whole community is proud of and which has saved the lives of tens of thousands of your friends and neighbors.

'As we go through this trial, and you hear evidence, I want you to think of a brick of cheese. I want you to picture what kind of cheese it is. The government will try to show you a solid block of cheese. But, as we proceed, you will begin to see a different kind of cheese. First you will begin to see a block of lorraine cheese; apparently solid, but actually full of small holes. And by the end of this trial you will see Swiss cheese, a block of cheese full of gaping holes—and the government's case will smell like limburger.'

The jurors smiled. Several of them chuckled openly.

White's choice of a cheese analogy wasn't merely a convenient visual image. He knew that there would be times during the trial—and, if not then, certainly during final jury deliberations—when lunch would be brought to the juror's from the delicatessen across the street. The deli menu included numerous offerings containing cheese, predominantly Swiss. He was setting up his own closing argument in which he would reemphasize his cheese analogy and hope to benefit further from the menu service provided by the Court.

'As the judge will instruct you at the end of this trial, the government has the burden of proving its case beyond a reasonable doubt. Ladies and gentlemen, you will hear about more than reasonable doubt. You will hear about leads the government chose not to follow. You will hear about conflicts on the hospital board. You will hear about factions who would do anything to be rid of Mr. Bower. You will hear about a board so concerned with its own reputation that it would do anything to blame Mr. Bower for all the financial woes the hospital has suffered. You will hear about numerous other people who had motive, means and opportunity to commit the acts Mr. Bower is accused of committing. You will learn how others may have benefited from those acts and how they may benefit from pointing the finger at Mr. Bower. When this trial is over, you may not know who committed these acts, but you *will* know the government has not proven that it was Mr. Bower.'

* * * * *

When Elizabeth Powell returned to her office, Managing U. S. Attorney Dwight Madison was waiting for her.

'I hear your opening statement went well,' Madison said.

'Sarcasm doesn't become you, Dwight. I'm not in the mood.'

'Well, you better get in the mood, and quick,' Madison responded. 'This is a major case, and this office has a lot riding on it. You screw it up, and you'll be trying misdemeanor drug possession cases for the rest of your career . . . short as it may be.'

'I can handle it,' Powell muttered.

'You'd better,' Madison admonished, and left the office.

* * * * *

Powell's day didn't end with her confrontation with Dwight Madison. She wanted to go home and pour herself a stiff scotch before facing the reality that her career was hanging in the balance. But before that, she needed to know how much White really knew. Randall Harrington had gotten her into this position, and by God Randall Harrington would have an explanation that would get her out of it.

Early in the case, Harrington, then all smiles and cooperation, had given her his home telephone number, as well as his cell phone number, his car phone number and his wife's car phone number. She started with the home number. It was answered by a woman, and Powell heard voices in the background. Probably dinner time, she thought.

'I'm sorry to interrupt your meal,' she said. 'This is Assistant United States Attorney Elizabeth Powell. I need to speak to Randall Harrington.'

'Just a moment,' the voice replied.

'Randy, are you here for the U. S. Attorney?' Powell heard her ask.

A minute later, Harrington answered the phone. 'Hello, Elizabeth. What's up?'

'We have a problem. Are you still coming down here tonight?'

'Yes. I have a nine-twenty flight. It lands at ten-forty. I should be at my hotel by eleven-thirty. What's going on?'

'I'll meet you at your hotel,' Powell said bruskly and hung up.

* * * * *

Powell wasn't happy about having to meet with Harrington at eleven-thirty at night. Her trial was starting in less than twelve hours, and she had more important things to do with her time. White's news changed all that. White knew something that she didn't, and Harrington was the only one who could tell her what it is.

'You're getting bent out of shape over nothing,' Harrington assured Powell after she had reported the events of the day.

'That's easy for you to say. You don't have to try this case.' Powell made no effort to hide her anger. 'White knows something, and I want to know what it is.'

'And you think I know what he knows?'

'I'm sure of it.'

'How?'

'Don't jerk me around. My case is based on your information. Lucius White and his little band have been one step ahead of me all along.'

'You knew he was a good attorney. What else did you expect?'

'Damn it,' Powell snapped. 'My case is built on the documents and information you provided.'

'I don't know what you're concerned about,' Harrington said, looking away from Powell and taking another swallow of his vodka martini.

'Then what is Kevin Wilson doing on White's witness list?'

Harrington stiffened. 'Who?'

'Kevin Wilson. According to White, he's one of your former associates.'

'Not mine. I don't even recognize the name,' Harrington lied. 'Maybe he worked in one of our other offices.'

'Then why would he know anything about the information you've been providing?'

'I can't tell you what I don't know. My guess is that White is just trying to rattle you.'

'Well, he's succeeded. '

'Just take it easy. You have a solid case,' Harrington assured her.

'Yes, based on information you provided,' Powell said. 'I better not lose this case because your documents don't stand up.'

'You weren't concerned about our help when we were making your case for you. Isn't it a little late to be getting picky about your sources?'

'You've given me documents, and I've accepted them at face value. You can't prove I knew they were anything but what you said they were. If Lucius Fucking-God-Almighty White proves your documents are phony, I'll have your ass.'

39.

Even the morning drizzle didn't deter the flock of media vultures from crowding the promenade in front of the courthouse. Money. Power. Scandal. Everything the press loved was at stake. Flood lights blazed, and microphones were thrust into his face as White rounded the corner and headed up the ramp to the promenade.

'*Mr. White. Are you going to consider a plea bargain?*'

'*Mr. White. Is it true your client's wife has filed for divorce?*'

'*Mr. White. Did your client really use the money to buy cocaine?*'

'*Mr. White. Mr. White. Mr. White.*'

White suppressed the urge to shout, *Shut the fuck up.* and smiled. He nodded to a few reporters he knew while staying between the cameras and Martin Bower. By design, they stayed close to the building so the media couldn't surround them. Harry Harris trailed behind White and stayed beside Bower. His wheelchair blocked access to their client.

U.S. Marshal Ed Bailey appeared at the door and pushed the throng away while holding the door for the defendant and his lawyers. The betting pool among the court staff was substantial and Bailey had his money on White. White smiled his thanks and Bailey nodded a *no problem.*

Elizabeth Powell appeared from the parking garage across the street. The throng left the promenade and closed in on her. By official policy, she couldn't answer questions about a pending case, but the policy didn't prohibit facial expressions. Ed Bailey watched as she crossed the street. She would have to open the door for herself.

* * * * *

The government's first witness was its forensic accountant. It was likely to be a long and dry testimony. White was tempted to offer No-Doze to the members of the jury. He would have been perfectly happy for the jurors to sleep through Powell's examination of her expert, but he wanted them to be alert for his cross-examination.

White knew Powell was taking a risk putting the accountant on the stand early in her case. The accountant would describe the money transfers at the core of her theory of the case. Later witnesses would fill in facts supporting the various elements of her theory.

White also knew, or at least assumed, that most of what the accountant had to say would be based on documents provided by the hospital and its attorneys, rather than being based on a personal examination of the hospital's computer programs. Under the rules of evidence, White could only cross-examine the witness on matters he testified to on direct examination by the prosecutor. The prosecutor had to walk the narrow line between getting all the facts needed to support her case without exposing the accountant to examination on facts she would prefer the jury didn't hear. Her stress showed on her face as the judge asked, 'Ms. Powell, are you ready to call your first witness?'

'Yes, Your Honor. The government calls Peter Kish.'

Kaleidoscope

The bailiff escorted Peter Kish into the courtroom and up to the witness stand where he was sworn in and took a seat.

'Please state your name and occupation for the record,' Powell instructed.

'Peter Kish. No middle initial,' Kish said evenly. 'I am a forensic accountant with the Federal Bureau of Investigation.'

He had a New England accent, crisp and with a touch of the lost 'r' common to the Boston area. It was appropriate. For reasons wholly unknown, juries assigned more credibility to experts who spoke differently and traveled great distances. A jury would accept anyone as an expert as long as he was more than a hundred miles from home and carried a briefcase.

'Would you please describe your professional education and training for the court,' Powell said.

'Your Honor,' White interrupted. 'The defense will save the court some time and stipulate that Mr. Kish is an expert.' Juries tend to be impressed by credentials. White knew Kish was an expert in his field. He didn't want the jury to know just how qualified he was.

'Your Honor,' Powell said. 'The jury has a right to know about Mr. Kish's *extensive* background as a forensic accountant and his *twenty years* experience with the F.B.I. and his *dozens* of books and articles and lectures.'

'I think you just told the jury all they need to know about the witness,' the judge said. 'Let's move on.'

'Mr. Kish,' Powell began confidently. 'Have you had occasion to examine certain records of the Coastal Regional Hospital and the Gulf Coast Bank relating to transfers of funds from the hospital to the Bank?'

'Objection,' White said, standing slowly as he did so. 'No documents are in the record yet. Until the documents are authenticated by the appropriate records custodian, and admitted into evidence, the court cannot allow a witness to testify about them.'

'Approach the bench, counsel.' the judge ordered. White, Powell and the court reporter moved to the side of the bench, away from the jury, where the attorneys could argue their positions without being overheard.

'I ask the court to allow the government a little latitude here,' Powell said. 'The relevant documents will be introduced in due course. In the interest of justice, and for the benefit of the jury, the government should be permitted to offer expert testimony describing the overall scheme undertaken by the defendant. If the court decides that any documents referred to by the witness are not admissible, it can give the jury an appropriate instruction to disregard parts of Mr. Kish's testimony.'

'Your Honor,' White objected. 'A jury instruction will be meaningless after the jury has had many days to think about what the witness says.'

In fact, White was more than happy to let the witness say things that couldn't be supported by later evidence. Juries do not like broken promises. If White could later prevent supporting documents from being admitted as evidence, he could point to both the prosecutor's opening statement, and to witness testimony, as places where the government promised to establish facts that it was unable to prove with admissible evidence.

'I'll give you a little latitude, Ms. Powell,' the judge ruled. 'But I'm warning you. If you fail to introduce evidence supporting each and every fact this witness testifies about, I will give the jury the strongest possible instruction to ignore his testimony.'

'I understand, Your Honor.'

'Good. Now step back.'

White returned to his seat and Powell resumed her place at the podium.

'Objection overruled,' the judge said.

'Mr. Kish,' Powell resumed her examination of the witness. 'Please describe what you found in your examination of the documents obtained from the hospital and the bank.'

Kaleidoscope

For the next hour and a half the witness described the transfers of funds from the hospital to the bank and their subsequent transfer to a bank in the Cayman Islands. Under Powell's guidance, the witness described the intricacies of wire transfers and the methods used by the F.B.I. to trace wire transfers and identify their points of origin and destination. It was early in the trial and the jury was, to White's consternation, mesmerized by the testimony. By the time Powell turned the witness over to White, the jurors knew more about wire transfers than they would ever care to know.

When Powell announced, 'No more questions of this witness,' the judge asked White, 'Do you anticipate a lengthy cross-examination of this witness?'

White conferred briefly with Harris.

'Yes, Your Honor,' White said, not knowing how long his examination might really take, but needing time to make some decisions about his examination.

'Then we will take an early lunch break,' the judge announced. 'Court will resume at one o'clock.'

* * * * *

White, Harris and Bower took their lunch in the conference room of the federal public defender, courtesy of Charles Halperin, who ordered sandwiches from the deli across the street. The attorneys and their client chatted casually while they ate, ignoring the morning's testimony. Peter Kish had not said anything damaging, and the attorneys didn't want to increase Bower's anxiety by rehashing his testimony. Nonetheless, Bower wanted to talk about it.

'They didn't show any connection between me and the account, did they?' Bower asked anxiously. 'That's good, isn't it?'

Like most defendants, Bower was fixated on the one fact he could understand—the one critical fact he knew couldn't be proven. His signature didn't appear on any bank documents, so the government couldn't prove he was involved.

'They haven't hurt you so far, Marty,' White agreed, trying to minimize the significance of Kish's testimony. 'But he isn't the one who would be testifying about that.'

'Who will?'

'They'll probably use the bank's manager to introduce the account documents that have your name on them.'

'But I didn't sign anything.'

'We know that,' White agreed. 'But it's the only thing they have connecting you to the account.'

'They can't convict me without more than that . . . can they?'

'We've talked about this before, Marty. Their case has always been circumstantial,' White said, as he had so frequently in the weeks preceding the trial. 'The jury knows the account was opened. The jury will also soon know your name is on the account cards. Those are facts, and we can't do anything about them.

'We're going to argue that the government can't prove *you* opened the account. The government is going to argue that *someone* opened the account without signing any of the account documents. Once the jury accepts the fact that the account could be opened without *anyone* actually signing the account documents—and they have to accept that—they'll be willing to accept circumstantial evidence that it was you. At least, that's what the government hopes.'

Bower gave an exasperated sigh.

Charles Halperin joined the attorneys and their client just as they were finishing their sandwiches. 'Still up to your old tricks are you, Lucius?'

White responded with an exaggerated smile. 'I don't know what you mean, Charles.'

'You damn near put Powell into cardiac arrest yesterday,' Halperin said. 'What did you tell her?'

Kaleidoscope

'I just added a few surprise witnesses to my list.'

'I'd say *surprise* is an understatement,' Halperin said. 'I saw her opening statement. Whatever you told her really shook her up.'

White and Harris chuckled but said nothing.

Halperin slid into a seat beside White. 'Dwight Madison also chewed her out. I've never seen her as pale as she was when she left the building last night.'

'But that's not all you came to tell me,' White said.

'No, as a matter of fact it isn't,' Halperin confirmed. 'I was working late last night myself, and I stopped by the Harbourside Hotel for a quick refreshment. Who do you suppose I saw?'

'I assume that Powell was one of the people you saw. Who else?'

Halperin grinned. 'Randall Harrington. He checked in sometime after eleven, and Powell showed up right after that. They met in the lounge.'

White smirked. 'A happy reunion?'

'Hardly. She had a look that would melt granite.'

'I don't suppose they sat at the table next to you—and you overheard everything they said.'

'You get lucky, but not that lucky.'

'What's this supposed to mean?' Bower injected himself into the conversation.

'It means,' Harris said, 'that Powell wants to know what a former associate with Johnson, Kutter and Stump is doing on our witness list.'

'You're *not*.' Halperin said. 'You're not going to put one of their attorneys on the stand against them.' It was a rhetorical question. Halperin's eyes lit up at the prospect of an attorney testifying against the conduct of his former employer and former client. 'How are you going to get past the problem of attorney-client privilege?'

'Crime-fraud exception,' White said. 'Conversations between an attorney and his client aren't privileged if the subject of the conversation concerns the commission of a future crime or fraud.'

'Can you prove the attorneys are involved?'

'I think so.'

'Dirt.' Halperin demanded happily. 'I want dirt.'

'All in good time, Charles. All in good time.'

40.

'Mr. Kish,' White began when court had reconvened. 'You testified this morning that the hospital's computer made the monthly transfers from the hospital account to another account at Gulf Coast Bank. Is that correct?'

'Yes.'

'Did you personally examine the computer program?'

'I didn't examine the computer program's source code, if that's what you mean,' Kish said, without emotion.

'Then how do you know the transfers from the hospital bank accounts were initiated by the hospital's computer program?'

'The bank's records of the hospital account indicate that.'

'Could you be more specific?'

'Yes. When checks are deposited, the account records show the number of the check and the amount of the check. When a transfer is made by a wire transfer, a special code is recorded where the check number would have been recorded if the payment was made by check.'

'And are the wire transfers you discussed this morning the only wire transfers identified in the bank's records of the hospital account?'

'No. There are many others,' Kish admitted. 'Transfers made in the ordinary course of the hospital's business.'

'And how are these transfers made?'

'Objection,' Powell interrupted. 'The question is too vague.'

'Sustained. Rephrase the question.'

'The transfers you have just identified; are they made by the bank or the hospital?'

'Generally, they're made by the bank.'

'So it was the *bank* computers, not the hospital's computers that make these transfers?'

'Objection.' Powell spat. 'Mr. White is trying to tell the witness how to answer the question.'

'Sustained. Let the witness make up his own answers.'

'Are these transfers made by the *bank's* computers or the *hospital's* computers?' White said.

'The bank makes these transfers. In the case of special, one-time transfers, the bank acts based on specific instructions given by the hospital. In the case of regular transfers, such as direct deposit of employee paychecks, the bank has a separate program that makes this kind of transfer based on written authorization from the employee.'

'Are you talking about any bank, or Gulf Coast Bank in particular?'

'I'm talking about how banks usually do things.'

'But you have not inquired into how such transfers are made in the case of the hospital and the Gulf Coast Bank, have you?' White was taking a chance, and breaking the fundamental rule of witness examination, learned by every law student—never ask a question you don't already know the answer to. White didn't know whether the witness had examined the procedures of Gulf Coast Bank, but he was sure he knew the answer to his question. In any event, he knew what he would ask next, regardless of the answer.

'No,' Kish said cautiously.

White paused, studying the witness. He knew Kish was an experienced witness—and probably knew White was trying to undermine the testimony by planting questions in the jurors' minds about the thoroughness of his investigation. 'And you previously testified that the transfers we're talking about were made by the hospital's own computer. Is that correct?'

'Yes.'

'Well, if all *other* wire transfers were made by the *bank*, why were the transfers you described this morning made by the *hospital's* computer system?'

'Objection.' Powell shouted. 'Calls for speculation on the part of the witness.'

'Sustained.'

White knew the question would be objected to—and that the objection would be sustained. It didn't matter. Now the jury had another unanswered question to consider.

'Mr. Kish,' White continued his attack. 'In your testimony this morning, you traced the funds from the hospital's bank account to another account with Gulf Coast Bank, and from there to a bank in the Cayman Islands.'

'That's correct.'

'Where is the money now?'

'Objection,' Powell shouted. 'It's irrelevant where the money is now.'

'I think it may be relevant,' the judge announced after a moment of thought. 'Overruled. The witness may answer.'

'I don't know,' Kish admitted.

The jurors became more attentive.

'Do you know the name of the person who opened the account in the Cayman Islands bank?' White said.

'No,' Kish said. 'But the Cayman Islands have banking secrecy laws that prevent discovery of such information. That's probably why the defendant chose a bank in the Caymans.'

Now it was White who objected. 'Move to strike the witness's gratuitous and unsupported supposition. He has not been qualified as an expert on Cayman banking laws.'

'Sustained. The jury will disregard the witness's last statement. And the witness will confine himself to answering questions.'

'So . . . not only do you not know where the money is, you don't even know if the money that went to the Cayman Islands bank was ever controlled by the defendant?'

'No,' Kish said softly, almost as if he didn't want the jury to hear his answer.

'You'll have to speak up,' the judge instructed.

'No. I don't know any of that,' Kish said, firmly.

'And isn't it also true that the account at the Gulf Coast Bank—the account that initially received funds from the hospital account—wasn't in the defendant's name?'

'That is also true.' Having been admonished by the judge for volunteering information, the witness said nothing more about the name on the bank account or the government's contention that it was controlled by Martin Bower.

'In fact,' White continued in a voice charged with contempt, 'you have never seen *any* document *signed by the defendant* relating to the bank account that received the funds from the hospital account, have you?'

'No. But . . .'

'Thank you,' White cut the witness off before he could say more. 'Let's return to the hospital's computer program for a moment.'

It wasn't a question, but the witness, eager to leave the previous line of inquiry, nodded his agreement anyway.

'You previously testified that the money transfers were controlled by a routine in the hospital's own computer.' White paused, making sure he had the jury's attention. 'So *someone* had to program the computer to make these transfers. Is that correct?'

'Obviously,' Kish agreed

Kaleidoscope

'To the best of your knowledge, does Mr. Bower know anything about how to program the hospital's computers?'

White knew that the witness had no knowledge about Bower's abilities. Getting a witness to admit his lack of knowledge of a seemingly significant point was important. White wasn't disappointed.

'I don't know, but he . . .'

Again, White cut the witness short with a curt 'Thank you.'

'So the hospital's computer program must have been changed by someone *other than* Mr. Bower. Isn't that true?'

'I . . . I suppose.'

The significance of this admission was immediately apparent to the jurors who looked at each other in shared understanding.

'And you previously described an arrangement to transferred funds from the hospital account to some other account at Gulf Coast Bank.'

'Yes.'

'And they were subsequently transferred to a bank in the Cayman Islands.'

'Yes.'

'And was this a transfer made by the bank's computers?'

'Yes.'

'So someone *in the bank* must have programmed the bank's computer. Isn't that true?'

The courtroom spectators held their breath. All eyes focused on the witness. The witness hesitated, looking apologetically at Powell before answering. 'I suppose so.'

White walked to the defense table, leaned over and whispered something to Bower. Bower shook his head. White turned and quietly studied the witness as he returned to his place behind the podium, still considering his next step.

Attorneys frequently ask questions they know will be objected to. Sometimes it is merely so the opposing attorney will object and make it appear that they're trying to keep the jury from learning something important. Sometimes it is merely to plant a question in the jury's mind. And sometimes it is intended to stretch the limits of the rules in hopes of discovering something new. White had all three objectives in mind when he asked, 'Then why hasn't the government charged anyone in the bank?'

'Objection,' Powell shouted as she leapt to her feet. Her words could barely be heard over the eruption of chatter in the spectator gallery. 'Irrelevant and beyond the scope of the witness's knowledge,' she said as she fought for the judge's attention.

Three times the judge gaveled for silence before the spectators quieted.

The judge sustained the objection, but White's point wasn't lost on the jury. The fact that the prosecutor had objected so aggressively only emphasized the potential importance of something she didn't want them to know.

Throughout his early questioning White had intentionally asked questions in a form that would be objected to. The more the prosecutor objected, the more curious the jury got. As White intended, Powell's outburst had refocused the jury's attention.

'Just so that we're clear, is it your testimony that *all* the money that was removed from the hospital account to another account at Gulf Coast Bank was wired out to another account?'

'Yes.'

'And Mr. Bower himself never took any money from any account at Gulf Coast Bank. Isn't that so?'

'Yes.'

'In fact, you have no proof that Mr. Bower *ever* received *any* of the money, do you?'

'I guess not.'

'I have no further questions for this witness,' White announced, ending his cross-examination on a high note.

'We'll take a fifteen minute recess,' the judge announced.

* * * * *

During a break in the proceedings, Bower asked White, 'Are we getting anywhere with this?'

'So far he hasn't said anything that hurts us,' White said. 'And he's admitted little things that don't necessarily fit together.'

'What does that do for us?' Bower asked.

'The problem with little inconsistencies is that they keep adding up, like flies on road kill. If we can put them all together for the jury, the government's theory will smell like a dead carcass to them too.'

41.

When Court reconvened, Powell called Connie Baker. Baker was duly sworn and took her seat in the witness chair.

'Please state your name and occupation for the record,' Powell instructed.

'Connie Baker. I'm Regional Manager for Gulf Coast Banks.'

'Is your correct name Connie or Constance?' the court reporter asked.

'Connie,' Baker said.

'Your Honor, I ask that the courtroom clerk hand government exhibits 1 through 16 to the witness.'

'So instructed,' the judge ordered.

'Ms. Baker,' Powell continued, "can you identify the documents you have just been handed?'

'Yes.'

'For the record, would you describe, for the Court and the jury, what these documents are?'

Connie Baker paused while she removed her reading glasses from her purse and settled them on her nose.

Slowly she paged through the bank records, describing each as she went.

Kaleidoscope

'To the best of your knowledge, are these true and correct copies of the records of Gulf Coast Bank?' Powell asked.

'Yes.'

'Your Honor, the government offers the documents identified by Ms. Davis into evidence.'

'Any objection, Mr. White?' the judge asked.

'No objection,' White said, his tone suggesting that the documents were irrelevant.

'In whose name was this account opened?' Powell asked.

'The account card says Walco, Inc.'

'Do you know who owns Walco, Inc.?'

'No.'

Powell stepped back from the podium just, enough to give the jury an unobstructed view of the defendant. For a moment she said nothing; waiting for the jury to focus on her next question. "And whose name is on the account card as the authorized signatory on the account?'

'Martin Bower,' Baker said evenly.

'*The Defendant.*' Powell spat, as if the jury didn't already know who Martin Bower was.

'It's the same name,' Baker agreed, without emotion.

'And from the annual statements of account activity, can you determine what transactions occurred in this account?'

'Yes.'

'Please describe them.'

'There was a wire transfer into the account on the first of every month. There was a corresponding wire transfer out of the account on the same day.'

'Was there any other activity in this account?'

'No.'

'From these documents, can you tell where the wire transfers into the account originated?'

'Yes. The deposits came from the general account of Coastal Regional Hospital.'

There was a murmur throughout the gallery and the jury box.

'Order,' the judge demanded as he hammered his gavel. 'I have no further questions of this witness.'

White stood and walked to the podium, smiling at the jury and the witness. Unlike the prosecutor, White didn't carry any notes or prepared questions. The absence of notes was intended to convey the subtle message, *There is nothing here to be concerned with.*

'Ms. Baker,' White began. 'Isn't it true that *none* of the documents relating to the establishment of this account were ever signed by Mr. Bower?'

'Yes. That's true. The account was opened without any evidence that Mr. Bower was involved in opening the account. The account could have been opened by anyone.'

'So, for all you can tell from these documents, the account could have been opened by someone who wanted to make it *look like* it was Mr. Bower's account. Isn't that true?'

'Absolutely. For all I know the account could have been opened by the prosecutor.'

The silence that smothered the courtroom was broken by the thud of Elizabeth Powell's leg slamming into her table as she leapt to her feet.

'Objection. Move to strike.' Powell was enraged. She glared at White, on the verge of accusing him of coaching the witness.

'Sustained. The witness's answer following 'Absolutely' will be stricken, and the witness is instructed not to speculate.'

'Yes, sir,' Baker said.

White continued as though nothing unusual had happened. 'Was this account opened at Gulf Coast Bank?'

'No.'

Powell's head snapped up, followed by the heads of her two assistants. Their collective response set off a chain reaction. The jurors, seeing the prosecutor's response, shifted forward in their seats. The judge leaned toward the witness. The spectators stopped whispering among themselves

'Where *was* this account opened?'

'It was opened at the Peoples Bank of Sarasota.'

'Is that bank connected to your bank?'

'Not at the time the account was opened. Peoples Bank was later acquired by the Gulf Coast Bank. That's how the records happened to be in our bank.'

Powell and her assistants exchanged puzzled looks. Powell scribbled something on her legal pad.

'Now, returning your attention to the documents you identified for the prosecutor.' White built his question slowly. 'Were those documents given to the government by the bank?'

'No.'

The silence and tension grew.

'How do you know that?'

Spectators and jurors alike moved forward in their seats.

'The bank has no record of receiving a subpoena from the government.'

'So how did the government get the documents?'

'Objection. The witness has no way of knowing the answer to that question.'

'Your Honor. The government obtained the documents somehow. If it didn't get them through legal means, it got them through *illegal* means.'

White was treading on thin ice, and he knew it. Just as he knew that Powell's objection would be sustained. He also knew what was coming next.

'Counselor, that's enough,' the judge admonished harshly. 'The court reporter will strike Mr. White's last comment from the record and the jury will disregard Mr. White's outburst.'

'Just one more question, Ms. Baker,' White said, a signal to the jury that the other shoe was about to drop and they should pay attention.

'To the best of your knowledge, has the bank ever released any of the records on the Walco, Inc. account pursuant to any legitimate and proper request?'

'No. Never.'

'Nothing further,' White said, again smiling at the jury. Most of them smiled back.

White took his seat at the defense table and looked toward Powell. She was huddled over her notes, conferring with her assistant. White knew she was thinking about the fundamental rule of litigation—always end on a high note. Powell needed to do something to counter the effect of Baker's damning testimony, but anything she might ask would only fix Baker's testimony more firmly in the jury's mind. It was a classic problem.

Powell took the safest way out.

'No redirect, Your Honor.'

Sensing the prosecutor's situation, the judge asked, 'Would you like to call your next witness now, or should we adjourn until tomorrow?'

'Your Honor. My next witness will be Mr. Morgan, and I believe that we should delay until the Court can make a ruling on the issues relating to his testimony.'

This wasn't something Powell should have said with the jury in the room, but she wasn't in control. The judge glared at her with no attempt to disguise his anger.

'Very well. Court is adjourned until nine-thirty tomorrow morning.'

When the jury had been escorted out of the room, the judge called the attorneys to the bench.

'I will have my order on Mr. Morgan's testimony by nine o'clock tomorrow,' the judge announced. Then, looking squarely at Powell, he added, 'And I hope you will spend some time this evening reviewing proper courtroom conduct, Ms. Powell.'

Powell glared at the judge, but said nothing.

Kaleidoscope

42.

Harry Harris wasn't in court for the afternoon of the first day of the trial. He was in the office of State's Attorney Paul Parker.

'Well, I'll be damned,' Parker said when he looked up from his desk and saw Harris at his office door.

'You probably will be,' Harris said. 'But that's another story.'

'I told my secretary not to let any lowlife defense attorneys in here without a guard.'

'I guess Gretchen doesn't consider me one of the lowlife types,' Harris said. 'Besides, I've known her longer than you have. And I was trying cases in this court long before you became the State's Attorney.'

'And maybe she's just taking pity on you,' Parker said. He immediately regretted his choice of words. 'Jesus, I'm sorry, Harry. I didn't mean . . .'

'I know you didn't, Paul.'

'I'm really sorry.'

Harris waved a hand dismissively. 'Forget it. I know it was just a figure of speech.'

'So how are you doing these days?' Parker asked, quietly changing the subject. 'I don't see you around the courthouse.'

'I don't spend much time in court these days. This,' Harris patted his wheelchair, 'doesn't lend itself to persuasive representation.'

'That's bullshit, Harry. The chair doesn't affect your mind. Even in a chair, you're a better trial lawyer than ninety percent of the attorneys I see.'

'Maybe. But juries aren't always that open minded. It wouldn't be fair to my clients. I can't let their freedom depend on the feelings a jury might have about a crippled defense attorney.'

Parker tensed at Harris' reference to himself as a cripple.

'Do you want some coffee?' Parker said. 'It's probably left over from this morning. It'll tear your guts out.'

'With such a ringing endorsement, how can I refuse?'

As they waited for their coffee, Parker changed the subject again. 'I hear you've partnered up with Lucius White,'

'Yeah. Lucius and I have been together for a couple of years. I was pretty far gone after the accident.' Harris paused as the painful memory passed through his mind. 'Lucius stuck by me. He helped me through rehabilitation, got me dried out, and gave me a home. I owe him a lot.'

'He's a good attorney.'

'And a good friend,' Harris added. 'I don't know where I'd be without him.'

'He kicked my butt in a probable cause hearing the other day,' Parker said.

'I heard. No hard feelings?'

'Of course not.'

'Actually,' Harris said, 'the way I heard it, U. S. Attorney hung you out with a bad warrant and bad law.'

Parker shook his head slowly. 'That bitch really did me in. That was the last time I do anything to help *that* broad.'

'I guess you won't be taking her to the prom?'

'You can be sure of that.'

'Lucius also wanted me to thank you for the heads-up on the surveillance operation.'

Kaleidoscope

'It probably wasn't the smartest thing I ever did,' Parker said. 'But I've never believed it's appropriate to tail attorneys. Their clients, and maybe even their operatives, but not the attorneys.'

'Powell has never been concerned with such niceties,' Harris said. 'And the lady is continuing with her ways.'

Parker slid his coffee cup to the side of his desk and leaned forward. 'Why do I think you're throwing me a hook baited with my favorite goodie?'

Harris shrugged.

'Okay,' Parker said after a short pause. 'I'll bite.'

'We think,' Harris began, then corrected himself. 'No, it's more than that. We're sure that the Ice Princess is basing a significant part of her case on falsified documents.'

'Does she know the documents are phony?'

'Truthfully, we're less sure of that,' Harris said. 'We think so, but we can't prove it. Not yet.'

'Who's making up the documents?'

'We think it's Joe Morgan, the hospital's in-house attorney—with or without the participation of outside counsel.'

'Joe Morgan?' Parker said. 'Medium height, overweight, greasy dark hair and a mustache?'

'That's him. Do you know him?'

'He was with Powell when I got suckered into the Worthington fiasco,' Parker said. 'He struck me as a weasel at the time. A fat weasel, but a weasel nonetheless.'

Harris began to feel optimistic about his mission. 'That's the guy.'

'What's he doing?'

'Obstructing justice, fabricating evidence, giving false testimony.'

'Not wise things for an attorney to be doing,' Parker said. 'The Bar Association would probably want to hear about this. But I have the feeling that you want me to take a personal interest in his doings.'

'Filing false police reports is still a State crime, isn't it?'

'So?'

'The initial criminal complaint was filed with the State's Attorney. That's you, isn't it?'

A knowing smile formed on Parker's lips. 'What do you have?'

For the next half hour, Harris explained what they had discovered about the copied documents. He didn't mention the suspicions about Morgan's involvement in the AIDS drugs. That information would have assured the State's Attorney's interest, but Harris had other reasons for wanting to get the State's Attorney interested.

When Harris finished, Parker leaned back, his hands clasped behind his head, and looked at Harris with narrowed, skeptical eyes. 'I assume you brought this to me for a reason,'

'Yes,' Harris admitted, without hesitation. 'I need a favor.'

'I'm listening.'

'Right now, all we have are suspicions.' Harris said. 'It would help our case if we *knew* these documents passed though Joe Morgan's home printer-copier. It would be even better if we discovered that some of the questionable documents originated on Morgan's computer.'

'And since you can't get a search warrant, you thought you could sucker me into doing your work for you,' Parker concluded, his voice a mixture of irritation and admiration.

'That's about right,' Harris admitted.

Parker thumbed through the documents and scanned his notes. Finally he broke the silence. 'Harry. I don't like being used, even by you.'

Damn. He's not biting.

'But I'm even more pissed that I was used by Elizabeth Powell and the hospital in the first place, especially if Morgan committed a crime when he used me.'

Harris showed a hint of a smile, but remained silent—waiting for Parker to announce his decision.

Parker continued to thumb through the documents.

'This should be enough for a warrant,' Parker said. 'I suppose you're also going to tell me when you want the warrant executed.'

'I wouldn't presume to tell you how to do your job. But Morgan will be taking the stand tomorrow morning. You might find it convenient to go to his house about eight-thirty in the morning. His housekeeper arrives about eight o'clock, but Morgan will have left for court.'

'You think of everything, don't you?'

Harris smiled. 'Just trying to be helpful.'

43.

Clyde's is *the* watering hole for the Fort Myers power brokers. It is locally said, not without some truth, that every deal of any significance originated in, or had been finalized at, Clyde's. Equally true is the proposition that you were not among the elite until Jack, the bartender to the after work crowd for longer than anyone could remember, knew your favorite beverage and had it on the bar by the time you reached your customary seat.

Clyde's is reminiscent of the era of White's warehouse. It was originally a private home, a mansion by the standards of the day, built in the Victorian style. It had brick walls and hardwood floors. A mahogany bar, imported from an exclusive London men's club shortly after World War II, extended along one wall, from the door to the corner of the room, and halfway down the left wall of the room. A large mirror, held in place by a heavy, carved mahogany frame, covered the wall behind the bar. A table at the end of the bar held two steamer trays filled with grilled chicken wings and chicken livers wrapped with bacon. A shiny black grand piano stood in the center of the room.

Soon the piano would be surrounded by patrons stuffing bills into the brandy snifter to hear their favorite songs. But it was only four o'clock, too early for the regular crowd, when Amanda Gregori entered and took a seat at the end bar farthest from the door. From her seat, she could watch the entrance without being obvious.

Gregori attracted attention wherever she went. She was a willowy five-foot-six-inches with shoulder-length dark brown hair. She had mahogany eyes, as moist and sultry as a rain forest, framed by delicate, arched eyebrows and high regal cheeks reminiscent of a Grecian statue of Aphrodite. Her complexion was a natural tan suggesting a hereditary link to the Mediterranean. Although none of her roots reached that historic soil, she did do anything to dispel the first impression of her heritage. To the contrary, she often cultivated the impression with vague allusions to troubles faced by her grandparents in the old country.

Gregori provided her services to Lucius White when he needed confidential information. She described her profession as entertainer, which was accurate as far as it went. The police would use a different term, but she had no police record. She was very discrete, very selective and very expensive.

Gregori ordered a glass of Pinot Chardonnay and waited as Clyde's filled with weary professionals in need of a couple of stiff drinks before facing the chore of being devoted family men. They gathered around the bar and the few small tables, debating the movements of the stock market and the future of the prime.

Randall Harrington entered shortly before five o'clock, took a seat half way down the bar from Gregori. He was hard to miss. He was six feet tall, had dark hair, worn fashionably long, and was dressed in a dark, tailored suit with the mandatory monogrammed white shirt with French cuffs, gold monogrammed cufflinks and a crimson tie.

Harrington ordered a vodka martini and lit a cigarette. Gregori watched as he exhaled, accepted his drink and took a sip. For five minutes, she watched him smoke and drink, never turning from the bar or checking his watch. *Perfect,* Gregori thought as she opened her cellular telephone and placed a call.

'He's here,' she said, when Horse answered the telephone. 'Alone. And he doesn't seem to be waiting for anyone.'

'Then go ahead,' Horse said.

Gregori closed her cell phone, slipped it into her purse and glanced at the mirror behind the bar. Harrington was looking at her reflection in the same mirror. She looked away, feigning a lack of interest in the growing number of patrons. When she returned her attention to the mirror, Harrington was gone. She was tempted to look around the bar, but was afraid she might give herself away.

A moment later, she heard a voice behind her. 'Would it be too obvious if I were to offer to buy you a drink?'

Gregori turned and studied Harrington. 'I already have a drink. But you can take a seat if you like.'

Harrington slid onto the barstool next to Gregori and introduced himself.

'I don't think I've seen you here before,' Gregori said, tapping the rim of her glass with a polished fingernail. 'Are you new in town, or just passing through?'

'Just visiting,' Harrington said. 'I'm in town for a trial,' he said, implying his status as an attorney.

'Really. That sounds exciting,' Gregori said. Her feigned enthusiasm gave her an opportunity to lean forward and give Harrington a view of her cleavage—and let him know she wasn't wearing a bra. It had the desired effect. Harrington's eyes were momentarily riveted on her charms, his mind considering the possibilities they presented.

'Real trials are actually pretty boring.' Harrington said.

'But the trial of that guy from the hospital seems exciting.'

'Now *that*'s another story.'

'Is that the trial you're here for?' Gregori asked, leaning forward to give Harrington another look at her breasts.

'Yes. But I'm not involved in the trial.'
'Oh. What are you doing?'
'I'm an attorney for the hospital.'
'Good for you. I hope you get that guy.'
'We will,' Harrington said, confidently.
'Are you helping get them?'
'You could say that.'
'But would you . . . say that, I mean?' Gregori teased.

Careful now, Gregori thought. She knew she was taking a risk. Showing too much interest in Bower's trial could make him suspicious.

'Yes. I've been working with the government.' Harrington said smugly. Harrington's second martini—they were each doubles during happy hour—and Gregori's ample cleavage were having their desired effect. Harrington wasn't thinking about the hospital, or his role as its attorney.

'Are you ready for another drink?' Harrington asked, tapping her empty glass with his own.

'Are you trying to seduce me?' Gregori purred.

'The thought crossed my mind. But seduction sounds so crude. I prefer to think of it as letting nature take its course.'

'Well, if you aren't going to do it right, you shouldn't do it at all.'

'Then let's be sure we do it right,' Harrington said directly. 'Would you care to join me for dinner?'

* * * * *

After dinner in the restaurant at Harrington's hotel, during which Harrington boasted about his role in building the case against Bower, Gregori and Harrington rode in silence up the glass elevator to Harrington's suite. At dinner, Gregori limited herself to a glass of wine. Harrington had consumed two more vodka martinis, most of the bottle of wine—ordered to ply Gregori—and a brandy after dinner. Work wasn't on his mind.

Harrington's suite on the top floor of the hotel had a sitting area with a sofa and two chairs plus a small, round conference table and four more chairs—the businessman's home away from home. A few files lay open on the conference table, but they held little interest for Gregori.

'I have to make a call,' Harrington said as they entered the room. 'Can I get you a drink from the mini-bar?'

'No thanks,' Gregori replied. 'If you don't mind, I think I'll take a shower.'

'Be my guest.' Harrington smiled at her tacit suggestion that she was there for the night. 'You'll find an extra robe on the back of the door.'

The shower stopped and Gregori stepped naked from the bathroom just as Harrington entered the spacious bedroom, disrobing as he went.

'Are the oysters working?' Gregori whispered softly, as she pulled him close and nibbled on his ear.

'We'll know soon enough,' he said as he lifted her in his arms and carried her to the bed. He kissed his way down her center, leaning into her until she was lying on her back.

As he moved to the bed beside her, there was a knock on the door.

'Who the hell can that be?' Harrington muttered irritably, awkwardly grabbing a robe and stumbling to the door. 'Who is it?' he demanded.

'Delivery,' came the voice from the other side of the door.

'Slide it under the door,' Harrington ordered.

'You have to sign for it,' the voice insisted.

Harrington looked through the peephole and saw two men, neither of whom looked like a member of the hotel staff or a delivery agent. The man standing in front of the door looked familiar, but Harrington couldn't place him. He knew instinctively that something wasn't right, but was equally sure that ignoring them would only delay the inevitable. Better to find out what was going on and get back to his carnal bliss, if it was still possible.

Harrington removed the chain, turned the lock and slowly opened the door. The second man, a large man Harrington didn't recognize, pushed the door open and the two men entered.

'What do you want?' Harrington again insisted.

'You know who I am, don't you, counselor?'

Harrington suddenly recognized the stranger—Dr. John Wiley—and answered, 'Yes.' It was all Harrington could say as he struggled to make sense of this late night intrusion and the identity of his surprise visitor.

'Good,' Wiley said. 'Then no further introductions are necessary.'

'Who's that?' Harrington asked, indicating the large man accompanying Wiley.

'That isn't important, counselor.'

'Then what do you want?' Harrington demanded for the third time, now with much less authority than before.

'We have some business to discuss.'

'This is neither the time nor the place,' Harrington responded with controlled anger.

'But it will have to do,' Wiley said, his tone one of ambivalent disinterest.

'Look, I have company, and . . . '

'I don't think so,' Wiley said, looking past Harrington to the bedroom hallway where Amanda Gregori, now dressed, was walking toward them. As she passed between them, she smiled thinly at Harrington and pressed a small black box into the hand of the unidentified visitor. Harrington's jaw went taught as he recognized the tape recorder. He had been set up, and he knew it. He just didn't know why.

'Sit down, counselor,' Wiley instructed. His commanding voice and military bearing made it clear who was in charge.

Harrington wasn't accustomed to being given orders. He gave the orders and people did what he told them to do.

Harrington was in unfamiliar emotional territory, and too surprised to ignore the instruction.

Wiley took the chair opposite him while the other man remained standing near the hallway to the bedroom.

'You've been a very busy boy, counselor,' Wiley began. 'And you have done a wonderful job of framing Martin Bower.'

Harrington was too preoccupied, trying to determine why Wiley was there, and where the conversation was going, to respond.

'I'm sure the hospital board appreciates your efforts to protect their collective asses.'

'Including yours,' Harrington interrupted.

'Perhaps,' Wiley said calmly. 'But I have not participated in your efforts to fabricate the evidence against Mr. Bower. Or hadn't you noticed that I never attended the meetings where you've been plotting your activities?'

Harrington said nothing as he waited for Wiley to say why he was there.

'You can put your mind at ease, counselor. I'm not concerned with your efforts to frame Mr. Bower. At least not at the moment.'

'Then what do you want?' Harrington asked, relaxing at the suggestion that his problem may not be serious.

'Money, counselor. I want the money that was siphoned out of the hospital by Marty Bower.' Wiley's polite veneer was now gone, replaced by a demanding tone bordering on the vicious. Wiley stared at Harrington with the cold intensity of a sniper with his target in the cross-hairs.

Wiley's tone made it clear that he knew something, probably something the rest of the board didn't know. There had never been any discussion of recovering the money, other than as restitution at the end of the criminal trial. Wiley, and apparently Wiley alone, knew the money was still intact.

Harrington was the master of years in the courtroom and was accustomed to controlling his expressions when confronted with surprises. His face showed no response to Wiley's demand. 'I don't know what you're talking about.'

'Don't underestimate me, counselor. You know exactly what I'm talking about. You know where the money is, and you know who controls it.'

Harrington started to respond when he heard a noise from the bedroom. His attention shifted to Wiley's companion who was standing in front of the open door of the television cabinet—removing what Harrington immediately recognized to be a compact video tape camera.

'Counselor,' Wiley said, resuming his polite tone, his alternative persona having achieved its purpose. 'You're a happily married man, notwithstanding your predilections for companionship when traveling. That would probably change if these tapes were sent to your wife. In that case, you would lose everything—including the benefits you enjoy as the husband of a wealthy wife, and son-in-law of your firm's biggest individual client.

'You are also a successful and well-respected lawyer. That, too, would change if your involvement in the fabrication of evidence against Martin Bower were ever disclosed to the authorities and to the Bar Association.

'In addition to which, there are other people, far more inclined to violence than I, who would be upset by disclosure of the means by which certain drugs have been made available to their customers. Such a revelation would not be conducive to your continued physical well-being.'

Harrington was unable to speak, even if he had been able to think of something to say. For the first time, he knew how defendants felt when, as a former prosecutor, he demanded cooperation, or guilty pleas. He knew that Wiley could, and would, do exactly as he had said—with the predicted consequences.

'What do you want?' Harrington finally asked.

'We want you to convince your friend that the Caymans are no longer a safe place for the money. We found it, so the authorities can, too. Especially if we choose to tell them what we know. Convince your friend to transfer the money to this account in the Bahamas,' Wiley instructed, removing from his coat pocket an envelope containing the transfer authorizations White had prepared. He threw the envelop on the coffee table in front of Harrington.

'How am I supposed to do that?'

'You're a good lawyer. Use your talents of persuasion.'

Harrington continued to stare at Wiley with a mixture of hatred and helplessness.

'Morgan begins testifying tomorrow,' Wiley said. 'How much comes out on cross-examination depends on when we hear from the bank, so I suggest you act quickly.'

Harrington stared at the envelope before returning his attention to Wiley. 'Even if I can do what you want, how do I know you won't still hold everything over me?'

'You think too highly of your importance. We don't care about you. You are merely a means to an end. But just to be fair, I'm going to put these tapes in an envelope,' Wiley said, removing another envelope from his coat and putting the tapes inside. 'When we receive confirmation that the funds have been transferred, you get the envelope.'

'But you can make copies.'

Wiley sealed the envelope and passed it to Harrington. 'Sign across the seal. You'll know the seal hasn't been broken and we haven't made any copies. And just so we understand each other, if word of this conversation gets back to anyone other than your friend with the money, everything we just discussed will happen.'

'You're telling me to violate my obligations to my client,' Harrington whined.

'Your friend with the money isn't your client; the hospital is. And, as a member of the board, I am. You've already violated your duty to the hospital, and to me, by helping keep the money hidden,' Wiley said as he and his companion turned and headed for the door.

Wiley paused and turned, as if forgetting an important point, "In case you can't sleep, I believe your partner, Jim Davis, may be looking for you. You might give him a call.'

* * * * *

John Wiley was smiling when, ten minutes after leaving Harrington's hotel room, he stepped off the elevator into White's apartment.

'I take it the evening visit went well,' White said as he led Wiley into his study and closed the door.

'He may have soiled the hotel's nice robe,' Wiley said.

White smiled at the image.

'My guess,' Wiley began, 'is that your hunches were right. At least, they were close enough to scare the pants off Mr. Harrington.'

'Did he even *try* to deny anything?'

'Not a word. He was in shock the whole time.'

'Good. Now we know we're on the right track. But that doesn't really get us much closer to the facts.'

'By the way,' Wiley asked, 'what was all that business about Jim Davis?'

It was all going to come out soon enough, so there was no harm telling Wiley. 'Jim Davis is a partner in Harrington's firm. He practices criminal law out of their office in Tampa. Mr. Davis represented a small-time drug dealer who was convinced to plant drugs in the home of Jim Worthington, one of Marty's friends. Then, he told the F.B.I. about drugs in exchange for his freedom.'

'And Harrington didn't know about this?'

'To the contrary, I'm sure Harrington knows everything about it. In fact, he was probably behind it from the beginning. What Harrington didn't know is that I also know all about the arrangement to implicate Worthington. In fact, late this afternoon the druggie called Mr. Davis and told him that he was dissatisfied with his representation. He also told Davis that he had decided to engage a new attorney, me, and had told me everything Davis had done.'

Wiley thought about this for a moment, his smile spreading. 'Rather *Machiavellian*. Is this news the lawyer's equivalent of a nuclear bomb?'

'That's the hope,' White agreed. 'But even a nuclear bomb wouldn't be enough to destroy Harrington.'

Wiley gave White a puzzled look.

'Cockroaches are great survivors.'

Wiley smiled before asking, 'Do you think he'll transfer the money?'

'Until tonight, we didn't even know there was any money left to transfer.'

'Christ. You were bluffing.'

White nodded. 'Yeah. It was a calculated risk. If there wasn't any money left to transfer, he would know we still haven't discovered everything.'

'Remind me not to play poker with you.'

* * * * *

As Wiley was leaving White's apartment, the telephone rang. For the briefest moment, White's thoughts returned to the middle of the night telephone call that had started it all. With the same apprehension, he lifted the receiver. 'This is Lucius White.'

'Lucius, it's Tony.'

'Oh, shit.' White muttered, just loud enough to be heard.

'You could say that.' Tony said.

'What happened?'

'Your friend from the parking lot was released.'

Visions of an attack on Leslie filled White with apprehension. 'How the hell could that happen?'

'I don't know, Lucius. I'm on the night shift now. I just reported in, and I called you immediately.'

'I thought you were going to lose the paperwork and hold him for a couple of days.'

'That was the plan, but the guy has serious juice. A Miami lawyer showed up this afternoon and got him sprung. According to the guys on the early shift, your boy was royally pissed. The bastard even left a message for me to give you.'

White stopped breathing. 'What did he say?'

'The note says *All bets are off*. He told the guy he left the message with that you'd know what it means.'

White's grip on the telephone tightened.

'What *does* the note mean?'

'It means I could get a paper cut,' White said.

'Huh?

'Where is he now?' White asked, ignoring Tony's implied question and knowing he wasn't going to like the answer to his own.

'We don't know, but he's out there somewhere.'

White leaned back in his chair and looked toward the ceiling. The pieces were falling into place, but there were still too many loose ends. They still didn't have a motive. They still couldn't prove Bower wasn't involved. Now someone who might want to kill them was on the loose.

White reached for a legal pad and pencil. For a long moment, he sat unmoving, arms on the desk, pencil poised over the pad, waiting for. . .

He took a deep breath and exhaled, stared at the blank pad, and threw his pencil on the deck. It bounced once and came to rest on the sofa across the room.

He wanted a drink. God how he wanted a drink. But he knew it wouldn't stop at that.

44.

At eight-thirty the next morning, Horse entered the conference room just outside the double doors to the courtroom. White and Harris were waiting, reviewing the examinations planned for the day. They looked up in unison and asked, 'Do you have anything?'

Horse laughed. 'Oh, yeaaaaaaaah.' Horse pulled a chair from the table and sat down. 'After Dr. Wiley left, I had a little chat with the night clerk at the hotel. I'll bet we weren't even at the elevator before Harrington was on the phone to Jim Davis. They talked for almost twenty minutes. I think we can guess the topic.

'Then Harrington made another call. The call lasted less than two minutes. My guess is that Harrington didn't go into any details. He probably just said something had happened and they had to meet.'

White was past being amazed with the amount of information Horse could come up with. His only question was whether money had passed hands or whether Horse had merely charmed the night clerk out of the information—and perhaps her panties as well. It was better than even money that it was the latter.

Kaleidoscope

'Now, here's where it gets good,' Horse continued. 'Would anyone like to guess who Harrington met first thing this morning?'

'Morgan?' White guessed.

'Dr. *Sommers*. Harrington met Sommers at six-thirty at the Shoney's on North Cleveland Avenue. They took a booth in the corner of the restaurant. I couldn't go inside because Harrington would have recognized me from last night. I found a parking spot by the window near their booth. Sommers was facing me, so I could see his face while Harrington was talking.

'I wish I had a camera with me.' Horse had everyone's attention and was thoroughly enjoying telling the story. 'Harrington must have laid it on heavy. For a while, Sommers was arguing with Harrington. My guess is that he was saying something like *There has to be a way out*, because Harrington was hanging his head and shaking his head. Finally, Harrington took the envelope out of his pocket. Sommers spent a few minutes staring into space. Then he signed the papers, the ones authorizing Harrington to make the transfers.'

'They left the restaurant a little before eight. I don't know where Sommers went because I followed Harrington back to the hotel. I called his room from the house phone in the lobby every minute for half an hour. It was busy the whole time.'

'Probably letting the other guys in his office know what had happened, and setting up the money transfer,' Harris said.

'Probably,' White agreed. 'Horse, I want you to go back to the office and alert the manager of the Bahamian bank that the transfer may be coming through. Make sure we know the minute it's there.'

'Then what?' Horse asked.

'Just stay by the phone.'

'We have a serious problem,' White said to Harris after Horse had left. 'Our theory of the case is based on the assumption that *Morgan* controlled the money and was behind the frame-up. Now we find out that it was Sommers.'

'That's not necessarily a problem,' Harris said. 'We already suspected that Sommers was involved. The fact that Sommers controlled the money doesn't mean Morgan wasn't involved. In fact, it doesn't change any of the reasons we had for looking at Morgan in the first place.'

'But a lot of our case was based on the fact that *Morgan* went to the Caymans right after Marty was fired. If he didn't control the money, what was he doing there?'

Harris shared White's troubled look.

'It's too late to change our theory now,' Harris said. 'What we have is still enough to create reasonable doubt, unless the prosecutor comes up with more than we think she has.'

'Let's hope you're right.'

* * * * *

The judge's deputy came out of the courtroom, knocked once on the open door and handed White a document. 'The judge wanted me to give you this.'

White and Harris eagerly read the judge's order on the scope of Morgan's testimony.

'It beats the hell out of me,' Harris muttered quietly, answering a question that no one had asked.

'It isn't the way I read the law,' White agreed. 'Let me see if we are reading this the same. Powell has a choice. She can either acknowledge that Bower's conversations with Morgan were attorney-client communications. In that case, Morgan can't testify about the conversations themselves. But she can still use the information Morgan dug up *after* those conversations if she can prove it would have been inevitably discovered.'

'Or,' Harris interjected, 'she can introduce the communications between Bower and Morgan, regardless of the existence of the attorney-client privilege, because the crime-fraud exception vitiates the privilege. But if she goes that way, she can't introduce any evidence discovered as a direct result of that communication because it was discovered as a result of communication that Marty *believed* to be privileged.'

'That's how I read it,' White said.

'What was the judge *thinking*?'

'Who cares,' White said. 'It puts Powell on the spot—and it gives us grounds for an appeal if things don't work out.'

'Let's hope it doesn't come to that.'

'Let's hope,' White agreed.

'She can't possibly go with the first option,' Harris said, analyzing the prosecutor's choices. 'We know there was no independent discovery by her investigators, because the hospital gave her everything to make her case. Without Morgan's testimony about what the hospital discovered, she won't have anything to support her theory.'

'We may be wrong about how much independent investigation was done.'

* * * * *

At twenty minutes past nine o'clock, Elizabeth Powell entered the courtroom, followed by her assistants. She was holding a copy of the judge's order in her left hand. There were dark circles under her bloodshot eyes, and her face showed all the stress of the decision she had to make in the few minutes remaining before she would begin her examination of Joe Morgan. She desperately needed Morgan's testimony to get her case back on track. White knew how she felt. Whatever decision she made, her prepared examination, based on her assumption that she could examine Morgan without restriction, was in shambles.

Powell was still considering her alternatives when court was called to order.

'The government calls Joseph Morgan.'

Spectators in the know whispered their shared understanding that Morgan was a key witness. The courtroom quieted as the rear door opened and Morgan lumbered heavily down the aisle. He looked at Powell, the jury and the judge, but avoided looking toward the defense table.

Morgan was sworn in and took his seat in the witness chair.

'Mr. Morgan, state your name, occupation and current employer.'

'My name is Joseph Morgan. I am an attorney, and I am currently employed as in-house counsel by Coastal Regional Hospital.'

'In testimony yesterday, the F.B.I.'s forensic accountant testified to the discovery of a bank account at Gulf Coast Bank that was opened by Mr. Bower,' Powell opened, taking the opportunity to reemphasize the credentials of her witness and restate the basic facts of her case. 'He also testified that this account received monthly transfers of $50,000 from the hospital's account,'

White could have objected to Powell's statement as a speech rather than a question. He could also have objected on the grounds that her conclusory statement of facts had not been established. A quick study of the eight men and four women who would decide Martin Bower's fate made him decide that an objection made this early in her examination of Morgan would offend the jury.

'Do you know how the hospital discovered Mr. Bower's account?'

'Yes. I discovered it.'

'How did you happen to discover the transfers of money from the hospital?'

Harris leaned over the defense table and whispered to White. 'She's going with option one, *What did Bower tell you?* Now she's trapped.'

Kaleidoscope

'We'll see,' White whispered in response. His eyes never left the jury.

'Mr. Bower came to me with a problem involving the executive accounts,' Morgan said.

'What kind of problem?'

'Some of the accounts were out of budget—higher than they should have been.'

'Why did Mr. Bower bring this matter to your attention?'

'Objection,' White said. "The witness has no way of knowing what Mr. Bower may have been thinking.'

'Sustained. Rephrase the question.'

'Did Mr. Bower tell you why he wanted you to look into the matter of the out-of-budget accounts?'

'Yes.'

'What did he tell you?'

'He said he wanted me to take care of the problem.'

'What did you understand that to mean?'

'I understood him to mean that he wanted the problem to go away—to make sure it wasn't brought to the attention of the board.'

'So he wanted you to hide the problem?'

'Objection. It's a leading question and requires the witness to testify as to what Mr. Bower may have been thinking.'

The objection was sustained, but it was too late. The jury had heard the question. The suggestion that Bower asked Morgan to a cover-up of the account discrepancies had been planted in their minds.

'When did this occur?' Powell continued.

'When we decided to conduct an internal audit of the hospital accounts,' Morgan stated flatly, smiling.

'That's it,' Harris again whispered to White. 'She doesn't have anywhere else to go with this.'

White shook his head. 'She has something else. She's looking too smug.'

Powell looked at White and smiled before continuing her questioning. 'Mr. Morgan, have you ever seen a document showing *that the defendant* caused the hospital's computer to be programmed to make the transfers we have been discussing?'

'Yes'

'Objection,' White said. Unlike the prosecutor, White made his objection in a voice that was unhurried and virtually unconcerned. 'No document such as the prosecutor has described is in the government's exhibit list and no such document has been provided to the defendant.'

'What's going on here Ms. Powell?' the judge asked angrily.

'Your Honor. This document was just produced this morning.'

'Your Honor. This is unfair surprise,' White shot back. 'We haven't had an opportunity to examine or authenticate any such document.'

'I'm going to overrule the objection for the time being, Mr. White. If you need time to examine the document and want to challenge its authenticity later, I will entertain a motion at that time.

'And you, Ms. Powell,' the judge continued, glaring at the prosecutor, 'have just reached the limits of my tolerance. Do you understand me?'

'Yes, Your Honor.'

'Good. Now ask your question.'

'Do you recognize this document, Mr. Morgan?' Powell resumed, unable to resist a quick glance, and smirk, in White's direction.

'Yes,' Morgan said.

'What is it?'

'It's a memo from the defendant to the hospital's director of information systems.'

'And what does the document say?'

Kaleidoscope

'It instructs the director of information systems to reprogram the computers to make the transfers you were talking about.'

A murmur filled the courtroom. Everyone knew this was devastating. The jurors were looking at each other and shaking their heads.

Martin Bower turned pale, a mixture of astonishment and disbelief.

Harry Harris leaned over to White and whispered, "She sandbagged us. We've been had.'

White nodded, never letting his eyes leave the jury.

'But this document is unsigned,' Powell pointed out, anticipating White's basis for attacking the document. 'How can you be so certain it's from Martin Bower?' This was the first time Powell referred to the defendant by name. She wanted to make perfectly clear whose name was on the memo.

'It isn't uncommon for routine internal hospital memos to be unsigned.'

'Thank you,' Powell concluded smugly. 'Nothing further.'

As she returned to her seat, Powell gave White a take-that-you-son-of-a-bitch look.

White stood slowly, almost lazily, and approached the podium.

'When did the hospital produce this document?' White asked, waving the memo that had just been introduced by the prosecutor.

'This morning.'

'Why was this document produced this morning?'

'It seemed relevant,' Morgan said smugly. For the first time he looked at Martin Bower. He had crossed the line and was now on record as a nail carrier for Bower's crucifixion.

'And did the hospital voluntarily produce this memo?'

'Yes.'

'So the government didn't have this memo *supposedly* linking Mr. Bower to the computer program when he was indicted?'

'I guess not.'

Harris signaled White to come to the defense table.

'May I have a moment to confer with co-counsel, Your Honor?'

'Make it quick.'

Harris slid the copy of the damning memo in front of White and pointed to a corner of the document.

White shook his head, not understanding what Harris was getting at. Then it dawned on him and he smiled.

'Your Honor. May we have a brief recess?' White asked.

'But we've just gotten started,' the judge said in a voice that asked White for some justification for his request.

'Your Honor,' White said. 'I appreciate the Court's concerns, but the defense needs time to consider this surprise evidence.'

White emphasized the word surprise, hoping the jury would blame the prosecutor for the inconvenience they were about to suffer.

'Recess for fifteen minutes,' the judge announced.

45.

Harris and Bower sat at the table in one of the conference rooms outside the courtroom. White leaned against the wall looking at the document provided by Morgan.

'What's going on?' Bower asked. 'I never wrote that memo.'

'We know,' White assured him.

'You *know*?' Bower said, puzzled by how the attorneys could have reached this conclusion.

'Show him, Harry.'

Harris smiled as he took the copy of the government's memo from White, slid it in front of Bower and pointed to the now familiar telltale markings of a desktop printer-copier on the corner of the copy.

'What are you thinking, Marty?'

'The date. Look at the date on the memo.'

White and Harris looked at the memo and then at each other, neither seeing anything significant.

'The memo is dated a month before the first money transfer.'

'So?'

'I didn't have a computer in my office then,' Bower announced proudly. 'I didn't get a computer in my office until two years later.'

White and Harris let this sink in.

Finally Harris spoke. 'And someone who didn't work at the hospital at that time, someone who didn't come to work at the hospital until after you got an office computer, wouldn't have known that.'

White smiled as he said, 'Joe Morgan.'

* * * * *

Joe Morgan returned to the witness chair.

White approached the podium where he stood quietly for a full minute, waiting for the jury to focus its undivided attention on him. Just as he began to speak, Powell jumped to her feet and shouted, 'Sidebar, Your Honor.'

White glared at Powell, knowing that her outburst had been timed to break the mood of tense anticipation his silence had built.

Judge Greene motioned the attorneys to the side of the bench. 'What's the problem, Ms. Powell?'

'Your Honor. I have asked this witness about only two matters. Under the rules, Mr. White's cross-examination is limited to the matters raised on direct examination.'

'We are all familiar with the rules, Ms. Powell,' the judge said impatiently.

'But . . .'

The judge cut Powell off with a wave of his hand and turned to White. 'Do you intend to go beyond the issues raised by the government, Mr. White?'

'Yes, Your Honor. We do.'

Before the judge or Powell could say anything, White continued. 'The credibility of a witness is always relevant. It's the defendant's position that he is being framed. We also believe that the frame-up may be based on advice provided to the hospital and its board by Mr. Morgan. And finally, we believe that Mr. Morgan himself may be an active participant in this frame-up.'

The judge was considering this argument when Powell interrupted. 'Your Honor. Mr. Morgan is the in-house counsel for the hospital. As such, any information he has is subject to attorney-client privilege. He can't be required to testify about his communications with any of the hospital's officers or employees on anything he may have learned in the course of his duties as hospital counsel.'

'I believe I addressed that problem in my order, Ms. Powell,' the judge said. 'Now, unless there is something else, Ms. Powell . . .'

'Your Honor,' Powell protested. 'Your order only addressed the scope of Mr. Morgan's testimony regarding information disclosed to him by the *defendant*. It didn't address the disclosure of any communications between Mr. Morgan and his employer, the hospital board, on any other matters.'

The judge nodded and rubbed his chin.

Powell pressed her position. 'I believe it is appropriate to require the defense to disclose the matters on which he intends to examine the witness before the jury hears any questions. If he is allowed to raise an issue in his questions, it will plant seeds with the jury and they will want to know what is being hidden when you sustain any objection the government may make.'

'You'll have to do better than that,' the judge said with growing irritation. 'Your concern is no more relevant to the examination of this witness than any other time an objection is made and sustained. Do you have anything to add, Mr. White?'

'Two things, Your Honor. First of all, I don't intend to inquire into Mr. Morgan's conduct as hospital's counsel. Second, because it's the defendant's position that he is being framed by the hospital and Mr. Morgan, the crime-fraud exception applies. Anything Mr. Morgan may have discussed with the hospital board loses its status as privileged communication.'

Powell couldn't control herself. 'Your Honor, this is *crap*. Mr. White is on a fishing expedition in an effort to confuse the jury.'

'Ms. Powell, you will *not* use that kind of language in my courtroom.'

'Yes, Your Honor,' Powell said, sounding contrite but looking otherwise. 'But the government demands an offer of proof.'

The judge considered the prosecutor's request for a moment, then turned to the jury. 'Ladies and Gentlemen of the jury. A matter has come up that requires a meeting with the attorneys. I apologize for the inconvenience, but it will be necessary to take another brief recess. The jury is excused.

'In my chambers, both of you,' he ordered.

46.

When Joseph Morgan returned to his seat in the witness chair, White wasted no time on preliminaries. 'Mr. Morgan, you testified on direct examination that you provided the government with the memo, *allegedly* written by Mr. Bower to the director of information systems, instructing him to insert a subroutine in the hospital's financial accounting system.'

It wasn't a question, but Morgan nodded his agreement.

'You will have to respond verbally, Mr. Morgan,' the judge instructed. 'The court reporter cannot record gestures.'

'Yes, that's correct,' Morgan said.

'*When* did you provide this document to the prosecutor?'

'This morning,' Morgan said, glaring at White. 'I already told you that.'

Morgan's reaction was what White expected. Trial attorneys make dangerous witnesses. They're skilled in preparing their own witnesses, insisting that their witnesses limit their answers to the questions asked without volunteering anything, and instructing their witnesses not to argue with counsel. But when attorneys are themselves witnesses, they have a difficult time suppressing their combative instincts. Their egos--and trial attorneys have the biggest egos of all--

compel them to engage in a battle of wits with another attorney. Morgan's reminder that he had already answered White's question was personal. It didn't go unnoticed. White knew he could use Morgan's ego against him if it became necessary.

'Did she ask you for this document?'

Morgan hesitated. 'Not exactly.'

'Did the prosecutor ask you for *any* document?'

Morgan repositioned himself in the witness chair. His discomfort was obvious to White, but was probably not yet apparent to the jury.

'Not really.'

'Did she ask you for *anything*?' White said.

'Yes.'

'What did she ask you for?'

Morgan looked to Powell for help.

'Look at *me*, Mr. Morgan,' White said. 'Not the prosecutor.'

'Yes, she asked me for documents.'

'I asked you *what* documents she asked you for,' White insisted.

'She wanted to know if there were any documents showing that the defendant knew about the changes in the computer system.'

'When did she make this request?'

'Yesterday. After court recessed.'

'Where were you when she made this request?'

'Here.'

'Do you mean here in the courtroom?'

'Yes.'

'So you were here in the courtroom yesterday when the prosecutor's forensic accountant admitted that he had never seen any document connecting Mr. Bower to the changes in the hospital's computer system. Is that correct?'

White knew this wasn't a completely accurate summary of the testimony of the government's witness, but he also assumed that Powell would be too concerned with the direction of White's examination to notice and object.

'Yes.'

'Why did she come to *you* with her request?'

'I don't know.'

'Where did you get this document?' White pressed.

Morgan's eyes flickered with indecision. 'From the hospital files.'

'So you went to the hospital *after* court recessed yesterday. Is *that* your testimony?'

Morgan glared at White for a moment before responding. 'Yes.'

'Mr. Morgan.' White paused, looking at the jury to be sure they were paying attention. 'What would you say if I told you that my investigator followed you when you left court yesterday, and he will testify that you didn't go to the hospital after you left court?'

Powell was immediately on her feet. 'Objection. Assumes facts not in evidence.'

'Counsel. Approach the bench.'

Judge Greene put his hand over the microphone and addressed White. 'Are you playing games, or do did you really have Mr. Morgan followed?'

'He was followed, Your Honor.'

'Fine. Step back.'

'I'm going to overrule the objection. The witness may answer.'

'I don't know anything about that,' Morgan said evasively.

'And what would you say if I were to tell you that the hospital's director of information systems is prepared to testify that *his* files didn't contain any document of the type you gave the prosecutor?'

'Overruled,' the judge said, even before Powell could make her objection.

Like everyone else in the courtroom, the jury included, the judge stared at Morgan.

'I wouldn't know about that either,' Morgan said nervously.

White shuffled his papers, giving the jurors time to consider the implications of Morgan's testimony, before abruptly shifting to a new line of inquiry. 'Mr. Morgan, who is Erica Matheson?'

Morgan tensed, gripped the arms of the witness chair and stared at White—then at Martin Bower.

Powell almost left the floor as she leapt to her feet. 'Objection. Beyond the scope of direct examination,' she shouted. 'Mr. White knows he is not allowed to cross-examine the witness about matters not raised on direct examination.'

'Your Honor,' White said quickly, 'the question goes to the matters we discussed in chambers and . . .'

'Enough.' the judge said, glaring at White. The substance of what is discussed in the judge's chambers cannot be discussed in open court with the jury present. White was stretching the limits, and he knew it. But now the jury was curious about what had been discussed.

'And besides,' Powell took the opportunity to press her argument, 'the question can have no possible relevance.'

'I believe we can show relevance,' White said.

'I'll give you a little latitude, Mr. White,' the judge ruled. 'But very little. Be quick about it.'

White repeated the question.

Morgan remained silent, studying White's face and searching for some sign of where he was going.

White knew the look, just as he knew that Morgan was wondering how White knew about his e-mail correspondence.

As the silence extended, White looked at the judge and requested, 'Your Honor, we ask that the witness be instructed to answer the question.'

'Answer the question,' the judge ordered sternly.

Powell knew her witness was in trouble. She had no idea where White was going, but she could see the effect White's question had on Morgan.

'Objection,' she shouted. 'The person Mr. White is asking about has not been identified on the defense's witness list and is not an employee of the hospital. Who this person is cannot possibly have any bearing on these proceedings.' She was making it up as she went along, buying time for Morgan to collect his thoughts. When in doubt, object. Hearsay; no foundation; speculative; kitchen sink.

Morgan's silence, and suddenly pallid look, were enough to indicate that White was going somewhere meaningful. Without waiting for White's argument in opposition to the objection he ordered, the Judge said, 'Overruled. The witness will answer.'

'I . . . I don't know.'

'Isn't it true,' White pressed, 'that *Erica Matthison* is the name, or pseudonym, of a woman you have been communicating with through a matchmaking service on the internet?'

Again, Morgan hesitated before responding. 'Yes,' he said, his response barely audible.

'And what is the nature of your communication with Erica Matthison?'

Morgan moved uneasily and hung his head, not wanting to face the jury. Finally, he answered. 'Personal, I guess.'

'You *guess*?' White asked firmly, his voice challenging the credibility of Morgan's response. 'Don't you *know* what you communicated with Erica Matthison about?'

'Objection,' Powell shouted. 'The question has been asked and answered. And besides, Mr. White is badgering the witness.'

'Sustained.'

The door at the rear of the courtroom opened and a uniformed policeman entered, came to the bar and handed a package to Harris.

White looked from the judge to Morgan, then to the jury. 'Your Honor, may I have a moment to confer with counsel?'

'Make it quick.'

White stepped from the podium to the defense table and leaned close to Harris.

'What are you doing?' Harris whispered.

'Letting the jury wonder what's going on.'

'What *is* going on?'

White ignored the question. 'How certain are we that Morgan is involved in the hospital takeover?'

'Hold on,' Harris said, as he opened the package and quickly studied the contents. 'These are the documents Parker got from Morgan's computer. We've got him.'

White nodded and returned to the podium. 'Isn't it true that your communications with Erica Matthison concerned your *own* involvement in a plan to take control of the hospital?'

'Objection.' Powell was livid. 'Mr. Morgan is not on trial, and his own activities, whatever they may be, have no bearing on this case.'

'Your Honor. The defense contends that Mr. Morgan is himself involved in criminal activities . . .'

'That's *enough*.' the judge said. 'Mr. White's comment will be stricken from the record and the jury will disregard everything Mr. White has said about Mr. Morgan.

'Counsel. Approach the bench.' the judge ordered.

'Mr. White,' the judge said, 'unless you can show a basis for your accusation, you are going to find yourself in contempt of court.' The judge stared coldly at White. 'Now step back and continue.'

'Mr. Morgan,' White said, 'who filed the initial complaint regarding Mr. Bower's alleged embezzlement of hospital funds?'

'I filed it . . . at the instruction of the hospital board.'

'And is this a true copy of the statement you filed with the State's Attorney?' White asked as he handed a copy of the complaint to Morgan.

'Yes,' Morgan said. His expression said he knew White was taking him somewhere he didn't want to go.

'Offered as Defense Exhibit 1.'

'No objection, Your Honor,' Powell said.

'Mr. Morgan, have you ever been to the Cayman Islands?'

'Objection. What possible relevance can this line of inquiry have?'

'Your Honor, these questions will be brief and I believe the relevance of these questions will become apparent.'

'Objection overruled.'

'Mr. Morgan,' White repeated, 'have you ever been to the Cayman Islands?'

'Yes'

'When?'

'About a year before Marty . . .' Morgan caught himself. 'About a year before the defendant was fired.'

'Have you been back since then?'

'No.'

'Mr. Morgan, can you identify the handwriting on this matchbook cover?' White said, handing Morgan the matchbook on which he had written his cell phone number when he met with Horse at the T&A bar.

'Objection,' Powell said, without commitment. The judge was obviously interested in White's line of questioning and would overrule the objection.

The judge signaled White and Powell to the side of his bench. 'Where is this going, Mr. White?'

'Your Honor,' White began, 'the witness testified that he has not been in the Cayman Islands for at least a year before my client was terminated. The matchbook the witness has identified is from the Turtle Reef Hotel. The defense will produce evidence that the Turtle Reef Hotel was, at the time of

Mr. Morgan's claimed visit, still under construction and didn't open until *after* the defendant was terminated.

'The government has already shown that the money supposedly taken by my client was transferred to a bank in the Cayman Islands. My inquiry goes to both the credibility of the witness and to defense's theory that Mr. Morgan was himself involved in the transactions my client is accused of committing.'

'But, Your Honor,' Powell protested. 'Mr. White is attempting to impeach his own witness.'

'He's not my witness,' White argued. 'He's the government's witness. I'm conducting a cross-examination.'

'But you're the one who raised the issue of travel to the Cayman Islands, and now you're trying to impeach the witness on issues you raised in the first place.'

Powell was correct. Subject to only limited exceptions, an attorney cannot impeach his own witness. But White was also correct; Morgan wasn't technically his witness, even though he had indirectly made him his own witness when the judge allowed him to examine Morgan on issues not raised in the prosecutor's direct examination.

The judge removed his glasses and pinched his nose.

'All right. Move back,' the judge said. 'The objection is overruled.'

White returned to the podium and repeated his question. 'Mr. Morgan, can you identify the handwriting on this matchbook cover.'

'Yes. That's my handwriting and cell phone number.'

Morgan's eyes said that he was trying to determine where this line of questioning was going. Wherever it was, it wasn't good.

'We offer the matchbook as Defense Exhibit 2,' White said.

'So ordered,' the judge agreed, not waiting for a response from Powell.

'May we assume that you stayed at the Turtle Reef Hotel when you were on Grand Cayman?' White said.

'No. I just went to the bar there. I must have picked up the matchbook then.'

'Mr. Morgan.' White stepped away from the podium and looked at the jury as he asked, 'Are you aware that the Turtle Reef Hotel didn't open for business until *after* Mr. Bower was fired?'

White's tone was both demanding and accusing. A resonant murmur raced through the courtroom.

'Objection. The question assumes facts not in evidence.'

'Mr. White has already provided an offer of proof, Ms. Powell,' the judge reminded her.

'And besides,' Powell continued, unchastened, 'counsel is arguing with the witness.'

'Sounds like a pretty good argument to me,' the judge said. 'The objection is overruled.'

'I wouldn't know,' Morgan said evasively.

Morgan's response was irrelevant. The jury had heard the question, and that was all that counted.

'Mr. Morgan, who is Paul Smith?'

Morgan tensed at the mention of the name of the supposed F.B.I. agent he had met at the T&A bar.

'Objection,' Powell shouted. 'No one named Paul Smith is on the defense's witness list and . . .'

'I withdraw the question,' White said casually. The jury had seen Morgan's reaction to the name and heard the prosecutor's objection. Now they were curious about things they would never learn. That was all White wanted.

'Mr. Morgan, who is Parker Boles?'

Morgan again tensed at the mention of another name he had communicated with on the internet. His eyes moved quickly from White to Powell. He had the look of the recipient of a prostate exam.

'Objection . . .'

'Withdrawn.'

Powell had no idea who Erica Matthison or Parker Boles were. She knew even less about how they might be connected to the case. All she knew was that the mention of their names frightened Morgan. She also saw the reaction on the faces of the jurors.

White knew Morgan's mind was confused—fearing what else White knew and what was coming next.

'Mr. Morgan, do you own a personal printer-copier?' White asked, again changing the subject and keeping Morgan, and Powell, off balance.

His look said Morgan saw what was coming. His look, and the implications of White's question, were not lost on Powell. The only thing she could do was buy Morgan some time.

'Objection. No possible relevance.'

Once again the judge called the parties and the court reporter to a sidebar conference.

'I'm inclined to agree with the prosecutor, Mr. White,' the judge said. 'Where is this going?'

'Your Honor,' White began. 'As we previously discussed, it is the defense's theory that Mr. Morgan is involved in a scheme to frame the defendant.

'Many of the documents the government has *already* introduced into evidence contain a distinctive marking. Our expert will testify that the documents the government has introduced were either originally prepared, or were copied, on the same machine. Yesterday, I provided the State's Attorney with information relating to our theory that Mr. Morgan was involved in criminal conduct. On the basis of that evidence, the State's Attorney obtained a warrant to search Mr. Morgan's house and home computer and obtain samples of printouts made on Mr. Morgan's home computer and printer. That search was conducted this morning. Just before trial resumed, I was provided with evidence showing that documents prepared on Mr. Morgan's personal printer-copier contain the same telltale markings found on other documents

Kaleidoscope

introduced by the government. The search of Mr. Morgan's computer also revealed that certain documents the government has introduced as hospital records were, in fact, found on the hard drive of Mr. Morgan's computer.'

Powell was turning more pale by the minute.

'Your Honor,' she stammered. 'I can assure you that I have no knowledge of any of the matters Mr. White has raised.'

'That better be the case, Ms. Powell.' The judge's eyes narrowed and his jaw grew taut. 'If I find out you knew even a little bit about any of the conduct Mr. White is alluding to, I will personally see to it that you never practice law again. And you may very well be charged with criminal conduct,' the judge added. "Now step back.'

'Objection overruled. The witness will answer.'

'Yes. I have a home computer.' Morgan knew the trap was closing.

White walked slowly to the evidence table and picked up the bank records previously entered into evidence by the prosecutor.

'Your Honor, may I approach the witness?' White asked.

'Go ahead.'

'Mr. Morgan,' White began. 'these documents have previously been received into evidence.' As he spoke, he handed the documents to Morgan. 'Do you recognize these documents?'

'Yes.'

'From where do you recognize these documents?'

'They're documents the hospital provided to the government.'

'How did the hospital come into possession of these documents?'

Morgan's face took on a blank, stunned look. For several moments he said nothing, merely staring at White.

'Mr. Morgan,' White said. 'Yesterday the regional manager of Gulf Coast Bank testified that the bank never released these documents to anyone.' White was speaking for the benefit of the jury. 'Now, I ask you again. How did the hospital come into possession of these documents?'

Morgan continued to stare blankly at White. Suddenly, he gasped, clutched his chest and slumped over.

A startled murmur filled the courtroom. Half the jurors gasped.

The judge was immediately on his feet, shouting orders. 'Bailiff. Remove the jury and call the paramedics. We're in recess.'

* * * * *

Half an hour later, Joe Morgan was sitting up in the witness chair, breathing oxygen administered by a paramedic.

'I think he'll be okay, judge,' the paramedic said. 'He probably just suffered an anxiety attack. But just to be sure, we need to take him to the hospital.'

'Yes. Of course,' the judge said as he gazed across the empty courtroom.

47.

Martin Bower sat between Lucius White and Harry Harris at the defense table to the left of the podium. Elizabeth Powell sat with her assistants at the prosecutor's table to the right of the podium. The gallery was full of reporters and a few citizens whose interest in the proceedings had been piqued by the news of the previous day's proceedings. Everyone was talking in muted tones, all asking each other the same question: 'Where is Joe Morgan?'

The door to the judge's chambers opened and the bailiff emerged. He had a troubled look as he walked to the counsel tables, speaking first to Elizabeth Powell and then to Lucius White. 'The judge would like to see counsel in his chambers.'

White and Powell followed the bailiff across the courtroom and into the judge's chambers. They exchanged puzzled looks, but didn't speak to each other.

'Ms. Powell,' the judge began, before White and Powell had taken their seats. 'Court was to resume an hour ago. Where is your witness?'

'I have no idea, Your Honor,' Powell said, her own concern evident in her voice. 'He was released from the hospital about an hour after he was taken in yesterday.

Someone from the hospital took him home. I spoke with him last night, and he said he was all right. I expected him to be here by now.'

'Have you tried to locate him?'

'Yes, Your Honor. My assistant has called his home, but there was no answer.'

'Doesn't he have a wife?' the judge asked.

'Yes, he does,' Powell said. 'But when I spoke with him last night, he said his wife was out of town.'

'Does he have a cellular phone?'

'Yes. And we've tried that number too. He doesn't answer.'

The judge took a long breath.

'We've also called the police, to see if there has been an accident,' Powell volunteered. 'And the hospital—just in case.'

The judge looked at her hopefully.

'Nothing,' she answered his unspoken question.

The judge thought for a moment, then picked up his telephone and summoned the Marshal. 'I'm going to issue a bench warrant and send the Marshal to Mr. Morgan's home,' the judge announced. Then, looking at the courtroom bailiff, standing by the courtroom door, the judge said, 'Inform the jury that we have some procedural matters to be addressed and the proceedings will be in recess until one o'clock this afternoon.'

'Yes, sir,' the bailiff said and slipped quietly out the door and into the courtroom.

'I don't know what else we can do right now,' the judge said. It wasn't clear whether he was talking to the attorneys or thinking out loud.

'You two,' the judge continued, addressing White and Powell, 'had better stick around. I don't know what's going on, but I want you to be handy as soon as we find Mr. Morgan.'

Kaleidoscope

* * * * *

At ten minutes before noon, White and Harris were standing in the hallway outside the courtroom, discussing, as they had all morning, what might have happened to Joe Morgan. Their attention was diverted from their conversation when a Marshal appeared at the end of the long hall, heading stern-faced toward the judge's chambers. He didn't say anything to the attorneys as he passed, knocked once on the hallway door to the judge's chambers and entered without waiting for a response.

A minute later, the judge's law clerk emerged from the judge's chambers and summoned the attorneys.

When the attorneys were assembled and seated, the judge looked at them as if he didn't know where to begin. Finally he spoke. 'Mr. Morgan's body was found at his home. He had been shot twice in the head and his study had been ransacked.'

No one seemed to know what to say. The judge broke the tension. 'I'm not sure whether to let the trial continue or declare a mistrial. We'll meet here at three o'clock, and I will hear arguments from counsel.'

48.

Lucius White, Harry Harris, Horse McGee and Leslie Halloran gathered in White's office waiting for the evening news. It wasn't likely to have anything they didn't already know, but they were physically and mentally exhausted and too tired to do anything else—so they waited.

> *'In today's top story, Judge Horace Greene declared a mistrial in the criminal trial of Martin Bower. Sources close to the case suggest that the decision was required by the death of Joseph Morgan, Coastal Regional Hospital's in-house attorney, whose body was found late this morning. Mr. Morgan's examination by Mr. Bower's attorney, Lucius White, seriously undermined the government's case. Mr. White's examination of Mr. Morgan was scheduled to continue today.*
>
> *'Mr. Morgan's body was found at his home by U.S. Marshals. Morgan had been shot in what police describe as a gangland-style execution.*

> '*Managing Assistant U. S. Attorney Dwight Madison announced that the government would not seek a new trial of Mr. Bower. Although he refused to acknowledge that Mr. Bower was innocent, he conceded that the defense's inability to examine Mr. Morgan raised serious questions about the government's ability to prove its case.*
>
> '*Police refuse to speculate as to whether there is a connection between Mr. Morgan's death and the death of Randall Harrington, outside counsel for Coastal Regional Hospital, who died when he fell from the balcony of his suite at the Harbourside Hotel. Initial reports blame Mr. Harrington's fall on alcohol.*
>
> '*In an apparently unrelated incident, two Pennsylvania men were found dead in their motel room in East Fort Myers. Police speculate that the killings were drug-related.*
>
> '*We'll be back with details after this message.*'

Harris pressed the mute button on the remote control. 'Do you think we'll ever know the truth?'

'Probably not,' White said. 'There are still too many loose ends.'

The trial was over, and his client was free, but other issues remained unresolved. The government had not prevailed. But the frame-up had not been exposed.

White put aside his thoughts of the government's conduct and returned his attention to Harris. 'Morgan was obviously involved in the set-up. In fact, he was probably behind it,' White said lazily, without emotion. 'But I don't know how he was connected to the original plan.'

'We won. Maybe we should just forget it and count our blessings.'

'Winning isn't everything.'

'No, but it's the only thing that counts.'

Silence again filled the room until Harris asked, 'Do you think we could have gotten Marty off if the trial had gone the distance?'

White sighed. 'I honestly don't know.' His thoughts were interrupted by a beep from his computer and a metallic voice announcing, *You've got mail.* White stood slowly and walked to his desk where he clicked his computer mouse and displayed the message:

> '*Amigo*
> *You did well, as I knew you would. You have done us all a service. We didn't want to deal with those Yankees anyway.*
> *I've been looking out for you, and I am assured that you are now safe. But now I suggest, as a friend looking out for a friend, that some things are best forgotten.*
> *Hasta luego*'

A smile formed on White's lips as he pressed a button deleting the message. *You sly son of a bitch.*

'What was that about?' Harris asked.

White smiled. 'It was a message from my godfather.'

Kaleidoscope

49.

Martin Bower entered the Trade Winds Lounge at shortly after eight o'clock. Jim Worthington was waiting in a corner booth. Bower forced a smile as he eased into the booth opposite Worthington.

'Congratulations.' Worthington said. 'Lucius did a wonderful job.'

'It helps that I hadn't done anything,' Bower said without enthusiasm, the strain of the trial still showing on his face. 'Lucius showed the U. S. Attorney what we discovered, and convinced them that they couldn't get a conviction.'

For a minute, Bower said nothing as he gathered his thoughts. Finally he looked directly into his friend's eyes and asked, 'Why did you do it, Jim?'

The question caught Worthington by surprise, but the conviction in Bower's voice told him it was senseless to deny it.

'Why does anyone do anything?' Worthington said. 'How did you know?'

'I started thinking about it when we found out Morgan was using the internet to communicate with someone. It seemed a lot like the system you set up in Philadelphia.'

'So why didn't Lucius use that?' Worthington asked.

'I never told him everything I knew. At first, I didn't want to believe it. Then, Joe started pointing fingers at you, and I began having doubts. When I was ready to tell Lucius what I suspected, your house was broken into. I didn't think Joe knew enough to put the scheme together, but I still had too many doubts to turn on you.'

'How did you finally put it together?'

'It fell into place when we found out Nat Sommers controlled the money in the Cayman account. We knew Nat was involved in the theft of the AIDS drugs, but Lucius couldn't find anything connecting him to the money. At first, he assumed Joe was behind the money transfer scheme. But Joe wasn't at the hospital when the transfers started. We still don't know how the drug deal got started in the first place.'

'That was Morgan and Sommers,' Worthington said.

'But how?'

'I don't really know which one of them came up with the idea, but Morgan put it together.'

'How? Morgan didn't have access to the computers.'

'No, but Sommers was on the committee charged with changing the computer system, and I was helping with the project.'

'You? How did you get involved?'

'Halfway through my case, Morgan demanded more money, and threatened to withdraw from my case if I didn't come up with it. I didn't have it, so Morgan proposed a solution. If I would reprogram the hospital computers, he would let me off the hook. I took the only way out.'

'That wasn't your only way out,' Bower said.

'Probably not. But once you've screwed up, any excuse will do.'

'But how did you get into the computer system?'

'That was easy. After Sommers arranged to get himself on the committee that was working on the revision of the old system, he had access to all the information we needed about the program and the account codes. I wrote a simple program to do what we wanted. Then I broke into the computer and planted my program.'

'So you were involved in the deal from the beginning?'

'Not really. Originally, all I got for my efforts was Morgan's legal representation in my drug case.' Worthington smiled. 'Under the deal Morgan worked out with the feds, I had complete immunity for anything I'd done *before* the deal was agreed to. They obviously didn't know what I had done for Morgan, but it was before the immunity deal was signed. Even if the feds discovered what I had done for Morgan and Sommers, they wouldn't have been able to do anything to me . After my deal was finalized, and I went into the Witness Protection Program, I told Morgan and Sommers that I'd go to the feds if they didn't cut me into the deal. They were between a rock and a hard place, so I got my share.'

'And you made up the story you told Lucius about having the money all along?'

'I had to. There wasn't any way I could have legally accumulated that much money after Philadelphia. If I couldn't explain the money, Lucius would have gotten curious.'

'I think he had his suspicions. He just couldn't do anything about them because you were his client.'

After a moment of thought, Bower changed the subject. 'How were you able to control the bank's computers to transfer the money to the Caymans?'

'That was also Sommers' idea. He went to medical school with this doctor up in Sarasota.'

'That was Dr. Hart?' Bower said.

'Yes,' Worthington said with some surprise. 'Anyway, Dr. Hart was the head of this multi-specialty medical group—about twenty doctors. But you probably knew that, too.'

Bower nodded.

'Peoples Bank of Sarasota handled all of the group's money. The bank financed its buildings and equipment and handled all of its business accounts and managed its pension money—more than eleven million.'

'So the medical group was a major client.'

'The biggest . . . by far. And when the bank's biggest customer wants a favor. . . . You know how it is.' Worthington paused, idly running his finger around the rim of his glass. 'Anyway, the banker, Brian Lester, was responsible for keeping Dr. Hart and his medical group happy. If he lost their business, he would likely be out of a job. So he did what they asked. It wasn't hard. I showed him how. He got one of the bank's computer people to add a simple routine to their program.'

Bower said nothing.

'When did you figure it out?'

'I didn't know the whole story until just now.'

'Ironic, isn't it?' Worthington muttered.

Again there was silence as Worthington waited for the questions he knew were coming.

Bower swirled the ice in his drink before looking at Worthington. 'Why did Joe set *me* up?'

'Originally, it was just to cover up the thefts. Morgan was afraid that an audit would reveal the money transfers. When you asked him to look into the irregularities in the accounting, he knew he had to do something.'

'But Morgan could have covered it up if he wanted to.'

'Maybe. But that was a big risk.'

'How do you know all this?' Bower asked.

'When you were fired, and the hospital filed its criminal complaint against you, I went to Morgan. I tried to get him to back off you. He said it was too late.'

'Why?'

'He said Harrington had taken over the management of the merger. Harrington had a hard-on for you and White.'

'Did Harrington know the whole plan?'

Kaleidoscope

'I don't think so. Morgan never trusted Harrington, so he never told him everything. Harrington didn't even know who was behind the corporation that wanted to buy the hospital.'

'Then why was Harrington killed?'

'My friends don't like loose ends.'

Bower nodded numbly. *What have you become? How can you justify a murder so casually?* 'Why was my name on the transfer account in the first place?'

'When Dr. Hart opened the account, he had to name an authorized account signatory. You were the common connection between Morgan, Sommers and me, so he picked your name. Other than that, it didn't mean anything. It's almost funny, if you think about it.'

'Not to me it isn't,' Bower said.

Worthington shrugged and sipped his drink. 'When you guys made the AIDS connection, Morgan and Sommers panicked. They were afraid you'd put the whole thing together. At least, that's what Sommers was concerned about. Morgan seemed to have something else on his mind.'

'We know,' Bower said.

'What do you know?'

'The AIDS drug thing was ancient history as far as Morgan was concerned. Getting rid of me was all part of a plan to take control of the hospital and sell it to an organization in Philadelphia. It was a mob front organization. But Morgan had a problem. If the thefts of the AIDS drugs was exposed, the hospital's drug accounting procedures would have come under scrutiny by the D.E.A. With the D.E.A. nosing around, the hospital would have lost its value to the syndicate, and Morgan's deal would have fallen through.'

'Lucius is smarter than I gave him credit for,' Worthington said. 'I didn't think he'd be able to put it together so fast.' There was something in Worthington's look, a look of prideful satisfaction, that held Bower's attention.

'You *knew*.'

Worthington nodded. 'I put the deal together,' Worthington confessed in a tone of smugness. 'After Lucius' examination of Morgan, it was obvious he had figured everything out. Another day on the stand and Morgan would have cracked.'

'So he was murdered,' Bower murmured.

'There was too much at stake. Morgan knew too much about the people in Philadelphia.'

Bower shook his head. 'The only thing Lucius couldn't figure out was who sent Horse the codes.'

Worthington made no effort to suppress his smile.

'It was you.' Bower said, his suspicion confirmed by Worthington's look. '*You* sent Horse the computer codes.'

'Payback can be sweet,' Worthington gloated. 'Morgan tried to double-cross us all.'

'How?'

'When the hospital started its audit, Morgan said he had to stop all the money transfers. Under the circumstances, it seemed prudent. What I didn't know was that Morgan kept the money transfer system going. He wanted it all for himself. I didn't know that part until you guys found out the money wasn't completing its circle.'

'No honor among thieves after all, huh?' Bower said.

'None at all. And it's not like there was anything I could do about it. When I discovered the drugs planted at my house, I knew Morgan must have been behind it. I couldn't tell anyone what I knew. But I started paying more attention to your situation, just in case there was an opportunity to return the favor.'

'So you gave us the codes.'

'I couldn't let you get convicted, Marty,' Worthington said. 'It was the least I could do after everything you've done for me.'

'What happens to you now?'

'My friends weren't completely pissed at me after Philadelphia. The program I told the feds about was an early version. The only people who were still using it when I was busted were small-time local dealers. None of the really serious players were hurt. But this is different. Now they'll be after me.'

'I'm afraid that's not your only problem,' Bower said, sadly.

Worthington waited.

'The prosecutor had to salvage something from this. After your probable cause hearing, she kept on looking and discovered that you were in the Witness Protection Program. She figured you must have withheld the $100,000 found in your safe when you entered the program.'

'Which is just what I told Lucius, even though it wasn't true.'

'It doesn't make any difference now. Whatever the source, it was criminal. The feds will probably be waiting when you get home.'

'So after all that has happened, they're finally after me—and it's for the wrong reason.'

'The final irony,' Bower said softly.

'Why are you telling me all this?' Worthington asked.

'In spite of everything, we have a history. I owe you at least a couple of hours head start.' Bower shook his head sadly as he stood and started to leave the bar.

'At least the million dollars Morgan had in the new Cayman bank account is still there,' Worthington said. 'I won't starve.'

Bower didn't have the heart to tell him the money was no longer there.

'Goodbye, Jim. And good luck.'

50.

'*Good evening ladies and gentlemen. This is Lynn Thomas here with the latest news.*

'*This afternoon a federal grand jury handed down indictments against four members of the Board of Trustees of Coastal Regional Hospital. The indictment charges them with perjury, tampering with evidence and obstruction of justice in connection with the criminal charges brought against Martin Bower, the hospital's former president and chief executive officer. The trial of Martin Bower ended in a mistrial after Joe Morgan, the hospital's in-house attorney, collapsed during his examination by Bower's attorney and was murdered before returning to Court.*

'*It is unknown whether there is a connection between the charges announced today and the resignation of former Assistant U. S. Attorney Elizabeth Powell who prosecuted Mr. Bower and left the United*

State's Attorney's office shortly after the government announced it would not pursue a second trial of Mr. Bower.

'The indictments handed down today also charged Coastal Regional Hospital board member Dr. Nathan Sommers with conspiracy in connection with the theft of experimental AIDS drugs from the hospital.

'In other news, Congressman Richard Marks announced today that he will not seek re-election to a ninth term in Congress. The congressman cited undisclosed personal considerations and health problems as the reasons for his decision.'

Leslie reached for the remote, turned off the television and rolled over. 'So that's the end of it.'

White reached around her and pulled her closer. 'The end? Maybe. But it isn't over. It never is.'

-- THE END --

Alan Woodruff

About the Author

Alan Woodruff is a former engineer, educator, management consultant and lawyer. He holds degrees from Virginia Polytechnic Institute (Engineering), Harvard University (Administration), Florida State University (Law) and the University of Washington (Tax Law). Mr. Woodruff has been a consultant to the Ford Foundation, the World Bank, the U.S. Department of Education, the National Institutes for Education and the Department of Defense. Mr. Woodruff has also been a law professor and CEO of a financial services company. Mr. Woodruff is the author of more than one hundred articles in professional journals and authored, or contributed to, books on education and economics and law. Mr. Woodruff lives is eastern Tennessee and is a member of the board of directors of the Knoxville Writers Guild. *Kaleidoscope* is his first novel.

www.ingramcontent.com/pod-product-compliance
Ingram Content Group UK Ltd.
Pitfield, Milton Keynes, MK11 3LW, UK
UKHW041634060226
10557UKWH00018B/63